GONE

A Deadly Secrets Novel

OTHER BOOKS BY
ELISABETH NAUGHTON

Deadly Secrets Series
Repressed

Aegis Security Series (Romantic Suspense)
Extreme Measures
Lethal Consequences
Fatal Pursuit

Stolen Series (Romantic Suspense)
Stolen Fury
Stolen Heat
Stolen Seduction
Stolen Chances

Against All Odds Series (Romantic Suspense)
Wait For Me
Hold On To Me
Melt For Me

Eternal Guardians Series (Paranormal Romance)
Marked
Entwined
Tempted
Enraptured
Enslaved
Bound

Twisted
Ravaged
Awakened
Unchained

Firebrand Series (Paranormal Romance)
Bound to Seduction
Slave to Passion
Possessed by Desire

Anthologies
Bodyguards in Bed

GONE

A Deadly Secrets Novel

ELISABETH NAUGHTON

Published by Montlake Romance, Seattle

www.apub.com

Amazon, the Amazon logo, and Montlake Romance are trademarks of Amazon.com, Inc., or its affiliates.

ISBN-13: 9781503942592
ISBN-10: 1503942597

Cover design by Michael Rehder

Printed in the United States of America

For Alia,
my favorite book lover

CHAPTER ONE

If Alec McClane had a heart left, it might have been shattered on the floor. As it was, sitting on the cracked plastic chair in the sterile hallway, all he could think about was how someone else's heart was about to be shattered. And how he was going to have to live through that all over again.

He rubbed his aching forehead with his thumb and first two fingers and waited. He'd known the news wouldn't be good when he'd gotten the call, but he'd come anyway. Raegan, on the other hand, was probably so excited she could barely think straight. Just knowing all her hope was about to be crushed left a knot in the pit of his stomach that he'd carry with him for at least the next damn week.

Man, he wanted his old friend Jim. Unfortunately, he and Jim Beam weren't on speaking terms going on close to three years now.

He shifted on the uncomfortable chair, leaned back, and crossed his arms over his chest. A nurse rushed by, stethoscope in hand. Down the hall, a couple of doctors conversed quietly in their white coats and shiny shoes. Pressure formed in his chest the longer he waited. A pressure he knew was rooted in guilt and self-disgust even Jim Beam hadn't been able to ease.

He leaned forward again, rested his elbows on his knees, and clenched his hands into fists, only to release them in a feeble attempt to take the focus off the heaviness between his ribs. He should have called Raegan as soon as he'd seen the girl. Should have told her not to come. Then, at least, he wouldn't be sitting here waiting for the love of his life to walk through the door only to leave him wrecked and more empty than he'd awoken this morning.

Holy hell, he needed a drink.

"McClane?"

Alec glanced to his left where an FBI agent strode toward him down the long hallway, a grim expression on the man's angular face. Slowly, Alec pushed to his feet. "Hey, Bickam."

Jack Bickam had worked Emma's case. He was the one who'd called both him and Raegan when the four-year-old in the other room had been found in a park not far from the one where Emma had vanished three and a half years before.

Vanished when Alec had turned his back for two minutes to help a kid who'd fallen off the swings.

His stomach churned with another wave of guilt, and bile rose in his throat. But he swallowed hard and forced both back.

"Glad I caught you before you left," Bickam said. "Got a minute?"

Alec glanced over his shoulder toward the lobby of the small hospital. Still no sign of Raegan. Nerves rolled through his gut along with the guilt, but there wasn't a whole lot he could do about either. "Yeah." He turned back toward Bickam. "What do you need?"

"Sorry the kid wasn't Emma," Bickam said, brushing the dark bangs off his forehead.

There wasn't any good way to respond to that, so Alec shoved his hands into the pockets of his worn jeans. "That what you came out here to tell me?"

"No. I wanted to talk to you about the tip we received on the girl. It came from the Santiam Correctional Institution."

All the worry and stress faded to the background, leaving behind nothing but a simmering anger that was as insistent as any liquor craving. "Are you sure about that?"

"Yeah, I triple-checked the call records. It came in at one thirty-five p.m. SCI's a minimum-security facility that transitions inmates back to society. They have access to phones from six a.m. to ten p.m. so long as they're not out on a work crew. And your father wasn't on a crew when that call was placed. I just checked."

A thousand memories of a neglected and filthy childhood rolled through Alec's mind. The man in that prison wasn't his father. Fathers took care of their kids. They didn't knock them around, make them fend for themselves, or use them as mules to move their illegal shit. No, John Gilbert wasn't his father. He was just the son of a bitch Alec shared DNA with.

He was also the asshole who had every reason to want to see Alec suffer. "I'm gonna kill him."

"No, you won't." Bickam stepped in Alec's way before Alec could move toward the lobby. "I already sent someone out to question Gilbert."

"He won't tell you shit, and you know it. If he knew about this missing girl, it means he had a part in my daughter's disappearance."

"I'm not so sure," Bickam said. "The caller mentioned Emma specifically. That's why I notified you when we found the girl. I was hopeful this would be a major break in the case, but if Gilbert was the caller, as we think, it wouldn't be a stretch to say he did it to mess with you."

"You mean to fuck with me."

"Yeah, that." Bickam's jaw clenched. "Look, he could have learned about the missing girl from the news or overhead some of the correctional officers discussing the case. The caller didn't name the park where the girl was picked up; he named the one where Emma disappeared. It could just be a coincidence."

3

Not for Alec. There was no such thing as a coincidence when it came to John Gilbert.

"I also listened to the call," Bickam went on. "It didn't sound like Gilbert to me, but I know that doesn't mean much to you."

No, it didn't, not to Alec. The dickhead could have altered his voice or even conned another inmate into making the call for him.

"I just wanted you to know," Bickam said. "When I hear back from my people out at SCI, I'll fill you in. Either way, you need to watch your back. Gilbert's scheduled to be released next week. His six-month sentence for probation violation is almost up, and he's completed his community reintegration program. If we can link him to that call, I'll take the info to the judge, but if not, he'll be out on the streets soon."

Alec rested his hands on his hips and fought back the rage that wanted to consume him. Regardless of what Bickam thought, Alec knew John Gilbert had killed his daughter. He was the only person who had motive, the one person in the world who wanted to see Alec suffer. It was Alec's testimony as a teen that had sent Gilbert to prison for fourteen years. No matter how long he lived, Alec would never forget that day in the courtroom when Gilbert had been convicted, the way he'd stood at the defendant's table, stared at Alec across the gallery with enraged eyes while he was cuffed, and screamed that he'd make Alec pay. And Alec had paid. He'd paid every day since that awful day in the park. Gilbert had been released from prison less than a month before Emma had gone missing. Alec knew Gilbert had been there, that he'd taken Emma in his sadistic need for revenge, just as Alec knew Gilbert had killed her as soon as he got her away. Alec had just never been able to prove it.

"Yeah, okay," he said for the agent's benefit, though inside he was already planning how he'd wring the information from the son of a bitch's throat. "Thanks for letting me know."

Bickam nodded and glanced over his shoulder toward the lobby. "Any sign of Devereaux?"

Alec's stomach twisted, and with just the mention of Raegan he was transported right back to the reason he was standing in this empty hallway. "No. Not yet."

"Okay. Well, I'll be down the hall if either of you need me."

Alec muttered, "Thanks," as Bickam headed back the way he'd come. But as he sank into his chair once more and rubbed his throbbing forehead, the dread spiraled right back through his veins.

The automatic doors at the end of the hall pushed open long minutes later, followed by the click of heels on the tile floor. Lifting his head, Alec glanced to his right, and the minute he saw her, all the air drained from his lungs.

Raegan Devereaux rushed down the hall toward him, her curly auburn hair flying around her face, her tan trench coat flapping behind her. Pushing to his feet, Alec swallowed hard as she approached, remembering all the times he'd run his fingers through that silky hair, the countless hours he'd wrapped his arms around her slim waist and held her against him, and the nights he'd spent worshipping her perfect body like a peasant worships a goddess whose station is miles above his lowly class.

"Where is she?" Hope reflected deeply in Raegan's meadow-green eyes, but her angelic features were drawn and tight, and her soft pink lips quivered with a fear he knew threatened to overwhelm her.

"It's not her." Alec caught her by the forearms before she could rush past. The scent of her jasmine perfume filled his senses, a hard punch to his gut filled with memories he couldn't get sucked into. Not now. "Raegan. Stop. It's not her."

"How do you know?" Panic lifted her voice. "Agent Bickam said she fits the profile. He said—"

"It's not her," he said louder, ignoring the way her scent made him light-headed and how the warmth beneath the sleeves of her coat heated his chilled skin. "I saw her. It's not our daughter."

The hope in her pretty green eyes died like a flame being snuffed out. She searched his gaze as if willing him to say something more, but he couldn't. He couldn't, because hope was a dangerous thing. It was a mirage in the distance, flickering in the fading light and dragging a person forward like water draws a parched man. Only, when you got there, all you found was sand. Dry, grainy, throat-clogging sand that could kill you if you gave it the chance.

He stood motionless, unable to do anything to salvage her hope. Watched a familiar pain seep into her eyes and dampen her gaze. And he felt it filter deep into his bones, tugging at that heart he was sure no longer existed.

"I don't believe you." Just as quickly, another familiar emotion overtook her gentle features. One that hardened her jaw, darkened her eyes, and pulled her lush mouth into a tight line. She drew back from his grip. "You just don't want it to be her."

Alec's arms fell at his sides, and something in his chest deflated like a balloon losing air. There was nothing in this world he wanted more than for the four-year-old girl in the other room to be their daughter, but she wasn't. No girl who showed up in this hospital or any other ever would be because of John Gilbert.

He didn't tell Raegan that—they'd already argued about it a million times. He didn't try to stop her when she stepped around him. Didn't warn her against what she was about to see. Knew it would make no difference. He'd come to terms long ago with the bitter truth that Emma was gone and never coming back. Raegan, on the other hand, still chose to cling to a hope that would only torment her for the rest of her life.

He turned to look after her. Watched as she pushed past the doctors still talking, and rushed toward Bickam standing outside a room at the end of the hall with a uniformed officer. Pain lanced his chest as she nodded and followed Bickam into the room. When he could no longer see her, he clenched his jaw and rubbed the back of his neck.

Yeah, hope was a very dangerous thing. More dangerous than a loaded .45 aimed right at your head. And, shit, he should know. Because thanks to his splintered hope, he'd lived through that horror too.

All because of a man he planned to confront as soon as he walked out of this hospital.

———

She should have listened.

Raegan stepped out of the hospital room, rubbed a shaky hand against her forehead, and drew in a deep breath, desperate to settle her racing pulse. Nothing helped. It felt as if a jackhammer were chipping away at what was left of her heart, the pain nearly as intense as the day Emma had gone missing.

She pressed her hand to her chest and focused on breathing. He'd tried to warn her. Alec had tried to keep her from rushing into that room and getting hurt all over again, but she hadn't listened. He might have decimated her once, but he still cared. If he didn't, he wouldn't have waited for her here at the hospital. He would have left as soon as he realized the girl in that room wasn't their missing daughter.

"Excuse me, miss?" The officer outside the door stepped toward her. "Are you okay?"

Tears burned Raegan's eyes. Tears of pain, of frustration, of trampled hope, but she blinked them back, breathed deeply, and pulled herself together. "Yes," she managed. "I'm fine."

She turned away and swiped at her eyes. One look and Raegan had known the girl wasn't Emma. Her hair had been too dark, her eyes too round, and she'd been missing the small, strawberry birthmark on the outer edge of her right eye that Emma had been born with. Raegan had known not to get her hopes up. Had known the chances were slim, but she'd hoped anyway. And she'd go on hoping regardless of what Bickam or Alec said. Because hope was all she had left these days.

7

Be tough. You can get through this.

Lifting her head, she drew a deep breath and smoothed her blouse over her slacks. She was no worse off than she'd been this morning, right? This didn't have to wreck her. She wouldn't let it.

She turned away from the officer and headed back down the hall toward the lobby, her heels clicking along the tile floor like an ominous warning. Her pulse was still too high, but as soon as she got back to the office and dove into her work, she'd be fine. Maybe she'd even cut out early and get a drink before she had to meet Jeremy and his friends for dinner.

Her footsteps fumbled when she spotted Alec sitting on a chair midway down the corridor, massaging his forehead as if he had a whopper of a tension headache. Her treacherous heart squeezed tight, thumping a bruising rhythm against her ribs as she stared at him.

They'd been divorced nearly three years, but every inch of her body still responded to him as if they'd just met. Her skin heated, her mouth watered, and a low tingle spread through her belly and inched its way downward until her knees were literally shaking.

He stopped his vigorous rubbing and lifted his head. And when his sky-blue eyes caught hers and held, that heat in her skin combusted.

He pushed to his feet, watching her carefully. Swallowing hard, she forced her legs forward and told herself not to get worked up. This was Alec. The man who'd told her their marriage was a mistake. The one who'd trampled all over her heart. The one who'd left her alone and broken when she'd needed him most.

"You okay?" he asked quietly.

Dammit, she wanted to hate him but couldn't. He'd been as broken as she had when Emma had gone missing. He'd simply dealt with it in a very different way. One that now—years later—she'd accepted but would never understand.

"Yeah," she managed, slipping her hands into the pockets of her trench coat because she didn't know what to do with them. "I'm fine."

He nodded, but she could see in his eyes that he didn't believe her. She found herself wanting to lean into him for comfort. Found herself wanting to scream at him for being here when she was emotionally wrecked and physically drained. Found herself wishing so many things between them could be different.

Nothing was different, though. This was her reality: a missing child, a failed marriage, and a life left tattered and crumbling around her when all she was trying to do was move on.

He slid his hands into the front pockets of his worn jeans, the movement pulling at the black Henley over his strong shoulders. A low pulse beat through her belly as she studied him. He was just as gorgeous as he'd always been—blond hair, a lean, muscular body he obviously still took care of—but the years had aged him in ways no thirty-two-year-old should be aged. Fine lines that hadn't been there before creased his temple, and she could see a hint of gray in the blond scruff covering his jaw. Dark circles marred the soft skin beneath his lashes, telling her he hadn't slept much recently, and worry churned in her belly at the thought he was drinking again. But one look at his clear blue eyes told her he'd exorcised that demon from his life, at least. The guilt, though, she still saw swirling in their cerulean depths.

She hated that she still loved him. Hated that she wanted to comfort him the way he'd never let her comfort him. Hated especially that even after all the misery and heartache and time apart, he was still the one. The one who made her heart beat faster and her palms sweat. The one who could rock her world with just one look. The one who would forever ruin all other men for her from now until the end of time.

"I saw you on the news the other night," he said in the awkward silence.

Her journalism career was the last thing she wanted to talk about, especially with him, but she recognized he was trying to be polite. And knowing he was probably feeling the same disappointment she was, she told herself to suck up her crappy day and deal with it. "It's not a regular gig. I was just filling in at the anchor table."

"Yeah, well, you did good. I liked the human-interest piece on the Little League coach encouraging handicapped kids to play sports."

"Really?" Knowing he'd watched the whole newscast sent a pitiful thrill through her. "That was my piece."

"I could tell."

Of course he could. He knew the things that were dear to her heart.

She pulled her gaze from his and looked back at the floor because staring into his fathomless blue eyes, remembering all the times he'd kissed her and held her and told her she was his everything, was just too painful.

She struggled for something to fill the uncomfortable silence. "I'm a little surprised you're in-country. I thought you'd be overseas somewhere."

He was an incredible photojournalist. The best she'd ever seen. He had a way of capturing the human element in a crisis that made a person see conflict from a completely different perspective. It was one of the reasons she'd been so drawn to him when they'd met six years before. That and the fact that she'd felt as if she'd come alive the moment he'd looked at her.

She'd been a new beat reporter then, covering a colorful local election rally for her station. He'd been photographing not the politician but the faces of the spectators for the Associated Press. She'd caught him watching her through the crowd, and that had been it. She'd been entranced with just one look. Then she'd learned about his work and gotten to know the gentle heart he kept hidden beneath all those ruggedly handsome good looks, and she'd fallen headfirst into something that, even now with all the misery they'd lived through, was still the sweetest thing she'd ever known.

He shrugged. "I probably would be. Family stuff going on now, though."

Her heart pinched all over again at the thought of his family. What had been *her* family until the divorce. More of a family to her than her own distant relatives. "I heard Ethan's engaged. That's great."

"Yeah. For him."

That pinch turned into a quick stab, and the urge to run, to flee, to get out of this painful conversation, consumed her. "Well, I—"

Voices echoed from the lobby down the hall. Raegan glanced past Alec to see what was going on. Alec turned to look. A disheveled woman in her thirties with a jacket hanging halfway off her shoulder rushed toward them, flanked by a man in slacks, a white button-down rolled up at the sleeves, and a skewed tie.

The couple hustled past them, bypassed the doctors, and drew to an abrupt stop near the officer at the end of the hall. Even from this distance, Raegan could hear the woman's excited words.

"Where is she? Where's Maggie?"

"Ma'am," the officer said, "you have to calm down. We can't let you in until you're calm."

The woman didn't seem to hear the officer's words. She stepped past him and looked through the window into the small room. A gasp sounded down the hall as the woman reached for the man's arm. "Gary, it's her. Oh my God, it's her."

The two pushed past the officer and rushed into the room. Their joyous voices drifted out into the hall as they were reunited with their daughter. The happy sounds swirled around Raegan, reminding her of everything she didn't have, and might not ever find.

"Shit," Alec muttered. "You didn't need to see that."

"I'm fine, Alec." Raegan swiped at the stupid tears already spilling over her lashes. "Happy for them, is all."

He stepped close and reached for her elbow, and as his familiar body heat surrounded her and his fingers grazed her arm, a thousand memories bombarded her. Lazy Saturdays curled on the couch with him. Candlelit dinners at midnight when she'd worked the late shift and stumbled in exhausted and in need of only him. The night he'd come home from an assignment in Afghanistan and she'd told him she was pregnant.

Her gaze lifted, landed on his. Sparks shot between them. Sparks that warmed the coldest places deep inside her. Her heart beat faster as his gaze raked her features. And all the things she should have said to him long ago stumbled on her tongue.

"Raegan?"

Raegan startled when she heard Jeremy Norris's voice, and a new wave of discomfort rolled through her blood as she caught sight of him striding down the hall toward her.

"Darling." Jeremy walked right up to her as if Alec weren't even there, stepped between them so Alec was forced to let her go, and pulled her against him. "I came as soon as I heard the news."

The breath left Raegan on a shocked gasp, and she looked over Jeremy's shoulder toward Alec. Alec's jaw clenched and his shoulders tightened, but he didn't say anything, and Raegan found herself both relieved and disappointed by that fact.

Jeremy drew back but still held her at the elbows as he stared down at her with dark eyes. "What did they say?"

"It's not her." Prickles of heat rushed all over Raegan's skin. Not the good heat, though. The kind that made her itch.

She tried to push out of Jeremy's arms, but he sighed and pulled her close once more, trapping her in a claustrophobic embrace that made her want to scream. "I'm so sorry, darling."

Alec's gaze shifted from the back of Jeremy's head to Raegan, and the minute their eyes locked and she saw the disappointment in his, guilt rushed in, forming a hard knot in her belly.

She eased out of Jeremy's arms and swiped at the perspiration forming along her forehead. "Um, Jeremy, this is Alec."

Jeremy turned on his news-personality charm as if Alec were another mindless viewer, and reached for Alec's hand. "McClane, right?

Saw a spread you did on the refugee situation in Kenya in *Newsweek*. Interesting choice. The real refugee story's in Europe right now, don't you think?"

Alec's eyes narrowed, and Raegan tensed all over again because she recognized that look as disdain. "I've never been interested in reporting what's popular at the moment." He dropped Jeremy's hand. "Who are you again?"

"Oh, sorry." Jeremy smiled and wrapped an arm around Raegan's shoulders in what she knew was a possessive move. "Jeremy Norris. Station manager at KTVP."

Alec's gaze shot to Raegan, and she winced when she read the *you're dating your boss?* disbelief in his eyes.

Raegan glanced at Jeremy, desperate to get out of this uncomfortable situation. "I'm almost done here. Would you do me a favor and get me a water from the gift shop around the corner?"

"Sure." Jeremy leaned down and pressed a kiss to her cheek. "Anything for my girl." He looked toward Alec. "McClane."

Alec frowned but nodded. "Norris."

Jeremy finally let go of her and headed back down the hall. Mortified that had all just happened, Raegan swiped at her forehead again and said, "Sorry. I didn't call him. Someone at the station must have told him why I left work."

"Yeah."

Alec's expression didn't soften, and his shoulders seemed even tighter than before. Guilt consumed Raegan. A guilt she had no reason to feel.

She looked down at her pumps, unable to meet his gaze any longer. "I, um, was surprised when I came out and saw you. I thought you'd be gone already."

He glanced down the hall where Jeremy had been. "Kinda wishing I had been." She winced again as he looked back at her. "Guess I wanted to make sure you were okay."

She almost laughed. She hadn't been okay for three and a half years. Wasn't sure she ever would be again. And he had to know that. "I'm a big girl, Alec. You don't need to worry about me."

"Contrary to what you think, I do. Especially with this."

Her gaze lifted, and when their eyes met and she saw the regret lurking in his, every emotion she'd endured over the last three years hit her smack dab in the center of her chest until all she knew was loss.

She blinked back the sting of tears and looked away, knowing that, with Alec, there would never be anything but the reminder of that loss, no matter how much she craved something more.

"Well, I'd better go," she said weakly.

"Yeah, me too." He stepped back. "Take care, Raegan."

Cool air washed over her, replacing all the sultry heat she'd felt near him, and rejection—a familiar, bitter rejection—hardened like ice in her belly. One she thought she'd gotten over. One that, even now, chilled her to the bone.

She swallowed the rejection back. Repeated the mantra in her head, the one that had gotten her through the worst of times: *Be tough. You can get through this.* Even managed to say, "You too."

But as she turned and walked away, she knew that loss was going to consume her all over again. She just hoped it happened when she was alone tonight and not where anyone could see.

CHAPTER TWO

Alec's stomach rolled as he waited in the visitor's room at the Santiam Correctional Institution. The room was big, with a series of tables and chairs littered throughout the space. As it was Saturday, thirty minutes before the afternoon visiting hours were up, several of those tables were occupied by inmates, spouses, and children.

Alec looked away from a woman bouncing a small girl on her knee while she spoke with a man dressed in an orange jumpsuit seated across from her. The woman could have been Raegan from the back. Or maybe Alec was just hallucinating after seeing Raegan at the hospital.

Damn, but he hadn't needed that today. Hadn't needed the in-your-face reminder that she'd moved on and he had no one to blame for that but himself. She deserved to find a scrap of happiness in this world, and he had nothing to complain about, considering the number of women he'd dated. But none of his so-called dates ever got close to being serious. Raegan's relationship with that dumbass Norris had looked serious. That whatever-they-were-to-each-other had looked serious as hell.

The heavy door across the room opened, and a corrections officer walked in with John Gilbert at his side.

Alec tensed, and all thoughts of Raegan faded into the background.

John Gilbert scanned the room with his muddy blue eyes, spotted Alec, and smiled a malicious grin. He was roughly Alec's height, close to six two, and their eyes were both blue, though different shades. That was where the similarities ended. Gilbert's skin tone was a shade darker than Alec's, his hair a dingy brown instead of blond, and he was thin and bony, whereas Alec was strong and muscular. But even without the effects of years of drug use, Alec knew his looks came from his biological mother. A mother who'd cared about him so much, she'd dumped him with this prick and taken off to he didn't know where.

Once, as a teenager, when he'd been stuck at the Bennett Juvenile Detention center on a drug charge thanks to the man now striding toward him, he'd thought about finding her. Thought about begging her to take him back. But then he'd met Michael McClane, a man who, in a short amount of time, had become more of a father to him than Gilbert had ever been. When Alec had seen what a real family was like, he'd never thought about the woman who'd given him life again.

"Wondered when I'd see you," Gilbert said, stopping across the table from Alec with a sinister gleam in his eye. "'Bout damn time you came to visit your old man."

Alec refrained from telling the piece of shit he'd never be his old man and clenched his jaw. He hadn't come here to beat a confession out of Gilbert. As much as he wanted to do just that, he knew Gilbert was too cunning to admit to anything. No, he'd only come here to see the asshat's eyes when he mentioned the girl from the hospital. One look was all Alec would need to determine if Gilbert was somehow involved in what had happened to her.

Alec's gaze passed over the bright-orange jumpsuit hanging from Gilbert's thin frame. "Looks like the food in this place sucks. A strong gust of wind could knock you over, *old man*. Pity for you."

Gilbert's eyes hardened. "What the fuck do you want?"

Neither of them sat. This wasn't a friendly conversation. Alec glanced past Gilbert toward the guard who was watching them closely as if he expected fireworks to ignite. "I heard you like using the phone."

A smug smile broke across Gilbert's weathered face. Deep lines marred his cheeks and mouth, aging him long past his fifty-four years. "Oh, you came out here for the same reason those FBI hotshots did. You think I had somethin' to do with that missing girl. I'll tell you the same thing I told them. I don't know nothin'."

The twinkle in Gilbert's eyes contradicted his words. Just as Alec suspected, the fucker knew a hell of a lot. "If I find out you had something to do with that gir—"

"You'll what? Kick my ass like you threatened to do three years ago? We both know you ain't got it in you, son."

Alec's hand clenched at his side. He saw his fist come back. Saw it plow into Gilbert's face. Saw the blood splatter and spray across the table and floor. But he held back from unleashing the rage inside him. Knew it was what the asshole wanted him to do and that it wouldn't fix the situation or get Gilbert to admit to a damn thing.

"'Sides which," Gilbert went on, "I done tol' those FBI people that wasn't me. Not my fault they can't do their fuckin' job right."

That was bullshit and they both knew it. Alec narrowed his gaze. "You stay away from me. You stay away from everything that has to do with me. Are we clear?"

"Oh, we're clear," Gilbert muttered.

Alec turned and headed for the door.

"Hey, boy," Gilbert called at his back. "How's that pretty wife of yours? Or should I say ex-wife. Maybe I'll look her up when I get outta here next week. Seein' as how you ain't got no use for her no more, that is. I bet that newscaster mouth of hers could do all kinds a' naughty things. She's just waitin' for the right man to show her how."

The cap on Alec's temper shot free, and all the anger and rage he'd been holding back bubbled up and over. He whipped back, grasped

Gilbert by the shirtfront, and yanked the man halfway across the metal table. "If you touch her, if you so much as look at her, I'll kill you, you son of a bitch."

Two guards hollered and rushed over. One shoved Alec away with a nightstick, and the other grabbed Gilbert by the arm and hauled him back.

Gilbert chuckled, a malevolent gleam in his eyes as the guard put space between them. "Still get all worked up about that news whore, huh? Oh yeah, she's a fine piece of ass. I think I will look her up."

Alec growled and struggled against the guard holding him back.

"Gilbert," the other guard yelled. "That's enough. Your visitation time is over."

The guard holding Alec was close to six five, a wall of solid muscle preventing the annihilation Alec wanted to unleash. "You need to calm down," the guard yelled as Alec struggled. "Rogers," he hollered at the other guard. He nodded toward Gilbert. "Get him the hell out of here."

Rogers hauled a laughing Gilbert across the room and through the far door, and only when Alec couldn't see the son of a bitch anymore did the red haze finally lessen.

Alec stopped struggling when he realized the guard was talking to him and tried to focus on the guard's words. The guard was threatening to call the local cops if he didn't chill out.

"I'm fine," Alec said several minutes later, still breathing heavily but no longer fighting to get free. "I got it," he said to the guard, hoping the man would release him.

The guard frowned as if he didn't believe him but finally let go. "Get out of here. And don't come back, you hear?"

Alec stepped back, but his pulse didn't slow even when he was outside in the cool winter air, staring at the cars in the parking lot. Because he now knew that, even from behind bars, his father had definitely had a hand in what had happened to that girl back at the hospital, just as he'd been involved in Emma's disappearance three years ago.

No matter how much Alec wanted to ignore that fact, he couldn't. He couldn't because he knew as soon as John Gilbert was free next week, he'd be involved in some other child's abduction before long.

———

Raegan sat at the desk in her cubicle at the KTVP studio, scanning reports of missing children in the Portland metropolitan area.

She'd spent the first two years after Emma's disappearance scouring the web for similar cases. Many had seemed promising, but none had panned out. There were always inconsistencies . . . the manner in which the kids were taken, the circumstances of the families, even the ages of the children. She'd passed all the information off to Jack Bickam at the FBI, and he'd checked into each and every one, but none had ever been linked to Emma's case, and after a while, when Raegan had realized her searches were getting her nowhere, she'd spent less and less time looking and more and more time trying to adjust to her new life alone.

But this girl—the one she'd seen today in that hospital—was eerily similar to Emma. Not just because of her hair color or because she'd sort of looked like Emma, but because she'd shown up in a park near where Emma had disappeared.

Raegan's fingers stilled on the touch pad of her laptop when she came across a case from two years before. The boy had been two years old, African American, living with his parents in northeast Portland. He'd disappeared on a field trip with his day care center. Nothing about the case was at all the same as Emma's. Nothing except one small detail Raegan might have missed if she hadn't read the whole report: the fact the boy had disappeared in the same area where Emma had gone missing, at the same park where the girl today in the hospital had shown up.

Raegan's heart beat fast as she scrolled through the article, searching for a photograph of the boy. There wasn't one. She'd known there wouldn't be one. But she scrolled back up and stared at the name of the day care center anyway.

The Giving Tree Center.

Emma had never gone to day care. Raegan and Alec had hired a private nanny who'd looked after Emma at their home in the Pearl District when they'd been at work. But that park . . . the connection to Emma's disappearance and to that girl today was too much to ignore.

Raegan hit "Print" and gathered the article from the printer on the corner of her desk. Excitement pulsed inside her, but as she looked down at the papers in her hands, uncertainty rolled through her belly. More than anything, she wanted to show this to Alec, wanted to know what he thought, but part of her already knew what he'd say. He'd tell her she was reaching. That she was making connections that weren't really there. That she was getting her hopes up for nothing. He believed Emma was dead. He wouldn't want to hear any of this.

But still . . . If he saw this, maybe he'd—

"There's my girl." Jeremy's voice made Raegan jump, and she quickly flipped the papers over and set them on her desk as he came around the corner of her cubicle. "All set?"

Raegan blinked several times, unsure what he meant. Then it hit her. Their dinner plans with Greg Jamison, the five o'clock news anchor, and Chloe Hampton, his current flame. "Oh. Um, I lost track of time."

Jeremy stepped into her cubicle and brushed a hand over her hair. "Are you alright, darling? You look rattled."

Of course she was rattled. Her emotions were on a whiplash roller coaster today, and now she'd just found what could be a lead. She was just about to tell Jeremy that when she remembered the look on his face as they'd left the hospital together earlier in the day. An emotion she could only define as relief.

Jeremy Norris had no use for children. He made it clear that kids weren't welcome in the building during working hours. Oh, he loved to run a tearjerker piece now and then because a good human-interest segment on kids boosted ratings, but his career was center stage in his life, and according to him, it should be in each and every life of the people who worked for him as well.

Raegan slowly closed her laptop. No, she couldn't tell Jeremy what she'd found because he'd see it as reaching as well, but for very different reasons than Alec. And as much as she wanted to just head home and keep researching, she knew if she bailed on this dinner with Jeremy and his friends, he'd get suspicious. The last thing she needed was a lecture about not doing her job during normal business hours.

Great move there, dating your boss.

"I'm fine," she said, shaking off the thought. She pushed to her feet and tucked the papers she'd printed into her bag along with her laptop. "Just a long day."

Jeremy smiled and squeezed her shoulders when she turned. "Then this dinner out is perfectly timed, because it'll take your mind off everything that happened today."

Raegan doubted that. Looking into Jeremy's dark eyes, she knew she wasn't going to be able to stop thinking about Alec tonight or tomorrow or even next week.

Or how much today had to have affected him.

———

Standing in the middle of a big family party was the last place Alec wanted to be tonight.

With a bittersweet longing, he watched his parents, Michael and Hannah McClane, on the far side of the private dining room in the trendy Portland restaurant, shaking hands and doling out hugs to close friends who'd come to help celebrate their twenty-fifth wedding anniversary. His own marriage hadn't made it three full years before it had crashed and burned, and he had no one to blame for that but himself.

Clearly, he hadn't been paying attention to his father's shining example of what it took to make a successful husband.

"You know," his sister, Kelsey, said at his side, also watching their parents, "when people find out they've been married twenty-five years, I still get weird looks."

Alec snorted as he watched his father pull the newest member of the McClane family, Thomas, to his side and introduce the gangly teenager to the group of adults around him. "Only from the chumps who don't know we were all adopted."

Dressed in a sleek black cocktail gown she'd designed herself, Kelsey smiled up at Alec with warm brown eyes while wisps of curly blonde hair floated around her face from her stylish updo. "And those who don't know how old we all were when we were adopted."

That was true. Alec lifted his soda and sipped, wishing it were Jim Beam more with every passing second. He hadn't been a whole lot younger than Thomas when the McClanes had adopted him, six months or so after they'd adopted Ethan. Alec and Ethan had known each other briefly at Bennett, the juvenile detention center where Michael McClane had occasionally counseled troubled youth. Ethan had been at Bennett on a murder charge pled down to assault. Alec had been there on repeat drug trafficking charges.

His gaze strayed to Michael's salt-and-pepper hair, strong jawline, and warm smile as he chatted with his guests. It took a saint to adopt two kids from such fucked-up backgrounds, but Michael and Hannah had done so because they believed everyone deserved a second chance. Alec had found that second chance with them. A chance to get away from John Gilbert, and a chance to start over. No matter how he continued to fuck up his life, he owed Hannah and Michael for that. Owed them more than he could ever repay.

Kelsey leaned close. "Look at Rusty over there. Who's the girl he's talking to?"

Alec's gaze strayed to the corner of the second-floor dining room where their other brother Rusty stood in the shadows in black slacks and a long-sleeved black sweater that covered his scars and matched his hair, conversing with a brunette Alec vaguely remembered meeting once or twice. "I think she's the Kleins' daughter."

"The senator's daughter?" Kelsey harrumphed. "Ten bucks says her parents don't know she's flirting with the dark side."

Alec's gaze narrowed as he watched the two. The girl seemed to be extremely invested in the conversation, talking animatedly with her hands and smiling in abundance. Rusty, on the other hand, sported that same detached look he always had when he was itching to get out of an uncomfortable situation.

You and me both, buddy.

Alec caught Rusty's dark gaze as he lifted his drink and shook his head. Rusty clenched his jaw and glanced toward the ceiling in a *get me the hell out of here* look only an idiot could miss. One side of Alec's lips twitched.

It was good for Rusty to get out, even if he was stuck talking to some chick he wouldn't normally look twice at. The youngest McClane brother spent most of his days alone on his fledgling vineyard in the hills outside the city, and Alec often wondered how he didn't go nuts from the isolation. But Rusty had always preferred solitude to company. Even after he'd joined the McClane family, about a year after Alec, he'd spent most of his time alone, and Alec knew that had a lot to do with his own fucked-up background. Unlike Ethan and Alec, Rusty hadn't been a resident at Bennett. Hannah McClane had found him in her ER, taken one look at his bruised and battered body, and decided he needed a home too.

Rusty had gotten his second chance. As had Kelsey when the McClanes had adopted her at ten a few years later. Their family was the proverbial melting pot, but Alec wouldn't have it any other way. And it was only because of them that he wasn't at the bar right now tossing back shots. He didn't want to let any of them down again, not when they'd done so much to raise him up.

Alec's gaze strayed to Ethan, dressed in a suit, standing with an arm around his fiancée, Samantha, who was wearing a green dress, the pair smiling and chatting with friends of their parents'. Though he didn't want it to, his chest pinched with another bite of bittersweet longing. He was happy for his brother, happy Ethan had found someone and that the someone was Sam, but he couldn't stop the burst of jealousy coursing through him when he looked at the happy couple. Especially not today, when his interaction with Raegan was still tumbling through his mind.

He took another sip of his soda, cursing the fact it wasn't alcohol and that he hadn't brought a date tonight. He always brought dates to family functions because they distracted him from looking around and seeing everything he was seeing now. And tonight he could have used that distraction because what he was seeing was everything he didn't have and wouldn't ever find again.

Kelsey tensed at Alec's side. "Julian's here."

Alec tore his gaze from Ethan and Sam and glanced toward the stairs where Kelsey's shit of a husband shrugged the dark hair out of his eyes, waved, and headed in their direction.

Every muscle in Alec's body contracted, ready for a fight. He and his brothers all suspected Julian Benedict was hitting Kelsey behind closed doors, but she denied it every time they tried to talk to her, and whenever she showed up with a new bruise she blamed it on being clumsy. "I thought you said he was in Seattle on business."

"He's supposed to be."

Kelsey plastered on the fake smile she used on all her fashion customers and awkwardly moved toward Julian's side. "I thought you weren't going to make it."

Julian slid a possessive arm around her, pulling her a little too tightly to his side for Alec's comfort. "You said this was important, so I came back early." He didn't make eye contact with Kelsey, just stared at Alec with his soulless black eyes. "You look like shit, Alec. Rough day?"

Alec wanted nothing more than to draw his fist back and pop Julian Benedict in the nose. Today, especially, it would feel good to let loose on the jerk. But he held back for Kelsey's sake. And because Alec knew he was the last person who should be doling out relationship advice, even if he were convinced her husband was a total dick.

"Yeah, I guess you could say that." Alec turned his gaze on his sister. "I need to get some air. I'll be back."

He set his drink on a nearby table and headed for the door. At his back he heard Julian mutter, "What the hell is his problem?" and Kelsey whisper in response, "It's not you."

Alec almost huffed and said, "Yeah, buddy, it is you," just to piss the guy off, but he didn't. Because it wasn't the truth. The truth was that he was jonesing for a drink. And every second he spent around people who were happy—or, in Kelsey's case, pretending to be happy—made that craving harder to ignore.

He pushed the heavy door open and stepped out onto the restaurant's second-floor patio, drawing in a deep breath of cold, January air. Lights in potted trees twinkled as he moved up to the railing and looked out over the Pearl District neighborhood.

Shit. This view didn't do a thing to improve his mood. Just made the pressure in his chest grow tighter and his need for that oblivion only alcohol could provide that much stronger. Leave it to his parents to pick a restaurant in the same neighborhood where he'd once lived with Raegan to celebrate their anniversary. The universe was clearly telling him tonight was not his night to hold it all together.

"Hey. You doin' okay?"

Alec glanced over his shoulder toward Ethan, striding toward him. He hadn't heard his brother follow him out onto the patio, but he should have expected it. "I'm fine."

Ethan moved up next to Alec, his hands in the pockets of his slacks, his brow lifted in a *don't bother trying to lie to me* expression Alec knew all too well. "Holding on to that railing a little tightly for someone who's fine."

Alec's gaze dropped to his hands, which gripped the metal railing so tightly his knuckles were white. Shit. He didn't remember doing that either.

He let go and flexed his hands against the cramps shooting down his fingers. "I just needed some air. Is that a crime?"

"No. Definitely not. I should know." Ethan flashed a smile, and Alec didn't miss the inside joke about their time together at Bennett. Drawing his hands from his pockets, Ethan leaned his forearms against the railing. "It's just the reason you need air that worries me."

Sometimes it sucked having your family know your greatest weakness, and Ethan was the worst since Alec had never been able to hide his drinking from Ethan. Back when they'd been teenagers, Ethan had witnessed Alec's weakness for alcohol in times of stress. He'd even covered for him with their parents when they'd found an empty bottle in the trash or when Alec had been too hungover to do his chores after a wild night of partying. Alec knew that was part of the reason Ethan rode him so hard now. Because he felt guilty he hadn't helped Alec quit back then before the addiction had ruined his life. But it still irritated the hell out of Alec, especially when he hadn't touched a drop in three damn years. "I'm not drinking, if that's what you're asking."

"That's not what I'm asking."

Alec's jaw clenched. "I'm not gonna have a drink either, even though after the day I've had, I deserve one. Or ten."

"Wanna talk about it?"

No, Alec didn't want to talk about it with his therapist brother. Ethan was just like their father. He'd dig until he got what he wanted, then he'd talk you to death until you told him exactly what he wanted to hear. Unfortunately, aside from a jump off this second-story ledge that would likely just cripple him instead of put him out of his ever-loving misery, Alec knew he was stuck.

He exhaled a hard breath, hating that he was such a pansy, wishing this never-ending day would just hurry the fuck up and finish. "Jack Bickam called. They found a four-year-old girl wandering alone in a park today. Asked me to come down and try to ID her."

Ethan pushed away from the railing and stared at Alec with wide green eyes. "What?"

"It wasn't her," Alec said quickly, sensing Ethan's excitement. "I knew it wasn't her before I even saw her, and I was right. Bickam asked for a DNA sample, but her parents showed up while we were at the hospital. It definitely wasn't . . . her."

Ethan's gaze darted over Alec's features. "Maybe they're wrong. If she'd been missing as long as Emma, she might look totally diff—"

"Ethan, it wasn't her. She didn't have the birthmark near her eye. And even if you don't want to admit it, I can. My daughter's dead, and we both know who killed her."

Ethan's shoulders sank, and the disappointment on his face was too much to bear. Alec leaned his own arms against the railing and looked out at the view. Itching—again—for . . . shit. He didn't know what he wanted anymore.

"Who's we?" Ethan asked long minutes later.

"What?"

"You said 'while we were at the hospital.' Who's we?"

Alec's chest squeezed tighter. "Raegan."

"Ah."

Alec hated the way that one word sounded. Dripping with pity and understanding.

"I take it things with Raegan didn't go so well," Ethan said quietly.

Alec's jaw flexed as he thought of Raegan standing in that hallway, looking gorgeous and broken all at the same time, and how much he'd wanted to wrap his arms around her and console her. "It went fine."

"Fine," Ethan repeated. "Which explains why you're standing out here in the cold, looking like you're ready to knock over a liquor store."

Alec scowled. "Fuck you, doc."

Ethan smirked and slipped his hands back in the pockets of his slacks. "You know, maybe it's a good thing you saw her. It's been almost three years since the divorce. You were bound to run into her again at some point. Portland's not that big a city."

Three years felt the same as one day, but Alec didn't tell his brother that. He stared out at the twinkling view again. "Yeah, whatever."

"Alec." Ethan's voice softened. "You have to stop beating yourself up over this. Emma's disappearance was not your fault. She could have wandered away from any of us. She could have wandered away from Raegan if she'd been the one at the park with her that day. I'm sure in the three years you two have been apart Raegan has realized that. I'm sure she's forgiven you."

Alec couldn't stop the pitiful laugh that pushed up his throat. Or the sharp stab right through the center of his chest where his heart used to be. "That's where you're wrong, smart guy. She never blamed me. She said the same damn thing you just did. Right from the start. But that's the thing." He looked over at his brother. "I'm the one who can't forgive her for that. Because no matter what you or she or anyone else says, it was my fault. And she of all people should know that."

He couldn't take this anymore. Couldn't stand here and rehash the past because his chest was on fire. He pushed away from the railing.

"Alec, wait."

He didn't. As he headed back into the party he didn't want to be a part of, he told himself he could get through this night the same way he'd gotten through every night for the last three years.

By sheer strength of will, even if he was holding on to life by nothing more than a fraying thread.

CHAPTER THREE

Raegan swirled her wine and watched the crimson liquid stick to the sides of the glass and then settle in the bottom and still.

That was how she felt. On the verge of something, swirling and waiting.

"Raegan."

She looked up at the sound of Jeremy's voice and glanced to her right. "Yes?"

A perplexed expression pulled at his features. "I called your name three times. Are you daydreaming?"

"No."

"You've barely eaten."

She glanced down at the salad she'd moved around with her fork and let go of her wine. "Oh. Just thinking, I guess."

She took a bite that tasted like cardboard and tried to smile. When Jeremy only frowned, she knew her smile had come out as a scowl.

"Sorry she's such a downer," Jeremy said to Greg Jamison across the table. "She ran into her ex today."

Shock rippled through Raegan. He was blaming her mood on Alec. Not on the fact that she'd thought she'd found her daughter, only to have that hope crushed at her feet.

Jamison's eyes widened, drawing Raegan's attention, and she knew the fifty-year-old anchor was trying to lift his brows, but his forehead didn't even move thanks to his regular Botox injections. "That's gotta suck."

Chloe Hampton, the twentysomething weather girl Jamison was currently dating, tossed back the last of her second wine and set the empty glass down with a click. "Exes are the worst. My last ex burned all my clothes when we broke up. I was pissed. I liked that red cocktail dress more than I ever liked him."

"That's because you were sleeping with me." Jamison chuckled and leaned toward the blonde, his facial muscles barely moving with his expression.

Chloe giggled and rubbed her newly shortened nose against the news anchor's. "That's true. Though I still miss that dress. Your wife wasn't much happier."

The two laughed. Jeremy smirked.

As conversation at the table turned to the day's media rankings, Raegan looked over each face, wondering what she was doing here. Jeremy was nice to her, and she enjoyed spending time with him alone—usually—but most of the people he surrounded himself with were as fake as their faces.

Her phone buzzed, and reaching around to where her coat hung on the back of her chair, she pulled it out of her pocket.

8:00 p.m. McClane Anniversary Party

Her heart felt as if it skipped a beat, and her stomach tightened as she stared at the screen.

Alec's mother had invited her to the party months ago via e-mail. At the time, Raegan had sent a polite thanks-but-no-thanks note, but she'd put it in her calendar anyway. Now, as the reminder flashed, all she could think was . . . *why shouldn't I go?* If she went, she could catch Alec before he left. She could show him the research she'd found on that missing kid. She could spend a few more minutes with him. Because God knew the bit of time they'd spent together in that hospital today had not been enough. Ever since she'd left she'd been thinking about him nonstop. About what he was feeling tonight. About how clear his eyes had been. About all the things she'd wanted to say but hadn't.

Nerves humming, she grasped her coat and pushed back from the table.

Jeremy stopped whatever he'd been saying to Jamison and looked up at her. "Where are you going?"

"Sorry. I forgot an appointment."

"Now?" He turned toward her. "It's dark outside."

"I know." She snatched up her purse. "And I'm sorry. It's a family thing."

"But . . . Raegan, you don't have any family here. Your mother's still in Europe and your dad's in New York."

He was right. Her parents were divorced and led very different lives on opposite coasts—her dad was a high-profile attorney in New York and her mother happily lived off her divorce settlement in California or wherever she chose to travel next. Raegan didn't have any family in the area to have an appointment with, but she wasn't about to tell Jeremy she was leaving him to see Alec's family.

She leaned in and kissed Jeremy's cheek halfheartedly, catching more air than skin. "I'll call you later. Thanks for dinner. And I'm sorry to run."

"But—"

"Greg, Chloe." She nodded and stepped away. "Have a good night."

Jeremy's sputtered protest echoed at her back as he pushed to his feet, but she ignored it and him and rushed toward the entrance of the posh downtown restaurant.

He wouldn't follow her. They hadn't been dating that long, and she knew she didn't mean more to him than his precious station, which was the purpose of this dinner in the first place. Pulling on her coat, she stepped out into the cool night and drew a lungful of air that felt like the first she'd breathed in days.

Hope swirled inside her like the wine in her glass as she stepped to the curb and waved for a cab. Tonight she wasn't about to let it go still. Tonight she was determined to show Alec he was wrong, that their daughter was out there somewhere, and that together they could find her.

She just prayed she could get him to listen for five minutes before he turned and walked away.

———

Twenty minutes.

Alec decided he'd give his parents twenty more minutes before ducking out of the cloistering party and beating feet back to his place where he could breathe.

"Alec." Ethan's fiancée, Sam, stepped up at Alec's side and slipped her arm around his. "There you are. Rusty here was just trying to explain to me why hair color and IQ go hand in hand." She peered up at Alec with an amused expression. "You're blond. What do you think?"

Alec cut a look at Rusty on Sam's other side. Hands tucked into the black slacks that matched his shirt and hair and eyes, Rusty shrugged his wide shoulders and waggled his brows in a *watch me get the smart girl going* way.

A frown pulled at Alec's lips. He was not in the mood to get caught up in sibling teasing. But it was better than the alternative—schmoozing with his parents' friends who knew he was the kid who, even as an adult, still had "issues."

"He's right," Alec said to Sam, flipping Rusty the bird at his side where she couldn't see. "Ethan's hair is brown, and we all know he's full of shit."

Sam rolled her eyes and smiled. "And what about Rusty?"

"That one's easy. He doesn't have an IQ."

"Why not?"

"Because that black mop of hair on his head was transplanted straight off his ass."

Sam laughed. Rusty scowled and narrowed his eyes.

"It's true," Alec said, feeling marginally better for the first time in hours. "When he joined the family, he was as bald as a newborn baby. Our parents took one look at all the hair on his ass and said, problem solved!"

Sam's shoulders shook with laughter. At her side, Rusty frowned and said, "Ha-ha, very funny."

"What can I say?" Alec muttered, glancing toward his parents, who were talking with someone in a tan trench coat on the far side of the room. "It's my blond IQ. Hey, who are Mom and Dad talking to over th—"

The words died on his lips when his father stepped to the side and his mother leaned in and hugged the mystery woman.

"Shit." The air left his lungs in a whoosh as he watched Raegan smile and hug his mother back.

"What the hell is she doing here?" Rusty murmured.

"She who?" Sam asked. "Who are you looking at?"

"Alec's ex-wife."

Alec didn't catch the rest of their conversation or what Rusty told Sam about Raegan. All he could hear was the pounding rhythm of his pulse thundering in his ears.

His first reaction was shock that she was here. His second was panic that something had happened. But as he headed toward her, all he could think about was how gorgeous she looked in the low light of the private room, how soft her hair appeared, how much he wanted to grab her and kiss her and never let her go. Just as he'd wanted to grab her and kiss her today at that hospital.

He stopped next to his father and didn't miss the happiness in his dad's eyes and the excitement in his mother's when she let go of Raegan and noticed him.

"What happened?" he said to Raegan, ignoring his parents and their reactions. "Is everything okay?"

"Nothing. I mean, yes, everything's fine." Her cheeks were rosy, her face flushed, but more than that, there was a light in her eyes he hadn't seen earlier in the day. A light that put him on instant alert.

"Then I don't understand. Why are you here?"

The light dimmed, and her unsure gaze skipped over his features.

"Alec." Hannah placed a hand on his arm. "I invited her."

He looked toward his mother. "You *what*?"

"She's family. Of course I invited her." Shooting Alec a scathing look, Hannah laced her arm with Raegan's and pulled her away. "Come on. I want you to meet Ethan's girl. She's really sweet."

Raegan flicked a wary look Alec's way, but Alec was too stunned to react. His mother had invited her? Knowing it would throw him for a loop? Knowing—even without being clued in to what had happened today—that just seeing her could send him spinning toward a bottle?

His father sighed at his side as the two women moved away. "Women. Never can tell what they're thinking."

"Or doing," Alec muttered, watching his mother and Raegan now chatting and laughing with Sam and Ethan. There was no awkwardness on Raegan's part. No worried smiles or cautious embraces. She still fit with this family like a missing puzzle piece sliding back into place. He was the one who didn't fit. An outsider on the edge looking in. The same outsider he'd been as a kid, watching families in the park when he'd pause from John Gilbert's "errands" and fantasize about a different kind of life.

"You okay?" his father asked quietly.

A hollow ache spread through Alec's chest. One that was wider than it had been earlier in the day at the hospital. He swallowed hard. Tried to tell himself this was no big deal. Failed miserably.

"Yeah," he managed. But all he wanted to do was run. Away from this party. Away from his family. Away from all the reminders of every way he'd fucked up in life.

Except he couldn't. Not now that Raegan was here. If he did, his parents would just get suspicious, and the last thing he needed was them hovering like he was an invalid again, just as they'd done three years before.

He glanced around for the waiter. "I need a drink."

His father's eyebrows shot up.

"Caffeine," Alec clarified, seeing the look. "I can still have caffeine, can't I?"

Michael McClane sighed.

Alec ignored him and went in search of as much caffeine as it would take to get through the rest of the night.

———

John Gilbert stood in a darkened section of the yard he'd never been to before and tried like hell not to shake. He'd been pulled out of his cell, handcuffed, and marched out here by the guards, then left alone to shiver in the frigid night air without so much as a fucking coat.

If he weren't ready to shit for fear a guard in one of those towers high above was about to send a slug right through his chest, he'd be spitting mad.

Footsteps sounded somewhere to his right. Heart pounding, he turned in that direction and tried to see through shadows and darkness. "Who's there?"

"Someone who can make your life heaven or hell, Mr. Gilbert."

His pulse shot up even higher. He didn't recognize the voice. It was male, deep, cultured. There was no twang to it. No accent. No bite. Whoever this was didn't reside at SCI, and he definitely wasn't one of the guards.

Puffing his chest out as much as he could, Gilbert shoved his hands into his pockets and squinted to see better. All he could make out was a shape. He didn't know how big the guy was, but he knew he could take him. He could take anyone. "What ya want with me?"

Cigarette smoke drifted his way. Fancy smoke. The kind rich people sucked in. The shape moved in the dark, and he couldn't be sure, but it looked as if the man snuffed out a cigarette with his boot and ground it into the blacktop. "You placed a call this morning to the FBI. One we found—how can I say this so you'll understand?— fucking stupid."

Nerves bounced all around Gilbert's stomach. He shouldn't have made the call, but he'd known it'd get to his damn kid. Just as he'd hoped, Alec had shown up here today hot as a chili pepper and ready to take him on—something Gilbert couldn't wait for so he could finally show the fucker who was really in charge. "I didn't tell 'em where that girl was. I had nuthin' to do with that. I mean"—he tried to laugh, but even to him it came off sounding scared and pathetic—"I'm locked up in here. I can't do nothin' from behind bars."

"Nothing except cause trouble we don't need. The package got away from its handler. Had you stayed out of it, the package would have been picked up, the transaction would have continued smoothly, and the FBI—and the police—would never have been involved. Because of your simpleminded need for revenge, Mr. Gilbert, you managed to fuck up an entire operation."

"Hold on." Gilbert's heart beat hard and fast because he saw where this was going. "I didn't know nothin' about the kid being there—I mean, package. That was a coincidence. All I done was give the name of a park to screw with the Feds."

"The name of a park you yourself have used for similar transactions. And don't lie to me about not knowing there was a transaction taking place. We know where you got your information."

A spotlight flicked on from somewhere above, but Gilbert didn't turn to see where. All he could focus on was the lifeless body lying facedown in the grass, illuminated by the light.

True fear curled through his gut like smoke twists along the ground. Even without seeing the face, he knew it was Rory Mills. A guy he'd worked with a few times and the visitor yesterday who'd told him about the missing girl.

His hands shook as the light went out, dousing the area in darkness once more. Squinting, he searched for the shadow—the man—who had him by the short and curlies.

"As I said before, Mr. Gilbert,"—a match flared in the darkness, illuminating a cigarette and masculine lips before going out and leaving nothing but the red hue of a lit end—"I have the power to make your life heaven or hell. Others in my organization, however, are ready to see you facedown like Mills."

Gilbert swallowed hard. "I was stupid. I see that now. I'll do anythin' you ask. Just give me a second chance."

The red hue of the cigarette darkened as the man drew in a puff of tobacco. "There is one thing you might be able to do for us, assuming you can make it to your release without fucking anything else up."

"I will. I mean, I'll make it to my release. Just tell me what you want me to do."

"Make sure your son doesn't dig into things that don't concern him."

"Alec? He wouldn't do that. He knows his kid's dead."

"His ex-wife doesn't. I heard from a reliable source that your son was with Devereaux today at the hospital where the Feds took the package."

"That don't mean nothin'."

"No, it doesn't. But Devereaux almost caught on to the truth three years ago. We don't want her restarting her search and uncovering something better left alone. If she does, we want you to make sure she's unable to tell anyone about what she finds."

A burst of excitement ignited inside Gilbert. They wanted him to watch Raegan. That would not be a hardship. The chick was hot, and keeping her in line would go one step further in sticking it to Alec. Gilbert nodded quickly. "I can do that."

"Good. Because if you fail this time"—the man pointed the smoldering cigarette toward Mills's lifeless body—"you'll be joining your friend down there in the dirt. We have connections in high places, and you can be found anywhere, Gilbert. Remember that."

CHAPTER FOUR

He'd left.

Raegan glanced around the private dining room and told herself she should have kept an eye on Alec. Sometime between Ethan's toast to Michael and Hannah's twenty-five years of marriage and the coffee and desserts being wheeled out, Alec had slipped out of the party and disappeared.

She glanced across the room and spotted Ethan speaking with an older couple. After setting her glass on a nearby table, she wove through the crowd until she reached his side, then waited—not so patiently—as he said good-bye and the couple wandered off.

"Hey, Raegan." Ethan turned her way. "Having a good time?"

"Sure. Have you seen Alec?"

A worried look passed over Ethan's features as he glanced past her over the crowd. "Not since before the toast."

"I was hoping to catch him for a few minutes, but I think he might have left."

Ethan's jaw clenched as he pulled his cell from the pocket of his slacks and started punching buttons.

"What are you doing?" she asked.

"Seeing if he left. As long as he has his location services on, I can see where he is."

"You track your brother?"

"I haven't needed to in quite a while. After what happened today, he's given me reason to be concerned again."

Raegan realized Alec had told Ethan about the girl at the hospital. She'd known it would throw him for a loop, even though he'd acted as if he were fine.

Ethan frowned. "Yeah, he left. Rat bastard."

"Where is he?"

"Sunset Highway. Looks like he's heading home."

Home . . . She'd known Alec had moved out of the city after their divorce, only she didn't know where. Something in the back of her head warned that tonight was not the night to talk to him about what she'd found. But something else told her he was hurting tonight, and even though she was the last person he wanted comfort from, she couldn't turn her back on him.

"Where is that?"

Ethan looked up. "You sure you want to go out there? It's supposed to snow tonight. And in the mood he's in—"

"I need to talk to him, Ethan."

Ethan's features softened. "I'll text you the address."

Relief spread through her, and she hugged him, this man who'd once been her brother-in-law. "Thank you."

"Don't thank me yet," he muttered as she released him. "Alec's not the same guy you remember."

She knew he wasn't. He was sober. Even if he railed at her for following him, tonight she wanted to make sure he stayed that way.

———

Alec looked out the window of his front room at the brake lights illuminating the darkness.

Snow fell in big white flakes that had already blanketed the countryside in a layer of white. Whoever was out there at this hour was obviously having trouble on the slick road.

He frowned because heading out into the cold to help a stranger at midnight wasn't his idea of fun. Especially after the day he'd had. But considering he wasn't getting any sleep anyway, there was no reason to sit here and be an ass.

He shoved his feet into his boots, grabbed a jacket from the hook near the door, and shrugged it on. Buttoning his coat, he jogged down the rickety porch steps of the old farmhouse he'd bought a year before and hadn't come close to renovating yet.

The wind bit at his ears and neck, and he shrugged deeper into his coat as he crossed the front yard and headed down the short driveway. An engine revved a hundred yards down the road, and he looked up just as the driver overcorrected on the ice and slid into the ditch.

"Son of a bitch." He jogged along the snowy gravel on the edge of the country road. By the time he reached the car, his ears were frozen, his muscles tight, and he wished he'd stayed at that stupid party so he wouldn't be out here freezing his ass off for someone he didn't even know.

He picked his way down the embankment. Luckily, the black Audi had been nearly stopped when it had slid off the road, so he didn't expect the driver to be injured, just rattled. He knocked on the window. "Hey. You okay in there?"

Long seconds passed, then slowly the window slid down, and he stared into Raegan's nervous face. "Hi, Alec. Um, I'm okay. I think."

Shock gave way to irritation. "Holy hell." He pulled the car door open and reached for her arm. "What are you doing out here?"

"I was—" She grasped his forearm as she struggled out of the car, slipping in the snow and falling into him. "You left the party before I got the chance to talk to you."

He closed his hand over her other arm and shifted his weight on the hillside to pull her up beside him. "So you drove all the way out here in the middle of a snowstorm? That's asinine."

Her trendy pumps slipped on the snow, and she almost went down, but he wrapped an arm around her waist and pulled her up against him.

When they reached the roadside, she huffed and pushed out of his arms. "I wouldn't have needed to come all the way out here if you hadn't run."

"I didn't run."

She brushed the snowy hair out of her face. "You sure didn't let anyone know you were leaving."

Resting his hands on his hips, he glared down at her, the cold and snow and biting wind forgotten. "Who told you where to find me?"

She crossed her arms over her chest and pursed her lips, just as she'd always done when she was irritated with him.

"Shit," he muttered, knowing exactly who'd told her where to find him. "My money's on my obnoxious therapist brother. He needs to learn to stay out of shit that doesn't concern him." He moved into the ditch again toward her car.

"What are you doing?" she called.

"Grabbing your stuff. You're not going anywhere tonight." He pulled her car door open again and leaned inside. "What else do you have in here besides your purse?"

"Um, my laptop bag is in the back."

"Of course it is," he muttered, grabbing the keys from the ignition and tossing the strap of her purse over his shoulder before slamming the door.

He moved around the car, slipping twice in the snow and grabbing on to the car to keep from going down. Once he had her laptop bag out of the back, he slung the strap over his head and hiked back up to the road.

"What about my car?" she asked as he grasped her elbow and ushered her away from the car toward the house.

"It's stuck until we can get a tow truck out here."

She glanced over her shoulder. "Aren't you even going to lock it?"

"Why? So vandals can trash it trying to get inside to search for anything valuable?"

"Vandals?" She glanced around the snowy road. "Out here?"

Frustrated she'd slowed her steps, he said, "Yes, even out here. Come on, already. It's fucking freezing and I'd like to get inside where it's warm."

She frowned but stepped forward. The heel of her pump slipped on the ice, knocking her off-balance. A yelp slipped from her lips and her hands flew up to stop herself as she went down.

"Dammit, Raegan." Alec tightened his hand around her upper arm and jerked her against him before she could hit the ground.

Her heart raced beneath her thin trench coat. He felt it all the way through his thick winter jacket. And even through the layers of cloth between them, he could feel her heat, warm, enticing, calling to him in a way nothing and no one had called to him in a long-ass time.

His pulse shot up, and sweat slicked his spine even in the cold night air. Pushing her away so their bodies were no longer plastered together from chest to hip, he kept his arm around her to make sure she didn't go down again. "The house is right over there." He pointed toward the glowing lights through the storm and started walking. "Just don't take me down with you if you fall."

"I'll try not to," she muttered.

Somehow, they made it back to his drive and up to the porch. Letting go of her as soon as they moved out of the snow, he shoved the door open and stepped inside.

Raegan shook the snow from her hair and coat and followed him in. Then slowed her steps and said, "Wow."

He knew what she was seeing. The same thing he saw every day when he walked in. Bare floorboards, open walls he'd yet to close up after he'd had the wiring redone, a worn-out couch, and the only nice thing in the house—the river-rock fireplace he'd replaced as soon as he'd moved in.

"You'll have to ignore the mess." He untangled himself from her bags and set them on the couch. "I'm in the process of remodeling."

She turned a slow circle in the living room, looking over the stack of hardwood in the corner he'd yet to lay and up the scuffed stairs that led to the even shabbier second floor. "No, it's fine. How long have you lived here?"

Shrugging out of his coat, he hung it on the hook near the door, desperate for space. "Just about a year." He turned for the archway that led to the kitchen. "I'll call you a tow truck."

The cordless sat on the counter under dinged-up white cabinets he couldn't wait to rip out. Since he couldn't count on cell service on a good day out here, and he knew the storm would only make that service worse now, he reached for the phone book from the drawer to look up the number for a tow. Just as he wrapped his hand around the book, the lights went out and the hum of the furnace clicked off, dousing the kitchen in darkness.

He glanced toward the water-stained ceiling and then to the cordless on the counter. All he could see were shadows. One click of the phone illuminated the LCD screen and confirmed the cordless had battery life but no signal. "Shit."

"I think the power just went out," Raegan said from the doorway behind him.

Yeah, no shit, Sherlock.

Fabric rustled at his back. "I still have some battery life in my cell."

"It won't work."

She lifted her head as he turned, cell phone in hand, her delicate features illuminated by the soft blue light from her phone's screen. "What?"

"The signal's spotty this far out. The whole area's a dead zone. With the storm you won't get anything."

Her cheeks paled as she checked her signal. Worry rippled over her face as she keyed into the reality that they were stuck together until the power came back on.

He tried not to be disappointed by that reaction, told himself *he* didn't want to be stuck with *her* either, but couldn't quite shake the familiar emptiness growing wider inside him.

Dammit. Why the hell had she come all the way out here in the first place?

His annoyance increased by the second. Shoving the cordless back on its stand, he moved by her and pulled the cabinet open where he kept candles and flashlights. "Does your boyfriend know where you are right now?"

"Alec, he's not my—"

He shot her a look over his shoulder, and the words died on her lips. Just before her cell's screen darkened he caught the guilt in her green irises. Guilt that only widened that emptiness inside until it was a vast canyon of nothing.

"No," she said quietly. "He doesn't know I'm here."

Alec found a flashlight and checked the batteries. "I'm sure he'll be thrilled when he finds out."

Flicking the light on, he moved past her and back into the living room where he set the flashlight on the hearth and reached for more firewood to keep the fire going.

"I'm sorry that I showed up here unannounced and put a crimp in your night," she said from the kitchen doorway. "I just . . ." She sighed. "I wanted to make sure you were okay after everything that happened today. You left the party so fast, I . . ."

The worry he heard in her voice caused a little of his irritation to ebb. She hadn't come here to mess with his head as he wanted to believe. She'd driven all the way out here in a snowstorm because she cared. More than she still should for someone like him.

"I'm fine, Raegan." He tossed a log onto the fire and moved it with the poker. He'd put her through enough hell when they'd been married. He could be civil now. "And I'm not drinking, in case that's what you're thinking. I don't even have anything in the house."

"No one would blame you if you wanted to. Not after this day."

He laughed, but the sound held no humor. "There are plenty of things you can blame me for. Not having alcohol on hand isn't one of them."

"I didn't—"

"Look." He turned toward her, ready to be done with this conversation for good. "I appreciate the concern but I'm fine. I know Ethan probably made you think otherwise, but he's just being his normal worrywart self for no reason. I'm not drinking, I'm not gonna drink, and I'm done discussing it, okay?"

She studied him in the firelight for several long seconds, and even though her face was cast in shadows, he knew what she was looking for. Proof he really was sober, that he was telling the truth, that she'd come out here for nothing.

The first he knew he could pass. His eyes had been clear ever since the day he'd awoken in that hospital with his family around him asking what the hell he'd been thinking. He hadn't touched a drop of liquor since. But the second . . . telling the truth . . . he was sure she could see right through that like a veil.

"Okay," she said softly, breaking the eye contact and looking down at the floor.

Okay. He exhaled, relieved they were off the subject of his addiction, but his heart rate still didn't slow. Because now that they had nothing pressing to talk about, the awkwardness of the situation hit him full force.

"It's late." He set the poker back in its holder. "I'll grab some blankets so you can sleep on the couch. The power should be back on by morning. If not, the neighbor up the road has a truck we can use to pull your car out."

"O-okay."

He stared at her for a heartbeat. Remembered all the times they'd snuggled together in the dark on a makeshift bed of pillows and blankets in front of the gas fireplace in their city apartment when all he'd ever wanted was her. Now the thought of being alone with her, and the weight of everything he carried, made him want to run.

"Okay," he repeated as he headed out of the room. But it wasn't okay. Nothing about the situation would ever be okay. And he had no one to blame for that but himself.

———

Raegan's stomach swirled with doubt and regret as she sat on the couch in the firelight and waited for Alec to come back downstairs with a blanket for her.

She shouldn't have come here. He didn't want her around, and he definitely didn't want to talk about the reason they'd crossed paths today. If she hadn't been so emotional, or if she'd been thinking clearly at all, she never would have gone to his parents' party. She would have stayed at dinner with Jeremy and accepted things the way they were. Then she would have soldiered on with her life like she'd done every day since she'd signed those divorce papers.

Lifting her phone again, she checked the signal. "No Service" flashed in the corner. Frowning, she dropped her hands in her lap and sighed. *Be tough. You can get through this.* She could. She had before. She'd just have to do so again.

Her gaze skipped over the table on the far side of the room. His oversized camera bag sat perched open on top, the strap of his expensive camera draped out over the wooden surface. He'd have at least three cameras in that bag, she knew. A dozen different lenses. Hoods. Soft cloths. A notebook and pen. All the things he used when he was working.

She thought of the pictures he'd taken that she'd framed to hang on their walls. One was a sunset over the devastation in New Orleans after Hurricane Katrina. Another was a young girl on the side of the road in Chile, covered in ash after Puyehue-Cordón Caulle erupted. His photographs captured life. Not the fairy-tale version of life everyone expected but the hard, brutal truth of it. His photos brought out emotion in every person who saw them, which was why she'd framed and hung them. It was also why she'd taken them down and put them in storage after he'd left. Because she'd already been dealing with so much emotion then, seeing the harsh reality of the world through his lens had been too much.

It was still too much.

The stairs creaked under Alec's weight, and she looked in that direction, happy for the distraction from the memories. Seconds later he appeared in the low light carrying two blankets and a pillow, the muscles in his shoulders and arms flexing beneath his Henley as he moved. Her memories skipped quickly from photos to the feel of those strong arms surrounding her, closing her in, drawing her tight against all that masculine perfection. And just that fast, a resurgence of emotions tightened her throat, and her stupid heart tripped all over itself.

"Here." He leaned over the back of the couch and set the items on the cushion beside her. "These should be enough. I'll come down and stoke the fire in a few hours to make sure it doesn't go out."

When he turned back for the stairs, she realized where he was going.

"Wait." She grasped the back of the couch and twisted around. "There's no heat in this house."

"You've got the fire, you'll be fine."

"Yes, but you don't. If it weren't for me you'd sleep down here where it's warm."

He gripped the scuffed banister at the base of the stairs. "I'll be fine. I have blank—"

"Alec." She pushed to her feet and faced him. "It's fifteen degrees outside, and judging from how cold it was in your kitchen, I'm guessing this old house doesn't have much insulation. You'll freeze upstairs with no heat."

"I'll be—"

"Fine. Yeah, you already said that." God, he could be so damn stubborn. She'd once found that endearing, especially when his stubbornness involved his wanting to spend time with her. Now it just made her want to pull her hair out. "If you're going to be a jackass about it, I'll just go sleep in my car."

"Don't be stupid."

"Don't *you* be stupid."

He pursed his lips and scowled.

"This room's plenty big enough for the both of us," she said, ignoring the look. "I'll take one end of the couch, and you can have—"

He scrubbed a hand through his hair. "You're not gonna quit with this, are you?"

"No, I'm not."

"Pain in my ass," he murtered. Then, "The power will probably be back on in an hour or so anyway, and we can call that tow truck."

Did that mean . . . ?

"Fine, I'll stay down here," he finished. "But on the floor. You get the couch. No arguments."

Relief whipped through her, but it quickly faded to a whisper of unease when she realized they were going to spend the night together in the same room. Something they hadn't done in over three years.

"I'm gonna grab some pillows and blankets for myself," he said, shooting her a look as he headed back up the stairs. "I hope that's allowed."

His familiar sarcasm calmed her rattled nerves. But alone, as she looked over the hard subfloor in front of the fireplace and wondered how he was going to get any sleep there, she knew those nerves wouldn't stay calm for long. Because even after everything that had happened between them, she was still crazy about this man who clearly didn't want anything to do with her. And that meant *she* might as well be the one lying on that hard floor, because there was no way she was getting any sleep in this room with him tonight.

CHAPTER FIVE

Hours later, the snow hadn't stopped and the power still wasn't on. Alec couldn't sleep, and it didn't help that the floor was hard as rock or that every time Raegan shifted on the couch feet away and grunted with the movement, images of the two of them wrapped around each other in bed flashed behind his eyes, bringing his senses even more awake.

"You're gonna wear a divot in my cushions if you don't stop flopping around," he said, staring at the shadows dancing over the ceiling from the fireplace, knowing there was no use even trying to sleep now.

She stilled. "Am I keeping you awake?"

"Just a little."

"Sorry. I guess I'm not as tired as I thought."

Neither was he. Not even close.

Several awkward beats of silence passed, then she said, "So Ethan's fiancée seemed nice."

Fabulous. She wanted to talk about his family. He was tempted to roll away from her and feign exhaustion but knew he could never pull it off.

"Yeah, Sam's pretty great."

"How long have they been together?"

"A couple months."

"And they're already engaged? Wow, that's fast. And your parents are okay with that?"

"Yeah, they like her."

"I see," she said quietly.

He knew what she was thinking. That his parents had not been so okay with the two of them getting married so quickly after meeting. But their reaction to the news had nothing to do with her and everything to do with him. His parents had always thought he was too impulsive. As a teenager, when he'd wanted something, he'd gone for it, and more often than not, that impulsivity had come back to bite him in the ass. Years later, as an adult, when Alec had told them Raegan was pregnant and that they were getting married, they'd seen his decision as impulsive yet again. It hadn't been, though. He'd been planning to propose to Raegan before she'd even told him about the baby. If it hadn't been for one horrible moment in a park he'd wished a thousand times he could redo, he'd have proved his parents wrong by still being married to her.

He couldn't tell Raegan that, though, and just the thought of it caused that hollow ache to reform in his chest. He cleared his throat. "Sam and Ethan survived a lot to be together. It's a long story, but if anyone deserves to be happy, it's those two."

"Well, good for them," she said quietly.

His chest tightened. He needed to change the topic. Talking about people being happy—especially another couple—was too painful.

"Sam and Ethan are partly responsible for my parents adopting Thomas too," he said. "He was one of Sam's students and the kid Ethan was observing when they met. When my parents found out he needed a home, well, they stepped in like always."

She was silent for several seconds, then said, "I think it's great your parents are giving Thomas a stable home and a real family. Every kid deserves that."

He couldn't stop himself from glancing over at her, and even in the dim light he didn't miss the tension in her jaw or the way she stared at the ceiling as if lost in memories of her own childhood.

That heart he was pretty sure he didn't have anymore contracted because he knew what she was remembering. Two parents who'd used her as a pawn in the war between them, bouncing her back and forth between LA and New York when she least expected it, rarely spending much time with her when she arrived at one or the other's home because their personal lives were too busy for their own child.

Raegan had grown up a child of immense wealth but massive neglect. She had a soft heart and a gentle nature, and she'd turned out okay mostly because she'd learned to take care of herself. And because she'd chosen a college in the Pacific Northwest far away from either of her parents and eventually made that her home. A big, nosy family was not something she'd had much experience with before she'd met Alec, but she'd quickly grown to love his parents and siblings in a way that, even now, surprised him. Losing them in the divorce had been hard on her. Maybe harder than he'd realized until just this moment.

She rolled away and faced the back of the couch. "I think I'm finally tired now. Good night, Alec."

"Yeah, me too," he said because he didn't know what else to say. "Night, Raegan."

He forced himself to close his eyes but knew there was no way he'd be able to fall asleep. His heart beat too hard, and a thousand different memories were spinning through his head, all centered on the woman only feet away. And even though he knew he shouldn't, he couldn't stop thinking about the feel of her curled up next to him. Couldn't stop imagining the warmth of her head resting on his shoulder. Couldn't stop wishing he could banish every fear and doubt and moment of sadness from her life.

But he couldn't. And he was the last person who should ever try.

She was a terrible liar.

Raegan wasn't sure how much time had passed, but it felt like an eternity, and she still wasn't the least bit tired. Rolling to her back as soundlessly as she could, she stared at the ceiling and focused on breathing. Thankfully, from the sound of Alec's soft snoring on the floor, he didn't have a clue she was still wide-awake.

Her stomach growled, reminding her she'd skipped dinner. Realizing lying there twiddling her thumbs wasn't going to do any good, she decided maybe a snack would help her settle down.

She folded back the blankets and pushed to her feet. The floorboards creaked, and she stilled, looking toward Alec to see if she'd disturbed him. He didn't move, just continued drawing in long, deep breaths and releasing them slowly.

She'd watched him sleep hundreds of times, but something in her heart turned over at the sight tonight. And in a rush of emotion, she realized why. Because *this* was the man she wanted, not the one she'd left at dinner. She was fooling herself into thinking she was ready to move on with someone else when she was still in love with Alec. Which meant tomorrow, when she finally got out of here, she needed to have a long talk with Jeremy and walk away from something she never should have started.

She frowned because *that* was a conversation she really didn't want to have. Dating her boss had not been a smart move at all.

She moved quietly into the kitchen, the thick socks Alec had loaned her soundless on the floor. Since her slacks weren't nearly warm enough overnight, he'd given her a pair of sweats and a sweatshirt. The sweatshirt was no problem—she'd always loved wearing his baggy shirts to sleep in—but the sweats were huge. Even after rolling the waist down three times, the legs were way too long. The only solution had been to tug the elastic hem on each leg up to her knees so she didn't trip over the fabric.

The kitchen was nearly as big as the living room with a central empty space and counters lining the walls to the right and left. The room was dark, but there was enough light reflecting off the snow outside for her to see the island jutting out ahead, separating the kitchen from the dining area, and the sliding glass doors that looked out over the battered back porch and the layer of white beyond.

She opened cupboards one by one as quietly as she could. Most were empty. Others held a few dishes and pots. The only food she found was cereal, a couple of boxes of macaroni and cheese, ramen noodles, peanut butter, and coffee. Moving to the fridge, she discovered a half-empty gallon of milk, a block of cheese, and a loaf of bread. Nothing else.

Typical bachelor food. It was the same sort of stuff he'd had in his apartment when they'd first met. During their marriage, she'd gone out of her way to make sure he ate healthy. Alec hated to cook, which had never bothered her because she enjoyed cooking, and she saw it as a winning trade-off because he'd happily done all the shopping. Clearly, though, he hadn't paid much attention to what she'd put on her lists back then because none of it was in his fridge now.

Sighing, she decided a peanut butter sandwich would do the trick. Grabbing the milk and bread, she moved to the counter, set the items down, and reached for a glass from the cupboard.

"What the heck are you doing?" Alec asked just as she lifted a glass of milk to her lips.

Raegan jerked in surprise, and the glass slipped from her fingers. Wide-eyed, she watched as the tumbler hit the edge of the aged tile counter, ricocheted off the surface, and shattered at her feet.

Glass and milk sprayed over her socks and across the floor. Something sharp stabbed into the flesh at her shin. She winced and was about to step back, when Alec yelled, "No. Don't move." Then, "Shit. There's glass everywhere. Just stay still."

He disappeared through a doorway she hadn't noticed to her right and reappeared with a flashlight, which he flicked on and set on the edge of the counter, a broom and dustpan, and a towel. "Here." He pushed the towel into her hands. "That's for the milk. Wait until I get the glass out of the way first, though."

"You scared me." Taking the towel, she pressed it against her chest and breathed, trying not to move so she didn't slice up her feet. Her socks—correction, his socks—were soaked.

"Sorry." He pulled the broom through the milk, sweeping up the glass. "I didn't see you had a cup in your hand. I—dammit."

When the broom stilled, she looked down. "What's wrong?"

"You're cut." He leaned the broom against the counter and stepped toward her.

"Wait, you're going to step on gla—"

His strong arms swept her up off the floor, and he carried her across the kitchen and set her on the far end of the island counter. Tugging her left pant leg up, she saw what she'd missed because of the thick, blousy fabric: a piece of glass at least an inch long and an eighth of an inch thick sticking straight out of her shin.

"Oh my." Her head grew light, and she must have swayed because Alec's arm was suddenly around her waist and she was leaning into his weight.

"Don't pass out on me." He shifted her injured leg so it was stretched out on the counter, then moved her back so she could rest against the wall where the counters formed an *L* shape.

"I don't do well with the sight of blood," she managed in a voice that sounded far away and weak.

"I remember. Here." He lifted the towel in her hands up toward her face. "Cover your eyes while I pull out the glass."

Her stomach rolled, and she knew better than to try to look again. Covering her head with the towel, she held her breath and waited.

With one hand on her thigh to hold her leg still, Alec said, "Okay, on three. Ready?"

She nodded.

"One, two—"

A sharp, burning pain shot across her shin, and she cried out. Something warm and soft covered the spot.

"Done," Alec said. "You can look now."

Breathing heavily, Raegan lowered the towel and glared at him. "That wasn't three."

He flashed one of his charming, devilish, adorable grins that made him look ten years younger. "It's out, isn't it?" He lifted a hand towel from her leg she didn't remember him grabbing and checked the wound, angling the towel so she couldn't see the blood. "Damn but that was a big piece of glass. Bet it hurt."

Her glare deepened, which only made his smile widen.

"Here." He reached for her hand, tugging her to sit more upright, and placed it over the towel at her shin. "Keep pressure on this. I need to go grab some first-aid supplies." He stopped a step away and glanced back at her. "Don't look at it."

She flashed him an irritated glower. With a roll of his eyes, he moved through the arched doorway back into the living room.

When the stairs creaked, indicating he'd headed up to the second floor, she lifted the dish towel from her leg. Blood oozed from the gash. Her stomach twisted, and her head grew light all over again. Lowering the towel back over the wound, she swallowed hard, but the room was already spinning like she were in the middle of a pendulum ride at an amusement park, and spots began to form all along her vision.

"Dammit, Raegan." Alec's voice sounded really far away. "I told you not to look."

"I didn't . . . look. I just . . . peeked."

Warmth seeped into her spine. Her head fell back against something solid. The familiar scent of pine and citrus surrounded her.

"Right, just peeked," he said somewhere close. Really close. "Good thing they're grooming you for an anchor job instead of on-scene reporting."

She rolled her head. When the tip of her nose brushed his throat and she inhaled his familiar masculine scent, she realized he was holding her up from behind, her back against his chest, his muscular arms wrapped around her waist so she wouldn't fall off the counter. "Don't know what . . . you're talking about."

He chuckled. "Yeah, you do."

God, he felt good. Strong, solid, warm . . . right. Her eyes slid closed as she relaxed, loving being close to him.

Long seconds passed where all she did was breathe and sigh.

"Feeling less woozy?" he asked softly above her.

"Mm. Yeah."

"Good. Because I need to get pressure on that wound."

He shifted behind her, pulling her back along the counter once more. Cool air swept along her spine, replacing all his sultry heat. Before she could stop him, his arms were gone and the wall was once more pressed into her back.

"Don't fall over." He stepped away and laid his hand over the towel covering her shin.

Pain spiraled outward from the spot, and she hissed in a breath.

"Sorry." He lifted the towel again so she couldn't see and inspected the wound. "It's deep, but I think it got you at an angle. It's not very long. Hold still while I get a bandage."

Raegan caught a flash of red on the towel and quickly looked toward the ceiling, breathing through her nose so she didn't pass out. She felt Alec's warm hands at her leg as he cleaned the wound, then pressure when he applied a bandage and finally wrapped her whole calf in gauze.

"I used a butterfly bandage," he said when he was done. "It still might need a stitch or two. We'll have to check it in the morning. You steady now?"

Raegan chanced a look down at her leg, covered in white gauze. The room was no longer spinning, and the nausea seemed to be lessening. Slowly, she nodded.

"Good." He moved around the island. Seconds later, a cupboard door opened and closed, followed by water running in the sink. The water quickly shut off, and when Alec reappeared, he held a blue plastic cup in one hand and two white pills in the other. "Acetaminophen. It'll help the pain."

Raegan reached for the cup and held out her other hand so he could drop the pills in her palm. "Don't trust me with glass, huh?"

"Not anymore."

She popped the pills in her mouth, swallowed them back with a mouthful of water, and lowered the cup to her lap with both hands. "Sorry about the mess. And nearly passing out."

"The mess is no big deal. And I remember how you are with blood." He lifted his right hand from the edge of the counter near her knee and turned it so she could see the thin white scar down the back of his middle finger. "Remember this? You hit the floor before I'd even completely unwrapped the towel from my hand."

Her cheeks heated with a memory of the night he'd broken his finger playing softball and she'd had to drive him to the ER. "Okay, in my defense, that wasn't just because of the blood. The bone was sticking out of your finger. Bones aren't supposed to protrude from the skin."

A wry smile pulled at his lips. "And the injured person's driver isn't supposed to wind up in an X-ray machine, but mine did because she hit her head on the side of the gurney on the way down. I was stitched up and in a hand brace before you were done having pictures taken."

She couldn't help but smile at the memory. They'd gone to the hospital for him, and she'd been the one who'd wound up needing the most medical attention. "You're lucky I have such a thick skull or that could have been one expensive night."

"Yeah, it would have been. It was already expensive enough with the surgery to fix my finger. If you'd needed a brain transplant, that would have decimated our savings." His clear blue gaze skipped over her features in a familiar, loving way, and when she remembered the thousands of times he'd looked at her like that just before he'd kissed her, the heat in her cheeks spread down her neck and straight into her belly.

This was the old Alec she remembered. The easy-going, sarcastic, fun-loving Alec who'd always been able to make her laugh, whose quick smile and warm eyes could brighten even her worst day. The one she desperately wanted more of right now.

Nerves jumped around in her belly. She swallowed and tried to settle her suddenly racing pulse. Told herself this wasn't then, that things were different now, that he didn't feel the same. But when his gaze dropped to her lips, she couldn't help but wonder . . . maybe.

Slowly, she set the cup at her side, braced her hands on the edge of the counter near her legs, and looked up at him. His body responded. She saw it in the way the vein at his throat pulsed. Watched the way his skin flushed. Felt the heat all but seeping from him into her at this close distance. And when his hand drifted to the edge of the counter, brushing hers, and she recognized the way his eyes darkened with need, she knew he wasn't just *thinking* those same things, he was feeling them too.

The same combustible chemistry they'd always shared flared hot inside her. She leaned forward, wanting to touch him, to kiss him, to taste him. His body drifted her way, and her eyes fell closed. Heat surrounded her, but seconds later she still felt nothing. No warmth of his touch. No brush of his lips. No lingering slide of his tongue over hers that she could sample and savor and get lost in.

Confused, she opened her eyes and looked up. Then wished she hadn't.

Unease filled Alec's blue eyes as he angled back, away from her, out of her reach. "Raegs, don't."

Her heart contracted, not because he'd moved away but because he'd used that long-ago nickname, the one he'd called her by a million times when things between them had been happy, loving, and perfect.

"Alec—"

"It's late." He stepped farther back, putting more space between them. "You're tired, I'm tired, and it's been a really long day. Neither one of us wants to do something we'll regret in the morning."

That one word—"regret"—was like a swift punch to the stomach. Rejection burned like lava in her veins, heating her skin all over again, this time not with arousal but with mortification.

She looked away. Sat up straighter. Told herself he was right. But all she wanted to do now was run.

Except she couldn't. She was trapped with him here tonight because of the snow. Trapped with an ex-husband she'd just tried to kiss and who'd made it more than clear he was no longer interested.

"Yeah, it has been a long day." She scooted off the counter. Winced when her foot hit the floor and pain echoed around the cut. Turned quickly away so he couldn't see. "If you'd just show me where the cleaning supplies are, I'll take care of that mess."

"No, I'll do it. You just go on back to bed."

Go back to bed. Like a child. Yeah, that made her feel *waaaay* better.

The etiquette her wealthy socialite mother had ingrained in her screamed she should argue and offer to help, but she didn't want to help. She wanted to go back out to that couch, throw the blanket over her head, and pretend like the last twenty minutes had never happened.

"Yeah. Okay." She stepped away. Tried like hell not to limp so he wouldn't feel guilty about her injury again and try to help her back to the couch. Because the last thing she needed was him anywhere near her ever again.

"Raegan," he called out at her back.

Not Raegs. She was back to Raegan again. Which—honestly—was probably fine. Better in the long run. Safer for her heart, for sure.

She didn't stop. Just hobbled to the arched doorway that led to the living room, unable to bear looking back.

Because she knew if she did, she'd be lost forever.

CHAPTER SIX

Several hours later, Alec still felt like shit. And that feeling had nothing to do with the fact that he'd gotten zero sleep or that he'd frozen his ass off most of the night upstairs in his room.

No, this feeling had to do with the fact he'd made Raegan feel like shit. And he didn't have a flippin' clue how to fix that for her.

At least the power was back on. As the coffee finished brewing and sunlight slanted through the kitchen windows, casting a glare on the layer of white outside, he moved to the fridge, pulled it open, and frowned. No half-and-half. Raegan always liked half-and-half in her coffee. Man, he couldn't even get her damn coffee right.

Shuffling sounded behind him. When he turned and saw the woman who'd occupied his thoughts all night long standing in the doorway to the living room, her shiny auburn hair sticking out all over, her eyes sleepy, and his sweats all but hanging off her thin body, something in his chest felt as if it took a long, hard roll.

"Is that coffee?" she asked, staring at the coffeemaker.

"Yeah." He pulled a mug from the cupboard and held it out to her. "Here."

"Thanks." She took the mug without touching his fingers and reached for the carafe.

He watched in silence as she filled her cup, feeling like an even bigger louse because she couldn't look at him. "Sorry there's no creamer."

"It's fine." She lifted the mug to her lips and sipped without turning.

Whatever he'd felt in his chest dropped like a stone into his stomach, because this was worse than yesterday at the hospital. Worse even than that awkward meeting at his parents' party. He racked his brain for something—anything—to say. "How's your leg?"

"Fine."

Fine. That was a word he knew well. One he used to get people to back off. Guilt twisted tighter inside him. "Raegan, about last night—"

"Nothing happened last night." She moved back toward the living room, limping slightly in a way that told him her leg wasn't fine at all. "I already called a tow truck. It should be here in a half hour. Can I take a quick shower?"

"Yeah." Why did knowing she'd already called the tow make him feel like more of a schmuck? "I mean, that's fine—good," he corrected, silently cursing his word choice. "There's a shower in the bathroom at the top of the stairs. Towels are beneath the sink."

"Thanks."

He followed her back into the living room. Watched, helplessly, as she grabbed her purse and headed up the stairs with her mug. He looked after her until all he could see through the spindles of the staircase was her bare feet and then finally nothing as she moved into the bathroom and closed the door with a snap, never once glancing his way.

His chest stretched tight as a drum, and a thousand emotions he didn't want to feel pummeled him from every side.

Turning away, he scrubbed his hands over his face and told himself this was why he couldn't be around her anymore. Because just the slightest smile or touch or brush of her skin against his made him miss her. And missing her—needing her—was a slippery slope for him. Tumbling off the edge of that slope had nearly killed him once before.

But even as he tried to listen to his own sound reasoning, he realized he was taking the easy way out. One of the steps in his recovery program had focused on making amends. He'd done that with his parents and siblings, but he'd never made amends with Raegan. At the time, he'd rationalized that she wouldn't want to see him and that interrupting her life would just make her miserable all over again. But he wasn't interrupting her life now. She'd come to him.

His feet stilled. He could make amends with her now. Even if it sent him into a funk for the next month, he could apologize and, hopefully, give her what she needed so she could finally let go of the past and move on.

Heart racing, he lowered his hands and turned back toward the stairs, already thinking through what to say. His elbow knocked into her laptop bag sitting on the back of the couch and sent it toppling over. Cringing, he tried to grab the straps before the bag hit the floor, but he wasn't fast enough. Papers, a calculator, and a half-empty water bottle dropped out.

He knelt for the bag, relieved there was no laptop inside. Righting it, he shoved the water bottle and calculator back inside, then shuffled up the papers and was just about to replace them as well when he realized they were news printouts. About missing-child cases in and around the Pacific Northwest.

Unease spread down his spine as he scanned the top page, flipped to the next, and scanned it and the others. He counted eight different articles about eight different kids, some as young as a year, others as old as three, who'd gone missing under questionable circumstances. A few he'd seen before, but several others were new.

New and in Raegan's bag. Research, he realized. Not for a story but for an obsession she still hadn't let go.

Slowly, he pushed to his feet and stared at the papers as his unease shifted first to disbelief and then to shock.

She hadn't driven out here last night in the middle of a snow-storm because she'd been worried about him. She hadn't shown up at his parents' party because she missed or cared about his family. She'd done both of those things because she wanted to suck Alec back into a useless search. Into a search he'd never survive if he let her. And she wanted that so much she'd even been willing to make a pass at him in his kitchen to get it.

"Thanks for the shower," Raegan said, the stairs creaking as she came down. "Where do you want me to put my tow—"

She stopped two steps from the bottom. Lifting his head, Alec noted she was back in the clothing she'd worn yesterday, her purse slung over her shoulder, her hair pinned up, and her face clean of any of yesterday's makeup. Only now that face was pale and full of guilt.

Without even asking, he knew he was right.

He lifted the papers in his hand. "What are these?"

Her gaze flicked from his eyes to the papers. "Just some research . . . for a news segment."

"These were all printed yesterday. The time stamps say"—he glanced at the top paper again—"an hour before my parents' party last night."

Twisting the damp towel in her hand, she moved down the rest of the steps. "It's not what you think, Alec."

"It's exactly what I think."

"Don't—"

"No, you don't." He stepped away from her, slapping the papers against his thigh, unable to believe he'd been so gullible. "I can't believe you're doing this again. You did this three years ago, and it got you nowhere."

"Things are different now."

"No, they're not. You just want them to be different."

"This isn't about Emma." When he pinned her with a look, she said, "I mean, okay, maybe it is a little, but it's mostly about these kids. They came from somewhere. That little girl yesterday was taken by someone. Each of the kids on those papers didn't just wander away. They were abducted."

"And you think it's the same someone who took our daughter? That's ridiculous." He held the pages out, flipping through each one. "Most of these are inner-city kids with divorced or unmarried parents. Parents who were probably involved in drugs or gangs or worse."

"Not all."

"*Most* of them."

"So what if they were? Those parents still deserve answers. Those kids deserve to have people looking for them. Searching. Never giving up. The same way people searched for our daughter and didn't give up."

He didn't want to talk about Emma. Didn't want to think about her. He looked away and shook his head. "And here I thought you came all the way out here because you really were worried about me."

"I was. I am." She stepped toward him. "I'll admit I wanted to talk to you about some of this at your parents' party, but that's not why I drove out here. I knew you weren't in the best frame of mind to discuss it, so I didn't even bring it up. I really did want to make sure you were okay after yesterday."

"That makes me feel a whole lot better. You worrying about my frame of mind. Did Ethan tell you to come out here? Did he make you think I was a breakdown away from getting stinking drunk?"

"No."

"Because it's none of his damn business or yours what I do." He slapped the papers on the top of her bag.

"Alec—"

"She's dead, Raegan. She's dead and buried somewhere, and we're never going to find her. The sooner you accept that, the better off you'll be. And the better off I'll be, because I won't have to hear about this shit ever again."

She recoiled as if he'd slapped her, and for a split second he regretted being so harsh, but she needed to hear it. Needed to admit it to herself. Needed to let go so she could finally move on.

Like you've moved on?

He pushed the thought aside. This wasn't about him. It was about her and a stupid need for answers that she was never going to find.

"What happened to the man I fell in love with?" she asked quietly. "The one who would do anything to help another person?"

"He died. The same day our daughter did."

Her gaze drifted to her bare feet, and even though he tried not to, he couldn't help but notice the way her shoulders slumped and the fight seemed to seep right out of her.

Son of a bitch. He was not going to feel guilty over that too. Not this time.

The telephone rang. Clenching his jaw, Alec strode past her into the kitchen and jerked it from the wall. "What?"

"Is this Alec McClane?"

"Speaking. Who's this?"

"Jeremy Norris. We met yesterday at the hospital."

The edge of Alec's vision turned red. Raegan's boyfriend. *Fucking fantastic.* "What do you want?"

"I'm actually trying to reach Raegan. Is she there by chance? She's not answering her cell."

Alec was tempted to tell the prick she was there all right, in his bed, just to mess with the douche. But he didn't. Because all he wanted right now was for both of them to get out of his life and leave him the hell alone.

Mood growing darker, he lowered the phone and stalked out into the living room where Raegan was zipping her bag. "It's for you."

Surprised, she looked up, then hesitantly took the receiver. "This is Raegan."

A whisper of guilt rushed over her features before she turned away and mumbled, "Hey," into the phone. "No, everything's fine," she said.

Alec tried not to listen, but dammit, this was his house. If she wanted privacy she could go outside. In the cold and snow.

"Um, I don't know," she said in what sounded like a dazed voice. "I'm not sure I'm comfortable with that."

A rumble sounded from outside, and Alec stepped around her toward the front window to see what it was. The tow truck she'd called rolled to a stop down the road near her Audi.

"Oh my God," Raegan mumbled. "Are you sure?"

Crossing his arms, Alec turned to look back at her. Shock rushed over her suddenly pale features.

"Yes, okay, I'm just about to leave. I'll call you from the car."

She clicked "End." Stared down at the cordless receiver. Turned in a daze as if searching for the base.

"I'll take it." Alec moved toward her. She handed him the phone, careful not to touch him, he noticed, but as her gaze skipped past him, over the room, he was sure she saw none of it. "Raegan, what's happened?"

"Nothing." She grabbed her coat from the back of the couch, pulled it on, then reached for her bag. Slinging it over her shoulder, she picked up her purse and moved around the couch.

Unease rolled through his gut as she slid on her impractical pumps. An unease that caught him off-balance. "Something's happened." He stepped in her path so she couldn't reach the door. "Tell me what's going on."

"You don't want to hear about it."

Suddenly, he did. "Tell me."

Sighing, she looked up at him. And when their eyes met he saw that she wasn't just shocked from her phone call or hurt from their earlier conversation, she was mad. Spitting mad, judging from the fire brewing in her deep-green eyes.

"A two-year-old boy was abducted from his backyard early yesterday evening in North Portland. The babysitter didn't notice he was missing until close to eight p.m. An Amber Alert was issued, but the police found no sign of him until this morning. Cops discovered an abandoned blue Ford Focus on the shoulder of Highway 26, about ten miles from Banks. Looks like it had engine trouble. The boy was in the backseat alone." She stepped around him and pulled the door open.

Cool air swept over Alec's spine as he stood in the center of the room, his heart beating fast, his skin tingling not from the sudden drop in temperature but from a prickly heat that swept all over his body. An uncomfortable heat he didn't like. He turned after her. "Raegan, was he—"

She stopped on the snowy porch. "He's alive. Just scared. Sorry I bothered you last night. It won't happen again."

She tugged the door closed with a snap and rushed down the steps. Heart pounding hard, Alec stared after her through the rectangular windows in the top of the door, unsure what to do, what to say, what to think for that matter.

Another missing kid. Gone without a trace. Almost the same age as Emma.

Was it a coincidence? It had to be a coincidence. But no matter how hard he tried to convince himself of that fact, he couldn't quite believe it.

Raegan's voice echoed in his head. *What happened to the man I fell in love with? The one who would do anything to help another person?*

His mind stumbled back over the papers he'd scanned this morning. All those missing kids. Too many missing kids. The heat searing his skin intensified, and his pulse turned to a whir in his ears.

He didn't believe Emma was still alive. He knew she was dead. Knew John Gilbert had killed her, even if he could never prove it. But the kids who'd shown up in the last two days weren't dead. They were alive. They had parents somewhere who were probably as desperate to find them as Raegan was to find Emma. And if they were somehow connected to the other missing cases in Raegan's bag—and that was still a big *if* at this point—someone needed to figure out how. The police weren't doing it. The FBI so far hadn't been able to find a link. He and Raegan were both journalists. Their whole lives were spent investigating things others gave up on.

Make direct amends with the people you have harmed . . .

The ninth step in his recovery program echoed in his head. He still hadn't made amends with Raegan. He'd wanted to this morning, then he'd found those papers. Something was always stopping him. Time, distance, work. Excuses. The heat in his skin turned to a tingle he couldn't ignore. If he didn't make things right with her now, he might never have the chance again. If he let her walk away this time, something inside told him he'd regret it for the rest of his life.

His gaze drifted down the road to her car already out of the ditch and parked on the shoulder. The temperature had warmed up enough so the ice was beginning to thaw. He focused on Raegan standing next to her car, writing a check for the tow-truck driver.

Urgency sent him into the kitchen. He shoved his feet into his boots and pushed the back door open. Moving quickly around the side of the house, his boots crunching on the snow, he headed down the drive. Out on the road, Raegan's engine started, and exhaust spilled out of her tailpipe. Alec pushed his legs into a jog and reached her just as she pulled out onto the road.

He rushed in front of her car. Her Audi jerked to a stop, and she stared through the windshield as if he'd lost his mind.

The driver's side door swung open. "What the hell are you doing?" She stepped one foot out of the car, her hand on the top of the door, her other hand still on the wheel. "Get out of my way."

He held up both hands. "Just wait."

"Wait for what? You already said everything there was to say."

"No. I didn't."

Her features tightened with an anger he didn't miss. "Just get out of my way, Alec."

She climbed back into the car, slammed the door. Panic spread through his chest. A panic he couldn't contain. He moved to the driver's side door and stood close—too close for her to pull away without running over his feet—and knocked on the glass.

Her jaw clenched down hard as she lowered the window halfway. "What?"

"Just . . . wait. Okay?" He floundered for the right words. Now that he was out here, he wasn't sure what he wanted to say.

"I don't have all day." She glanced at the clock on her dashboard. "I have to be back in Portland for work."

It was barely six a.m. She didn't have to be at work this early. She just wanted to get away from him. And he couldn't blame her for that. Not after the things he'd said to her in his house.

He rested his hands on his hips, searching again for the right words. "I'm sorry, okay? I know you think I'm an ass, and you're right. I just . . ." Shit, this was harder than he thought. "I can't go back there. Rock bottom is a place I won't survive a second time. I can't put my family—" No, that wasn't right. "I don't want to put you or anyone through that again."

Her shoulders relaxed, and her gaze drifted to the steering wheel. He watched the fight seep out of her like a helium balloon losing air. She knew he was talking about his drinking. Knew she was thinking about how bad it had been in the weeks before he'd finally left her. The only thing that kept him from losing it right now was the knowledge that she'd never seen him at his very worst.

He scrubbed a hand through his hair and sighed. "She's gone, Raegan. I know you want to believe otherwise, but I can't. Not if I have any hope of making it to tomorrow. Because the alternative . . ."

His throat grew so thick he had to look away from her. "The alternative is something I can't think about."

Silence spread between them like a vast, empty chasm. And when the wind blew Alec's hair away from his forehead, a shiver rushed down his spine, reminding him it was still close to thirty degrees, in the middle of winter, and that he was wearing nothing but jeans, a black long-sleeved T-shirt, and boots, laying himself bare before the only person he'd never wanted to hurt.

"Okay," she said quietly, still staring at the steering wheel. "I get it. I—I won't bother you with any of this again."

She reached for the drive stick, and knowing she was about to leave pushed him right back into urgency mode. He slapped a hand on her window so she couldn't roll it up and shut him out. "That doesn't mean I want anyone else to go through what we did, though."

Her gaze lifted to his, and in her soft green eyes he saw surprise and doubt.

Do it. Make amends for all the shit you put her through. Set at least one part of this nightmare right.

"I'll help you," he said before he could come up with an excuse. "With these cases. There might be some similarities. Something the cops are missing. If you want my help looking into them, I'll do it."

Their eyes held. He didn't have a clue what she was thinking or feeling. All he knew was a burning desire to help her.

"Are you sure?"

"No." His stomach tightened. "But it's the right thing to do for those kids." *And for you.*

Her gaze drifted back to the steering wheel. Slowly, she nodded. "Okay. I—I appreciate the help. You have a good eye for research. That's part of the reason I wanted you to see the files."

He wanted to ask what the other part was but forced himself not to. As much as he wanted to hear that she still cared about him, he knew it would be too much.

Letting go of her car, he stepped back. "You have to go to work, and I have a few things I need to do here. Let's meet tonight. You can show me what you've found, and we can go from there."

She nodded, bit her lip. Looked up as if she wanted to say something more but held back.

Finally she nodded again and reached for the drive stick. "My number's the same. Text me later and we'll set up a time."

"Okay." He watched as she slid the window up and carefully pulled out onto the road. As her brake lights faded in the distance, shining red over wet pavement, he couldn't help but notice they looked like two giant warning beacons.

And like the fool he'd always been where she was concerned, he was about to ignore them and charge headfirst into something that just might kill him.

CHAPTER SEVEN

The coffee shop where Alec suggested they meet later that evening wasn't at all what Raegan expected.

The chic establishment on the west side of the city, a twenty-minute drive from her apartment in the Pearl District, sported trendy purple couches, gold chairs, and low tables. It also included a long bar, displaying rows of wines and craft beers.

Wine and beer had never been Alec's vices. He'd liked the hard stuff—Jack, Jim, Johnnie, Jose, even Captain Morgan when he'd been in the mood. But alcohol was alcohol, and Raegan's nerves kicked up as she watched patrons sipping from wineglasses or pilsners, wondering if he knew the place he'd picked wasn't just a coffee shop but also a wine and beer bar.

She pulled her phone from her jacket pocket and was just about to text Alec when the door opened behind her, and a wave of cold rushed down her spine.

"Did you get a table yet?"

Startled, she turned, heart pounding, fingers tingling, and stared up into Alec's blue eyes.

For a moment, she was blinded by his beauty. Those mesmerizing eyes, his shaggy blond hair, and the two days' worth of light stubble on his square jaw. Then he lifted his brows, and she realized she was staring. Heat rushed down her cheeks, forcing her to glance quickly away. "Um, no. I wasn't sure if—"

"Hey, Alec." A cute twentysomething brunette walked up to the check-in table to their left, winked Alec's way, and reached for two menus. "Don't usually see you in here this late."

"Hi, Molly. Working tonight." He held up two fingers. "Two of us."

The brunette gave Raegan the once-over and turned. "This way."

Raegan followed the brunette, weaving through tables toward the back of the restaurant, and didn't miss the way the girl kept glancing back past Raegan, smiling at Alec as if the two were close friends.

"Here you go." The brunette stopped at a table near a purple velvet drape and set out both menus. "Your regular table."

"Thanks," Alec said with a grin.

Irritated for reasons she didn't want to admit right now, Raegan moved around the girl and pulled out her chair. On the other side of the table, Alec did the same, but the waitress's hand on his arm stopped him. "Can I get you a beer? Or maybe some wine? We have a new pinot from Ribbon Ridge that's fantastic. I sampled it last night."

"Not for me." Alec's smile was warm and friendly, and he didn't make any move to dislodge his arm from the girl's grip. "Just coffee."

"Decaf or regular?"

"Regular, please. Thanks, Molly."

The brunette grinned and squeezed his arm. "You are so predictable." She finally looked toward Raegan. "And you?"

"Coffee's fine for me too. Black."

The girl let go of Alec—finally—and turned without another word. Even though Raegan tried to stop the burst of jealousy, it bit her just the same.

Alec peeled off his leather jacket, slung it over the back of his chair, and sat. "Since when do you drink black coffee?"

"Since I became single."

His hand stilled against the napkin.

And, dammit, knowing that had come out just as bitchy as she suddenly felt, she relaxed her jaw and told herself not to get worked up. They were no longer married. He could flirt with and date whomever he pleased.

Just please don't let it be that skinny tart.

She cleared her throat and reached for her bag from the floor, working for nice. "There's never any creamer or half-and-half in the break room at work. I started drinking black coffee there. Besides, I hate to go—"

"You hate to go to the store alone after work. I remember."

He laid the cloth napkin over one thigh and rested his muscular forearms on the table. "Okay, show me what you've got."

For a second, she studied his arms, the thick blond hair on his tanned skin, his wide palms and long fingers threaded together in front of him. Then her gaze lifted to the light-blue T-shirt that matched his eyes stretching over toned shoulders and chiseled pecs. And in a rush, she remembered how good it had felt to be surrounded by those arms only last night.

"Raegan?"

"What?"

"The papers?"

"Oh. Right." Her cheeks heated, and she looked quickly away, searching through her bag for her research. God, she'd been staring. And he'd noticed. "Yeah. Here they are."

She pulled out a stack of papers, more than he'd seen this morning, and set them on the table.

Unease passed over his features, and she remembered his admission out by her car about hitting rock bottom. About not being willing to go back there. She'd known he was talking about his drinking then, but now she couldn't help but wonder if he'd meant something more.

She wanted to ask about it. Wanted to know what had happened in the time they'd been apart. Wanted to know why he'd turned to alcohol instead of to her. After they'd lost Emma, all she'd wanted was him. But he'd needed the bottle. She'd tried to tell herself it had nothing to do with her, that his addiction went back years, but she'd never truly believed it. In her heart, she'd always felt as if he'd made a choice, and it hadn't been her.

He scanned the first page, then flipped to the second. "How's your leg?"

Chitchat. He was making chitchat. She could do that too. She focused in on a young couple laughing over a bottle of wine. "Fine."

"Did you have someone take a look at it?"

"No, it's better today." That wasn't exactly a lie. It was still sore but definitely better. God, she remembered laughing like that with Alec. Remembered smiling. Remembered so many things. Did he remember any of them?

From the corner of her eye she watched as he frowned and flipped to the next page.

Silence stretched between them. An uncomfortable silence she hated. "How often do you come here?"

"Whenever I can," he said without looking up. "They have the best coffee in town."

Raegan frowned as the bubbly brunette with eyes only for Alec headed their way with two steaming mugs.

"Here you go." The girl set Raegan's cup on the edge of the table and placed Alec's directly in front of him so she could lean way in and brush his arm with hers while drawing attention straight to her breasts, which were practically falling out of her low-cut, black, V-neck T-shirt. "Anything else I can get you, Alec?"

Raegan rolled her eyes. Across from her, Alec leaned back and smiled. "No, thanks, Molly. We're good for now."

"Okay." The girl rested both hands on the table, leaning in a little too long, then finally winked and turned, never once looking Raegan's way.

Jealousy came roaring back, a jealousy Raegan knew she shouldn't be feeling, considering she was—or had been until this morning—dating someone else.

Not wanting to think about the awkward conversation she'd had with Jeremy at the station or about the fact he hadn't seemed too upset when she'd told him she thought it was best they stopped seeing each other, she glared after the brunette. "I'm surprised you come here, considering the atmosphere."

Alec lifted his coffee and sipped. "You mean the booze? They don't serve it in the mornings, and wine and beer don't tempt me."

No, of course wine and beer didn't tempt him. Because obviously the tight-assed, big-boobed brunette distracted him from the alcohol around him.

She crossed her arms over her chest, her taste for coffee long gone.

Alec shuffled the papers in his hands, then laid them on the table in front of him. He handed three across to her. "These I think we can disregard."

She took the papers with a scowl and scanned them.

"The first looks like a classic custodial abduction to me. Separated parents, kid is picked up at day care and disappears. The description the day care provider gave is way too similar to the father. The second we can disregard because the kid was too old. He was snatched from an elementary school. That puts him at five or six, maybe even seven. It's outside the age range for the rest of these cases."

"And the last?" Raegan flipped to the bottom paper.

"Geographically, I don't think it fits. The kid went missing from a farm in the Coast Range. Unfenced yard, property bordered by woods. Kids wander. Even toddlers. You hear about it all the time. I bet they'll find that boy in the spring after the snows melt."

Sickness rolled through Raegan's stomach. If Alec was right and that child had simply wandered off, she couldn't imagine the guilt those parents would feel when he was finally found.

Actually . . . her gaze lifted to Alec seated across from her, sipping his coffee once more. Memories flickered behind her eyes, all the times she'd told him what had happened to Emma wasn't his fault, and the guilt that had lingered in his gaze.

Yeah—she swallowed hard—she could imagine it. She'd lived it. Was still living it.

Looking back down, she set the papers aside and reached for the ones he'd laid out in front of him. "So why these? What about them caught your attention?"

"The kids are all young enough not to communicate well."

Raegan's brow lowered. The ages varied by case. Some were as young as one, others as old as four. A one-year-old she could buy as not able to communicate, but a four-year-old could definitely talk . . . and in some cases never stop talking. "This one here is very verbal." She held up a page. "She was three when she was taken, and her parents reported she started talking at eleven months."

"True, but even a highly verbal three-year-old kid isn't going to be able to articulate well. You asked me why these. I look at these cases and see a pattern. Remember that story you were researching a few years ago? The Coast Killer? The one who was murdering all those girls?"

"Yes." Raegan glanced down at the papers again. The Coast Killer, as the news had labeled him, had murdered five young women in a six-month span and dumped their bodies in the Coast Range. It had been one of the biggest stories in the area when Raegan was first starting with the station.

"You have to think of these cases like that. There are patterns if you look hard enough."

"Are you saying you think these cases are linked? If they were linked, the police would have picked up on that."

"Not if they weren't looking deep enough. And isn't that what you think? That they're linked? Isn't that why you asked me to look into them with you?"

His eyes were as clear and focused as she'd ever seen them. He spent his life photographing others. Saw things most people didn't. He could do the same with a case file, which was exactly why she'd wanted to show him all this. But thinking the cases were connected and hearing that stated out loud were two very different things.

"So what's the connection?" she asked. "If we're saying these cases are linked, there has to be something more than just the fact each of these kids were young at the time of their disappearance and likely didn't communicate well. The Coast Killer went for blonde-haired, blue-eyed, early-twenties women. Most he met in bars. One he picked up on the side of the road when her car broke down. I don't see those kinds of similarities here." She held up a paper. "This boy is African American, this one Hispanic, this girl is Caucasian, and this one's Korean."

"Yeah, I noticed that." He shifted in his seat, rested his elbow on the table, and brushed a hand over his mouth, looking uneasy. "It's almost as if . . ."

"As if what?"

Frowning, he dropped his hand. "It's a stupid thought."

"There are no stupid thoughts when we're brainstorming, remember?"

Something in his eyes told her he did remember the often-used phrase from when they'd worked on something together in the past, but he clenched his jaw and looked down at the papers before she could tell what he was thinking. "On the surface, race could seem random. But something tells me it's not. It's almost as if someone's targeting certain kids for a reason. Like whoever's doing this is going shopping. One African American kid here, one Korean kid there. It's very specific, almost like someone's checking off a list."

"For what?"

"I don't know. But I bet if we get a map and plot where each of these kids lived, we might see other similarities."

Raegan looked back down at her paper, confusion wrinkling her brow. "They all came from urban addresses, I see that, but these are all over the Northwest."

"Right. A couple of these kids went missing in Seattle, a few right here in Portland. There are two from Spokane. They're all metropolitan areas, like you noticed, but look at the Portland addresses." Raegan's gaze followed his finger to an address listed on the paper. "You know where that is, don't you?"

Yeah, she did. One of the worst neighborhoods in the city.

Alec leaned back in his seat. "Maybe I'm wrong, but I don't think race is the link here. I don't even think it's age so much as it is the parents. How they lived, what kinds of neighborhoods they lived in. I bet if we search deeper we'll find that each of these kids came from low-income families. Maybe noneducated or drug-addict parents. People who don't have the resources or connections to support a lengthy search for a missing child."

Like the resources they'd had when they'd searched for Emma.

Raegan swallowed hard as she stared at the papers. The police would have looked into the possible links between these cases. They would have checked race and age and location. Would they have seen what Alec saw, though? That it wasn't just the location but type of location that could link these kids together?

Alec reached across the table and pulled three papers from the stack still in her hands. "These are the ones I say we start with. All three kids went missing here in the Portland area. They're local. Should be easy enough to check out. Neighborhood alone isn't going to tell us anything. We should interview the parents to see if our hunch is correct and if there are any other similarities between the kids we're missing. After that we can widen our search and look into the others."

"And what about the other two. The kids who were found yesterday? The girl in the hospital and that little boy found in a car on the side of the highway?"

"They may or may not be connected. We can find out pretty quickly, though. Remember my friend Hunt?"

Hunter O'Donnell. Of course she remembered him. Hunt and Alec had gone to college together. "Yes."

"I'll give him a call and see if he can look into those two for us. He has a way of digging up things even the press can't."

Hunt was a former-military man who now ran his own PI and securities firm somewhere in Portland. Raegan had never approved of some of his questionable methods of obtaining information, but she'd been willing to look the other way when Emma had disappeared, and she was willing to look away now. "Okay."

Alec finished the rest of his coffee. "Why don't you pick which one you want to start with tomorrow and we'll set up a meeting with the parents." He pulled his phone from his pocket and checked the screen. "I have a conference call about an upcoming assignment in the morning, but I could meet you around one o'clock if that works for you."

"Yeah, I think I can do that." Jeremy had given her free reign to investigate these cases. He'd told Raegan when they'd met today that he knew she needed closure and was hoping looking into these cases would do that for her. She wasn't stupid, though. She knew what he really wanted was a story, which was the real reason he hadn't been the least bit upset when she'd called things off between them. A story—and the ratings it could provide—was always more important to Jeremy than anything else.

"Okay, then." Alec pushed back from the table and reached for his coat. "It's late. I need to get going."

"Yeah, me too." Raegan rose as Alec pulled a twenty from his wallet and dropped it on the table. A generous tip for two black coffees, even with all the flirting from Molly the wonder server.

"You want to take that to go?" He nodded at her untouched mug.

The last thing she wanted to do was take any memory of that waitress with her. She shoved the papers back into her bag and shook her head. "I'm fine."

Alec shrugged and turned toward the door.

With nothing else to do, Raegan tugged on her coat and followed. The air was chilly as they stepped out onto the sidewalk, the bell on the door jangling after them. A few dirty piles of snow from last night's storm still lingered against the edge of the building, but as the temperature had warmed up into the forties during the day, they were almost gone.

Alec tucked his hands into the pockets of his jeans and looked toward her. "Did you drive or take a cab?"

"Drove."

"Where'd you park?"

She angled her chin ahead. "Just around the corner."

He tipped his head the other direction. "I'm this way. You okay getting to your car alone?"

Something in her chest pinched tight. "Yes, Alec. I've managed to get to my car just fine the past few years alone."

He nodded again but looked away, and she sensed the flex in his shoulders had nothing to do with the temperature and everything to do with this awkward situation between them.

What was between them? History. A little of the same old chemistry they'd always shared, judging from the way he'd looked at her last night in his kitchen. And guilt. Not a whole lot more, though. As much as she wanted the old Alec back in her life, she had to accept the fact that he never would be. And even though that truth hurt her heart, at least she had this—whatever it was they were doing together—to tide her over, and hopefully help her move on.

"Well, I guess I'll see you tomorrow," he said. "I'll text you when I'm on my way into the city."

"Okay."

She watched him walk away from her and remembered the last time she'd seen him before the divorce. When he'd moved out of their apartment. He hadn't spoken much to her when he'd been packing his clothes, hadn't asked to take any of their pictures or even the furniture they'd bought together. Just zipped his bags and left without so much as a good-bye. And when she'd realized he really was going for good, she'd rushed down the stairs after him, stopped him on the street, and told him that even though he was leaving, she wouldn't give up. She'd never give up on them.

Her heart twisted with the memory. At the way he'd laughed in that cold, heartless way and said, *"We only got married because you were pregnant. Now that she's gone, there is no us."*

A familiar wave of grief washed over her, one that threatened to suck her down into a funk if she let it. Breathing deeply, she looked away from him and headed for her car, wishing a hundred things could be different between them, knowing they never would be. It was finally time to accept it all and get on with her life, even if her heart didn't want to agree.

She pulled her keys from her bag and hit the unlock button on her fob as she rounded the corner. Three cars down, her Audi's headlights flashed, and the driver's side door clicked as it unlocked. She crossed to her car, tugged the door open, and tossed her bag on the front seat as she slid inside and drew another deep breath that did little to make her feel better. Fragmented memories of everything Alec had said tonight swirled in her mind as she looked up and spotted a flyer of some kind stuck under her windshield wiper, blocking her view.

Frustrated, she climbed back out and reached for the paper, expecting news about a rave or some Sunday sermon invite. But the paper in her hand wasn't an invite or an advertisement. One look told her whoever had placed it there had known this was her car.

They'd known because it was meant specifically for her.

YOU ALWAYS THOUGHT SHE WAS ALIVE.

STOP WHAT YOU'RE DOING OR SHE'S DEAD.

CHAPTER EIGHT

Alec's nerves were shot by the time he pulled his truck to a stop in front of Raegan's building the next day.

He'd stupidly suggested he pick her up so they could drive together to the first interview. It had seemed like a logical plan. Now that he was sitting outside her building—the same building they'd once lived in together—he wasn't so sure.

He'd thought she'd moved. Hadn't realized she'd stayed in the same place until she'd texted him her address after he'd already been on his way into the city, And now that he was here it was too late to back out and change plans.

Why the hell hadn't she left?

Common sense told him it was because this was a nice building in the highly desirable Pearl District of Portland, close to shopping and restaurants and entertainment, all things Raegan enjoyed. But he couldn't imagine walking into that apartment day after day, knowing Emma would never toddle out to greet him. And when he thought of all the nights he and Raegan had spent there together, in their bed, on the floor, in the shower, on the couch in the living room, even on the dining room ta—

"Shit." He ran a shaky hand down his face, trying to ignore the bruising rhythm against his ribs. He did not want to go up there. Knew he'd never survive it.

Grabbing his phone from the console, he texted her. I'm downstairs.

An ellipsis blinked on his message screen, indicating she was typing. Seconds later her response flashed on his screen. Come on up. The door's open. I'm not quite ready. The code to get in the lobby is 6429.

"Dammit." His pulse beat faster, and nerves bounced all around in his gut. He couldn't go up there. Didn't need the memories or the flip it could trigger inside him. But the longer he sat in his truck, the more he knew he looked like a coward, and the whole reason he was doing all this was to make amends, right? He could spend five minutes in her apartment—hers, not theirs—to make that happen.

Muscles tight, he climbed out of his truck, slammed the door, and moved onto the sidewalk. He punched the code into the security panel near the door and waited until he heard a click. Pulling the door open, he drew a last deep breath of fresh air and told himself to relax. He could get through this. It was no big deal.

But man, a shot of Jim Beam sure wouldn't hurt any.

He bypassed the elevator for the stairs, hoping the physical exertion would kill the alcohol craving. Unfortunately, by the time he reached the fifth floor he was still keyed up and jonesing for a drink, only now he was sweating too.

"Son of a bitch," he muttered as he stood outside the apartment he used to share with Raegan and knocked. "She better seriously appreciate the effort here."

"Come in," Raegan's muffled voice echoed through the door. "It's open."

Fuck. He didn't want to go in. He wanted her to *come out.*

His palm grew damp as he forced himself to reach for the handle. Like she'd said—unfortunately—the door was unlocked, and the knob turned in his hand.

The short entry hall swirled around him as he forced his feet forward and let the door snap closed at his back. The coat tree Raegan had picked up at the Saturday Market stood to his left, the trench coat she'd been wearing yesterday hanging from one side. To his right, the antique hutch he'd bought for her birthday was still pushed up against the wall under a decorative mirror she'd had in her old place when they'd first met. The air seemed to close around him, and his chest grew tight. Feeling boxed in, he moved into the living room, hoping more space would help him relax, but the sight of the familiar room drew his feet to a stop at the threshold and sent pressure spinning through his chest like a top.

The furniture was exactly the same—same burnt-orange couch they'd saved three months for when they'd first been married, the same gold throw pillows Raegan had picked out at a flea market they'd wandered through one drizzly Saturday afternoon still scattered across the seat. The scuffed round coffee table was just as he remembered—also a flea market find—as were the mismatched, oversized side chairs, one off-white, one gold. He looked across the living room to the kitchen with its wide island and familiar stainless-steel appliances where he'd watched Raegan cook more times than he could count. Even the round, shabby-chic table and four upholstered gold-striped chairs that he'd bought Raegan for their first Christmas were the same. Still sitting in the breakfast nook with its wide windows that overlooked the patio and the city view, waiting to be used.

The air caught in his lungs. It was like stepping back in time, like walking through a memory.

"Sorry I'm running late," Raegan called from the hall that led to the two small bedrooms. "I'll be right out."

Her voice jolted him out of his memories, shocking him back to the moment. Swallowing hard, he flexed his hands and closed them into fists, did it again and again and focused on the sensation as he forced back the pain threatening to suck him under.

Thankfully, it worked. The memories faded, the ache subsided. But as they did, his alcohol cravings intensified. In a rush, he looked toward the kitchen cupboards, wondering if Raegan had anything hard stashed behind those doors. He took a step in that direction but faltered when he noticed subtle differences in the apartment, ones he hadn't seen on first look.

The high chair that had sat against the wall between the kitchen and breakfast nook was gone. The magnetic alphabet letters were missing from the fridge. There were no toys in a basket near the fireplace. No outlet protectors covering the plug-ins low on the walls.

The hole in his chest that he lived with daily seemed to grow, creating a crater beneath his ribs. Turning away, he stared at the bookshelves on both sides of the fireplace, scanning titles and tomes in a desperate attempt to take his mind off everything that was missing. But instead of helping, all that did was tear at something in his chest. Because two seconds was all it took for him to spot the framed photo on the third shelf. The one of him and Raegan, both kneeling down behind Emma in her high chair on their daughter's first birthday.

He'd been wrong. He did still have a heart. A shadow of one that twisted so hard in the center of his chest it felt as if it were ripping in two.

The backs of his eyes burned as he stared at the photo. At Emma's little hands covered in blue icing. At the cake smeared all over her cherub face and in her auburn hair. At the way she was laughing hysterically as she pressed her frosting-covered hand against Alec's cheek while he smiled at the camera and Raegan looked at both of them with nothing but love and happiness in her eyes. A thousand emotions hit him like daggers driving deep into his chest, stealing his breath, blinding him with pain, robbing him of the ability to think of anything but that long-ago, precious moment.

"Sorry to keep you waiting," Raegan said from the hallway. "I was at the station this morning, and one of the interns spilled coffee all over my blouse. I had to come home and take a quick shower because I smelled like a barista."

Alec blinked quickly, turned away from the photo, but couldn't bring himself to look at Raegan. Focusing on breathing, on taking one lungful of air at a time, he glanced over the room again, only everything he saw reminded him of Emma. Of Raegan. Of a time when he'd been happy and loved and whole.

He couldn't stay here. Needed to get out. Was going to lose it if he didn't leave *right fucking now*.

"That's fine." He strode past her, careful not to look at her or anything except for the carpet in front of his shoes. "Let's go."

"Um, okay," she said after him. "Let me just get my coat."

He didn't wait for her. Pulling the door open, he moved into the hall as fast as he could. "I'll grab the elevator."

He moved quickly down the hall, punched the elevator button, leaned a hand against the wall, and closed his eyes. Sweat slicked his skin everywhere, and his pulse still raced like he'd been in a fight. But at least out here in the hall he wasn't about to hyperventilate.

A click sounded behind him, followed by footsteps. Seconds later Raegan moved up on his right. "Everything okay?"

The elevator dinged, and the door swept open. Still feeling unsteady, Alec stepped inside and said, "Fine."

He punched the lobby button and stared at the wall panel as Raegan moved into the car next to him. "Fine." There was that word again. The one he'd gotten good at using over the years. He wasn't fine. Couldn't remember the last time he'd been fine. Was shocked people couldn't see through his bullshit like tissue paper.

The car jolted to a stop at the third floor, and the doors whooshed open. Six teenaged boys dressed in shorts and tanks, one holding a basketball, moved into the car, chatting and laughing as if they were alone.

Raegan stepped toward Alec to give them room. The car was small, built for five people max, not a group of almost-men. Alec turned sideways and angled closer to the wall, desperate for space, but doing so only made Raegan move closer, and the next thing he knew, they were pressed together at their fronts, the teens behind her rehashing last night's Blazers game like the superfans they obviously were.

"Dude, did you see McCollum's dunk? That thing was sick."

"Yo, man. He brought the house down last night. That guy's the real deal. I'm tellin' ya."

"Plumlee cleaned the glass too. They're fuckin' all-stars. We're goin' all the way this year."

Heat surrounded Alec as the doors closed and the car began to move again. A heat that had nothing to do with the number of bodies in the cramped space and everything to do with the soft curves pressed up against him, making all the dead places inside him suddenly come to life.

He knew it was a bad idea, especially when he was already still shaken from being in their apartment, but he couldn't seem to stop himself from looking down at her. And when he did, his pulse beat even faster because Raegan wasn't watching the teens or paying even an ounce of attention to what they were saying. She was staring up at him with the softest green eyes he'd ever seen. Eyes he still dreamed about every damn night.

All that heat around him intensified. Seeped from her into him or him into her, he wasn't sure which. The only thing he knew was that the temperature was growing warmer in the tiny car. So hot his skin tingled, his fingers twitched, and his body grew hard and hot and achy.

The elevator dinged, and the doors whooshed open. The boys' voices faded as they stepped out of the car and disappeared around the corner. But Raegan didn't move, and neither did Alec. He couldn't because all he felt was a growing urge to slide his hands into her silky auburn hair, to tip her mouth up to his, to taste her the way he'd wanted to taste her last night in his kitchen.

She blinked and stepped back, breaking the connection. Without a word, she moved out of the elevator, leaving him alone. Alone to wonder what the hell was happening and why he'd thought helping her with these silly cases had been a good idea at all.

He took a second to clear his head. When the elevator doors began to close, he still wasn't ready, but he pushed a hand between the doors, forcing them open again, and finally stepped out.

The cool air of the lobby surrounded him, easing at least one of his problems. Ahead, though, Raegan tied the sash of her coat around her waist and fixed the strap of her purse over her shoulder, averting her gaze in a way that told him she hadn't missed what had almost happened in the elevator and that she was just as rattled as he was.

Irritation pulsed inside him. An irrational irritation, all things considered. What the heck did he expect? That she'd want him to kiss her? After last night when he'd shut her down? She had every right to be confused by the mixed messages he was sending, but holy hell . . . he was just as confused by them himself.

She pushed the lobby door open and moved out onto the sidewalk. "Are you driving or do you want me to?"

"I'll drive. Black Dodge over there." Body still vibrating with things he didn't want to think about right now, Alec pulled the keys from his jacket pocket, desperate for something—anything—to do with his hands so he wouldn't be tempted to put them on her. "Do you have the address?"

"Yeah."

They headed toward his truck. In the old days, he would have opened the door for her, would have helped her in, but today he didn't trust himself, so he walked around to the driver's side and let her fend for herself.

Once inside, she set her purse on the floor at her feet and fluffed her hair from her jacket collar, then rattled off the address. "I called ahead. The wife was home. She didn't sound excited to talk to us, but said she'd give us a few minutes."

A few minutes. Wow. He was fucking up his whole day for a few minutes.

As he punched the address into his GPS, he tried to ignore Raegan's familiar jasmine perfume, the scent that always made him hot, but failed miserably. That urge to touch her again came back full force, messing with his head and heating up his body in a way he didn't want.

"This is in east Portland," he said, trying to focus on anything other than the fact she smelled good enough to eat. "Probably take us about twenty minutes in afternoon traffic."

"Yeah, probably."

He punched in the last number and put the truck in drive. The navigation voice echoed in the speakers, telling him where to turn.

Raegan was quiet for several minutes as they left the Pearl District and headed over the Broadway Bridge. On the east side of the river, she shifted in her seat, and out of the corner of his eye, Alec noticed her tight shoulders and clenched jaw.

That didn't seem like confusion. It screamed stress—or anger.

"So," she said in the silence. "Last night after we said good night, I had a little bit of a surprise."

He glanced sideways at her, unsure how to read her. "What kind of surprise?"

"A note on my windshield kind of surprise."

He wasn't sure why she was telling him about some silly flyer. He merged onto I-5 South.

"It was handwritten. Only contained two lines." She exhaled. "I'm not even sure I should tell you what it said."

He switched lanes and shot her a look. "What do you mean you don't know if you should tell me? Why are you bringing it up then?"

"Because Jack Bickam might call you about it. I gave it to him this morning."

A tingle ran down Alec's spine. "Bickam? Why? What did the note say?"

She pursed her lips and didn't answer.

That tingle intensified. Glancing sideways at her, he said, "What did the note say, Raegan?"

She sucked her lips between her teeth and stared ahead at the freeway. Stress and worry radiated from her, putting Alec on instant alert. "Raegan? Tell me what the hell the note sa—"

"I'll tell you if you don't freak out, okay?"

That did not put Alec at any kind of ease. He was just about to explain that to her when a heavy sigh slipped from her lips.

She glanced his way. "It said, 'You always thought she was alive. Stop what you're doing or this time she's dead.'"

For a moment, everything stopped. The cars on the freeway whizzing by disappeared. The radio went silent. Even his pulse seemed to halt as the words circled in his head. Then reality slammed into him, shooting his pulse straight through the roof and his adrenaline into overdrive.

He cut the truck across the lanes, onto the shoulder, and slammed on the brakes.

Raegan lurched forward, but the seat belt pulled her back. She braced a hand against the window at her side and gasped. "Oh my God. Alec. What are y—"

"Where is it? Where's the note?"

"I told you. With the FBI."

"You didn't keep a copy of it? I know you kept a copy. Show me."

"Maybe we should talk about this later when you're not so—"

"Raegan, show me the damn note."

Her lips snapped closed. She stared at him for several seconds. Then with a disapproving shake of her head, she leaned forward and reached for her purse, but the seat belt stopped her. Alec hit the button on her belt, freeing her so she could grab her purse from the floorboards. The sound of his pulse returned, morphing to a roar in his ears as she fumbled inside her bag.

Or this time she's dead.

Or she's dead . . .

Did that mean she *could be* alive?

Raegan pulled out a full piece of paper folded in half. "This is just a photocopy. I took the original straight to Jack Bickam. He said they'd run it for fingerprints." Hesitantly, she held the paper out to him. "I wanted to show it to you first, but I thought the smartest thing to do would be to give it to the FBI. But, Alec"—her voice lifted with both excitement and hope as he unfolded the note—"this could be proof Emma is still alive."

Alec stared at the photocopied handwriting. And in a rush, his blood cooled and the tiny thread of hope he'd let himself believe in dropped free like scissors slicing through yarn. "It's not proof."

"What do you mean? It could be. It says 'or she's dead.' This could be someone trying to tell us Emma is still alive."

"It's not proof of anything."

He shoved the paper toward her and shifted back into drive, glancing in the rearview mirror for a break in the traffic so he could pull back out onto the freeway. A renewed rage simmered beneath his control. A rage centered on one person.

"Why?" Raegan said softly beside him when they were a mile down the road. "Why can't you believe, even now?"

Alec's jaw clenched so hard, pain ricocheted across his cheekbones. He took the exit onto I-84 East. "Because I'd know that chicken scratch handwriting anywhere. It's John Gilbert's handwriting. He's messing with you. And me."

Goddamn son of a bitch. Gilbert was still in jail, but he had plenty of lowlife friends he could have pegged to follow Alec.

"Your father?" Raegan looked down at the photocopy in her lap with shock and disbelief. "Are you sure?"

"Yes, I'm sure." Alec swerved around a school bus going entirely too slow. "And he's not my father. He's just the asshole who fucked the woman who abandoned me. He's taunting you, Raegan. Taunting you because he knows we were together last night. Goddamn fucking prick." His hand tightened around the steering wheel as he thought of all the ways he wanted to kick the fucker's ass.

Raegan's shoulders slumped, and knowing he'd just killed her faith—again—dimmed a little of the rage brewing inside.

"I'm sorry he did that." He slowed the truck when he realized he was going eighty in a fifty-five. Moving carefully into the right lane, he glanced at her again, forcibly softening his voice. "He's in jail on a probation violation right now, though, so you have nothing to worry about."

Yet.

A new sense of worry rippled down Alec's spine as he refocused on the road. His father was set to be released at the end of the week. John Gilbert had mentioned finding Raegan when Alec had gone to see him at the jail. At the time, Alec had considered it an empty threat, but if his goons had seen her with Alec and one had left her that note, it meant she might not be safe alone once Gilbert was free.

"Then I don't understand how his handwritten note got on my car."

"Gilbert's a loser, and he has plenty of loser friends who visit him in that shithole. I'm sure he conned one of them into leaving that note on your windshield."

"But how would he know I would be at that coffee shop on that night?"

"He wouldn't." Alec turned off the freeway and headed east on Glisan toward the Hazelwood neighborhood, keeping his eyes on the road so she couldn't see just how much this news rattled him. "He knows I go there. Ever since he got out of prison three and a half years ago, he's kept tabs on me. I guarantee that note was meant for me and that whoever delivered it saw us together and decided to give it to you instead."

At least that was what he hoped, because the alternative—that they really were targeting Raegan—left a pit in the bottom of his stomach.

Raegan was silent while he made a turn, staring down at the note in her hands.

Alec tried to settle his frayed nerves as he followed the GPS directions until he pulled to a stop in front of a one-level dump on a dilapidated street. The lawns on the street were all brown, covered with junk, trash cans, and even car parts. The gray house to Alec's right was the worst of the bunch, with chipped and peeling paint, missing shutters, and one window covered with duct tape to close up a hole in the glass.

"God, this place looks happy," Alec said as he shifted into park and killed the ignition.

Raegan looked up at him with sad eyes. "Maybe you're wrong. Maybe this note wasn't written by John Gilbert. Maybe—"

"I'm not wrong." He knew where she was going. Hated that he was dousing her hope all over again. But he couldn't let her wish for something that was never going to happen. Not when he knew his fucking father was back to his old ways, tormenting him—them—in any way possible. "This isn't the evidence you've been looking for. You have to let it go and forget about it."

Her gaze dropped back down to the paper, and even though he couldn't see her eyes, he read the heartbreak in her expression. More than anything he wanted to take her into his arms and comfort her, but he couldn't. Couldn't, because it was his fault she was suffering right now. His past had caught up with him and was ruining not only his life but hers once more as well.

Guilt swamped him. A familiar guilt that threatened to drag him under. Before it could, he pushed his door open and climbed out of the truck. "Come on. Let's get this over with so we can get the heck out of here. This place reminds me way too much of a childhood I'd rather forget."

She nodded. Folded the paper and slipped it back into her purse. But when he rounded the hood and watched her climb out, that guilt sank in deeper.

Because something had died in her eyes. A light he hadn't even realized was there until right this moment. A light that had dimmed because of his father. His good-for-nothing, selfish prick of a father.

As they headed up the front walk toward the dilapidated house, he swore to himself then and there that if John Gilbert so much as touched her, he'd kill the fucker once and for all.

———

Raegan couldn't stop thinking about John Gilbert as she stood on the broken front stoop of the worn-down house and waited while Alec knocked.

She'd never met Alec's biological father. When they'd first started dating and gotten married, John Gilbert had still been in prison for providing drugs to a minor and using Alec as a mule to move his supply. Raegan knew Alec's testimony as a teen had sent Gilbert to prison, and she knew from talking to both Alec and Michael McClane that Gilbert blamed Alec for his incarceration. But after Emma had disappeared, she'd never been convinced John Gilbert was involved. Alec believed without a doubt that his father had taken her to get back at him, but there'd never been any proof. And this note in her purse that Alec claimed was from Gilbert now didn't prove his involvement either.

She needed to believe Emma was still alive. Couldn't let herself think of the alternative. Because if she did . . .

Something hard and sharp stabbed straight into her chest, and she swallowed the silent scream that pushed at her throat as she blinked back the sting of tears threatening behind her eyes. Believing anything else would lead her straight into the darkness, and she couldn't go there and stay sane.

Emma was *still* alive. Somewhere. Waiting for her. If this note was nothing more than John Gilbert trying to harass his son, it didn't change that belief for her.

The door pulled open, and a thin woman dressed in a tank top and leggings with dark hair pulled back in a tail eyed them speculatively. "Yes?"

Raegan pushed aside her emotions, shifting into reporter mode as she held up her station ID. "Mrs. Willig? I'm Raegan Devereaux from KTVP. We spoke earlier on the phone?"

Barbara Willig looked like she was in her midthirties, but Raegan suspected she was quite a bit younger, aged by stress and circumstances. She narrowed dark-brown eyes on Raegan. "You don' look like that blonde newsgirl on the TV."

"I'm not. That's Allie Ziegler. But I do fill in for her at the anchor table from time to time. This is my colleague, Alec McClane. Can we come in for a few minutes and talk with you about your son?"

Barbara Willig's brow wrinkled, and for a moment, Raegan feared the woman might change her mind. Then Alec flashed that thousand-watt smile at Raegan's side and shivered in what Raegan knew was a very calculated way.

"Dang, it's getting cold out here." He glanced at Raegan then back at Barbara Willig. "I think Chloe Hampton was wrong with last night's weather forecast. Feels like it's about to snow again to me. What do you think, Mrs. Willig?"

The woman's gaze shifted to Alec, and her expression relaxed. "It just might. And the name's *Ms.* Willig. Not missus. Not after I kicked that louse out once and for all. But you can both call me Barbie." She pulled the door open wider. "Come on in."

She turned, leaving the door open, and sauntered down the long hallway toward the back of the house with a sway in her step Raegan bet ten bucks hadn't been there a few minutes before.

Lifting his brows in a *you can thank me later* move, Alec waited for Raegan to step in front of him, then closed the door at his back. She had to hand it to him. He had a way with women. He'd charmed their way into this house when Barbie Willig was ready to toss Raegan out simply based on her looks. For a moment, she wondered if that's what she'd witnessed last night—Alec charming that waitress so she'd give them an isolated table in the back of the coffee shop away from the bar—rather than the blatant flirting she thought she'd seen.

The dark hallway opened to a living room filled with scuffed furniture, a flickering TV, and toys strewn over the coffee table and floor. Three small children in underwear and T-shirts lay on the floor on their stomachs, eyes wide and glued to the screen.

Barbara stepped in front of them and flipped the TV off. All three sat up, whining and complaining. She shushed them and pointed toward a doorway on the far side of the room. "Go play in the other room. I got someone to talk to. You can watch TV when I'm done."

The children grumbled under their breaths but shuffled out of the room. Barbara shook her head and motioned toward the couch. "Have a seat."

Raegan sat next to Alec on the couch, pulling a small notebook from her purse. "Thanks for meeting with us, Ms. Willig. I know you talked to the police and several reporters last year when your son went missing, but we're doing a follow-up piece and wanted to ask you a few questions."

Barbara sank into a recliner on Alec's side, looking cautiously between them. "Are you trying to catch the guy who took my son?"

"We're looking into similar cases, seeing if there's a connection," he answered. "Sometimes stories like this spark viewers' attention. We can't guarantee we're going to find anything, but keeping your son's name in the press can't hurt, right?"

She nodded, but a frustrated look pulled at her brows. "No one much seemed to care about my Billy disappearing. Oh, there were reporters hanging around when it first happened, but then after a few days . . . nothin'. You're the first people who've come to follow up since just after it happened."

Raegan wasn't sure why that would be, but before she could ask, shuffling sounded at her back, and she turned to see a young girl with curly dark hair walk out of the kitchen, her gaze locked on a smartphone in her hand.

"Ginny, what are you doing?" Barbie pushed out of her chair and swiped the phone from the girl's hands. "I told you your time was up."

The girl didn't answer. Just dropped her hands and stared up at the woman.

Barbara waved a hand toward the hallway the other children had disappeared through. "Go do your homework."

The girl's expression dropped, and she turned away, heading for the hall with a huff.

Barbara sighed as she sat back in her recliner and set the girl's phone on the table beside her. "That girl thinks I'm the Wicked Witch of the West, when all I'm trying to do is make her smarter than me."

"Are all of these your children?" Raegan asked.

She shook her head. "Just Ginny. The other three are kids I take care of durin' the day. Not as good money as, say, being a reporter, but I get to work from home."

"Yes, that is a nice perk," Raegan said.

Barbie reached for the soda can at her side and tipped it back for a sip. "Sometimes I think homeschooling that kid was a bad idea. She doesn't appreciate it none." She glanced at Alec and Raegan with a scowl. "You'll have to excuse her bad manners. She's mad at me right now 'cause I wouldn't let her run up to the elementary school to play with some of the older kids in the neighborhood."

"Do you not like those older kids?" Raegan asked.

"Oh, those kids are fine. It's the school I don' want Ginny near. That's where my Billy was taken."

Raegan sensed the woman didn't let her daughter out of her sight very often, and for that reason she felt for the girl. But could she blame Barbara Willig? If she'd had other children, Raegan probably would have been the same way after Emma's disappearance.

"Your son went missing at the elementary school?" Alec asked.

Barbara nodded. "Last year. I wasn't doin' day care then. I was . . ." She frowned. "Well, I was a dancer. It was good money, but my old man—Bob—he didn't want me doin' it anymore. He used to get wicked jealous. So I quit, and I'd just gotten a job as a cashier down at the Save and Go. When I was dancing I used to work nights, and I'd take care of the kids during the day, but the new job had me working days, so Bob had to take care of them on the weekend when he was home. It was a Saturday. Bob was working on his truck in the driveway. I guess Billy wouldn't stop bugging him about going to the playground. Billy, he was a sweet little boy, but so full of energy." She shook her head. "He could run circles around you and leave you wondering what the hell happened. Used to run up to my legs and say, 'Go walk. Go walk!' and wouldn't let up 'til I took him outside."

A far-off look filled Barbara's dull brown eyes, and for a moment, Raegan pictured her as she must have looked before Billy's abduction—young, full of life, with a light in her eyes that wasn't there now. Raegan knew how stress could age a person. She guessed Barbara Willig had aged ten years in only a few short months.

Barbara shook the look away and scowled. "Good ol' Bob didn't want to take the time to run Billy up to the school, so he told Ginny to do it. She took Billy up to the playground and let him climb all over the jungle gym. There was a bunch of kids there that day, and Billy was runnin' all over the place. At some point . . ." She paused, and that faraway look came rushing back. "She lost track of him. And then . . . poof. He was gone."

Raegan's gaze strayed to Alec, and she wondered what he was thinking, what he was remembering. His eyes were fixed on Barbara Willig, but not a single muscle in his features moved. His face was as stone-cold unreadable as she'd ever seen it.

"What happened then?" Raegan asked softly.

"Then?" Barbara's voice hardened. "Then I got a call at work sayin' Billy was missing. I rushed right home. Bob was in a state, screaming at Ginny, but it wasn't her fault. She was only six years old. He never should'a sent her up to that playground alone with Billy. I called the police. They came out and looked around, but they didn't do much. Once they found out I used to dance, they figured it might have been a customer or stalker or something. But then they found out about Bob's old girlfriend who used to cause trouble for us. Used to vandalize the house and mess with our cars and stuff. They decided she must have taken my Billy as revenge or somethin', but no one was ever able to prove that."

"What did Bob think?" Alec asked.

"Oh, Bob thought she did it too. Went nuts all over her, trying to get her to admit it. She never did, though."

A yapping sounded from the other room, then seconds later a tiny Chihuahua mix with a blinged-out pink collar streaked into the room, barked at Raegan and Alec like a loon, and jumped up on Barbara Willig's lap, waggling her tail with an excited whine.

Barbara Willig frowned but immediately started petting the attention-demanding dog. "This is Ginny's dog. Ginny!" she yelled.

A door somewhere in the house opened. "What?" the girl called.

"Come get Daisy."

Ginny rushed into the room and scooped the dog from her mother's lap. "Did those mean people scare you?" she cooed, showing emotion for the first time. "Your Ginny's here now, baby." The dog lapped at the girl's nose and lips. Ginny laughed and held her like a doll.

Barbara sighed as the girl walked away with the dog, watching the two disappear down the hall. "That dog's the only thing she really cares about. Ever since her brother went missing . . ." Her voice hitched, and she coughed to try to cover it. "Well, she's not been the same since."

Raegan could only imagine how something like that would scar a child. "It's good she has the dog."

"Yeah, sometimes." Barbara took another sip of her soda. "And other times I worry she's too attached to that dog. She uses it like a shield, focusing all her emotion on that dog while she blocks out everyone else. If something were to happen to Daisy, I don' know what Ginny would do."

Raegan glanced at Alec, who hadn't spoken in the last few minutes. He was watching Barbara Willig, but something in the way he sat expressionless told Raegan he was lost in his own thoughts and memories.

Thinking about the alcohol he'd used as a shield? About how he'd blocked her out when all she'd wanted to do was help him? Raegan didn't know, and wondering hurt too much, so she glanced down at her notes and refocused. "So you mentioned that you're divorced now, Ms. Willig. Do you know where we could find Mr. Willig to ask him some questions about what he saw that day?"

"Sure do. He's at CRCI."

"Columbia River Correctional Institution?" Alec said, finally joining the conversation.

Barbara nodded. "He lost it after Billy went missing. He always had a bit of a temper, but he went off the deep end when we couldn't find Billy. We fought all the time. Then he got arrested for roughing up that ex-girlfriend. I couldn't look at him after that. It was his fault Billy disappeared. His fault Ginny changed. His fault because he didn't watch the kids like he was supposed to do when I had to work. When he got sent to jail, I divorced him, and I'm not sorry."

Alec's shoulders tensed. Raegan saw it from the corner of her vision. Her gaze drifted down his arms toward his hands clasped tightly together in front of him, his knuckles turning white.

Her back tingled because she knew what he was thinking. Barbara Willig's story had hit way too close to home for him.

"We're very sorry for your loss, Ms. Willig." Raegan pushed to her feet. "I know you're busy, so we don't want to take up any more of your time."

Barbara rose as well, surprise pulling her brows together. "That's it?"

"Yes," Raegan answered, watching Alec carefully as he stood. His jaw was as hard as she'd ever seen it, and something dark lurked in his gaze. "I think that's all we need."

"Do you see any similarities between my son and those other cases you're looking into?" Barbara asked with wide eyes.

Raegan didn't want to get the woman's hopes up. The only thing that stood out to her was that this family had been poor and uneducated, and she suspected the person who'd taken Billy had known that and used it to his advantage. "I'm not sure."

Raegan moved toward the door, but Barbara Willig stopped her with a hand on her arm. "If you figure out who took my Billy, I'd appreciate it if you'd come tell me. That person didn't just steal my boy, he ruined my whole family. That's something he needs to pay for."

Raegan nodded and squeezed the woman's hand. "We will."

Outside, Raegan drew a deep breath that did little to ease the heaviness in her belly. Alec didn't speak to her, just walked up to the truck, opened the passenger door, then moved around to the driver's side as she climbed in. Dim barking echoed from inside the Willig house, but Raegan didn't turn to look. Because the only thing she could focus on was the man sitting next to her. The one who was dredging up a truckload of guilt over something that was not his fault.

Alec put the truck in drive and pulled away from the curb. Raegan waited until they were out of the neighborhood before she glanced his way and said, "You okay?"

"Me? Yeah, I'm fine."

She frowned because she knew he wasn't fine. He was spiraling all over again. She just didn't know what to do about it or if there was anything she could do to help. And that hurt more than anything else, because that's all she'd ever wanted to do. Just help the man she loved.

CHAPTER NINE

Alec flexed and squeezed his hand against the steering wheel. Knew if he didn't focus on breathing and finding control that he could easily lose it. As much as he tried not to, though, all he could think about was what Barbara Willig had said.

"They didn't just take my baby, they ruined my family. That's somethin' they need to pay for."

She didn't know who'd taken her child, but Alec knew who'd taken his. And that person was sitting in a prison yard right this minute, only an hour away, planning all the ways he was going to mess with Raegan.

Well, Alec wouldn't let him.

"You know that woman's situation is completely different from ours, right?" Raegan said softly at his side when they were on the freeway.

Alec huffed. Of course she knew what he was thinking because she knew him better than anyone else ever had. "No, it's not. The only difference between us and her is that she's uneducated and has no money."

"That's not true. That woman's husband clearly had issues before their child disappeared. And so did she."

"We all have issues."

"Alec." She looked toward him with sad green eyes. "It's not the same. We are not the same. I never blamed you."

This time the pain was so sharp it was all he could do to keep from steering the truck over the divider and into oncoming traffic to ease the misery. "And that right there is your issue."

"No, it's—"

He flipped the radio on and turned the volume up to drown out her voice so he wouldn't have to talk. A sports analyst was running through the Blazers stats from last night's game, but he barely heard what the man was saying. All he could think about was his father. About the note Gilbert had arranged to be left for Raegan and about how satisfying it would be for Alec to walk into that correctional facility and slam his fist into the fucker's face.

He finally turned the radio down as he pulled to a stop in front of Raegan's building. Worry settled over her features, a worry he saw from the corner of his eye but wouldn't acknowledge.

"Why don't you come up for a little while?" she said. "So we can talk."

"No, I've got things to do."

"Alec—"

"There's nothing to talk about, Raegan."

Her shoulders slumped even further, and knowing he was being an ass, he drew a calming breath and tried like hell to chill out. For a few minutes. For her sake.

"When you get the next interview set up, let me know. I'll go with you. Today, though"—he stared out the windshield—"I need to be alone."

"Are you going to be okay?"

Probably not. But he'd lived through worse than this. "I'll be fine."

She stared at him. Bit her lip as if she weren't sure whether to believe him or not. Then finally popped her door open. "Okay. I'll text you later."

Great. Fabulous. She was gonna check up on him as if he were a five-year-old.

She climbed out and closed the door, but she didn't move toward her building. And unable to handle that worried, heartsick look on her face one more minute, he pulled away from the curb and followed the surface streets back to the freeway.

He didn't breathe easier until he was halfway to Salem. Make amends. That's what this was all about, right? And the best way to make amends with Raegan was to make sure his father stayed away from her for good.

That, above all else, was one thing he knew he could control in this nightmare that had become his life.

———

Raegan stood on the sidewalk long after Alec's truck disappeared from view, worry and fear mingling inside her. More than anything she wanted to help Alec, but he wouldn't let her in. He was pushing her away, just as he'd done three years before. And there was nothing she could do to stop him.

She went back upstairs to her apartment, tossed her purse and jacket over the back of the couch, and tried to call Jack Bickam. He didn't answer, so she left him a message explaining what Alec had said about the note and asked him to compare the handwriting to John Gilbert's. For the next hour she typed up notes on their meeting with Barbara Willig, then called out to the Columbia River Correctional Institution and tried to arrange a time to speak with Bob Willig, only to discover the man was in solitary confinement for attacking another inmate. It would be at least a week until he could have visitors.

The light in her apartment dimmed as dusk settled in. Unable to sit anymore, she pushed away from her laptop on the dining room table and moved into the kitchen to grab a Perrier from the fridge.

The bottle hissed as she opened it, but when she took a sip, the sparkling water did little to calm her frazzled nerves. Her gaze skipped over the apartment, and she remembered how tense Alec had been there earlier in the day.

Had he been remembering living there? She'd considered moving a dozen times after he'd left, but she'd never been able to force herself to go. She'd kept the apartment pretty much the same on purpose, because when Emma finally came home, she wanted her daughter in familiar surroundings. But she could see how that would rattle a man. Knew it was part of the reason Alec had been so off even before they'd visited the Willig woman. Especially a man who carried as much guilt as Alec did. But . . . couldn't he see this was the only place she could be? Couldn't he, for once, think about someone other than himself? He wasn't the only one who'd suffered these last few years, dammit.

For a fleeting moment, she wondered what she would do if Emma never came home. Wondered what she'd do if the police ever showed up at her door to tell her they'd found Emma's bod—

No. She wasn't going there. Couldn't. Recapping the bottle, she set it on the counter and moved for her coat. She needed to get out of this apartment, needed to get out of her head for a few hours. When her stomach rumbled, she remembered that she'd barely eaten today and decided she'd grab dinner out. After shoving her phone and credit card into the inside pocket of her coat, she grabbed her keys and headed for the door, ignoring the way her fingers shook and her heart raced against her ribs.

The temperature had warmed up enough so the snow had all melted, and a cool drizzle forced her to pull up her hood as she moved down the sidewalk. Oregon winters were like that, though. Frigid one minute, wet and dreary the next. As it was just after five, the sidewalks were busy with people trying to get home. Raegan moved around a young couple holding hands and told herself she'd feel better after a drink and some food. Alec would be fine too. He was a grown man, after all. He made his own decisions. She had to stop worrying about him when he clearly didn't want her concern.

She pushed the pub doors open three blocks down and shook the rain from her hood as she stepped inside. The Irish bar had opened a few months ago, and she passed it every day on her way to work, but she'd yet to try it out. Tonight seemed like the perfect time. Bypassing the tables, she found a spot at the bar and pulled her coat off to drape over the back of her barstool.

"What can I get you?" the female bartender asked, a twentysomething attractive brunette with long hair pulled back in a messy tail.

Raegan glanced over the bottles on the shelves behind her, then finally decided to go for a Guinness. "I'll have a dirty apple."

"You got it. Want a menu?"

"Sure."

The bartender went about filling Raegan's pint glass with Guinness and cider, then set the drink in front of her. "Wave me down when you know what you want to eat."

"Thanks." Lifting her drink, Raegan took a sip and closed her eyes as the bitter and sweet tastes rushed over her tongue. Unlike Alec, she'd never been one for hard liquor, but she could see how a person could grow addicted to this. It had a calming effect, even just one sip, and hinted it could help you escape from the hell that was your reality if you just kept on drinking.

Raegan's eyes opened, and she stared at the wall of bottles across from her as she thought of Alec. That was why he'd started drinking as a kid. To escape the nightmare of his childhood. He'd told her multiple times that his biological father had been an alcoholic, that alcohol had always been available in his trailer. She glanced down at her glass, remembering the way Alec had rarely drank when they were together and how after they'd lost Emma he'd turned to the bottle instead of to her. He'd been reverting back to what he'd done as a kid. What was

Elisabeth Naughton

comfortable. What was easy. Opening up to her, dealing with the pain of their reality, had definitely not been easy.

A new sense of appreciation for what he'd lived through as a child trickled through her. And when she remembered how bad things had been when they'd separated and how often he'd been drinking then, another wave of awe swept through her over the fact he'd pulled himself out of that pit.

She set her glass down. Pulled her cell from her coat pocket and stared at the screen. She wanted to text him. Wanted to make sure he was okay, but she didn't want to push because she knew it would just send him running in the other direction. A frown pulled at her lips when she remembered the way he'd sped off today. Apparently, she didn't even need to push to send him running. One bad day had done that without even a nudge from her.

Sighing, she lifted her drink again and took a long swallow. That was the frustrating thing about Alec McClane. He was unpredictable in a million different ways. When they'd first met, when they'd been dating—even when they'd first been married—she'd loved that about him. Now all it did was twist her heart into knots because she didn't have a clue how to reach him.

A young couple sidled up next to her at the bar, chatting and laughing and touching each other at every opportunity. She listened to their banter for a few minutes, but when the man leaned in and kissed the woman, Raegan knew she was done for the night. The drink wasn't making her feel any better, and her appetite was long gone. Pulling a ten from her pocket, she left it on the bar next to her half-empty glass and reached for her coat. She'd grab a sandwich from the deli around the corner and go back to her apartment. If she was lucky, she'd find a movie to veg out to on the couch. If she wasn't lucky . . . well, then it would just be like every other night, and she'd lie awake wondering where Alec was and what he was doing.

"You are a fool for still being so in love with the ass," she muttered to herself as she tugged on her coat.

110

And she was. A giant fool, because he'd made it more than clear over the last few days that he was no longer in love with her.

She didn't bother buttoning her coat as she stepped out of the pub. Cool air whipped across her neck and down her spine, but she didn't care. It gave her something else to focus on besides how clueless she was.

The sidewalks had cleared out, and darkness pressed in. Moving around a homeless guy standing in a doorway, she rounded the corner and headed for the deli. She hated this side street because the overhead light had gone out last fall and the city had yet to replace it, but it was faster than taking a different route.

Footsteps sounded behind her, and a chill slid down her back. Picking up her pace, she shoved her hands into her pocket and closed them around her key ring, just in case, wanting only to get her dinner and get home so she could forget about this miserable day. Just as she reached the edge of the alley, something slammed into her from the back, sending her stumbling forward. She yelped, and her keys and cell phone went flying. Before she could cry out, a hand slapped over her mouth, and she was jerked sideways into the darkness.

She struggled against the arm at her waist and the hand over her mouth. Tried to scream but couldn't make more than a muffled sound as she was dragged deeper into the alley. The scents of filth and cigarette smoke filled her nostrils. The person who'd grabbed her pulled her past a Dumpster and hurled her to the side.

Her body hit the cement wall of the building with a crack, and pain spiraled all across her cheek as she ricocheted off the wall and stumbled to the ground. Groaning, she tried to get up, but something hard—a knee, she realized—pressed into her spine, keeping her pinned to the ground.

"You don't listen very well, do you, anchor girl?"

Fear consumed Raegan, and her blood turned to ice when she realized she was trapped. She opened her mouth to cry out for help, but the pressure in her back intensified, spiraling pain all through her lower half.

"Well, you're gonna listen now, bitch. Stop looking into things that are only going to get people killed."

Tears burned Raegan's eyes, and she tried to twist her head against the asphalt to see her attacker, but he pressed a hand to the side of her head, holding her still.

"So fucking pretty," he said in an almost singsongy voice as he fingered her hair. "Yeah, you'll listen this time, won't you?" He stroked a finger down the side of her neck. One that sent a new terror straight down her spine. "'Cause if you don't, I promise this'll only be a taste of what I can do."

———

Alec pulled up to the check-in station at the gate of the Santiam Correctional Institution and rolled down his window. Rain blew into his cab as the guard moved out of the small building, carrying a clipboard.

"Visiting hours are almost over, sir."

"I know," Alec said. "I'll only be a few minutes."

The guard frowned and looked down at his clipboard. "Inmate name?"

"John Gilbert."

The guard scanned his paper, flipped it to the next page, then the following. Rain blew into Alec's cab as he waited, sending a chill across his skin that did little to cool his blood.

"I'm not seeing that name on the list. Hold on." The guard moved back into the small building and lifted a phone. Through the window, Alec watched as the man called up to the facility, a whisper of foreboding tingling along his spine.

The guard hung up and moved back to Alec's window. "John Gilbert was released yesterday morning."

A mixture of disbelief and dread churned through Alec's gut. "He wasn't supposed to be released until the end of the week."

The guard shrugged. "Looks like he was let go early."

Dread turned to fear, then to horror. Alec shoved the truck into reverse, whipped around, and peeled out of the gravel drive.

Because only one thought circled in his head.

The note on Raegan's car yesterday hadn't come from any of Gilbert's buddies. It had come from Gilbert himself. He'd followed Alec to that coffee shop, had seen Alec and Raegan together, and had changed his plans to go after her instead of him, just as he'd promised Alec he would when they'd met. And if he'd tailed Raegan home after that, he could be watching her right now. He could be hiding outside her door. He could be waiting for the perfect moment to strike.

Alec knew the fucker would do it too. He'd do it the minute Alec was gone and she was alone. Just as she was right this minute.

———

Every inch of Raegan's body hurt as she climbed out of Anna Chapman's Civic and looked back through the window at the twenty-three-year-old girl who'd been interning at KTVP for the last two months. "Thanks for picking me up from the police station and bringing me home. Sorry to bother you after hours."

Anna tipped her head from the driver's seat. "It's no bother, Raegan. I'm just sorry you got mugged like that. I always think Portland's so safe. I'm definitely not telling my mom about this. She'd want me to move home to Klamath Falls right away."

Raegan tried for a smile, but her cheek hurt too much from being shoved into the asphalt to do more than scowl. "I appreciate it just the same. I would have called Jeremy, but—"

"Yeah, I heard you guys split." Anna wrinkled her nose. "I wouldn't have called him either. You sure you're gonna be okay?"

"Yeah, I'll be fine. Just a few bumps and bruises. No real damage. Thanks again, Anna."

"Night, Raegan."

Raegan moved slower than she liked toward the double doors at the entry to her building. Her back was on fire, and she knew she'd have a nice-sized bruise in the middle of her spine by tomorrow, but she was glad whoever had attacked her had released her and run off without hurting her in other unthinkable ways.

Once she'd picked herself up from the ground and realized she was alone, she'd located her keys and cell phone. Her keys had been intact. Her cell phone shattered. All she'd wanted to do was limp home, but she'd known she had to report the attack, so she'd made her way to the police station where she'd filled out a report, then called Jack Bickam and relayed her attacker's cryptic message.

Alec was convinced John Gilbert had left that message on her car the other night, but he couldn't have been the one to attack her today because he was still in jail on a probation violation. Bickam had agreed with Raegan, but he'd promised to visit Gilbert at SCI and question him to see if he'd sent anyone after her. Raegan didn't have much faith Bickam would be able to pin this on Gilbert. She could have been attacked by anyone. It could have been someone who'd seen her at Barbara Willig's house earlier in the day. It could have been someone who thought she was looking into a completely different story at the station. Her attacker hadn't mentioned Emma or the missing kids she and Alec were looking into now. In fact, he hadn't mentioned anything except to stop digging.

Stop digging? That's what reporters did. Shaking her head, she keyed in her building code and pulled the lobby door open.

Thankfully, there was no one in the lobby, and she was able to ride the elevator up alone. She wasn't in the mood to talk right now and only wanted to take two Tylenol PM and fall asleep. The bell dinged, and the double doors opened. Looking down at the keys in her scraped hand, she shuffled forward, then drew to a stop when she spotted a shadowy figure at the end of the hall in front of her door.

Fear shoved aside all the pain, and her stomach tightened. Then the man turned and she recognized his dark hair and athletic build.

"Ethan?" She limped down the hallway toward him. "What are you doing here?"

"Holy hell." Ethan's eyes grew wide as she drew close. "I guess he had every reason to be worried."

"Who?"

"Alec. He called me from his truck about thirty minutes ago, asked me to come over and check on you. Said he couldn't get a hold of you. He gave me the building code to get in. I was just about to leave you a note."

Her frustration with Alec and her inability to let go of something he'd obviously let go of long ago got the best of her. She shoved her key in the lock and turned it with a frown. "Really? I find that hard to believe, considering he bolted away from me earlier as if I had cooties."

Ethan chuckled as he followed her into the apartment. "That's my brother. Totally suave." He closed the door at his back. "What the hell happened to you?"

Raegan dropped her keys on the entry table, moved down the short hallway into her living room, and sank onto the couch, feeling more tired than she could ever remember. "Someone jumped me on the street."

"You were mugged?"

"No, warned. To stop looking into things that don't concern me."

Ethan stared down at her with his hands on his hips. "A story you're researching for the station?"

She shrugged. "Not sure. He wasn't specific."

"Shit. Did you report it?"

She nodded. "A friend from the station picked me up at the police station and brought me home. It looks worse than it is, Ethan. It's just bruises and some swelling from hitting the ground. I didn't even need to go to the hospital."

He eyed her as if he wasn't so sure. "Alec asked me to check on you because he went to see John Gilbert at SCI tonight. Gilbert was released yesterday morning."

Raegan looked up with wide eyes. "Are you sure?"

"That's what he said."

Shit. It very well could have been Gilbert then. Unease tightened her stomach because she knew Alec was going to flip his lid when he saw her. And because he was going to insist Gilbert had left the note on her car and done this to her when he still had no proof.

Closing her eyes, she drew a deep breath that did little to make her feel better. "Tonight I really don't want to think about Alec or his estranged father. I just want to sleep."

Ethan chuckled. "That sounds like someone who knows how obsessive my brother can be."

She blinked and rubbed her throbbing forehead. "Unfortunately, I know that way too well."

"Yeah, I'm sure you do." Ethan smiled and pulled his cell from his back pocket. "I'll call Alec and tell him you're fine and not to come by. Do you want me to stay? I can sleep on the couch."

"No." She hated when people fussed over her. A direct result of her parents never fussing when it came to her, she was sure. "I'll be fine. You have Sam waiting at home."

"Samantha will understand."

"I'm really fine." Raegan pushed to her feet, fighting back a wince as pain streaked down her spine. "Security in this building is good. Even if whoever did this knows where I live—which I'm sure they don't—they can't get in. I'm not worried."

"If you're sure. It's really no bother."

"I'm sure." She walked him to the door, but as they drew close to her entryway, a thought rattled in the back of her mind. "I appreciate you coming by to check on me." She stopped and looked up at him, debated, then finally decided she might not ever have another chance to ask. "Can I ask you something before you go?"

"Sure. What's on your mind?"

She bit her lip. Ethan and Alec were roughly the same height, nearly the same build, and from a distance, most people assumed they were full-blood brothers, even though Ethan was dark and Alec was blond. They did share a deep brotherly bond, though, and she wasn't sure if her question would cross a line. She decided to go for it anyway.

"Alec said something the other day about hitting rock bottom. I thought he was talking about when we split up, but I got this funny feeling that wasn't what he meant."

Unease passed over Ethan's face, telling her loud and clear he knew exactly what rock bottom meant.

"It wasn't when we split, was it?" she asked.

Ethan stared at her several seconds as if debating his answer, then said, "No, it was after. He held it together for about three months. Then when he got the final divorce papers, he spiraled downward really fast. He's good at pretending everything's fine, but I had a hunch it wasn't. I went out to his place to check on him."

Ethan hesitated, and a tingle rushed down Raegan's spine when she sensed whatever he'd found had not been good. "And?"

He sighed. "And I found him facedown on his kitchen table, an empty bottle of Jack near his left hand, and a loaded .45 near his right."

"Oh my God." She lifted a hand to her mouth so Ethan couldn't see it hanging open in shock.

"When he came to in the hospital, he was pissed," Ethan went on. "Then apologetic after the buzz wore off. He swore he wasn't trying to kill himself, but Mom and Dad weren't convinced. They had him admitted to a rehab center. It was a ninety-day treatment program, which he agreed to go through. When he got out, he promised he wouldn't drink again. As far as I know he's lived up to that promise and hasn't touched a drop of alcohol since."

All the things Alec had said over the last few days ricocheted through Raegan's mind, and her heart hurt for him and everything he'd gone through. But something else was growing inside her, a frustration, a simmering anger that he'd let all of that happen instead of turning to her as she'd wanted him to do, as she'd *begged* him to do. She'd never once blamed him for what had happened to Emma. She'd done everything she could to get him to lean on her instead of the alcohol. To pick them over the bottle. But he'd tossed her aside as if she'd meant nothing to him. And as long as she lived she'd never forget what he'd said to her before he'd walked out of this apartment that last time. The words that still cut like a knife every time she remembered them.

"We only got married because you were pregnant. Now that she's gone, there is no us."

"Anyway," Ethan said, "I'm sure he never told you because—"

"Because it's none of my business." Her jaw clenched. "That's exactly what he'd think and say. Because Alec McClane makes all the decisions. Well, you know what, Ethan? I'm done letting him make them for me."

One side of Ethan's mouth quirked up, and his eyes crinkled at the corners with amusement. "You're a strong woman, you know that, Raegan Devereaux?"

Not strong enough, because her stupid heart was still tied up in knots over his brother. Starting tonight, she was changing that, though.

She reached for the door handle and tugged it open. "Thanks again for checking up on me."

Ethan closed his arms around her. "Anytime. Call me if you need me."

She wouldn't. They both knew it. "I will."

She let go of him. Forced a smile and turned.

And stared into Alec's wild blue eyes.

CHAPTER TEN

Alec's gaze shot from Raegan's scraped and bruised face to his brother standing next to her with a hand closed way too tightly around her upper arm. "What the hell?"

Ethan let go of Raegan and frowned. "Don't go getting any crazy ideas. I came over here to check on her, like you asked."

Alec pushed his way into the apartment, forcing them back, and slammed the door behind him. "I said make sure she was okay, not let this fucking happen."

"I'm standing right here, you know," Raegan said, crossing her arms over her chest.

"I can see that. Looking like someone's punching bag." Alec turned on his brother. "How the hell did this happen?"

"Oh, for God's sake." Raegan dropped her hands and looked toward Ethan. "Ethan, good to see you." She glared at Alec. "And you? For your information, I'm a grown adult who doesn't need you sending people to check on me like a five-year-old. You know where the door is, Alec McClane. Use it."

She turned for the hallway that led to the bedrooms, leaving them standing dumbfounded in the entryway as her bedroom door slammed shut.

"What the fuck was that?" Alec asked, staring after her.

"That," Ethan said, "is a woman who has finally had enough."

When Alec glared at his brother, Ethan shook his head as if he were a moron. "Word of advice? When you go in there to talk to her, like I know you can't stop yourself from doing, check the attitude at the door. She's been through hell tonight."

Fear and a renewed burst of rage spiraled through Alec, draining the blood from his face. "Was she—"

"She's fine. Already went to the police station and filed a report. Didn't need to go to the hospital. Some guy roughed her up a little, but that's it."

Relief whipped through Alec, but his heart still raced like a thoroughbred, and all he wanted to do was see for himself that Raegan was only bruised and nothing else. He stepped past his brother.

"Whoa." Ethan's hand landed hard against Alec's chest, stopping him from moving more than two steps. "I said she's fine. But you go in there all fired up like this, and I guarantee she won't be fine. She'll be more pissed than she is right now."

His pulse was a roar in his ears, but a little of what Ethan was saying got through, and he focused on his brother's green eyes. "Did she say who it was?"

"No."

He looked back down the hallway toward her bedroom door, fighting the rage building again inside. "We both know who it was."

"Maybe. But she's a tough chick. Tougher than you give her credit for."

She was. Alec knew that.

"Do me a favor and chill out before you go barging in there."

"Okay."

"Yes?"

Alec turned a glare Ethan's way. "Yes, okay?" He shoved at Ethan's hand, which was still pressed against his chest. "Now back the hell off."

Ethan released him but still didn't move. And several seconds of silence passed before he said, "Sucks when they don't need you, huh?"

Alec's heart twisted as he looked down the hallway again. It did suck. More than Ethan would ever know. Raegan had never really needed him. He was the one who'd always needed her. He'd just never been able to tell her that. And now it was way too late to even try.

Ethan's keys jangled in the silence as he pulled them from his pocket. "Too bad that's not the real problem between you two." When Alec glanced his way, Ethan moved toward the open door and shrugged. "The real problem is that you never thought you deserved her. Even before you lost Emma. You think you're like John Gilbert, but you're not. And until you let go of that kind of thinking, nothing's ever going to change for you or for her."

Ethan tugged the door closed softly at his back. His muffled footsteps sounded in the hall, then silence settled over the apartment. But that silence was short-lived as Alec's pulse sped up, turning to a roar in his ears.

Was Ethan right? Was he the one holding Raegan back from moving on? The tightness in his chest told him yes. He'd agreed to help her because he wanted to make amends, and he couldn't do that until he fessed up to all his shortcomings, not just his drinking. Because the drinking was really a result of everything else. Of not being able to let go of the past, of not being strong enough to face up to his guilt, of not being able to control his environment.

Nerves curled all through his gut like waves crashing against a beach. On legs not nearly as steady as he liked, he crossed to Raegan's door, lifted his hand, and knocked. No answer came from inside, so he reached for the door handle and turned.

The bedroom was empty. Water sounded from the adjoining bathroom, indicating she was in the shower. He debated his options, knew he needed to leave, but was also smart enough to realize if he did, he'd chicken out and never say the things he wanted to say. Ethan was right. He was the one holding them both back from healing. It was way past time he fixed things for her and for him.

He stood where he was for several minutes, looking over the room he'd once shared with her. This space was definitely different. She'd replaced all the furniture. Instead of golden oak, the dresser and side tables were white-painted pine. She'd gotten rid of the huge, king-sized sleigh bed that had taken up most of the room and replaced it with a queen-sized wrought-iron bed with scrolling detail that arched at the headboard. The bedding was puffy and white. The accent curtains were white. Even the club chair in the corner of the room was white striped, the blue throw pillow on its seat the only color in the entire room.

A whisper of sadness blew through his soul as he lowered himself to the edge of her bed, leaned forward, and rested his forearms against his knees. Not that she'd changed their room—he actually liked what she'd done—but that she'd done so to banish him from her private space. His thoughts drifted to her boyfriend, the one he'd met at the hospital, and even though he told himself not to go there, he couldn't stop wondering if she'd brought him here, if he'd slept in this bed, how many men she'd let in this room to expel all the memories of their marriage from this place.

The shower shut off, and he sat up straighter, his pulse ticking up again as he looked toward the door and waited. A little voice in the back of his head echoed it was time to go, that she'd be pissed if she came out and saw him, but he ignored it because he'd listened to that voice long enough. This time he was determined to do the right thing, even if his conscience screamed not to.

The door pulled open, and steam poured from the room just before Raegan appeared. A plush white towel was wrapped around her damp body and tucked together at her breasts. She held another in her hand, scrubbing the wetness from her hair.

She made it two steps into the bedroom before she saw him, jerked back with a yelp, and dropped the hand towel at her feet. "Goddamn it, Alec! You scared the crap out of me."

"Sorry." He pushed to his feet, trying to ignore the water droplets on her bare shoulders and the way her damp auburn hair hung in waves to the middle of her back.

"What the hell are you doing in here?" She tucked the towel tighter together at her breasts and held it closed with her hand. "I thought I told you to leave."

"You did. But we need to talk first."

Her jaw clenched down hard, and she glared at him, but all he could see was the scrapes and bruises on the right side of her face. And all he could think about was who had done that to her when he'd been driving away from her.

She stalked past him to the dresser and yanked out a T-shirt and a pair of sweats from the drawers. "I'm done talking to you."

He turned to look after her and cringed when he saw the bruise on the back of her left shoulder blade. *Hold it together. For her. Don't lose your shit here, moron.* "Ethan said you already went to the cops."

"I did." She tossed the clothes on the bed and jerked a pair of underwear from the top drawer of her dresser. Something white and lacy he knew he was going to fantasize about late at night for the next damn year.

Focus, idiot.

He forced his gaze away from the lingerie between her fingertips and up to her face. "Tell me what happened."

"No."

"Why not?"

"Because you don't get to know. You don't get to ask. At least not me. You want to get the information from your brother, go right ahead.

Call Jack Bickam if you want to know, but I'm done with this. I'm done with your secrets and your moodiness and your telling me what to do." She pointed the lingerie at him. "You're the one who walked away from me. From us. I was stupid to ask for your help on these cases. I know that now. You don't care about them. You don't care about me. You don't care about anything but wallowing in your own misery. So go ahead." She grabbed her clothing from the bed and stalked past him back toward the bathroom. "Go ahead and wallow but leave me the hell out of it. I've had way more than enough for this lifetime."

He grasped her by the arm so she couldn't shut the bathroom door and close him out. "You think I don't care?"

Her eyes narrowed, not the soft green he remembered but this time flickering with a flame he sensed was about to ignite. The same flame suddenly flaring hot inside him. "I know you don't."

"You don't know anything."

"I know everything. And thanks to you, I also know that the only reason we ever got married was because of Em—"

Grasping her by the other arm, he pulled her up against him and kissed her to cut her off. He couldn't let her say it. They were the words he'd regretted from the moment they'd left his lips.

Her eyes flew wide. She dropped the clothing and pressed both hands against his chest, lurching back from his mouth. "You also don't get to kiss me, you jerk. I'm not your wife anymore. You made sure of that. And this isn't your room, so get the hell out of my apart—"

He yanked her close and kissed her again, didn't know how else to get her to stop talking, knew he should probably release her and back away but desperately didn't want to. Because even though she was spitting mad, even though she hated him and had every right to hate him from now until the end of time, he didn't feel the same. He never had.

She pushed hard against his chest and stumbled back, breaking his grip on her arms. "I said you don't get to kiss me like that, you son of a bitch."

The towel slipped free of its knot and skimmed her body, exposing those luscious breasts he'd kissed and licked and laved so many times he'd lost count. That fire flared hotter inside him, bringing his body to life in a way it hadn't felt in years. He watched as she grasped the towel at her waist, as she yanked it back up and tucked it tighter around her breasts, blocking the gorgeous sight from his view. Heat rolled through his belly and shot through his veins as he lifted his gaze to her face, as he focused on her flushed cheeks, the way her chest rose and fell with her rapid breaths, and the fervor brewing in her eyes.

Instead of moving farther away, as he expected her to do, she stepped toward him. "I say who kisses me."

His pulse picked up. He didn't move. Knew he deserved the right hook or knee to the groin or whatever she was about to do to him. Knew he deserved way worse than that. Her fingers tangled in his shirt. She glared up at him. But she didn't lash out at him, didn't try to hurt him. Instead, she lifted to her toes and pressed her mouth to his.

For a heartbeat, he didn't move. Didn't think. Couldn't breathe. And then his brain kicked into gear and he realized, *she's kissing me.*

Biology overtook reason. Lust replaced common sense. History, passion, and need overwhelmed him, empowered him, spurred him forward. He closed his arms around her and tugged her tight against him. And opened to her kiss, drawing her into his mouth before the world could spiral in and tear her away.

She grunted, held on to his shirt tighter, drew a deep breath in through her nose as her tongue found his and stroked. The first lick of wet heat was electric, and he fisted the towel at her back, desperate for more. Turning her away from the bathroom door, he pushed her up against the wall. She groaned and kissed him harder. One sexy bare leg lifted and skimmed his hip. He caught it in his hand as he tipped his head and kissed her, trailing his fingers up the backside of her thigh. Trembling against him, she groaned again and rocked against his growing erection until the only word he heard echoing in his head was "more."

More of her, more of this, more of them. He stepped back, pulling her with him, wanting to feel her beneath him, above him, around him. Her foot hit the floor. Her fingers drifted up into his hair. Dragging her against him, he changed the angle of the kiss, exploring every inch of her lips and tongue and teeth, needing her with a desperation he'd all but forgotten. The backs of his legs hit the mattress. He tugged her down with him. She fell against his chest as he bounced on his back on the mattress. A grunt echoed from her as she pushed up on her hands and broke their kiss. Wide, glazed green eyes stared down at him with a mixture of anger and heat and need and passion. All the same emotions swirling inside him.

A thousand memories of the two of them together flashed behind his eyes, tugging at that heart he definitely knew he still had now. His throat grew thick. Gently, he brushed a lock of wavy damp hair back from her face and glanced over her beautiful features, bruises and all, as he fought for the right words to tell her what he felt. As he struggled with whatever this was happening between them.

Her gaze dropped to his lips, and the need to taste her again, to lose himself in her sweetness, rebuilt until it was all he knew. He skimmed the back of his fingers down her bruised cheek and lifted his mouth back to hers, whispering, "Raegs."

Her gaze lifted back to his as he drew close, and he watched something shift in her meadow-green irises. Watched her eyes harden, watched her lips thin, watched the blush of passion fade from her cheeks until they were as white as the bedspread beneath him.

She scrambled backward before he could kiss her, climbed off him, and tugged her towel back up around her breasts. Pushing up on one hand, he reached for her to pull her back, but she muttered, "No," and moved another step away, closer to the safety of her bathroom. "You need to leave, Alec."

He sat slowly up. Was having trouble thinking. Only knew he didn't want to let her go. But the waver in her voice kicked some part of his brain into gear, and in a rush he realized she was no longer vibrating with rage and passion but with fear.

"Raegan—"

"No." She stepped back again, into the bathroom, before he rose fully to his feet. And this time the panic in her voice brought him to a full stop. "Please"—her voice hitched, and she swallowed quickly to hide it, but he heard it just the same—"just leave."

Oh yeah, he still had a heart because it cracked right there in front of her. Cracked because the last thing he wanted to do was hurt her—he'd done that too many times to count—and he was obviously doing it again.

His throat grew so tight it was hard to breathe. He could never make up for the wrongs he'd done her in the past. All he could do was the right thing tonight. "I'm not leaving."

Her gaze lifted to his. Only this time when their eyes met he didn't see fear or anger or passion in her mesmerizing eyes. He saw desperation. "I don't want you here anymore. Can't you see that? I don't want or need—"

"I know my father did this to you." Her words hurt, more than he'd thought they could, but he held his ground. He was done running. Done hiding. Done ignoring the pain he'd caused. He'd done all of that before and it had only prolonged both of their misery. It was time he faced her and the past. And whether or not she wanted to admit it, she needed him now. He wasn't walking away from her until he knew she was safe. "You're not staying here alone."

"I don't need you to protect me. I don't *want* you to protect me. I'm perfectly fine by myself."

"I'm still staying." He turned for the door, moving on legs steadier than he expected. "I'll sleep on the couch. Try to get some sleep. We'll talk in the morning."

He closed the door before she could protest. Before she could rail at him again and throw him out. She was wearing nothing but a towel. He knew she wouldn't come after him. In fact, he suspected he'd shocked and confused her so much just now that she wouldn't come out of her bedroom until dawn.

His thoughts were a whir as he moved down the hall. This night had not gone at all as he'd planned. Breathing deeply, he tried to focus on something concrete instead of the emotions still swirling inside him. Like the cases and those missing kids. Reaching back for his phone, he decided to text his friend Hunt to see if he'd found any information on those two kids, but his feet drew to a stop when he neared the second bedroom. Emma's room.

All thoughts of the cases drifted from his mind. His skin tingled and his fingers twitched at his side. A little voice urged him to walk on by, that tonight of all nights was not the time to test his willpower, but his legs didn't seem to want to listen. They led him across the carpet, and before he could stop himself, he closed his fingers around the door handle and turned. Then stared into the dark room.

Light from the hall spilled past his feet, and his heart pounded hard and fast as he scanned the bookshelf still stocked with all of Emma's favorite stories, the rocking horse she'd spent hours playing on beneath the window, the basket in the corner she used to drag to the middle of the floor, dump the toys out of, and climb inside. Everything was the same—the stuffed animals, the books, the pictures on the lavender walls—everything except the bed. Gone was Emma's white crib, the one he'd spent two days putting together when Raegan had been pregnant, replaced now by a twin-sized big-girl bed with white trim, covered in a new pink-and-green-checked comforter.

In that moment, standing at the threshold of his daughter's quiet room, he realized why Raegan hadn't moved out of this apartment. Not because she was stubborn or couldn't face reality, but because she needed to believe that Emma would one day come home. Needed to believe it the way she needed air to breathe. Needed it because that belief was all she had left to keep her going.

Whatever was left whole inside him shattered right in the doorway of his daughter's darkened bedroom. Because in that moment he also realized that his father wasn't the real threat to Raegan's safety. He was.

All because he was a selfish son of a bitch who'd only ever cared about protecting himself.

———

Half a beer should not leave a person feeling hungover and wrecked, but that was how Raegan felt as she pulled herself out of bed late the next morning, paused in the doorway of her bathroom, and pressed her fingers against her throbbing forehead.

Her back ached, the palms of her hands were scuffed and sore, and while the bruise on her right cheek was no longer swollen, it hurt like a bitch.

Grabbing the glass from the bathroom counter, she filled it with water, pulled open a drawer, and downed two acetaminophen. Then she looked up at her reflection and wished she hadn't. The bruise wasn't bad. She could cover it with makeup easily enough. It was the dark circles under her eyes she'd have trouble hiding. Especially from Alec.

Irritation swept through her, followed by a good dose of mortification. The way she'd yelled at him last night tumbled through her mind. And the way she'd kissed him. Rolling her eyes, she moved out of the bathroom and pulled jeans from her dresser drawer. Why the hell had she kissed him?

Because you were mad. Because he kissed you first. Both correct answers, except she knew he hadn't kissed her because anything between them had changed. He'd kissed her because—she peeled off her sweats and jerked on her jeans—because she'd been wearing nothing but a towel and he was a guy. Because she'd been yelling and he'd been ready to do anything to shut her up. Because he'd been frustrated at the fact she wouldn't tell him what had happened to her, and he wanted to make that point known.

But those weren't the real reasons. The real reason hit her as she snapped her bra, pulled up the straps, and grabbed her brown cable-knit sweater from the drawer. The real reason he'd kissed her was because, after that miserable interview yesterday, he'd been feeling angry and self-destructive. And what better way to self-destruct than to make a pass at the woman who reminded you of the worst moment of your life and who you never wanted to be with again?

Her mood dipped even lower as she moved back into her bathroom, slapped on some mascara and lip balm, used powder to hide the bruise, and fluffed her hair with her fingers. She didn't feel like styling her hair. Didn't feel like making much of an effort, period. She knew Alec was still in her apartment because she could hear him moving around in the other room, but all she wanted was for him to leave. She didn't need his help anymore, he really didn't want to give it, and the sooner they both stopped pretending, the better off they'd be.

Knowing she'd spent as long as she could in her room and that it would soon be noon if she didn't get moving, she squared her shoulders, turned out of her bathroom, then crossed to the bedroom door and pulled it open. Only to falter when she smelled breakfast sausage and freshly brewed coffee wafting through the air.

Her heart picked up speed as she stepped into the hall, rounded the corner, and moved into the living room. Sizzling sounds echoed from the kitchen, and when she looked across the open space toward the island on the far side, she almost tripped.

Alec stood at her stove, cooking. Something he'd never done, not once in all the time they'd been married. Watching as he moved eggs to a plate, grabbed the toast as it popped up, and then buttered it, she realized he wasn't doing it like a guy who was just trying to be nice. He was doing it like a guy who'd done it dozens of times in the past.

An irrational burst of jealousy hit her hard. Who had he made breakfast for in the last two years? And how often was he doing it for that person that he'd gotten so good at it?

He must have heard her because he glanced her way. "There you are. I heard your shower running. This is just about ready. Why don't you grab some coffee?"

She told herself not to be stupid. It didn't matter who he cooked for. They weren't a couple, and it was none of her business anyhow. But her already bad mood took another header.

Clenching her jaw, she moved past him into the kitchen, pulled a cup from the cabinet, and reached for the carafe. Then she watched from the corner of her eye as he moved a plate to the table near the windows that looked out over the city and then came back into the kitchen to stand at her side.

"Sleep good?" he asked as if nothing had happened last night.

Raegan lifted the cup to her lips and sipped, then turned for the table. "No."

"That's too bad. I did." He poured more coffee into his mug. "I forgot how comfortable that couch is."

A memory flashed. One of Alec snoozing on that same couch with an infant Emma snoring softly on his chest.

Her heart pinched, but she pushed the memory away and sat, focusing in on the eggs and sausage he'd cooked. When he sat next to her with nothing but his coffee, she frowned. "Aren't you eating?"

"Already did. Dig in before it gets cold."

Dammit, he'd made sausage links, her favorite. He didn't even like sausage. He preferred bacon. Why the hell was he being so nice to her? She scooped up a bite of eggs and chewed begrudgingly.

"So I made us an appointment for an interview with the second family this afternoon. The husband gets off work around two. They said they could see us at two thirty."

Shock rippled through Raegan as she lifted a piece of sausage with her fork. "You already called them?"

"Yeah." He rose from the table, grasped papers she hadn't noticed were scattered all over the coffee table, and came back. "I was looking through these files last night, and I found something of interest. Each of these families in the Portland area was receiving social services through the state for food assistance, basic services like health care, or were part of the Family Support and Connections program that provides parenting classes and resources." He laid the papers out so she could see them.

Raegan was still reeling from the fact he'd taken the initiative to make those calls when his words hit her. "All three of them? Are you sure?"

He nodded. "I called Barbara Willig this morning. The Willig family's caseworker was a man named Conner Murray. I also put a call in to the Oregon Department of Human Services and left a message. Someone's supposed to call me back regarding the other two families."

"You think they might have the same caseworker?"

"Would be quite a coincidence if they did, don't you think?"

Raegan glanced back down at the papers. "Yeah, it would be."

He shuffled the papers together into a stack. "I also heard back from Hunt. The girl we saw at the hospital? She's autistic. Nonverbal. Looks completely normal but has trouble forming attachments. She'd been missing about a week when she turned up."

"Were any of the other kids autistic?"

"Not that I've been able to find."

She looked down at the papers. "Then I don't see how her being autistic has anything to do with anything else."

"Stay with me a second. We're brainstorming, right?" He shifted in his seat and smiled, and the rare curve of his lips pushed away the last of her irritation and made her focus in on him. "It's odd no child remains have been found or reported to the police. If we assume these cases are linked and that someone is kidnapping young kids and killing them, then someone would have found something by now. Let's face it.

Criminals make mistakes, and some of these cases go back at least ten years. Mistakes are how all serial killers are caught."

Sickness brewed in Raegan's stomach, but she listened to what he was saying because she knew they had to consider the fact this was a serial killer at work. His targets, for whatever reason, were just much younger. "Okay, go on."

"It's possible this person's taking kids for organ harvesting."

She'd already thought of that. That sickness rolled faster, killing her appetite. "We should check blood types on all these kids. See if there are any similarities there as well. We should also check out child transplant surgery lists in the Northwest and try to find which transplant companies were used."

"I agree. But I'm not convinced these kids are being killed."

Her brow lowered because that wasn't what she'd expected him to say. Especially considering what he believed had happened to their daughter. "Why not?"

He flipped through the case files in his hands. "All the kids here were healthy, normal children, and they're still missing. The only kid who's turned up is the autistic girl found wandering in a park, alone, ten miles from her house. No one has any idea how she got there, not even her."

"That's not true. There's the boy who was found in the back of that car on the highway."

"Right. A normal, healthy boy. In a getaway car. That had engine trouble." He pulled his notepad from the bottom of the stack of files and read off what he'd scribbled there. "I talked to the police this morning. The timing belt in that car was busted. It wasn't going anywhere anytime soon. It was also found not far out of the city where traffic's still pretty heavy. What if the kid was sleeping in the backseat, and the guy left to get help, and before he could get back someone checked the car? Or what if he freaked when the car broke down and just ran, leaving his cargo behind?"

Raegan wasn't thrilled with the way Alec used the word "cargo," but she set her fork down, understanding where he was going. "You're hypothesizing that if the same person is abducting all these kids, then the boy being left in the car was a fluke, but the autistic girl showing up alone in a park was not."

"Yeah. I think he dropped her off *because* she was autistic. He didn't want her anymore because she was different."

Raegan stared at him, her heart beating hard. "You're talking about abducting children for a reason other than killing them. That goes against your theory about what happened to Emma."

"I know." He didn't look away when she mentioned Emma's name. Just held her eyes with the same focused attention. He always looked away whenever anyone mentioned their daughter's name. "But kids are abducted all the time for sex trafficking. An autistic girl who doesn't like to be touched could never be trained for that."

What little breakfast Raegan had eaten threatened to come back up. She did not want to think about kids as young as one and four being taken for sex trafficking. Reaching for her coffee, she said, "You think it's possible this social worker could be involved in something like that?"

"I hope not." He lifted his coffee for a sip and watched her over the rim of his cup. "Tomorrow I think we need to try to meet with the family of that autistic girl."

Raegan nodded, but her head swam with information and the pieces Alec had put together this morning.

Alec jotted a few notes on his pad of paper. "I'll also look into the blood types and try to get some transplant lists. That's a good idea." His pen stilled against the pad. "There's one more thing we need to talk about."

The wary look on his face made Raegan's stomach flop, and her nerves came rushing back because she knew he was going to bring up that kiss.

Alec leaned back in his seat. "Before you got to the hospital the other day, Bickam told me the FBI received a tip about where to find that girl, and that the tip had come from the Santiam Correctional Institution. I had a hunch John Gilbert was the one who'd phoned it in, so I went to see him after I left the hospital."

Shock rippled through Raegan again as she looked up at him, only this shock was stronger than the one she'd felt before. In all the time she and Alec had been together, he'd only once gone to see his biological father, and that was right after Emma had disappeared. "You went to see him?"

"I just wanted to know if he was involved."

"And?"

"He didn't admit to it. There's no proof he's the one who made the call. He didn't name the specific park where she was found, but he did name one in the area. That's more than coincidental to me, even though Bickam seems to think Gilbert might have heard the story on the news and was just messing with me. We all know how he likes to do that."

Yeah, Raegan did know that. In the weeks after Emma's disappearance, John Gilbert had taunted Alec via phone and the mail. The cops had never been able to prove Gilbert had been involved in Emma's disappearance, but Alec had always believed the worst.

"Anyway, the conversation between us didn't go well, as you can imagine. And when he mentioned you, I might have reacted. Badly."

Her stomach dropped. She could only envision how that had gone over. "What happened?"

Alec's jaw clenched. "He threatened to look you up after he got out. Since he wasn't due to be released for a week, I didn't tell you. Then you got that note on your car, and I thought maybe he told a friend to mess with you since I'd just talked to him. But yesterday when I found out he'd been released, and then discovered what happened to you in that alley . . ."

A mixture of rage and regret flashed in his features when he glanced at her bruised cheek, and she knew in that moment that he'd talked to Bickam this morning and gotten the details on her attack.

"I know it was Gilbert. Bickam talked to the local cops about our case and said they're looking for him so they can question him about his whereabouts last night, but so far they haven't had much luck finding him. Which means"—he scrubbed a hand over his face—"you're not safe until they do."

"I'm fine. This building—"

"Is not as secure as you think." He dropped his hand and stared at her with very focused, very determined blue eyes. "Until they pick him up, you're not staying alone."

What little empathy she'd had for how awful it must have been for him to confront his father flew right out the window. "I don't need any kind of protection. I'm perfectly fine by myself."

"No, you're not." Alec rose with his coffee and moved into the kitchen. "And don't argue with me about this, Raegs. I know the man, and I'm not about to take chances with your life just because you want to be stubborn. We can either stay here or at my place, but until he's caught, you're not getting rid of me."

Raegan stared after him as he poured the rest of his coffee down the drain, a mixture of disbelief and frustration—and, yes, even warmth, since he'd used that stupid nickname again—tumbling through her.

"Now finish eating," he said, "so we can head over and find Conner Murray. I'm gonna grab a shower."

She watched him walk out of the room and disappear down the hall. Alone, she looked at her now-cold food and tried to decipher what, exactly, had just happened. They had a couple of leads—several that churned her stomach, but they were still leads. Alec had gone out of his way to not only take charge of their investigation but to be nice. And for the foreseeable future, they were living together.

Nerves jumbled in her stomach at the last thought, followed by a rush of heat she told herself she was stupid to feel. He hadn't mentioned their crazy make-out session last night, and part of her was relieved by that fact. But another part was disappointed too. Especially since she was even more wrecked now than when she'd climbed out of bed.

Were they friends now? Exes who were just trying to be civil and solve a case? Or were they something more? He'd called her Raegs—last night and today. As much as she tried to tell herself he was only being nice, that he really didn't care about her, she knew that was a lie. He did care. He cared a lot, judging by the fact he wouldn't leave.

Her hand shook as she reached for her coffee and sipped the cool liquid. Because she had absolutely no idea what she was supposed to do about anything.

CHAPTER ELEVEN

Alec's phone had rung just after he'd finished a shower that had been filled with too many thoughts of Raegan in the other room and the way she'd looked at him this morning with a mixture of confusion, surprise, and heat.

It was the heat that lit him up and made his body ache. Thankfully, the call had been from the department of social services for Washington County, refocusing him on the task at hand instead of on how much he wanted to pull Raegan into the shower with him. The receptionist hadn't wanted to give him much information, but she had confirmed that Conner Murray had indeed worked with all three families he and Raegan were checking into. And that news had shifted his plans for the day. After hustling to get ready, he'd found Raegan waiting for him in the living room, and they'd driven right over to Murray's office to try to catch the man.

The receptionist was young, with blonde hair pulled back in a neat tail and trendy glasses perched on her slim nose. She immediately grew nervous when they approached her, and Alec suspected she knew she'd already given away too much information. He poured on the charm, but the girl kept glancing at Raegan, and the most she would tell them was that Murray had just left for an appointment.

Alec thanked her, and they headed for the door. "Let's see if we can catch him."

Raegan nodded.

The employee parking lot was empty except for one man with dark hair climbing into a state-issued Ford Taurus.

"Mr. Murray?" Alec called.

The man turned with one foot in the car and glanced back over the top of his door as Alec and Raegan approached. "Yes?"

Bingo. "I'm Alec McClane, and this is Raegan Devereaux. We'd like to ask you a few questions about a couple kids under your watch."

Murray's blue eyes narrowed, and his gaze skipped between them. "What's this about?"

"It's about three missing toddlers over the last three years," Raegan said. "You were assigned to each of their cases."

Murray's face went ashen and quickly turned red. "You're reporters, aren't you? I've got nothing to say to the press."

He climbed into his car and slammed the door. Alec and Raegan watched as he whipped his car out of the space, glanced back at them through the rearview mirror, then sped out of the parking lot.

A tingle ran down Alec's spine. "Jumpy, wouldn't you say?"

"Very."

"Let's find out who he's scheduled to see tomorrow and get in his way."

Raegan glanced up at him. "That receptionist is not going to give it to us."

Alec wasn't so sure. "Let me see what I can get out of her. Wait here."

Raegan rolled her eyes as he headed back inside. The receptionist was more relaxed once Raegan was gone. Alec made up a story about writing an article on the hidden heroes in America's fight against poverty and told her he'd heard amazing things about Murray's work with at-risk youth. She was hesitant about giving him the info he wanted, but after turning up the charm and showing her some of his other work on his phone, she finally caved.

When he rejoined Raegan at his truck, she was already sitting inside waiting. He climbed in and handed her a piece of paper. "Got his schedule for tomorrow."

She scanned the page, written in the young girl's bubble script, frowned, and proceeded to rip the bottom line off and tear it in pieces.

"Hey," Alec said, feigning shock as he pulled out of the parking lot. "I might need that."

"Blondie's phone number? I don't think so."

Alec chuckled as they headed to their scheduled interview. She was jealous. He sorta liked that. When he'd seen her with Jeremy Norris at the hospital he'd been green with envy. He had no idea what was happening between them, and after last night's kiss he wasn't sure what he even wanted to happen between them, but he liked that she was jealous. It meant some part of her still cared.

Forty-five minutes later they pulled to a stop in front of a one-story Cape Cod in Forest Grove. Luis and Marie Ramirez had moved out of Portland a year after their son David disappeared. Their rental was small but well-kept. The yard was clean, the trees had recently been trimmed, and a three-foot-tall wooden snowman wrapped with an orange scarf sat on the porch welcoming guests.

"What did you say Mr. Ramirez does for a living?" Raegan asked as she followed Alec up the front walk.

"Concrete. He got a job out here with the city about fourteen months ago."

"And what about Mrs. Ramirez?"

"Food services at the local elementary school."

He knocked, and they both waited as footsteps sounded inside. Seconds later, the door pulled open, and a Hispanic man in his early thirties with dark hair and eyes, wearing a blue long-sleeved shirt but-toned all the way to his throat, said, "Yes?"

Alec offered his hand. "Hi, Mr. Ramirez. I'm Alec McClane. We spoke earlier on the phone?"

Luis Ramirez nodded. "*Sí.* Uh, come on in." He held the door open for them, closing it after they moved into the living room. "I'll get my wife. She just got back from picking our son up from school."

His English was choppy but clear. As he rounded a corner and dis-appeared down a small hallway, Raegan moved farther into the living area and sat on the couch. "This is nice. A lot nicer than the last place we visited."

It was. The room was small but clean with whitewashed beadboard walls, a leather couch and two recliners, a small TV on the wall above the fireplace, and a crucifix hanging near the door.

Luis reappeared holding the hand of a small Hispanic woman, her dark hair pulled back in a neat tail, a nervous expression on her face. "This is my wife, Marie."

"*Hola.*" Marie stepped forward and held out her hand. Alec rose and shook it. Raegan did the same.

"Thanks for meeting with us," Alec said.

The woman turned toward her husband and said something in Spanish Alec didn't catch. Seconds later, Luis looked their way. "Sorry. Uh, my wife's English is not so good. She wants to know if you want something to drink?"

"No, we're fine." Alec smiled at the wife, then sat. Raegan lowered herself to the couch next to him. "Thanks for talking to us today about David. We know how hard this probably is for you."

The Ramirezes exchanged nervous looks, then each sat in the reclin-ers opposite the couch.

"It is," Luis said. "But we agreed long ago if anyone, especially any reporters, wanted to talk to us, we would cooperate. We want to find our son."

Alec's chest tightened, but today he focused on the case, not his personal feelings. "David went missing twenty-nine months ago, is that correct?"

"Yes," Luis answered. "We were living in Northeast Portland then. It was September. We'd taken him to the State Fair down in Salem. It was packed that day. Hot. Over a hundred degrees. Our older son, Miguel, was eight at the time. He'd wanted to go on the rides. I took him. Marie stayed with David and went to get food from one of the vendors."

"How old was David then?" Alec asked.

"Barely two."

Marie spoke rapidly in Spanish, and Luis nodded, then said, "He was walking then. Never wanted to sit still. She pushed the stroller to a food cart, took her eyes off of him to pay, and when she looked back, he was gone."

Marie's eyes angled downward, and she fiddled with her hands in her lap until her husband reached for her. Tattoos Alec couldn't decipher stained the back of his hands.

"She looked everywhere for him," Luis went on. "There was no sign of him. It was like he just vanished. She found a security guard, but her English wasn't good, and he didn't understand what she was trying to say. She came and found me so I could translate. We searched the entire fairgrounds. Security helped us look, but there were multiple entrances and exits. By the time the authorities got involved, he could have been anywhere."

It was a parent's worst nightmare, and Alec knew that nightmare well because he'd lived it. "What happened then?"

The Ramirezes exchanged looks again, and Luis said, "The police came. We told them what happened. They said they would look into it, but . . ."

"But what?" Raegan asked.

Luis glanced her way. "We were both in the States illegally then. And we weren't married. I was also running with a gang in the city. The cops . . . they were sure whoever took David targeted him specifically because of the people we associated with. No one seemed interested in helping us. You are the first reporters who have ever asked about our son."

Alec wasn't surprised. Illegal immigrants, especially gang members, had very little voice. "You said you were living up in Portland. Was your son receiving help from the state? Health care, social services, that kind of thing?"

"Yes. Both of our boys were. They were both born here."

"Do you ever remember a man named Conner Murray?" Raegan asked. "He would have been with Washington County Health and Human Services. He would have come out to your home to check on the boys. About five eight, round around the middle, with thinning hair?"

Luis turned to his wife and spoke in Spanish. They conversed back and forth a few minutes, then he looked at Raegan once more. "Yes. The name and description are familiar."

Raegan glanced Alec's way, and in her green eyes he saw the same thing he felt. A hint of hope.

"Do you have e-mail, Mr. Ramirez?" Alec asked.

"Yes."

Alec pulled a business card from his pocket and handed it to the man. "Can you write down your address for me? I want to send you a photo of Conner Murray and see if it's the same guy."

"Okay."

Footsteps sounded from the hallway while Luis jotted down his e-mail. A squeal echoed from a back bedroom, followed by a child speaking rapidly in Spanish.

Raegan looked toward the hall. "What was that?"

Luis glanced over his shoulder. "Oh, that was our son Miguel. Sorry, he must have woke the baby."

"Baby." From the corner of his eye, Alec saw the way Raegan's face paled. "You had another baby?"

Shuffling sounded again, then a boy with shaggy dark hair appeared from the hall, holding a red-faced, chubby baby with tear tracks down his cherub face.

Marie jumped up from her seat and rushed to the boy's side, taking the infant from her son as she spoke quickly in a soothing Spanish tone.

Luis handed the card back to Alec. "That's Daniel, our youngest."

Raegan pushed to her feet and crossed to Marie and the baby, holding out her finger for the baby to grab. "Oh my goodness. He's adorable. Hi, there. Hi, little guy."

The baby sniffled, eyed her with big brown eyes, and wrapped his chubby hand around her finger.

Marie held the baby out to Raegan. "Here. You hold?"

"Oh. Um." Raegan's eyes widened, but she reached for the boy, taking him into her arms and pulling him close against her. Naturally. Like a woman who'd held a child a thousand times before.

"Oh my goodness," she said again, staring down at him with a mixture of wonder and sadness Alec didn't miss. "You are absolutely beautiful, aren't you? How old is he?" she asked, looking at Marie.

"Six months," Luis answered.

"Six months," Raegan repeated, staring back down at the baby as she began to sway from side to side with him in her arms. "What a big boy you are. What a sweet, big boy."

Tears glistened in her eyes as she smiled at the infant, and as he watched, Alec's heart contracted so hard, pain radiated all through his torso and arms and legs.

"We weren't sure we'd ever have any more kids," Luis said softly at Alec's side while the two women focused their attention on the baby. "Weren't really sure we'd even stay together after we lost David. Marie, she blamed herself. Couldn't let it go, even though it wasn't her fault. If I had been with him, he could have climbed out of that stroller just the same. Sometimes . . ." The man shrugged, and Alec looked his way. "Sometimes bad things just happen."

Alec's throat grew thick. "How did you get past it?" He nodded toward Raegan and the baby, forcing himself to keep going. "How did you get to this?"

"I don't know. We just did." Luis held his arm out, and the boy who'd carried the baby into the room moved to his side and sat. "We had Miguel. He needed us. When he started having trouble in school and with friends, it was a wake-up call for us."

"Geez, Dad," Miguel said with a sheepish smile. "I wasn't that bad."

Luis ruffled his son's hair. "No, not that bad. But we were." He looked at Alec once more. "Life goes on. That's what we learned. You never forget. You never stop looking. But you can't spend your time living in the past or you miss out on the present."

God, this guy sounded so freakin' healthy. Healthier than Alec had ever been.

"My wife and I both applied for citizenship after that. And we decided it was time we stopped pretending to be a family and finally got married. I stopped running with my gang and went to a trade school while she got a job with the school district. It wasn't easy, and there were times I thought we'd never make it, but then we moved out here where I could work, found this house to rent. She's still working for the schools here, but she's taking a class to improve her English, and she wants to go to school and get her degree so she can be a nurse."

Amazingly healthy. Especially considering all the obstacles against them. Alec stared in wonder at Raegan, shifting the baby in her arms and laughing at his puzzled expression. "And the baby?"

"He was Marie's idea. I wasn't sure at first. Wasn't sure we could handle it or that having a baby around wouldn't be a constant reminder of David. But Marie was insistent. She never wanted Miguel to be an only child, and now"—he looked toward his wife and their son in

Raegan's arms—"now I can't imagine life without him. Having him was the best thing we did for the both of us."

Raegan's gaze lifted from the baby and drifted Alec's way. And when she smiled, her eyes still glistening with unshed tears, her arms still rocking the baby, something inside his heart broke open wide.

He loved her. Had never stopped loving her. And he knew some part of him would always love her no matter where he went or who he was with.

Instead of warming him, though, that realization sent a whisper of fear through his chest because he didn't know what to do about it. He didn't know if they were as strong as the Ramirezes or if it was even smart to think about trying again, considering everything he'd put Raegan through. He just knew he was tired of fighting what he felt. Tired of pretending he didn't care. Tired of looking at her and wishing so much between them could be different.

He was just deathly afraid of fucking up all over again and making things worse for both of them if he took a chance.

———

Raegan stared out the passenger window as Alec drove them back to her apartment in the city. A light rain had begun to fall when they were talking with the Ramirezes, and now that it was dark, the city growing larger in the windows shimmered like white twinkle lights on Christmas morning.

She'd thought she could handle these interviews. Thought Alec was going to be the one who'd have trouble, but today he hadn't. Today he'd been the one to speak with the Ramirezes and ask all the right questions. She, on the other hand, had been useless the minute she'd seen that baby. That precious, adorable, chubby baby who'd looked nothing like Emma but made her ache in a way she felt deep in her soul.

Alec hadn't talked to her on the ride back, and for that she was grateful. Her throat was so thick she wasn't sure she'd be able to speak even if she tried. She told herself to pull it together, told herself she'd seen a hundred babies in the years since Emma had been gone and that she'd never reacted this way before. But then, she'd never met another couple like the Ramirezes. Now, every time she pictured them and their situation, all she could think was, *that could have been us.*

Her street was busy—as always on a weeknight—and Alec had to drive around the block several times before he found a space for his truck. She pulled her keys from her purse and popped the door as soon as he was parked, desperate to go upstairs, to be alone, to let these tears that were building finally fall in the privacy of her own room where no one could see.

She keyed in the building code at the front door, and they moved into the elevator in silence. The car seemed to take forever to go up to the fifth floor, and just when she was wishing she'd taken the stairs, the double doors finally pinged and opened.

Exhaustion pulled at her as she opened her apartment door, moved inside, and dropped her keys in the bowl on the entry table.

Alec closed the door softly at his back while she took off her coat and hung it on the coat tree in the entry. When she gestured for his, he slipped it off and said, "Thanks."

She forced a smile she didn't feel, hung up his coat, and moved into the great room. Alec's footsteps sounded behind her as she pulled the fridge open and grabbed a bottle of water.

"Are you hungry?" he asked.

She shook her head, popped the top on the bottle, and took a long swallow. "You're welcome to anything you can find. There's also a take-out menu near the phone."

Alec slipped his hands into the pockets of his faded jeans, looking just as worn and wrung out as she felt. "I'm not hungry either."

She glanced away, not wanting to think about how he was feeling tonight. Not on top of everything else. Knew she'd lose it even faster if she did. Moving for the hall, she said, "Well, I'm pretty tired. I think I'm just going to go to be—"

"You were a great mother, Raegan."

Her feet stilled at the edge of the hallway, and her heart skipped a beat.

"Emma was lucky to have you as her mom."

It was the first time he'd used Emma's name since she'd gone missing. Even before the divorce, when she'd known he was hurting and missing their daughter just as much as she was, he'd never used her name. He'd only referred to her as "she" or "her."

Slowly she turned to look at him. "I don't know if that's true," she said, unable to walk away, unable to move because, after all this time, he was finally talking. "I didn't have a clue what I was doing."

His lips curved in a sad smile, one that tugged on her heart. "Emma didn't know that. I didn't know that either. You always seemed to know exactly what she needed. I'm the one who didn't have a clue when it came to her."

"Yes, you did," she said softly. "Emma loved you."

His eyes glistened as he looked toward the ceiling. "I shouldn't have traveled so much. I should have taken assignments closer to home so I could spend more time with her. And you."

He looked down at her with so much heartache and regret, it felt as if someone were strangling her heart.

The backs of her eyes burned, and she knew she couldn't look at him anymore. Knew she was going to break if she did. Blinking rapidly, she focused on the water bottle in her hand. On something solid, something real instead of the pain swirling around her. "I think we could both spend our whole lives playing the 'I should have' game. It doesn't change anything."

"No, it doesn't," he said softly. "Are you still seeing that guy? The one at your office? The one I met at the hospital?"

The question threw her, seemed to come out of left field when they were talking about Emma. "No." Her brow wrinkled. "I ended it after . . . well"—her cheeks heated because she didn't want to give too much away—"after I started looking into these cases."

That made sense, didn't it? She had ended things with Jeremy after he'd called her with news on these cases. Of course, that was right after she'd spent the night at Alec's house, but he didn't need to know that.

"Good."

His footsteps sounded against the floor, and when she lifted her gaze, she discovered he was standing in front of her, focused solely on her. Sadness and heartache and regret still reflected in his clear blue eyes, but there was also something more. Heat and passion swirled in those deep cerulean depths now as well. So much her pulse shot straight into the stratosphere.

"That's good." He took the water bottle from her hand and set it on the end table beside him. Moving closer, he cupped her face in both of his big hands, his warm, rough fingers sending tingles all across her flesh. "Because I don't want you to have any reason to feel guilty about what I'm about to do."

She had one split second to suck in a surprised breath before he lowered his head and kissed her. Electricity arced through her body. Electricity and need and an awakening desire she didn't want to fight. Unlike last night, unlike every time she'd fantasized about this very moment, this felt right. This felt right and real and perfect, and she didn't want to ever let it go.

He drew back long before she was ready and gazed down at her, but he didn't drop his hands from her face. And that was all the encouragement she needed.

"Do that again," she breathed.

His eyes darkened, and his mouth covered hers once more, his kiss rocking the world right out from under her. She opened at first contact, slid her arms around his shoulders and hung on, kissing him right back until she was breathless. His tongue brushed hers with long, languid strokes she felt everywhere. And when his fingers slid into her hair, when he combed his hands through her long locks and trailed them down her spine to encircle her waist and pull her against him, she knew she was lost. Knew she could no longer go on pretending this wasn't exactly what she'd wanted from the first moment she'd seen him sitting on a chair in that hospital hallway.

Sensations rocked her body. The hot, wet slide of his tongue along hers. The firm, wide grip of his hand at her lower back drawing her closer. The hard, insistent length of his erection pressing against her belly, telling her he felt their connection as strongly as she did, telling her he wanted her just as much as she wanted him.

Her arms wound around his neck, and she trembled as he whispered, "Raegan," against her lips. He kissed the corner of her mouth, her jaw, the soft skin behind her ear, whispering, "Raegs," again and again until she melted.

Her hands slid to his cheeks, and she drew his mouth back to hers, kissing him hard. He answered by groaning against her, kissing her deeper, and wrapping his arms tightly around her waist as he lifted her feet off the floor.

She felt herself moving, didn't care where she was going so long as he was going with her. Didn't ever want to let go. "Alec—"

"Want you," he rasped, kissing the corner of her mouth, her cheek, the tip of her nose, cutting off her words. "Need you."

"Oh . . . *yeeees*." She pulled his mouth back to hers and kissed him deeply as she wrapped her legs around his hips.

An animalistic sound echoed from his chest, one that made her hotter and more desperate. She felt herself turning, knew he was taking her into her bedroom, couldn't wait to feel his weight pressing her into the mattress.

He crossed the floor, never once pulling away from her mouth. They reached the bed, and he wrapped one hand around her waist, stretched out the other to find the mattress. The soft comforter brushed her spine, and his tongue continued to tease and taste and taunt her with pleasure, but when his weight pressed into hers and he rose up above her, all she could think about was him and this and them. And more.

Cool air whooshed over her belly, and he pulled away from her mouth. Realizing he was tugging up her sweater, she let go of him and lifted her arms so he could swipe it free and then reached for him.

He tossed her sweater somewhere to his right, leaned down, and kissed her again. But not before she saw his flushed cheeks, his lips swollen from her mouth, and his eyes glazed with a lust that supercharged her blood.

His kiss drew her right back into bliss. Finding the hem of his shirt, she slid her hands up and under the fabric and all across his chiseled abs, desperate to touch him. Groaning, he let her pull his shirt free, and rocked against her until she saw stars.

"Raegs." He kissed her jaw, her throat, trailed his lips down to the V of her cleavage. "God, you smell so damn good. Better than I remember."

Tingles spread all across her skin, wherever he touched. She closed her eyes as he kissed her, slid her fingers into his silky hair, and trembled when he flipped the front latch of her bra, freeing her breasts.

He groaned in approval, and a tingle of anticipation rushed over her skin, tightening her nipples. It shouldn't feel like the first time, but it did. They'd made love hundreds of times, and it had always been wonderful, but she never remembered being this turned on. This excited. Wasn't sure she'd ever felt this roaring desire for more.

His hand closed around her right breast, pulling a groan from her lips. He pressed his lips against the fleshy mass, slid his tongue around the areola, licking and laving and driving her absolutely mad. But when he found the tip, when he drew her nipple deep into his mouth and suckled, the world rocked right out from under her.

She trembled. Lifted her hips, desperate for contact, for friction, for *him*. He answered by palming her other breast, by kissing his way to the other nipple and drawing her deep in his mouth all over again.

Her skin grew hot. Her body ached everywhere for his hands, his lips, his touch. She pushed up on her elbows and shrugged out of her bra straps. He eased back and helped her pull the garment free, tossing it onto the ground. Sitting up, she reached for him again, desperate to feel his naked body sliding over hers, but stilled when she saw the four tattooed letters in cursive right over his heart.

Emma.

Emotions swamped her—loss, heartache, sadness, regret—but the strongest, the one that had always been there, even through the pain, was love.

She trailed her fingers softly over the four letters etched into his skin, blinking back tears that seemed to come out of nowhere, and looked up at him, kneeling above her, his eyes as blue and fathomless as she'd ever seen them. "Oh, Alec."

He lowered his mouth back to hers, and she opened to his insistent kiss, opened her mind to possibilities she'd never thought she'd have again, opened her heart to the only man she'd ever loved.

His hands streaked down her sides and around her front to free the snap on her jeans. In one swift move he pulled them off her legs and dropped them on the floor. She groaned as he kissed her again, as his hand moved down her belly. And when his fingers slipped between her legs, she trembled, held on to his shoulders tighter, and rocked into his hand until the pleasure overwhelmed her.

He drew back from her mouth long before she was ready to stop kissing him. Startled, she opened her eyes only to realize he was wriggling out of his jeans faster than she'd ever seen him move.

She watched as he wrestled his wallet from his jeans, pulled a condom free, and ripped it open with his teeth. But the need to feel him overpowered every thought, and as soon as he was sheathed, she reached for him, pulling his body back over hers and his lips right down where they belonged. "Come back here."

He groaned as his tongue slipped into her mouth. And when his bare flesh slid along hers and his familiar weight pressed her into the mattress, she opened her legs and kissed him harder, drawing him inside her, right where he belonged.

She trembled at the way he filled her as if they were made for each other. Her body felt on fire, her skin ultrasensitive. Kissing her harder, he began to move.

"Ah, Raegan . . ." He kissed the edge of her mouth, her cheek, moved to her ear and sucked the lobe between his lips. "Need this. Need you . . ."

She needed him too. More than she'd realized until this moment. "Don't stop." Her eyes slid closed when he hit the perfect spot, sending sparks all through her body. "Don't let go."

"Never could," he rasped. "Ah God, not gonna last. Come with me, Raegs."

He groaned, and when she felt him grow harder inside her, the pleasure ignited, sending a shock wave all throughout her body. "Oh yes, Alec . . ."

She cried out as it consumed her, was unable to do anything but let it pull her under. In a daze, she heard him grunt, felt every muscle in his body tighten. And knew the shock wave was consuming him too. Exactly as it should. Right along with her. The way it had always been.

He stilled against her, his hot breath fanning her neck and shoulder where his face was tucked against her. Slowly, she became aware of the comforter beneath her, his sweaty skin against her, and the twitch of his back muscles under her hands. She realized something else too. That this wasn't a fantasy or a dream. Alec was on top of her, still *inside* her, and she didn't want to ever let him go.

She had absolutely no idea if he felt the same.

She knew their meeting with the Ramirezes had affected him. Knew by the way he'd been watching her that he'd felt something. Knew whatever that something was had pushed him to kiss her in the living room. But did he want more? Did he want any of the same things she did?

Panic rushed in. A panic that came out of nowhere and stole her breath. A panic that was rooted in the fact she'd barely survived losing him once. If this was just his needing comfort because he felt sad . . . if this was nothing more than casual sex—no matter how incredible it had been—she was in trouble. Because she wasn't anywhere near as confident and put together as he thought. And he had the power to destroy her if she wasn't careful about what she said and did right in this moment.

He pushed up on one hand and looked down at her, his face flushed, his eyes sexy and sated and . . . assessing. "Sorry that was so fast. It's been a while for me."

Oh no. She couldn't think about how long it had been for him or whom it had last been with. Not when her heart was already racing on a roller coaster. She focused on a mole near his collarbone. "It was fine."

"Fine." His eyes narrowed. "I see that wasn't the only thing that was fast."

She didn't have a clue what he was talking about, and right now she didn't want to ask.

One corner of his mouth curved in a sexy smirk. He lowered to his elbows and brushed the damp hair away from her temples. "I almost forgot how fast your brain can flip from pleasure to pondering."

She frowned, still staring at the mole. "I'm not pondering."

His smile widened. A mesmerizing Cheshire grin she saw from the edge of her vision and which made her blood hot all over again. "Yes, you are. Your brain always worked faster than mine." He leaned down and kissed her. "Don't think, wife. Just let it be. Just feel."

His lips moved to her ear, and she shivered at the wicked sensations rushing over her skin, but the pain cutting through her heart kept her from getting lost in him all over again. "I'm not your wife, Alec. Not anymore."

He eased back and looked down at her, but this time there was no humor in his eyes when they held hers. There was only truth. A truth that rocked her way more than his body ever could.

"You'll always be my wife, Raegan. A piece of paper doesn't change that." He reached for her hand and placed it over his heart, right where the word "Emma" was etched into his skin. "I don't have any answers to the questions rolling around in your head right now; I just know I want to be with you tonight. Because I miss you. I miss us. I miss this."

Tears burned her eyes. "I miss us too."

He lowered his mouth and kissed her. Tears streamed down her temples as she wrapped her arms around him and kissed him back. Tears rooted in hope and fear and love.

Whole, broken, fragmented, or shattered, it didn't matter how he came back to her. She'd take anything she could get. She just wasn't sure if he had anything more than tonight to give.

CHAPTER TWELVE

Alec rolled to his side in the middle of the night and reached for Raegan, only to find her side of the bed empty.

Pushing up on his elbow, he rubbed the sleep from his eyes and looked around the dark bedroom. "Raegs?"

No sound met his ears, and nothing moved. The adjoining bathroom was dark and quiet as well. A whisper of unease tickled his spine as he climbed out of bed and reached for his pants from the floor. He'd seen the worry in her eyes after they'd made love, knew she was probably overthinking everything right now and trying to figure out where they stood.

His heart skipped a beat as he rose and pulled on his pants. Where did they stand? He didn't have a clue. Nothing between them had really changed. She still needed to believe Emma was alive, and even with everything they'd uncovered the last few days, he was still pretty sure his father was the one who'd taken their daughter. They hadn't found any proof that Emma's disappearance was linked to these cases. Which meant neither of them was ever going to convince the other to change their beliefs, and no matter what happened between them here, at the end of the day they'd be right back where they were three years ago.

Except . . .

Pressure formed beneath his ribs, a pressure that brought his palm up to rub against the spot. Tonight, being with her again, was the first time in a long time anything had felt right. He wasn't sure he wanted to give that up. Wasn't sure of anything except that he didn't want to think about tomorrow yet.

Unable to find his shirt in the dark, he opened the door and moved into the hall. A light shone from the living room, so he headed that way, then drew to a stop when he spotted Raegan at the stove in the kitchen, flipping something in a pan with a spatula, her back angled his way, her sexy body covered by nothing but his black T-shirt.

Heat rolled through his belly as he watched her lift whatever she was cooking to a plate, the T-shirt pulling up to reveal her creamy thighs and long, toned legs. Her auburn hair hung halfway down her back, and her slim arms flexed in the oversized garment with her movements.

God, she was beautiful. More beautiful than she'd been six years ago when they'd met, because her body was curvy and filled out in all the right places now. He knew part of that was because she was older, no longer the twenty-five-year-old who'd been obsessed with working out. But another part knew it was because of her pregnancy, because carrying his child had changed her body from that of a girl to a woman, one he wanted more of right this minute.

Quietly, he crossed the living room and moved into the kitchen, his heart pounding, his blood warming with every step, and slid his arms around her waist from behind.

She startled and turned to look up at him. "Alec. Geez, you scared me."

"Sorry." He brushed his nose against her hair, drawing in a deep whiff of her sweet jasmine scent. She even smelled incredible. "That bed is cold without you in it."

He brushed her hair to the side with his hand, nipped at her throat, then pressed a kiss against the tender spot.

"Oh." Her body tensed, only to relax back into him, just as he wanted. "Um . . . I was hungry. I tried not to wake you."

He glanced past her to the grilled cheese sandwich on the plate in front of her. "If you're hungry, I'm sure I can find something to satisfy you."

She turned to look up at him, her cheeks shifting to a soft shade of pink, and he knew by her reaction that she'd cued in to what he meant. But instead of smiling, worry rippled in her eyes. A worry he knew was the real reason she'd left him sleeping alone in that bed.

He slid his hands back to her waist, maneuvered her around so her back pressed against the counter, and moved in at her front. "You're thinking too much again, Raegan."

A frown pulled at her lips. "One of us needs to."

"Why?"

"Because this"—she lifted her hands and dropped them on his biceps—"it makes no sense."

"When did it ever?"

The cute little lines between her eyes deepened, causing him to laugh.

He brushed his lips over the spot, then trailed kisses down the left side of her face until he reached the corner of her mouth. "I don't want to think about yesterday." Moving across her jaw, he kissed his way to her throat. "Or tomorrow."

Her eyes slid closed, and a sigh slipped from her luscious lips.

He pushed her plate out of the way and lifted her to sit up on the counter. "Right now I only want to think about you."

Surprised, she opened her eyes and gazed down at him.

He stepped between her legs and pushed the edge of his T-shirt up her creamy thighs. "And about how hungry you make me."

Her eyes glazed over with lust, and she groaned as she leaned down and kissed him, drawing his tongue into her mouth and wrapping her arms around his neck.

Yeah, this was all he wanted to focus on tonight. Just her and him and nothing else. His whole body tightened when he discovered she was naked beneath his shirt. She sucked in a breath when he touched her and kissed him harder. His erection swelled as he teased her. He just wanted to focus on her. Her and the way she made him feel. Everything else could wait.

He kissed the corner of her lips, nipped at her jaw, and worked his way down her throat. She groaned and tightened her arms around his shoulders. A ringing sounded from the living room, interrupting his plans to show her just how hungry she made him.

Lifting her head, Raegan looked past him toward the couch and in a breathless voice said, "That's not my cell. It must be yours."

He didn't care who was calling. Sliding a hand around her neck, he pulled her mouth back to his. "Whoever it is can wait."

She opened to his kiss again. The ringing stopped. Pushing the shirt up to her waist, he slipped his hand beneath the soft cotton and palmed her breast. Her groan deepened, and she kissed him deeper.

His cell phone rang again, causing her to jerk back from his mouth.

"Dammit." He didn't want to answer it, but he didn't want it to keep going off and distracting her from what he was about to do either. Reluctantly, he withdrew his hand, letting the cotton fall to her thighs. "Don't you dare move."

A wicked smile pulled at her lips. "Turn that thing off, and I won't."

Spotting his cell on the coffee table, he grasped it, flipped it over, and was just about to power it down when he read Jack Bickam's name across the screen.

His chest tightened. Wide-eyed, he glanced toward Raegan. "It's Bickam."

Her cheeks paled, and she immediately climbed off the counter, crossing quickly to his side. "Answer it. He wouldn't be calling in the middle of the night unless it was important."

That was exactly what Alec was thinking. Swallowing hard, he pressed the phone to his ear. "McClane."

"Alec, it's Jack Bickam with the FBI. Sorry to bother you so late, but something came up down here at the crime lab that I wanted to run by you."

The words "crime lab" didn't do a thing to ease the knot suddenly twisting in Alec's gut. "Yeah, okay. What is it?"

"Two days ago, a two-year-old boy was abducted from his yard in North Portland. He showed up the following morning in the backseat of an abandoned car we found out on Highway 26."

"Yeah, Raegan told me about him. What does that have to do with me?"

"I'm not sure it has anything to do with you, but . . ." Bickam paused, and the hairs on Alec's nape stood straight as he looked toward Raegan's expectant face.

"Well?" Raegan mouthed.

"A forensics team's been going through the car, looking for hair, skin, any kind of evidence they can use to identify the driver. So far we've got the lab running analysis, but the team found a bag in the trunk that led to my call."

Alec's heart pounded hard, and against the phone, his fingers shook. Part of him didn't want to know, but he had to ask. "What was in the bag, Bickam?"

"Oh. Damn. Not what you think. Sorry. I didn't mean to scare you. It was filled with stuffed animals. Nothing more."

Alec breathed easier and scrubbed a hand over his forehead. Nothing more than stuffed animals. The pressure building in his chest eased.

"The forensics team cataloged the items, but I didn't take a look at them until tonight. I was going to wait and call you in the morning but thought you might want to know now. In the bottom of the bag we found a stuffed white rabbit with a red collar. And it isn't new. It's worn, as if it's been held. A lot."

Alec's heart felt as if it came to a stuttering stop, right in the center of his chest. "Are you sure?"

"Yeah. I'm gonna text you a photo. I wasn't sure if I should show this to Raegan. She looked pretty shaken the other day at the ER. If—"

"She's standing right next to me."

"Oh." Surprise echoed in Bickam's voice. Since he kept up with them periodically about Emma's case, he knew they'd divorced not long after she went missing. "Well, good. It should be coming through now. Have her take a look at it too."

Alec's phone buzzed, indicating he'd received a text. "Hold on."

Pulling the phone away from his face, he paged to his text messages.

"What is it?" Raegan asked at his side. "What's going on?"

Alec opened the picture message. And felt the room sway under his feet.

"Oh my God." Raegan's hand covered her mouth. Wide-eyed, she lowered her hand and looked up at him. "That's Emma's bunny. Where did they find it? Where—"

"McClane?" Bickam's voice sounded from the phone.

Dazed, Alec lifted it back to his ear. "Yeah, I'm here."

"I heard her," Bickam said. "Any chance you two can come down to the lab tomorrow morning and take a look at this thing for me?"

"No." Alec stared down at Raegan. "There's no way we can wait until the morning. We'll be there in fifteen minutes."

———

Raegan couldn't take her eyes off the stuffed white bunny in her gloved hands, with matted fur and dirt streaking across one whole side. "It's Emma's. I know it is."

Beside her in the FBI's crime lab, Alec shifted his weight, jangling the keys in the front pocket of his jeans. "It might be. We don't know for sure that it is. Let's not get carried away just yet."

His skepticism barely fazed her. "It's hers. I remember when she pulled this button off beneath the bow. It went flying across the car. I saved it. I always meant to reattach it, but I just never found the time." She turned toward Jack Bickam, standing behind her in slacks and a dress shirt rolled up to his elbows. "I have it in a drawer at the apartment. I can get it for you. You can see—"

"I don't think that's necessary, Raegan, but I'll tell the tech."

Alec pulled his hands from his pockets and crossed his arms over his chest, a grim expression on his face, the good mood he'd been in back at her apartment long gone. "Let's say for argument's sake this is hers." He glanced at Raegan with a pointed look. "And I'm not saying it is hers." He looked back at Bickam. "But if so, what can it tell us?"

"Well." With his own gloved hands, Bickam took the toy from Raegan. Reluctantly, she let him have it, but her fingers felt cold when it left her grip, and it was all she could do not to yank it away from him. "We'll run tests on it. See what we can find. If there are any hair or skin cells in the fur, we'll find them."

"Can you tell how long it was in that car?" she asked.

"Probably not." Bickam set the rabbit back on the high counter behind Raegan. She turned to stare at it, unable to look away. "We'll run what we find on the toy against what we found in the car. That might tell us if the same person who abducted that toddler was ever near Emma. Assuming it's her toy, that is."

Beside her, Alec nodded.

"There's not much more you two can do here tonight," Bickam said, drawing Raegan's attention. "Why don't you head home? It'll be a few days at least before we get any kind of results. I'll call you as soon as I have any news."

"Thanks." Alec shook Bickam's hand and turned to leave, but Raegan's feet faltered, and when she looked back at the dirty toy, she didn't want to let it out of her sight.

"Come on, Raegs." Alec tugged at her elbow.

She finally turned away from the toy and followed him out into the hall. But the minute they were alone, everything started to shake. "Oh my God."

He drew her against him. "Don't do it, Raegan."

"Alec." She gripped his elbows and looked up at him. "It's her bunny. You know it's her bunny."

Doubt crossed his features. Doubt and fear. But she didn't let it deter her.

She held on tighter, pleading with her eyes, with her grip, with her voice. "You know it's her bunny. You saw it. It's the same one she used to drag everywhere. It's the same one she used to tuck under her arm when she snuggled with you on the couch."

His gaze searched hers, full of apprehension and pain.

"It's hers, Alec. I know it's hers."

"Maybe," he finally whispered.

Tears blurred her eyes. Tears of hope and of relief. She slid her arms around his waist and rested her cheek against his chest, the beat of his heart strong, steady, real. As real as that rabbit.

"Maybe, okay?" he said louder, closing his arms around her. "But it doesn't mean anything. Even if it's hers, it won't tell us where she is. It won't tell us if she's alive or . . ."

He swallowed hard, and just the fact he couldn't say the word anymore gave her a strength she hadn't felt before.

She lifted her head and gazed up at him through blurry vision. "She's alive, Alec. I feel it. I know it. I know you feel it too."

"Raegan." He framed her face with his hands, his eyes still pained but insistent. "I don't want you to get your hopes up here."

"She's linked to that boy they found in the car. To that girl we saw at the hospital. I know it."

"Those kids were missing for a day and week. Not three years. Even if she is alive, she could be anywhere."

"We'll find her."

"Raegan—"

"I know we'll find her." She closed her arms around his waist again and pressed her cheek to his heart. "This is a sign, Alec. A good sign."

He wrapped his arms around her again. Tight. So tight. "I want to believe that," he whispered. "I really do."

For the first time in three years, her heart, which had been empty for so long, slowly started to fill. She closed her eyes and this time didn't let any of the doubt in. "You will. I'll make you believe it. I promise."

Alec hadn't slept. He spent the night wrapped around Raegan while she dozed, but he couldn't get his mind to stop spinning long enough to relax. All he could focus on was that stupid stuffed animal. All he could see was the hundreds of times he'd watched Emma drag it through the apartment. All he could think about was the dozens of different scenarios she could be in right this moment if she really was alive.

If she was alive . . .

That was the kicker, right? If. He hadn't lied to Raegan. He wanted to believe their daughter was out there somewhere. But every time he tried, a new sense of fear grabbed hold and wouldn't let go—one focused on who she was with, what they were making her do, and what would happen to her if he and Raegan never tracked her down.

"Wow," Ethan said through the receiver pressed to his ear, pulling him back to his current conversation. "Have you told Mom and Dad?"

Alec frowned from the couch where he sat, dragging his attention from the hall and the sound of Raegan's shower running in the bedroom. "What do you think? I wouldn't be telling you if you hadn't called to make sure I hadn't lost my shit with Raegan."

"And have you?"

Classic Ethan. Always pushing. Alec scraped a hand through his hair. "No. You'll be thrilled to know she put me in my place the other night."

"She's the only woman who ever could. I'm not worried about Raegan. She's a survivor. I'm more concerned with how you're handling all this news about Emma."

"What news? We have no news. All we have is a stuffed animal that may or may not be hers."

"Come on, Alec."

He knew what Ethan was getting at. Alec looked down and scratched the back of his head. "I want a drink bad, okay? But I'm not going to have one."

If he'd heard the news alone, if he'd been out of the country when he'd gotten that call from Bickam, he might have gone straight to an airport bar and gotten tanked. But he wasn't about to do that now because Raegan needed him.

"I'm glad to hear that."

The shower shut off, and Alec lifted his head, peering back toward the hall once more. "Look, I gotta go. Raegan and I are heading out in a bit to do some interviews."

"Okay. I won't keep you any longer. Just one more thing. How are things between the two of you?"

How were they? Hotter than hell and better than they'd been in three damn years. "Fine."

"You and your 'fines.'" Ethan sighed.

"They're good, okay? We've talked some things out."

That wasn't a total lie. They had talked a little. And kissed and made love and slept wrapped around each other like neither wanted to let go.

"That's good to hear. It's long overdue."

Alec frowned because he heard the giant "but" coming. "I hate when you use the therapist tone. Just spit it out already."

"But," Ethan said, "she's a trigger for you. I'm just worried about you, that's all."

A mixture of appreciation and irritation rolled through Alec. "Well, don't be. I'm not going to do something reckless."

"Those have always been your famous last words."

Footsteps sounded in the hall, distracting Alec, and he looked up to see Raegan striding toward him dressed in slim jeans and a loose gray sweater, her damp hair hanging past her shoulders, and confusion pulling the brows over her gorgeous eyes together. Heat and need and a host of nerves coiled in his belly. "Look, I really gotta go. I'll call you when I know more."

"Okay. Stay strong, brother."

"You too."

He hit "End" and pushed to his feet, fighting back the burst of arousal he always felt at seeing her. As much as he wanted a repeat of what they'd done last night, now wasn't the time. "Hey."

"Hey. Who was that?"

"Ethan. Making sure I'm not driving you batshit crazy already."

She smiled, a warm, for-him-only smile that made him even hotter. "And what did you tell him?"

"That if I am, I'm sure you'll tell me."

Her smiled faded. "At this point, I'm just happy you're still here."

So was he.

They stared at each other. He wanted to reach for her, wanted to lose himself in her sweetness and forget everything else for the next three hours, but didn't. Ethan was right. She was a trigger for him. Not one that might push him to drink, but one that made him crave things he wasn't sure he was strong enough for. And after the news last night about that stuffed animal, he was already feeling shaky and weak and unsure about everything.

"Well." She pulled her gaze from his, looked down at his navy Henley, and bit her lip. And in that one small movement he saw that she'd wanted him to pull her in and kiss her just as much. "We should probably get going if we want to catch that social worker before we see the Colemans."

Yeah. The Colemans.

She moved toward the entry and reached for her coat. His heart contracted with a mix of wants and needs as he watched. For her, for Emma, for them. But mostly it squeezed tight because he realized he was lying to himself.

There was no way he could ever truly believe Emma was dead again. Not without proof. And that realization had nothing to do with what they'd learned last night. It had to do solely with the woman in front of him. With her unfailing belief. With her strength and compassion. With her hope that gave him hope and made him feel alive.

———

Raegan's gaze narrowed on the brunette in the red pantsuit walking out of a run-down ranch in Northeast Portland.

"That doesn't look like Murray," Alec said in the driver's seat of his truck, where they were parked on the street.

"Didn't the receptionist say this was where he was supposed to be today?" Raegan asked from the passenger seat, not taking her eyes off the woman.

Alec checked the notebook where he'd jotted notes. "Yeah, she did. Maybe he switched with someone?"

A tingle ran down Raegan's spine. "Maybe." She popped her door and climbed out. "Let's find out."

She rounded the hood and joined Alec on the street. They crossed and reached the blue Ford Taurus at the same time as the woman.

"Hi, there," Raegan said, putting on her journalist smile. "Sorry to bother you. We're looking for Conner Murray. We were told by DHS that he had an appointment here today."

A nervous look passed over the brunette's face. "Someone told you he'd be here today?"

"Yeah," Alec said. "Yesterday. He agreed to answer a few questions for a story we're researching." It wasn't a total lie, Raegan figured, as Alec pulled out his Associated Press badge and held it up. Just a little white one. To get the answers they needed, she didn't even care if he flirted.

"Oh." The brunette's face sobered. "Then you didn't hear the news."

That tingle down Raegan's back intensified. "What news?"

"Conner was killed yesterday."

Shock rippled through Raegan. "How?"

"Car accident in the hills outside Sherwood. The police still aren't sure what happened, but his car went off the road and tumbled down a hillside."

Raegan glanced toward Alec, catching the *holy hell* look in his eyes.

"Are you managing his caseload now?" he asked.

"Just until someone else can be brought on. It was too late to cancel his appointments for today. What story did you two say you were working on?"

"Missing children." Raegan handed the photos of the three children they'd identified as being Murray's cases to the brunette. "Do you recognize any of these kids, Ms. . . ."

"Johnson." The woman took the pictures and flipped through them. "The first two, no. But the third one . . ." She held up the photo of David Ramirez. "He has an older brother, doesn't he?"

"He does," Alec answered. "Miguel. He's almost eleven now."

"Right." The woman nodded. "I remember because I was trying to get his parents enrolled in the Family Support and Connections program when their younger son went missing. That's where I normally work. Only they didn't qualify because they weren't US citizens. Do you know what happened to them?"

"They're doing well. Both got their citizenship, and good jobs."

"Oh, I'm so happy to hear that. It was so sad when David went missing. Losing a child like that can rip a family apart."

Raegan's heart pinched, and she couldn't stop herself from glancing toward Alec. "Yeah. We've heard that."

"You don't recognize the other two children?" Alec asked.

"No, I'm sorry." She handed the photos back to Raegan. "I have to be going. I have a couple other families I need to visit today."

"Sure." Alec stepped back so the woman could open her car door. "Thanks for speaking with us."

The woman nodded and climbed into her car. As they watched her drive away, Raegan had another funny feeling. "What are you thinking?"

Alec looked down at her. "I'm thinking we might have missed a link. If the Ramirezes and the Willigs both had older children close to the same age . . ."

Raegan's breath caught. "Then we should check the other families and see if they had older kids as well."

"Right. And check to see what programs those older kids were enrolled in, if any."

"It's also interesting that Murray turned up dead the day after we questioned him about those missing kids, don't you think?"

Alec nodded. "Yeah. Very." He pulled out his cell phone as they crossed the street back to his truck. "I'm gonna call Hunt and see if he can tell us anything about the accident."

Hunt agreed to look into the accident for Alec, but as they drove into the Gorge to find the Coleman property, all Raegan could think about was the fact that two of the three families they were looking into had older children. And the fact that Emma had been an only child.

"I think this is it," Alec said, pulling off the highway and onto a long gravel drive. The drive wound at least a mile up into the hills before a run-down home, overgrown with brush and weeds, appeared in the distance.

Raegan turned to look back the way they'd come. Through the trees she could just make out the Columbia River far below. "How long ago did you say they moved out here?"

"About four years ago." Alec pulled the truck to a stop next to a beat-up Chevy 1500 and shifted into park. "Pretty sure this is where Brent Coleman grew up."

The house looked like something out of *The Silence of the Lambs*, and Raegan couldn't help but wonder if Brent Coleman's ancestors had lived here too. She reached for her door handle. "You called him and told him we were coming out, right?"

"Yeah." Alec pushed his door open. "Not exactly friendly, but he agreed to see us."

Raegan joined him at the hood. A dog barked inside the house seconds before the screen door creaked open and a thin man with graying hair who looked to be in his fifties stepped out onto the porch. "Can I help you folks?"

Alec stepped forward on the gravel drive, but a bloodhound pushed past the man's legs, howled, and streaked forward, rushing up to meet them with a rolling bark.

Alec moved in front of Raegan.

The man whistled and yelled, "Thunder! Get back here, you butthead."

The dog barked once more, then turned and galloped back up to the porch.

Alec looked once at Raegan, then hesitantly moved forward. "Mr. Coleman? I'm Alec McClane. We spoke yesterday."

Brent Coleman nodded. "Was wonderin' if that was you. Thunder don't like anyone with the press." He turned with a wave of his hand. "C'mon in so we can get this over with. I got things to do."

The look Alec sent Raegan said, *See? Told ya. Not friendly*. He moved up the porch steps in front of her, then held the screen door open so she could enter.

The inside of the house was just as bad as the exterior. Worn furniture filled a small living room decked out with light-brown wood paneling and brown shag carpeting Raegan guessed hadn't been vacuumed in years. An orange-and-green-floral-print couch with wooden arms sat to the right, a gold recliner and a TV straight out of 1980s to the left. Brent Coleman flopped down in the recliner while Thunder the guard dog fell into a pile at his feet.

Alec moved to the couch and sat. Trying to ignore the mildewy scent, Raegan joined him.

"This is Raegan Devereaux," Alex said. "Thanks for agreeing to see us."

"Not entirely sure why I did." Coleman reached for a tumbler on the table beside him, glanced at the ice and the little bit of golden liquid left in the bottom, and frowned before setting it down again. "My wife and I talked to a lot of reporters when Mary went missing. None of 'em ever did anything for us. Unless of course you two have some news, which is why you're here?"

The little bit of hope Raegan heard in the man's voice pulled at her heart, and when she saw the way his brows lifted, she realized he wasn't nearly as old as she'd initially thought. Barely forty, she guessed, remembering how much older Alec had seemed to her when she'd first seen him at the hospital. Stress and worry could age a person way faster than time.

"I'm sorry, we don't have any news for you." Raegan tucked a lock of hair behind her ear and tried not to be saddened by the man's slumped reaction. "We're actually looking into several old missing-child reports in the area, trying to see if there's any kind of link."

"And have you found any?" Coleman asked.

"We're not sure." She glanced down at the folder in her lap. "You used to live in Northeast Portland, correct?"

He nodded.

"And your daughter went missing six years ago, is that right?"

"Seven in July."

God, seven years. Raegan's heart hurt all over again. "And she disappeared at a park?"

"At the zoo. I'd taken her there on my day off. The wheel on her stroller locked up. I took her out because she was throwing a fit about seeing the bats. She went running ahead of me to check them out while I fixed the wheel." A dark look passed over his eyes as he reached for the empty glass by his side. "By the time I rounded the corner, the cave was packed with kids. I looked everywhere for her but couldn't find her. Just that fast she was gone."

The ice clinked in the glass, and from the corner of her eye, Raegan saw the way Alec's gaze dropped to the floor, reliving, she knew, the moment he'd lost Emma.

Raegan looked back at Brent Coleman. "You told the police that your wife wasn't at the zoo with you?"

"She wasn't." Coleman lifted the glass in his hand, tipped his head, and sucked back whatever alcohol was left, then set the glass back on the table at his side with a sigh. "Jules was shopping with her girlfriends that day. She'd just gotten this job at the mall, and she needed new clothes. I was glad, you know? I'd been working two jobs to keep things going, at the gas station and at the convenience store. And I was tired. But I wasn't a bad parent." He shook his head and stared off into space. "She never forgave me for losing Mary, though."

"Where is your wife?" Alec asked. "Is she available to speak with us?"

"I don't know. You'd have to ask her. Julie left me five years ago." He sank lower in his chair. "Took Brenda with her. I haven't seen either of them since."

"Who's Brenda?" Raegan asked, sensing they were about to lose Brent Coleman to a deep depression he'd yet to pull himself out of.

"Our older daughter."

Raegan's pulse sped up, and she glanced at Alec, saw he was thinking the same thing as her.

"How old is Brenda?" Alec asked.

"Gosh. She'd be in high school now." A blank look filled his eyes. "I don't even know what she looks like anymore."

Heat spread across Raegan's skin. Seven years ago, Brenda Coleman would have been close to the same age as Miguel Ramirez and Ginny Willig when their siblings went missing. The three families were definitely linked by more than just their caseworker.

"Do you remember a social worker by the name of Conner Murray?" Alec asked. "Five eight, pudgy, with thinning hair?"

Brent Coleman's gaze narrowed as he thought back. "Yeah. He helped Brenda get set up with some social programs. Why?"

"We're just checking into people who may have come into contact with different kids. Did he spend any time with Mary?"

"No." Coleman shook his head. "I mean, I'm sure he saw her a few times when he was at the house, but his focus was on Brenda and getting her the services she qualified for."

Alec nodded, but Coleman didn't seem to notice. His gaze had drifted to the window, and a faraway look filled his eyes. "Some days I try to pretend like it didn't happen, but it never works. Funny how one brief moment can change everything, isn't it? I didn't just lose Mary that day; I lost my whole family. If I had it to do over again . . ." His voice hitched, and he blinked several times before looking down at his hands. "Well, I'd do a lot of things different."

Raegan's heart squeezed tight, and as she stared at the broken man who'd lost everything, she couldn't help but think of Alec alone in that farmhouse out in the country, different in a million ways from this but also eerily the same.

Her gaze drifted to the glass. Is this what Alec had done? Sat around drinking himself to death because he felt so guilty about losing Emma? Yes, she knew, because she'd watched him do it in their apartment before he'd left her. But he'd pulled himself out of it. He'd gotten help. He'd gone into rehab. He'd been sober now three years.

"I found him facedown on his kitchen table, an empty bottle of Jack near his left hand, and a loaded .45 near his right." Ethan's words the other night in her apartment echoed in her head, making her chest squeeze even tighter. *"He swore he wasn't trying to kill himself, but our parents weren't convinced. They had him admitted to a rehab center. When he got out, he promised he wouldn't drink again."*

He hadn't gotten help on his own. He'd pulled himself out because he'd had people who wouldn't let him wallow. People, she realized as she looked at his strong jaw and his blue eyes focused on Brent Coleman, who hadn't given up on him, like she had.

Her heart stuttered as Alec pushed to his feet and held out his hand. "Thank you, Mr. Coleman. That's all we need."

"That's it?"

Alec nodded. "Yeah. We won't take any more of your time."

Coleman's gaze narrowed, and for the first time since they'd walked into his house, his eyes looked clear. "Why are you two so interested in my kid? In these other kids?"

Alec glanced once at Raegan as she stood, and before he even said the words, she knew what was going to come out. "Because our daughter went missing too. We're trying to see if other cases in the area are linked to hers in any way."

Coleman rose and glanced between them. "Your daughter? How long ago?"

"Three years," Alec answered.

"You think she's still alive?"

"Yes," Alec said. "We hope, anyway."

Raegan's heart stuttered. Last night he'd said he'd wanted to believe. Today he was saying he had hope.

"I'll pray you're right," Coleman said. "No one should go through what I have."

Alec shook the man's hand. Raegan said good-bye and moved toward the door, her head and heart spinning. Behind her, Alec and Brent Coleman exchanged quiet words on the porch, then seconds later Alec was beside her in the truck, starting the ignition and pulling away from the run-down property.

They needed to talk about the older siblings. Needed to figure out if the kids had possibly known each other. But all Raegan could focus on was what Alec had just admitted.

That he believed Emma was still alive.

She was just terrified to bring it up in case he hadn't really meant it.

CHAPTER THIRTEEN

Raegan made idle chitchat on the drive back into the city. Alec tried to pay attention but couldn't do more than mutter "Uh huh" and "Yeah" because his brain was stuck on what Brent Coleman had said to him on the porch.

"Hold on to her. The biggest regret I have is wallowing in my own pain and not being there for my wife. I lost her same as I lost Mary. Difference is, losing Mary was an accident. Pushing Jules away wasn't."

That was him. He'd pushed Raegan away when he should have held on to her. Pushed her away when all she'd needed to do was lean on him.

Her cell phone buzzed as he pulled to a stop in front of her building. Darkness was just setting in, and the lights from outside shone over her face and the frown lines breaking across her bruised cheek as she gazed down at the screen.

"What's wrong?" he asked, killing the engine.

"Nothing. It's just the station. I haven't checked in for a few days. I guess someone noticed."

She hit "Answer" and pushed the car door open. "Yeah, this is Raegan."

Unable to hear who she was talking to, Alec climbed out and moved around the car, waiting while Raegan keyed in the building code. When the door clicked, he pulled it open for her.

"Yes, sorry," Raegan said. "Things have been a little crazy. I'm going to lose you on the elevator. Can I call you right back? Okay."

She clicked "End" as they stepped onto the elevator.

"Who was that?" Alec asked.

"Anna Chapman. Jeremy's on the warpath because I haven't reported in."

Jealousy rolled through his belly. A jealousy he didn't have any right to feel, considering he'd been the one to leave her. "The boyfriend."

"Ex-boyfriend." She turned to look up at him as the elevator hummed. "And he wasn't even really that. We only went out a handful of times or so. It wasn't serious."

He wanted to ask what she meant by serious—I-love-you serious or sleep-with-you serious?—but the elevator doors pinged open before he could.

"Here." She handed him her keys then punched "Redial" on her phone and held it to her ear. "I'll be just a minute. Go on in."

He nodded as he moved toward the apartment's door, but he couldn't shake the strange feelings swirling inside him.

His life was exactly like Brent Coleman's. Even down to the drinking and self-deprecation. The only difference was that he'd had parents and siblings who'd looked out for him. Brent Coleman hadn't had that.

He moved into the apartment and closed the door behind him, dropping Raegan's keys in the dish on the entry table. He didn't want to end up like Coleman, bitter and alone. He didn't want to look in the mirror one day and see half the man he used to be.

He blinked, looking at the purple walls around him, realizing he'd wandered into Emma's room. His gaze strayed to the pink-and-white castle Raegan had painted above the bed when they'd learned that Emma was going to be a girl.

Pain lanced his chest. A pain that burned his eyes. A pain he knew he'd never be without. But one he didn't have to struggle through alone if he didn't want to.

Footsteps sounded behind him, then a sharp intake of breath. Turning slowly, he spotted Raegan standing in the doorway, her cheeks pale, her eyes wide and filled with a thousand insecurities.

She lifted a hand and flipped the switch on the wall. Light from the ceiling fixture illuminated the bed, the dresser, and the toys neatly put away in the corner of the room. But all Alec saw was her.

"You're probably wondering what this is," she said hesitantly.

"I'm not."

She looked over at the room, glancing, he realized, anywhere but at him. "I know you think it's silly. And maybe it is, but I—"

"I don't think it's silly. I think it's perfect. I want this in my house." When her gaze slid to his, he added, "I want it in our house."

"Ours?" she whispered.

"Yes, ours." His heart raced as he stepped toward her, as he brushed the hair away from her bruised cheek and gazed down at her as if he were seeing her for the first time. It felt like he was. In the center of his soul. Where his heart seemed to be beating hard and strong for the first time in years. "I want a second chance, Raegan. I want our life back. I want you and any future kids we might have, and I want to find Emma. My life means nothing without you in it."

Emotions played across her face as she looked up at him—fear, doubt, hope—but when her eyes grew damp and her lip quivered, he knew the strongest of those emotions was love. "I want those things too." Lifting to her toes, she threw her arms around him and whispered, "I want all of them. That's all I've ever wanted."

His eyes slid closed, and he held her close, pressing his face against her neck and breathing in the sweet scent of her jasmine perfume. This was where he was supposed to be. With her. He'd spent the last three years trying not to feel anything, trying to convince himself that being numb was better than hurting, but it wasn't. Numb was empty. Numb was Brent Coleman, waiting to die. Numb gave him no reason to live, and he wanted to live. He wanted to live with Raegan. He wanted to feel the highs and the lows. He even wanted to feel the pain because it meant he was human and real, not dead inside. As long as he was with her, he knew he could survive the pain. As long as they were together, he could survive anything.

Tears burned the backs of his eyes. Tears of regret, of sadness, of fear, but mostly of hope. A hope he felt because of her.

"I need you to know something." He swallowed the lump in his throat, the words like sandpaper on his tongue. "I'm an addict. I was an addict before we met, and I'm always going to be an addict, even now when I'm sober. I can give you a hundred different reasons why, but the simplest is that it was available when I was very young. Gilbert never cared if I drank. He encouraged it, actually. And when you're a kid, living in that kind of environment—" His chest grew tight. "It's how I learned to cope with all the shit going on around me."

She drew back and looked up with tear-filled eyes, and even though he just wanted to go on holding her so he didn't have to see her face when he admitted his faults, he knew he owed her this. Owed her way more than he could ever give her.

He drew a deep breath for courage and looked down into her gorgeous green eyes. Focused on them and not the raw emotions clawing at his chest. "I hid it," he said, closing his hands over hers and holding on to them for strength. "For a long time. After Michael and Hannah adopted me, I got caught at a few parties. They knew I drank now and then in high school, but I played off the fact all kids do it. I knew just what to say to reassure them it was no big deal. They didn't know how much or how often I was drinking, though. My siblings didn't really either. Ethan's the only one who had any kind of idea, but he never even knew how bad it really was. Anytime he or anyone else would bring it up, I'd make a joke and laugh off their concern. I got through college okay because everyone drinks in college, but before you and I met, I was drinking way more than before. I blamed it on the job. On the travel for the AP, on the long hours and the things I was photographing and seeing in war-torn countries like Afghanistan and Ethiopia. And I told myself when I got home I'd be better. But I wasn't. Not until I met you."

His heart squeezed so tight, as if it were wringing all the lies and half-truths from inside him as he thought back to that night. Seeing her through his camera lens in the crowd. Being mesmerized by her beauty and self-confidence. Knowing he needed to be a part of that. Somehow. In any way he could.

"I didn't want to just get by anymore," he said. "I wanted to live. To let go of the past. To start fresh with you. So I cut way back. I told myself I could be a social drinker. We could go out with friends and I wouldn't have to get loaded to have a good time. And I did have a good time. Anytime I was with you was the best time. But I was always thinking about having another drink. About stopping at the liquor store on the way home. About giving in to the urge and just letting go."

"You never told me you thought about that."

"I couldn't. No addict can. It's admitting your biggest weakness. I don't think even I knew how bad it was until we lost Emma."

She closed her eyes, and the pain he saw across her features hit him hard, right beneath the breastbone, right in his heart, which was already twisted into a knot. He squeezed her hands and forced himself to go on.

"I lost it then. I didn't know how to deal with it all. I couldn't look at you. I couldn't stop thinking about what had happened or how it was all my fault—"

"What happened to Emma was not your fault." Her eyes shot open, and this time when they focused on his, they weren't sad or heartbroken; they were determined. As determined as he'd ever seen them. "It could have happened to me. It could have happened to your mother if she'd been watching Emma that day. Whoever took her had been waiting and watching for the right moment when we looked awa—"

"I know that." God, he loved how she jumped to defend him. She'd done that before, when she'd had every reason to hate him, but he'd been so focused on his own pain and self-loathing then that he'd pushed her away. He didn't want to do that anymore. He brushed a shaky finger down her soft cheek. "I know that now. But then . . . then I couldn't face it. It hurt too much. So I did what I'd always done when things got to be too much. I had a drink. And another. And another, until I was numb to everything—the pain, the guilt. Especially you."

She looked down at his shirtfront, and he knew she was remembering all those nights he'd stumbled in drunk when she'd stayed up worried because she hadn't known where he was. All the times she'd needed to lean on him and he hadn't been there for her. The arguments, the tears, all the heartache he'd put her through. And the way he'd walked away from her when he should have stayed and fought for her. For them.

His fingers shook as he brought her hands to his lips and kissed them. Lowering them so they rested on his chest, right over his heart, he forced himself to get it all out. "I know Ethan told you about the night he found me passed out on my kitchen table. That was a wake-up call for me. Not because I'd hit bottom or whatever, but because I saw what I was doing to my family. And through them, I saw what I'd done to you."

He tightened his hands around hers, felt their warmth beneath his fingers, and knew he could do this no matter what she had to say when he was finished. "I hated myself for what I did to you. For how I treated you. And there hasn't been a single day that I haven't wanted to find you and tell you how sorry I am. But I couldn't because I . . ." He searched for the right word. Knew there was only one. "Because I was scared. Scared that you'd slam the door in my face or walk away. Scared it would push me right back to the edge even though I deserved that kind of response from you. Scared, mostly, because I don't know if I hit the very bottom that night or if there's something worse out there waiting for me. All I know is that I don't want to go there. I never want to go there again. I want you. I want us." The tears he'd been fighting back through his whole admission filled his eyes. "I want everything back that I fucked up so badly because I'm weak."

"Oh, Alec." A tear slipped over her lash and slid down her bruised cheek. "You're not weak." She brushed her soft fingertips over the stubble on his jaw, her voice just as thick and raspy as his. "You're stubborn. You're hotheaded at times. And when you want something, there's no stopping you. But you're not weak."

He closed his eyes and leaned into her touch, reveling in her comfort even as his own tears slipped free.

"A weak child couldn't have survived the upbringing you did. A weak teenager wouldn't have had the strength to testify against his father about all the horrible things that man made him do. And a weak adult could never stand here and tell me all the things you just did. I just wish you'd told me sooner. I wish . . ."

When her voice hitched, he opened his eyes and looked down at her. At the tears shimmering in her eyes, at the emotions playing over her face.

"I wish we hadn't spent the last three years apart," she whispered. "Because I would have been there with you through it all. I promised to love you through better or worse. Those weren't just words for me. I meant them. I still mean them. I love you, Alec. I've always loved yo—"

Every emotion he'd kept locked inside for so damn long burst free. He let go of her hand still resting on his chest, framed her face, and captured her mouth with his. She groaned against him, held on to his arms, kissed him back until he was breathless. But it wasn't enough. It wasn't nearly enough. He needed her to know he felt the same. Needed to show her. Needed to be with her now. Right now.

He dropped his hands to her waist and lifted her off the floor. She drew back from his mouth and gripped his shoulders. "What—?"

"Don't let go of me."

Her eyes darkened with understanding as he moved them both toward the hallway, and with another groan she lowered her mouth back to his and wrapped her legs around his waist, kissing him with such passion and heat and need, the blood pounded in his veins and pushed his desire for her past all sense of reason.

He carried her into her bedroom and laid her out on her bed. Her hands turned greedy, tugging at his shirt as she lifted her mouth to his, kissing him again and again. Her soft fingers grazed his abs, his chest. Breathless, he pulled away long enough for her to tug the shirt over his head, then kissed her again, melting into her against the mattress, loving the taste of her, the feel of her, loving everything about her. "Raegan . . ."

She pushed a hand against his shoulder. Taking the hint, he rolled to his back, tugging her with him. She shifted a leg over his as she continued to kiss him, to drive him crazy with her lips, her tongue, her taste.

He brushed her hair back as he changed the angle of their kiss and stroked his tongue against hers. Groaning, she pressed her lips to the corner of his mouth, his jaw, trailed wet, sensual kisses down his throat until he shivered.

"God, Raegs . . ." His eyes slid closed as tendrils of heat and electricity raced across his flesh. "You don't know how much I've missed this. You."

"Yes, I do." She shifted back, pressing her mouth down his chest, across to his right nipple. Her wicked little tongue flicked out, teasing the tip. Her lips closed around him, and she scraped her teeth against the spot until all that heat shot straight into his groin, making him hot and hard and ready.

He opened his eyes, looked down at her, tried to pull her back up to his mouth, but his hands were shaking and she was already moving lower, sliding her slick tongue around his belly button while her fingers flicked the button of his jeans free.

"Raegs, come here." His voice was raspy as he reached for her. She slithered out of his grip and moved back off the bed, dropping to her knees between his legs as her hands closed around his waistband and tugged.

"Lift," she ordered, breathless, frantic, insistent.

He pressed his feet into the floor and lifted his hips. In one swift move she pulled the jeans from his legs and threw them over her shoulder. He managed to get a hand on her sweater and tugged. She lifted her arms so he could slide it off, but before he could reach for her, she wrapped her fingers around his erection and lowered her mouth to the tip.

Heat, pressure, so much suction surrounded him, his brain short-circuited. His hands fell to the mattress as she pleasured him.

"Raegan . . ." His hands fisted in the comforter. Sweat beaded on his forehead and down his spine. He fought the screaming need for release and closed his shaking hands around her shoulders so he could pull her away before it was too late. Sitting up, he said, "I'm never going to last if you keep doing that, baby."

She stumbled to her feet as he pulled her up. "I don't want you to last."

Need roared through his veins as he pulled her mouth down to his. She melted into his kiss with a moan. Rolling her to her back, he pushed her down to the mattress then drew back and flicked the latch on her bra.

"Lose the bra." His fingers freed the button on her jeans, and as she wiggled out of the straps, he peeled her pants down her legs and tugged them off. "Hurry."

Her hands shook as she did what he said. He found a condom in his wallet on the floor and rolled it on. Her eyes were glazed with lust as he climbed over her, as he lowered and took her mouth, as he kissed her with a need stronger than any need he'd ever had for a drink.

"God, Raegs." He slid a hand down her stomach and between her legs to find her hot and wet and ready. "You have no idea how many nights I laid awake thinking about this. About you. About us."

"Oooh." Her head fell back, and she rocked into his hand. "Alec . . ."

He couldn't handle the desperation in her voice, the heat in her words, the feel of her beneath his fingers. Kissing her again, he moved between her legs and slid inside her.

Her whole body trembled, and she groaned long and deep, the sound turning his blood to lava in his veins. Kissing her deeper, he began to move, their bodies finding a familiar rhythm that pushed aside any last lingering doubt that this wasn't exactly where he was supposed to be.

"Oh, Alec." Her hot breath fanned his lips. "Yes, yes . . . don't stop."

He couldn't. Was past the point of reason. He knew she was close. Knew the signs, knew her body better than anyone. Rolling to his back, he pulled her on top of him so she could take the lead, so she could pull them both into mind-numbing bliss.

"Raegs . . ." He slid a hand around her nape, pulling her mouth back to his as her body moved faster. "God, I need you. Don't give up on me, baby. No matter what."

"I won't," she whispered against his lips. "I won't ever."

Her whole body contracted, and she squeezed him so tight the last of his resistance broke. And when the wave crashed over him, it swept her under as well, swirling them together into a pleasure so sweet and perfect and complete, he knew he'd been a fool to think he could ever live without.

She collapsed against him, sweaty, breathless. And he was just as wrecked, but more alive than he'd ever been. Holding her tight, he pressed his face to her throat and breathed her into his heart, into his soul, drawing her back where she'd always belonged.

Long minutes passed where the only sound in the room was their heavy breaths and racing heartbeats. She relaxed into him, sighing in pure contentment. He tightened his hold on her and closed his eyes, loving her damp skin against his and how perfectly she fit against him, even now. Loving everything about her—her compassion, her ability to forgive, the way she made him the man he'd always wanted to be.

"What are you thinking?" she whispered.

He opened his eyes and blinked up at the ceiling. "I'm thinking I'm the biggest fucking moron on the planet for ever letting you go."

She turned her head against him and smiled. "Yes, you are. No argument there."

He smiled. Couldn't remember the last time he'd really smiled and meant it, like this.

"I'm also thinking I like what you did to this room." His chest pinched. "And I'm trying really hard not to think of you here with anyone else."

She pushed up on her elbow, looking down with gorgeous green eyes that had haunted him for three damn years. "No one has been here with me."

His heart sped right back up as he looked at her. "No one?"

She shook her head, all those luscious auburn locks framing her face like ribbons of smoldering fire. "I only got rid of our bed because it was too big. It felt empty being in it alone."

Pressure formed beneath his ribs as he brushed a lock away from her cheek, so much pressure he couldn't find the words to tell her how sorry he was for hurting her, for leaving her. For being such an idiot.

Her gaze drifted to his chest, and she brushed her fingers over a mole near his collarbone. "And this will probably sound really pathetic, but . . ." She bit her lip, her cheeks turning a soft shade of pink. "I haven't been with anyone since you left. I mean, I've dated, but I haven't . . . you know."

"You haven't?"

She shook her head again and pursed her lips.

The relief was so sweet, it opened his lungs so he could draw air again, something he knew he didn't deserve. Unable to stop himself, he laughed and closed his arms around her, pulling her against him as he closed his eyes and smiled into her hair.

"You think that's funny?" she mumbled.

"Yes, because I nearly decked your boss at the hospital the other day."

Her muscles relaxed, and she trailed her soft fingers over his arm. "That would have gotten me fired, I'm sure. He's a nice enough guy, but I shouldn't have gone out with him. I don't really know why I did."

Alec's smile faded. He knew why. Because she'd been lonely and the guy had shown interest. Alec had no one to blame for that but himself.

It should have been me. It should have only ever been me. His throat grew thick. "I haven't been with anyone either."

Her fingers stopped their tantalizing strokes. "Really?"

He shook his head, knowing his admission wasn't going to be as sweet as hers. And he hated that too, but he owed her the whole truth if they had any hope of moving forward from here.

"I've dated a lot of women. Taking a date to family functions was a great way to make sure no one asked how I was doing or brought up my drinking or rehab or any of the past. And it was a way to forget and not have to feel anything." Her heart beat fast against his, making his hurt all over again, but he forced himself to go on. "I wasn't a saint, Raegan. I tried to sleep with several of them. I just . . . couldn't."

"Why not?" she whispered.

His brain tripped back over the nameless faces, all redheads he'd picked up in a pathetic attempt to purge Raegan from his heart. None of them had done the trick. All they'd done was make him miss her more.

He turned his head and pressed trembling lips against her temple. "Because none of them were you. You're the only woman I want. The only one I've ever wanted. I love you, Raegan. I love you so damn much. I'm sorry I left you. I'm sorry I hurt you. I never wanted that. I only ever wanted you to be happy, and I knew I was making you miserable. I thought if I left, you might be able to smile again. I thought—"

"Oh, Alec." Her hand grazed his jaw, and she turned her face toward his, claiming his mouth to draw every ounce of his pain and agony and fear away. Her kiss bathed him with sweetness. Caused that tiny heart he'd only recently realized he still had to swell. Gathered all the broken pieces inside him and wrapped them in love until he knew he was forgiven.

When he was breathless, she drew back and looked down at him. And smiled that for-his-eyes-only smile that told him he was loved. That he was home. That they could get through anything together. "I hope you have more condoms in that wallet of yours, because I want you again."

Heat rolled through his belly, making him hard—everywhere. Making him smile too. "There's still a drugstore around the corner, isn't there?"

"Yes."

He hooked a leg over hers and rolled her to her back. "Then we're good for at least another round. I have one left. After that, you'll need to stop mauling me long enough so I can run down to the store."

She laughed as he kissed her. And when her laughter turned to a sigh and her lips became greedy, he sighed too because he'd finally been given a second chance.

No matter what happened with their investigation, no matter what happened with Emma, he promised himself he wouldn't mess this chance up.

———

All Alec had wanted to do the next morning was stay in bed and show Raegan how much he loved her with his hands and mouth and body. But her boss had texted and told her she needed to come into the station to go over her research, and since that boss was the one who'd given Raegan the nudge about these missing-child cases, Alec had reluctantly let her go.

He pushed the drugstore door open and smiled as he remembered the way Raegan had brushed her lips against his when he'd dropped her off at her station. Her kiss had been filled with so much promise, his whole body had tingled. He couldn't wait for her to kiss him again like that. Couldn't wait to show her just how incredible that made him feel.

The brown paper bag crinkled in his hand as he slipped on his sunglasses, crossed to his truck, and tossed the bag inside. He hadn't made it to the drugstore last night for the condoms now in the bag. Hadn't wanted to leave Raegan for even five minutes. Instead, they'd used his last one and then gotten creative with their hands and mouths. Of course, it had been insanely hot and completely satisfying, but it wasn't enough. He wanted her in the shower, on her bed, against the wall, on the couch . . . His whole body tingled, as he thought about taking her on the floor in the entryway just as he'd done the night he'd come home from that assignment in Afghanistan, so desperate to touch her that they'd barely had time to close the door before they'd ripped each others' clothes off.

He hit the lock button on his fob, shoved the keys into his pocket, and pulled out his phone as he crossed the street toward the coffee shop on the opposite corner, feeling hopeful for the first time in years. Hopeful about his life and where it was headed, hopeful about his relationship with Raegan, hopeful even about finding their daughter.

His chest both tightened and warmed when he thought of that stuffed animal, when he thought of Emma. Raegan was right. This was the best lead they'd had in years. They weren't going to give up until they found her.

He dialed, held the phone to his ear, and shoved one hand in the front pocket of his jeans as he moved down the block.

Hunt answered on the second ring. "Was just about to call you, dipshit."

"My ESPN is on point today, then."

Hunt laughed at the old joke, but his humor faded quickly when he said, "So Gilbert seems to have disappeared off the face of the earth."

Alec's mood took a serious nosedive at just the mention of the man who'd tried like hell to ruin his life. "He hasn't checked in with his probation officer?"

"Nope. No one's seen him. I'm checking in with his old acquaintances, but so far I've got nothin'. Was the FBI able to match that note on Raegan's car to his handwriting?"

"Not yet."

"Of course not yet, because shit doesn't go down that fast in real life, only on TV."

Alec really wasn't in the mood to get into Hunt's ongoing prejudice against Hollywood. "What about Murray? Did you find out anything about his accident? Or what he was doing before it happened?"

"Yeah." Paper shuffled, and Alec imagined Hunt shoving aside folders and piles on his mess of a desk to find the scrap of paper where he'd jotted his notes. "I tracked his movements prior to the accident. He left work around five thirty p.m., stopped at a drugstore downtown, then headed northeast and entered the"—more papers rustled—"the Children Are Our Future charity offices on Morris. He was there for thirty minutes before heading to the West Hills."

Alec stopped at the corner and waited for the light to turn. "What's Children Are Our Future?"

"It's a youth-mentoring charity. They partner at-risk kids with adult volunteers in the community. Kind of a big brother–type thing, but they claim to only use professional, successful, business-minded mentors. Let me see, their website says, 'Successful men and women in the community who have passed vigorous background checks and are committed to being a stable, positive role model destined to shape the minds of our future generations.'"

"That's a tall order."

"No shit."

"And Murray was a volunteer mentor?"

"I'm not sure yet."

"Who runs the charity?"

"Um . . . I'm still looking into that. There's nothing on the site. You think this has something to do with your cases?"

"I'm not sure. I'll give the charity a ring later to see what I can find out. What about the accident?"

"Looks like alcohol was a factor. After he left the charity, he stopped at a bar, was seen drinking inside over the next hour, then he left. Accident happened roughly twenty minutes after that."

Maybe or maybe not. It was still way too coincidental that Murray had been involved in all three of these missing children's cases and now he was dead only one day after Alec and Raegan had tried to talk to him.

The sign flashed "Walk," and Alec stepped off the curb, following a man in a suit and a woman in a floral dress that was way too springy for Oregon in January. "Once they get the toxicology reports back, any chance you can snag them so I can take a look?"

"I'll try. I've got a buddy with the Portland PD who owes me a favor. Speaking of favors . . . what's the deal with you and the ol' ball and chain? And don't try to tell me nothin', because I know you so damn well that I know when you're lying."

Alec's stomach tightened as he crossed the street. Hunt was fiercely protective of his friends. It was his greatest strength. He'd been with Alec the day Alec had gotten the final divorce papers, and he'd seen how the news had wrecked Alec. What he didn't know was that Alec was the one who'd walked away from the marriage, and that he was the one who'd filed those papers, not Raegan.

"That's a conversation I think we need more time for."

"Shit, man. There is something going on between the two of you. What the hell are you doing, Alec?"

Alec sighed, not in the mood to get into it with Hunt today, and glanced at a woman on the far sidewalk holding a crying baby. His eyes widened when he spotted the shadowy figure behind her in the al—

He heard the pop a split second before pressure exploded in his shoulder. His body sailed backward. His cell phone flew from his fingertips. The woman on the sidewalk screamed and jerked her baby toward the building. The back of Alec's skull hit the pavement with a crack, but thanks to his time in Afghanistan and Iraq and the world's hot spots taking pictures for the AP, he knew exactly what had hit him.

A bullet.

The fucker had shot at him. Right in broad daylight like the coward he'd always been.

CHAPTER FOURTEEN

Raegan itched to throw her coffee cup across the desk and into the face of the man currently lecturing her. Since he was her boss, who she'd recently ended things with, she figured that wouldn't be her smartest move.

"Furthermore," Jeremy said, "contrary to what you think, this station is not here to fund your own personal agenda, whatever that may be. I gave you an assignment, I assumed you were working on that assignment, and now I find you've done nothing to get me the story? That's not the way things work around here, Raegan."

He was ticked she'd broken things off with him. He'd acted like he hadn't cared, but obviously he had. She knew that. She knew it was why he was laying into her now, and she knew she needed to be sympathetic. But it was hard. Especially because he knew this wasn't just any story; it was personal for her.

"You asked me to cover a story, Jeremy, and I'm covering it. I'm researching, which, as you know, is how one builds a story."

He rolled his brown eyes. "You're not building a story. You don't have a single goddamn person interviewed on camera. You haven't even once called Larry to accompany you to these so-called interviews."

Larry was the cameraman she often used on assignment, and Jeremy was right; she hadn't called Larry to join her because she wasn't ready to interview anyone on camera about these missing kids yet. Wasn't sure she ever would be, but she couldn't exactly tell him that.

Drawing in a calming breath, she reminded herself to keep her cool. "I'll call Larry when I'm ready."

He pushed to his feet and shuffled file folders together on his desk. "I already called him for you. He's waiting in the conference room."

"What?"

"I need something for the five o'clock news. He'll tape your personal connection to the story. We'll run it with video of the car the police discovered on Highway 26 where they also found that little boy. I'll let you add in any details you think are important from your research, but that story airs tonight. When you have more, we'll run the rest later."

A sick feeling rolled through Raegan's stomach as she pushed to her feet and watched Jeremy lift a folder and move around his desk as if he were done with her.

"This was never about the story," she muttered to herself.

"What did you say?" He glanced up.

Shock that she hadn't seen the truth before rippled through her. "You came up with the idea for this story the day I got the call about that little girl at the hospital."

"Don't be ridiculous."

"You saw how I reacted to that news." Her skin grew hot, but not in the good way. "You saw and you decided to use it to get your Emmy." Holy hell, that made total sense. They were getting close to the end of January. The deadline for Emmy nominations was in mid-March. She knew he had no other emotionally moving stories to enter in the stupid news awards. He'd been complaining to her about it for weeks on their dates before that night.

She lifted a hand to her forehead, feeling like a complete fool. "I can't believe I fell for it."

He dropped the file folder on his desk and pinned her with a *get real* look. But his brown eyes lacked the same angry focus they'd held earlier. "You're imagining things. Go do your taping and we'll talk when you're not so emotional."

No, they wouldn't. She wasn't about to let him use her personal tragedy for his professional gain.

She tugged the station ID badge from her jacket. "I quit."

A perturbed expression crossed his features. "I don't have time for theatrics today, Raegan. Throw your temper tantrum on your own time. I have work to do. So do you for that matter, so go do it."

She shook her head, stepped forward, and dropped her badge on his desk. It landed with a thud against the folders. "I'm sorry if I hurt you. That was never my intention. And I'd be all for this if you wanted to run this story to keep my daughter's name in front of the public, if I thought you wanted to help those other families, but that's not what you want. You want my personal connection to these kids, not Emma's connection, not details on these missing kids. I'm not just a story, Jeremy. *She's* not just a story. And neither are those kids. Their parents deserve to know what happened to their children just as much as I do. What they don't deserve is to be used as pawns in a ratings quest. So I quit."

She turned, pulled the office door open, and made it two steps out before she heard him swear and say, "Raegan, come back."

She kept walking, wanting nothing more than to get out of this station and back to Alec. He didn't follow her. She'd known he wouldn't because he wouldn't dare make a scene in front of his staff.

Just past the dark soundstage, Anna Chapman rushed up at her side. "Hey. There you are." Breathless, she said, "This note was left for you at the front desk."

Raegan stuffed the note in her pocket without looking at it and rounded the corner toward her cubicle. "Probably another lecture from Jeremy."

Anna hustled to keep up with her. "You two have a fight?"

"We had nothing." Raegan stopped at her desk, grabbed her purse from the bottom drawer, and pulled out her keys.

"What's going on, Raegan?" Anna stood in the doorway of her cubicle, clearly not getting the hint Raegan wasn't in the mood to chat.

"Nothing more than finally seeing the light."

Some kind of commotion sounded behind Anna. Raegan glanced that way to see a cluster of people around a salt-and-pepper-haired woman dressed in a fancy suit who looked like she'd just stepped off the pages of *Vogue Senior*.

"What's that about?" Raegan asked as she shoved lip balm, her brush, and the rest of her personal items from her desk into her purse.

"Oh that." Anna glanced over her shoulder at the small crowd and then back at Raegan. "Miriam Kasdan's giving an on-camera interview." Raegan recognized the name. The woman was some big philanthropist in the city who Jeremy had been trying to hook for a special interest piece. "So are you and Jeremy done for good? Chloe Hampton said he was really upset the other day after you were here."

A tiny bit of guilt pinched Raegan's chest, but it faded quickly when she remembered the way Jeremy wanted to use Emma for his ratings. She grabbed the framed photo of Emma from the corner of her desk and shoved it in her bag. "Look, Anna, I really have to go."

The phone in her purse buzzed. Raegan pulled it out as she moved past Anna and turned for the elevator. "This is Raegan."

"Raegan, it's Ethan."

"Hey, Ethan." A whisper of worry rushed down Raegan's spine when she realized his voice sounded tight. "What's up? Is everything okay?"

"No."

Her feet drew to a stop. "What's wrong?"

"It's Alec."

The blood drained from her face, and she gripped the receiver until her knuckles turned white. "What happened?"

"He was shot. Paramedics are transporting him to the ER right now."

———

"It's fine. It doesn't even hurt." Alec sat upright on the gurney in the ER bay, winced at the pain he didn't want the doctor and nurse to see, and tried to stand. "Just put a bandage on it and let me go."

The nurse typing on a computer in the corner of the room rushed over and pushed him back down while a doctor who looked to be in his forties removed the pressure bandages the EMTs had applied in the ambulance. Another twinge of pain shot through Alec's shoulder, making his teeth grind. "Sir, you need to calm down or we're going to have to sedate you."

Panic clawed at Alec's chest as his spine hit the mattress. The pain in his shoulder from that bullet and the throb in the back of his head where he'd cracked his skull against the pavement sucked, but they were the least of his worries at the moment. He didn't have his cell phone, didn't know where it was or what had happened to it. He couldn't call anyone to go find Raegan, and he was ready to scream if Nurse Ratched didn't let go of him soon so he could make sure Raegan was okay.

He struggled for patience as he tried to hold still so the doctor could work on his arm. "Okay, just do it fast. I need to get out of here."

"You're not going anywhere until we make sure this isn't more serious than it looks," the doctor said. To the nurse still holding him down, he said, "Let's get an IV antibiotic drip going. I also want images of the shoulder to make sure we're not missing any shrapnel."

"Yes, doctor."

The nurse rushed out of the room while the doctor looked back down at Alec's shoulder and reapplied the pressure bandage. "We'll know more after we take some pictures. Sit tight. Someone will come get you in a few minutes."

Pictures would take hours. That panic grabbed hold of Alec's chest and squeezed like a python. "At least let me use a phone. It's important. My wi—"

Footsteps pounded in the hall. Alec looked up just as a frazzled Raegan appeared in the doorway, her auburn hair a tangled mess around her face, her eyes wide and frightened, her coat hanging off one shoulder and down her arm as if she hadn't had time to pull it all the way on.

"Oh my God, Alec." Her gaze darted from his bandaged shoulder to the doctor and back to him as she rushed into the room and around the bed to his uninjured side. "Are you okay?" She looked up at the doctor. "Is he okay?"

"Raegan." Relief poured through Alec like a waterfall. He reached for her with his good arm as soon as she was close, ignored the sharp stab of pain in his bad one, and wrapped his hand tightly around hers to reassure himself she was safe, that the prick hadn't gotten to her too.

"He's going to be fine." The doctor rested one hand on the back of Alec's bed. "Looks to be mostly soft tissue damage. The bullet either ricocheted off the muscle on his outer arm or it went clean through. We'll know more after we take a few pictures." He looked down at Alec. "Do you still need a phone or are we good now?"

"We're good," Alec breathed, staring up at Raegan as he squeezed her hand.

"Okay." The doctor stepped back, tugged off his gloves, and tossed them in the trash can by the door. "The nurse will get your IV started, then someone will be in to take you to imaging. After that, we'll get you stitched up and out of here."

"Thanks," Alec said, still focused on Raegan, his relief so sweet it pushed aside the pain.

Eyes wide and not totally focusing, Raegan looked toward the door as the doctor left.

As soon as he was gone, Alec sat forward, wincing at the tug in his wounded shoulder, and pulled her down to hold her against him.

"Oh my God, Alec." She closed both arms around his neck and held on just as tight. "When Ethan called and said you'd been shot, I thought—"

"I know." Thank God he'd been on the line with Hunt when that shit had gone down. And thank God he'd been conscious to tell Hunt where he was. Hunt had obviously called Ethan right after calling 911.

He swallowed the lump in his throat, closed his eyes, and breathed in the sweet scent of her, not feeling the pain anymore, not feeling the ache in the back of his head, not feeling anything but her. He'd thought the same thing—that his time was up, that it was all over, that he'd never see her again. His throat grew thick. He wasn't ready to let her go. Knew he never would be.

"I'm okay," he said, fighting back the hitch in his voice. Knowing he needed to reassure her . . . and him. He swallowed hard. "'Tis but a scratch."

His stupid Monty Python reference pulled a half laugh, half grunt from her chest. Pushing back, she sat next to him on the edge of the gurney. But there was no humor in her shimmering green eyes when she stared down at him, just pure terror. "If it had been a few inches to the left—"

"But it wasn't." He squeezed her hand. "I'm okay, Raegan."

The nurse came in with the IV bag, dragging at his attention. She hung it on the pole and moved around the room gathering supplies.

"Don't freak out." Alec looked back at Raegan. "This is all just precautionary."

Tears filled Raegan's eyes. "I thought I'd lost you. Right after I found you again."

Emotions closed his throat—that she could love him so much after all this time. That he was so damn lucky to have her in his life. That he was such a fool for having ever let her go.

Wrapping his good arm around her once more, he pulled her against him and held her close. "You're not gonna lose me. Never again, okay?" He pressed his lips against her temple. "I'm not going anywhere."

She nodded and held him tightly, sniffling and fighting, he knew, tears that wanted to consume her.

The nurse cleared her throat. "Sorry to interrupt, but I need to get his IV going, and I need his good arm to do that."

"Oh." Raegan stood quickly and let go of Alec, swiping at her cheeks with trembling hands. "Sure."

She moved to the other side of the bed, near his injured shoulder, and looked down. Sickness rolled over her features while the nurse tied an elastic band around his good arm and searched for a vein.

"Look away, Raegan." To the nurse, he said, "Blood makes her light-headed."

The nurse glanced up. "You can wait in the hall if you'd like. I'll call you when I'm done."

Raegan crossed her arms over her chest. "I'll be fi—"

Footsteps sounded outside the door again, and Alec looked in that direction just as Hunter O'Donnell peeked his dark head around the corner. "Hey. Okay for me to come in?"

"Hunt." Alec breathed easier. "Yeah, come in and block Raegan so she can't see this."

Raegan frowned. "I'm fine."

No, she wasn't fine. She was emotionally wrecked and still shaking. Ignoring Hunt's raised eyebrows and his unspoken *what the fuck is she doing here?* question, Alec said, "I don't want her passing out."

Dressed in jeans, a black button-down, and a leather jacket, Hunt moved into the room and stood between Raegan and the bed. "I remember that. Didn't you end up needing your own X-rays? They thought you cracked your skull when you hit that gurney."

"It was only a bump," Raegan said with a note of irritation in her voice.

Hunt chuckled. "One hell of a bump."

Raegan sighed. "Ethan said you were on the phone with Alec when it happened. Did the police catch the person who did this? Do they have any leads?"

Alec winced as the nurse pushed the catheter into his vein.

"Don't know." Hunt slipped his hands in the front pockets of his jeans. "I'm sure they'll be here soon enough to get Alec's statement." He glanced over his shoulder at Alec as the nurse pulled the elastic band from his arm. "Do you remember what happened?"

"Yeah, I remember." Alec's jaw clenched as the nurse placed a sticky plastic cover over the IV. "I remember everything, even that asshole's face."

"You saw him?" Hunt turned Alec's way. Behind him, Raegan stepped close, glancing at his IV and then looking quickly back up to his face.

Alec nodded. "It was John Gilbert."

The color drained from Raegan's cheeks. "Are you sure?"

"Absolutely." A bitter betrayal whipped through Alec as he looked up at Raegan. He had plenty of reasons to hate John Gilbert, plenty of reasons to suspect Gilbert had been involved in Emma's disappearance, but he never in a million years would have expected that his father—his own flesh and blood—would try to murder him in cold blood in the middle of a downtown street.

Alec's vision turned red, and he wanted to reach for Raegan's hand to soothe him, but she was standing hear his injured shoulder and the nurse was still messing with his IV. Forcing himself to look at Hunt, he focused on the facts, not on the hatred brewing inside him. "I was crossing the street, talking to you on the phone, when I heard a baby on the far sidewalk cry. I looked up, and that's when I saw him. He was standing behind the woman and child in the opening to the alley."

"Did you tell the cops?" Hunt asked.

"Yeah. But by the time they got there, he was already long gone. I should have expected something like this." Alec shook his head, feeling like a complete idiot. "He left that note for Raegan. He roughed her up in that alley and threatened her. I'm just glad it was me and not her."

From the corner of his vision, he watched Raegan pull something out of her coat pocket and look down. Her cheeks paled even more. Worry seeped in to mix with the hatred as Alec glanced at her. "What?"

"I . . ." She lifted a piece of paper. "Someone left this for me in the lobby of the station. I . . . I didn't think to read it until just now."

She handed it to Hunt, who read it and scowled, then held it up for Alec to see. Only one line was scribbled on the page.

You didn't listen before. Maybe today you finally will.

Rage bubbled through Alec, a familiar rage linked to years of abuse and taunting, only now it was fueled by what had happened today and the fact that fucker had gone to Raegan. "It's Gilbert's handwriting." He looked up at Raegan. "He was at your station?"

"I don't know. I never saw him."

Hunt tugged his cell phone from his jeans. "I'll call my guy down at Portland PD and get them to send someone over to KTVP to get a statement. Who gave you the note, Raegan?"

"Anna Chapman."

Hunt nodded and stepped out of the room so he could get a signal.

Alone, Alec looked over at Raegan only to see both hands covering her face. A little of the rage ebbed, replaced with a wave of relief that Gilbert hadn't touched her.

"Hey," he said softly, desperate to reach for her but still unable to because she was standing on his injured side. "It's okay."

"It's not okay." She dropped her hands. "You told me it was him, and I didn't listen. When he left that note. When he . . ." She pointed to her face, unable to say the words. "I didn't want to believe it could be him, so I ignored it. He's your father. Fathers aren't supposed to do those kinds of things. And now you're lying in this bed, and—"

"Don't do that."

She swiped angrily at her cheek. "Don't do what?"

"Don't blame yourself for this. If you want to blame someone, blame him."

"They don't even know where he is, Alec. And if he had something to do with all these missing kids—"

"Then we'll catch him. He's not a smart man, Raegan. He's a drug dealer and an addict. If he's involved in whatever this is, I guarantee he's not the mastermind. He's a grunt, and grunts like him make mistakes. Like today. Today was a massive fucking mistake. I guarantee no one told him to take a shot at me. He did it because I went to see him the other day. He feeds off shit like that, knowing I'm upset."

Alec looked up at her worried face, sick to his stomach because he had a strong hunch none of this would be happening if he hadn't gone to that prison. "I triggered this. I basically told him we were looking into these missing-kid cases, and he jumped on that because he knew it would get to me. The same way he knows going after you will get to me because I still love you. If I hadn't gone to see him, I doubt he would have left you that note on your car. He wouldn't have gone after you in"—his stomach pitched at the thought of John Gilbert alone with her—"that alley. He wouldn't have gone to your station today."

She moved closer to the bed and sat near his injured arm. "If that's true, then why do this? Why try to kill you?"

"I'm not sure he was trying to kill me. I think he was just letting me know he could if he wanted to."

When her brow wrinkled in obvious doubt, he shifted his hand over hers and squeezed her fingers, even though it sent pain spiraling up through the wound in his shoulder. "Killing me wouldn't give him the thrill tormenting me does. He's a good shot. When I was young, he used to take me out into the woods so he could shoot beer cans with his pistol. He made me hold a couple a time or two. Scared the shit out of me, but he never missed. He thought it was funny as hell. He wants me to be scared, Raegan. That's why he went after you. That's why he did this. He was no more than twenty-five yards away from me when he fired today. If he'd wanted to kill me, I have no doubt he could have."

Raegan's eyes slid closed, and the look of utter torment on her face pushed Alec up to sitting. He cringed at the pain but lifted his good arm and slid his hand around the back of her neck, then rested his forehead against hers. "Don't worry, okay? What he did today was a stupid move. The cops will be all over him now. This is a good thing, Raegs. They'll catch him. He's not smart enough to hide for long. And when they find him, we'll know what he's been up to and how he's involved in all this. He won't be able to hurt us anymore."

"And what if you're wrong?" she whispered. "What if they never find him?"

Alec's stomach tightened. He knew one person who might have a good idea where to find Gilbert. He'd given Hunt her name, but when Hunt had contacted her, she'd told him she hadn't seen Gilbert in over a year. Alec suspected she was lying, knew she would always cover for Gilbert, but he hadn't gone out to talk to her yet because he hadn't wanted to leave Raegan alone. He'd also never wanted her to see the kind of dump where he'd grown up.

He couldn't ignore her any longer, though. He'd do anything to keep Raegan safe, even face all the old demons from his childhood, no matter how sickening they might be.

Throat thick, he said, "If they haven't caught him by the time we get out of here, I have a good idea where to look."

Raegan lifted her head and stared into his eyes. "Where?"

In the doorway, Alec spotted Ethan and his mother. Not the mother who'd birthed him but the one who'd raised him and shown him the true meaning of love.

"Alec?" Raegan asked.

Ethan had clearly called the whole family in. Things were about to get chaotic. He drew a breath that did shit to make him feel better and refocused on Raegan. "With Charlene Briggs. The woman I once stupidly thought was my mom."

————

Raegan's nerves felt as frayed and charged as a snapping electrical wire.

She watched Hannah follow the imaging tech as the man wheeled Alec's bed out of the room and down the hall to get pictures of Alec's shoulder. The woman had breezed in and taken control of the situation like the seasoned ER physician she was. It didn't matter that this wasn't her hospital or that her son was complaining he was a thirty-two-year-old man who didn't need his mommy going with him. Hannah knew what needed to be done and was making it happen. Something Raegan wished she had the strength to do at the moment.

She didn't even have a clue where to start.

Silence settled over the empty bay. Since Ethan had stepped out to call their father and other siblings to let them know Alec was going to be fine, and since Hunt was still off on a call to the Portland PD checking on John Gilbert's location, Raegan was alone. Lowering herself to the blue plastic chair near the wall, she tried to settle her strumming nerves but couldn't. And the way her hands wouldn't stop shaking wasn't helping at all.

Be tough. You can get through this.

Yeah, except this time that internal mantra wasn't working. Alec could have died today because of her. He could have died today, and she could have lost him all over again.

A tremble rushed through her, and she dropped her head into her hands. An hour ago, she'd thought quitting her job was the most traumatic thing in her life. That now seemed like nothing compared to this.

"Cops are heading down to KTVP to get a statem—" Hunt's voice cut off, and his boots squeaked to a stop in the doorway. "Where's Alec?"

Be tough . . . "They took him for pictures," Raegan answered, not lifting her head, focusing only on breathing so she didn't totally lose it in front of Alec's best friend.

Silence, then Hunt said, "Are you okay?"

No, she wasn't okay. The man she loved had nearly been killed all because she couldn't stop searching for answers she might never find. And on top of that, she couldn't shake the doubts circling in. The ones she'd worked so hard not to give a voice to over the years because if she did they would break her. The ones that were already whispering . . . *What if you're wrong? What if she's already dead? Are you willing to risk Alec too?*

"Raegan?" Something soft touched her elbow, and she realized Hunt was sitting in the chair beside her, clearly unsure what to say or do, but she couldn't even lift her head.

"I'm fine." Hot tears burned her eyes and spilled over her lashes before she could stop them. "I'm really . . . fine."

"Shit." Hunt slid an arm around her shoulder and awkwardly pulled her against him. He patted her shoulder while she fought the useless tears that didn't want to stop. "It's okay. Everything's gonna be okay. Alec's safe."

"I know that." She sniffled, hating that she was breaking down in front of Hunt of all people, but unable to stop it from happening. The weight of everything seemed to be crashing down around her. She wanted so badly to believe that Emma was alive, but at what cost? She couldn't lose Alec again. Not because of her stubbornness.

She swiped at the stupid tears, screamed at herself to *be tough*, and pushed away. "I know he's going to be fine, but he wouldn't even be here if it weren't for me."

"How do you figure? You didn't pull that trigger."

"No, I just gave John Gilbert a reason to do it."

Hunt's brown eyes narrowed. "What are you talking about?"

"I don't know." She swiped at her useless tears. "We don't have any proof Emma's alive."

"No," he said cautiously. "But you don't have any proof she's not alive either."

Raegan's shoulders dropped. "I know that. I just . . ." She blinked rapidly and looked across the room, hating what she was about to say. "I've been holding on to something so tightly these last few years, afraid if I loosen my grip at all I'll fall into an abyss. Just . . . cease to exist. And I worked so hard to make sure that didn't happen, I let everything else around me crumble—my relationship with my parents, my friendships, even my marriage." Tears welled up again, and she closed her eyes against the sting and shook her head. "I can't let that belief destroy Alec."

"Whoa." Hunt gripped her by the arms and turned her to face him. "Slow down. Let's start at the top . . . your parents, well, I don't know a whole lot about them except that Alec once told me you always had a tense relationship with them. If they haven't been there for you these last few years, then that's their issue, not yours. Your friends? I can speak from experience when I say that friends don't always know the right thing to say or do when a kid goes missing. I'm sure any friendships you let drop weren't your doing, and if those people bailed on you, then they weren't real friends to begin with. And as for your marriage . . . you need to remember that it takes two people to make a marriage work, just as it takes two to end one. You love your kid, Raegan. You want her to be safe. Believing she's alive isn't wrong."

Raegan's heart twisted. "Alec loved her too."

"Yeah, well." The edge of Hunt's lips turned down as he let go of her to rest his forearms on his knees. "Alec's got issues. We both know that. He dealt with Emma's disappearance the only way he knew how. Was it the right way? Hell, no. But he's not that guy anymore. And for what it's worth, from what Alec's told me about these cases, I think he's starting to come around to your way of thinking."

That's what she was afraid of. Her heart pinched so hard, she had to breathe through the pain. "And what if I'm wrong? Alec's already starting to think Emma's disappearance is linked to these cases, and no matter what you say, that is my fault. I asked him to look into these missing kids with me. I pushed him to investigate something he wouldn't have looked twice at otherwise. No, I didn't pull the trigger today, but if Gilbert's involved in all this, then I indirectly gave him a reason to go after Alec. I put Alec in jeopardy because of something I can't let go. I don't want to keep doing that."

"The cops are going to catch Gilbert. He can't hide after today. I bet he's already on the run. He fucked up, Raegan. I know you don't think so, but what happened today was probably a good thing."

"I'm not talking about Alec being shot."

Confusion drew Hunt's brows together. "Then what are you talking about?"

She drew in a shaky breath that did nothing to alleviate the crushing pressure in her chest. "What if Alec gets his hopes up that Emma is alive, and at the end of this search we find something terrible? Do you think he can survive something like that? Because I'm not so sure he can. Ethan told me what Alec tried to do after the divorce. When I heard he'd been shot today, I just . . ."

She blinked rapidly against the tears. "I know in my head they're two separate events. I'm not crazy, you know? But the whole time I was standing next to him by that bed, even when I knew he was okay, all I could see was that image of him in his kitchen with that bottle and that"—she swallowed hard and barely got the word out—"gun." Her eyes slid closed as the tears slipped down her cheeks once more. "I can't be the reason for that again. I can't let my need to believe destroy him."

Hunt sighed and stared down at the floor, and he was silent so long, Raegan wasn't sure he was still there. But then he surprised her when he said, "I know you've always thought I didn't like you, Raegan. I want you to know that's not true. I think you're smart and witty and fun. I think you're a really great woman. I never thought you weren't enough for Alec. Actually, I always thought the opposite was true."

She wasn't sure where he was going, but wondering gave her time to pull herself together and listen. Swiping at the tears, she looked at him and waited.

"Alec," Hunt said, looking up at the ceiling as if trying to find the right words, "has an addictive personality. It's why he turned to alcohol as a kid and why he's struggled with it since. It's why he got hooked on a career that puts him in dangerous places all over the globe and why he doesn't quit. And it's why he fell so hard for you when you two met." He turned to look at her. "I lived with him in college. I saw him date lots of girls. I never saw him fall as hard and fast as he did with you. You became his new addiction. You filled that empty place inside him in a way alcohol never could. And when it was great, it was like a high he never knew before. But when it wasn't, and when everything happened with Emma . . ."

Hunt looked across the room, his expression somber. "You have to know it wasn't just guilt that ate at him because he was the one who was with her that day. It wasn't just that she was gone. He loved her—you're right—he *still* loves her, as much as any parent could. It was you. When he had to tell you she was gone, when he saw how it shattered your heart . . . that's when everything tipped for him." He shook his head. "If you'd been any of those other girls Alec dated, I think he could have gotten through it. He would have hurt like a bitch. He would have missed Emma like crazy, and he still would have carried a shit ton of guilt because he was there when she disappeared, but I think he would have found a way through the pain. Maybe today he'd even have the same faith you do that Emma's out there somewhere. But because it was you, that didn't happen."

Tears welled in Raegan's eyes again, blurring her vision as she listened, the truth in his words slamming into her hard and stealing her breath.

"He loves you more than he should," Hunt said plainly. "More than is healthy. He always has. I saw it before, and I stayed out of it because it wasn't my place. But now . . . well, you asked." He turned and met her gaze. "Could he survive getting his hopes up about Emma and possibly having them crushed? Yeah, I think he could. What he can't survive is breaking your heart again. And I don't know how you stop that from happening when the odds things are going to work out the way you want are . . ."

He cut himself off and looked back down at the floor, and as Raegan struggled to breathe she knew he was trying to save her more pain. But she didn't want to be saved from it. Not anymore. She needed to face the facts and stop being blinded by hope because this wasn't about her. It was about Alec.

And these were the facts. In the United States, one child goes missing or is abducted every forty seconds. Stranger kidnappings target more females than males. In nonfamily kidnappings, 20 percent of children reported to the National Center for Missing & Exploited Children are never found alive. And 74 percent of children who are ultimately murdered are dead within the first three hours of an abduction.

Raegan knew those facts by heart. Had beat them into her brain after Emma's disappearance. And she'd rationalized that her daughter was not one of those statistics because they had no proof either way. For three years, blind faith had kept her going, had made her believe Emma would eventually be one of the 80 percent found alive. She'd even convinced herself that Emma had made it past that three-hour window because the other option was just too horrifying to consider. But now . . . now she didn't know what to believe. One stuffed animal found in the back of a car didn't mean anything. Every day that passed, their chances of finding her alive and healthy and whole decreased. And she was scared to death of pushing this investigation any further if they were only going to find out Emma really was dead. Because she knew that would break her heart. And it would inevitably tear Alec apart.

"Hey." Hunt's hand gently landed on hers. "That was probably too much brutal honesty. I'm sorry."

"No." She shook her head and sniffled. "You're right. You're right about all of it. I just . . . I don't know what to do."

"I don't think there's anything you can do. Not right now, anyway." He squeezed her hand. "And, shit, I'm the last person who should be giving relationship advice. Just . . . talk to him about your fears. If he'd opened up to you three years ago maybe things would have been different. You women, you do that better than we guys do. We're programmed to keep it all inside. Don't let him sink back into the darkness when things get rough. Make sure he knows he's not alone. And, by God, if there's any chance you don't love him the same way he loves you, then walk away now. Before things get out of control."

She nodded as she stared down at their joined hands. Loving Alec with every fiber of her being was the only thing she knew for certain. But even that scared her now.

Sighing, Hunt let go of her and pushed to his feet. "Look, since Alec's got the whole family here, and since it sounds like more will be descending soon, I'm gonna take off. Will you be okay?"

She nodded and tried to keep her voice from wavering as she said, "Yeah," but knew she failed miserably when he frowned down at her.

"Tell Alec I'll call him when I hear from my guy at PPD."

"Okay. Thanks, Hunt."

He cast her a sad smile and then walked out of the room, and alone, Raegan's mind tumbled through the last few days. Finding that stuffed animal. Hearing Alec say he believed Emma could still be alive. His admission that he wanted a second chance and that he loved her. Always loved her.

They were the words she'd longed to hear for three years, and she wanted that second chance for them too, more than she could ever express. But not if it meant she might one day lose him for good.

CHAPTER FIFTEEN

"This is a stupid idea." Raegan's jaw tightened as she sat in the cab of Alec's truck, her arms crossed over her chest and a frown pulling at her lips. "You don't need this stress on top of everything else. The cops can talk to her just as easily as you. You should be home resting, and you definitely shouldn't be driving."

Alec tried not to be irritated by her lack of support and looked back out the windshield as he drove. They'd already been through this a dozen times. "My arm feels fine. You heard the doctor. As long as I'm not taking pain pills I'm free to go back to my normal routine."

She huffed and looked out at the passing scenery. "This isn't your normal routine, and I don't care what that doctor said. You should still be in bed."

"I would be"—he shot her a smile, hoping to lighten her mood—"but someone wouldn't stay there with me."

Instead of looking at him like he wanted her to do, she scowled and continued to stare out the window.

Sighing, he refocused on the road and told himself not to read anything into her mood. He was having a hard time doing that, though. She'd been acting strange ever since he'd been discharged from the hospital. Two days had passed in which he'd spent most of his time in her apartment being waited on by her. She'd climbed into bed with him at night and wrapped her arms around him, but during the day she'd pretty much left him alone while she'd cleaned the apartment, done laundry, or worked on her laptop. She hadn't once talked about those missing kids, hadn't even mentioned Emma. And every time he brought up contacting Bickam at the FBI to find out if they'd learned anything about that stuffed animal, she'd told him someone would call when there was information to pass on and that they should be patient.

It wasn't like Raegan Devereaux to be patient. He liked her impatience. Liked that she knew what she wanted and went after it, even if sometimes he didn't agree. But on this he did agree. Ever since he'd seen that stuffed animal, he wanted to expand their search and find their daughter. Only now Raegan was the one dragging her feet.

He knew what had happened to him had scared her, but instinct told him this was more than that. Something was bugging her. Something she wasn't talking to him about.

He made a left onto a gravel road dotted with potholes. The truck jolted, sending a sharp stab of pain up his arm. He winced but covered it quickly so she couldn't see. "So you never told me what happened at KTVP the other day. Everything go okay?"

When she didn't answer, he looked across the cab. "Raegan?"

"Everything's fine."

"Fine." There it was again. His favorite word. There was definitely something going on with her.

Lifting his foot from the gas pedal, he pulled the truck to the side of the gravel road and killed the ignition.

"What are you doing?" Her brows snapped together. "Is something wrong with the truck?"

The lift in her voice at that possibility was just a little too hopeful, kicking his suspicions up even more. "Nothing's wrong with the truck."

He twisted in his seat toward her, ignoring the tug in his arm. "But something is wrong with you, so spill."

Her shoulders dropped, and she focused out the windshield, careful, he noticed, to keep her eyes off his. "I'm fine. Let's just keep going."

"Not until we talk. You've been acting weird, and I want to know why."

She pursed her lips but didn't turn his way.

The blunt approach clearly wasn't working. He'd have to try flirting. "Those little frown lines between your eyes are going to get stuck there if you're not careful." He leaned toward her and reached for her hand. "I could kiss 'em away if you want."

Her eyes fell closed, and the heartache he saw on her face pushed his suspicion to full-on worry. Drawing her hand to his lips, he kissed each knuckle, one by one. "Come on, baby. Talk to me. We said we wouldn't keep secrets anymore, remember? Tell me what happened at the station."

"It's not the job. I quit the other day. I don't even care about the station."

"You quit your job?"

Her eyes fluttered open. "Yes. I didn't tell you because of . . . everything. Jeremy wanted me to run my story. Not the cases we've been looking into but my personal story. About Emma. It was never about those other missing kids. He just steered me toward those articles because he hoped I'd dig until I created a link to Emma's case. Then he could use her disappearance to get his tearjerker, Emmy-winning story."

Alec's impression of the dickhead took a serious header. And that wasn't saying much because his impression didn't have far to fall. "You told him where to go, I'm guessing."

"Of course I did. I'm not about to let him use our daughter as a ratings ploy."

He thought about that for a moment. "Unless it could help us find her."

She sighed, and her shoulders dropped. "I know that. And I would have agreed if that were the case, but it wasn't. He wanted the focus on me, not on Emma." She glanced out the window. "Anyway, I can find another job. And I have my trust fund in the meantime."

The trust fund she hated to use because whenever she touched it—as she had when Emma had gone missing and they'd hired the best private investigators to find her—her self-absorbed parents made her feel guilty from thousands of miles away.

"You don't need to touch your trust fund. You have me."

"You're not going to start paying my bills."

"Raegs, that was our apartment."

"But it's not anymore," she said softly.

"What if I want it to be?"

Her gaze flicked over his, filled with a million doubts all playing across her gorgeous features. "Alec—"

"No, hear me out . . ." His chest drew tight as a drum, but it was a good tight. A right tight. One he liked because it told him he was alive. "I don't want to just spend the night at your place. I want it to be our place. I want you, every day and every night. The way we should have been the last three years."

She didn't reach for him. Didn't melt into his arms as he'd hoped. Instead, she looked down at their joined hands with a sadness that rocked him to his core. "And what happens if we don't find Emma? Or worse, what if what we find isn't what we both hope to find?"

He held her hand tighter because something in her sad voice made him feel like she was about to pull away. "Then we get through it together."

Her eyes slid closed. "Alec—"

"Do you want guarantees?" Panic spread beneath his ribs, drilling holes in that drum. He reached for her other hand, as if doing so could keep her with him. "I can't give them to you, Raegan. I don't know what we're going to find. All I can do is tell you that I love you.

That I have always loved you and that I *will* always love you. Nothing we uncover today or tomorrow or twenty years from now is going to change that fact."

A tear slipped down her cheek. One that tugged on his heart and drew him toward her like a lifeline. He closed his arms around her, feeling the wetness of her tears against his throat, hoping she felt the truth in the beat of his pulse where her cheek was pressed against his neck. "I know it's a risk. I know my track record is shit. But give me a chance, baby. Give us a chance. I love you so damn much, Raegan. More than you will ever know."

She sank into him and slid her arms around his waist, holding him just as tightly. "I love you too. I'm just . . . I don't want to lose you again. I don't want what happened before to happen again. I don't want any of this to be the reason . . ."

Her voice trailed off, but she didn't need to say the words for him to know what she meant. Their unspoken meaning slammed into him with the force of a freight train, twisting his heart like buckling metal.

She didn't want him to hit rock bottom again and decide he had nothing to live for.

Slowly, because his hands were shaking, he framed her face and gently drew her back so she could see his eyes. "Look at me. That's never going to happen again. Do you hear me? I was stupid and selfish that day, and I wish you didn't even know about it, but I promise you, I'm not going back there. I have too much to live for."

Her eyelids dropped. "But—"

"Raegan," He tightened his fingers on her jaw, forcing her eyes to flutter open and focus on his. "Even if we weren't together now, even if something—God forbid—happens in the future and you decide you don't want me anymore, I still won't ever go back there. Because if I did, if I left this world like that, there'd be no chance to win you back and prove to you this is the real deal. Because it is. This is for good or bad, for better or worse. Remember? This is forever."

"I'm scared," she whispered. Lifting her arms, she slid her hands around his neck and pressed her lips to his. "I'm just so scared."

He was scared too. Scared of what they'd find, scared of the truth, and scared to death of the unknown. But more than anything, he was scared of losing her again.

No matter what, he wouldn't let that happen.

———

Raegan closed her fingers around Alec's as she walked next to him on the pothole-laden gravel road and scanned the single-wide trailers to her right and left.

"How do you know she's here?" she asked, stepping over a mud puddle while she tried to ignore the smell around her. She couldn't quite place it. A mixture of urine and garbage that made her glad she hadn't eaten much lunch before they'd driven out here.

"Out here" was the only description she had for where they were. Since Alec hadn't let her drive and hadn't told her where they were going, she'd had to sit back and watch the scenery. She knew they were somewhere north of Portland back in the hills, but the trailer park was surrounded by such tall trees blocking all view that she had no idea in which direction the highway was or how she'd ever find her way out of here if she got separated from Alec.

"Because this is where she was the last time she contacted me, looking for money."

He didn't specify when "the last time" was, but Raegan knew he'd come out here after Emma had disappeared. He'd been looking for his father then, convinced he knew where Emma was. At the time, Raegan had tried to go with Alec, if for no other reason than to make sure he didn't kill John Gilbert and wind up in jail himself, but Alec hadn't let her tag along. Back then, in the days and weeks after Emma's disappearance, Alec hadn't wanted Raegan anywhere near him.

That memory sliced to the center of her heart, but she swallowed against the pain and told herself John Gilbert wouldn't be here. From what Alec had told Raegan, the cops had already questioned her. Hunt had already questioned her. Gilbert wasn't stupid enough to hide in plain sight.

Raegan squeezed Alec's hand and tried for a smile, hoping to reassure him—and herself—that everything was going to be okay. "Maybe she won't be here now."

He huffed. "She's here. She's got nowhere else to go."

Raegan continued to hold his hand tightly against hers, but her back tingled as they rounded a corner and four rows of trailers came into view. Most were old, with run-down, peeling metal siding. The cars parked in front of them weren't much better. Clunkers from the seventies and maybe eighties, most beat-up and dented, a few jacked up on blocks. Everywhere, garbage littered the ground.

"Oh my," she muttered before she could stop herself.

Alec's pulse jumped against hers, but when she glanced up he wasn't looking at her; he was staring at the trailers with a mixture of disgust and rage that told her he was absolutely remembering growing up in a place very similar to this. "She'll try to hit you up for money. It's what addicts do. Don't give her anything."

Addict . . . The word circled in Raegan's head as they continued walking, but her heart beat faster because it made her remember his words in the truck. He wanted them to move in together, and, oh, she wanted that with the same desperation he did, but she was scared. Scared of what their search for Emma might do to him. Scared of the things Hunt had told her at the hospital. Scared of his spiraling out of control once more and this time losing him forever.

He'd told her he wouldn't let that happen again, but he couldn't guarantee it. He'd even admitted as much when he'd said he'd always be an addict. Letting him go now, before either of them were too invested, would be better than wondering if and when it was all going to come crashing down, wouldn't it?

Her heart screamed no. She was already invested. She loved him more than she ever had, and she knew a big reason for that was because of everything he'd lived through to get back to her. She couldn't walk away from him now, knew if she even tried she'd regret it forever. All she could do was exactly what Hunt had told her to do at the hospital—talk to him, not let him sink into the darkness, and love him. Every single day, so he knew he was never alone. Then hope and pray that would be enough.

She squeezed his hand, wanting to reassure him, trying to reassure herself at the same time. His gaze was fixed ahead as he led her between two dilapidated trailers, on a mud path that sank beneath her black ankle boots. Her heart beat hard and fast as they sidestepped a metal garbage can lying on its side, then moved out from between the trailers into what she guessed could be considered a backyard.

It was mostly a flat muddy area bordered by trees. Cigarette smoke drifted Raegan's way, followed by a cough and a gruff voice muttering, "Holy shit. Thought you said you wasn't ever comin' out here again, boy."

Raegan stepped out from behind Alec and looked toward the back of the trailer where a bony woman with stringy hair and a pockmarked face sat in a plastic chair puffing on a cigarette.

"Charlene." Alec's voice was as strained and deep as Raegan had ever heard it. She swallowed hard, hoping this moment wouldn't be the trigger to send him spiraling.

The woman exhaled a long breath and eyed him with both disgust and superiority. "Still tryin' to class me up, I see. Name's Charlie, and ya know it." She lifted her angular chin Raegan's way. "Who's that?"

Raegan stood still as she tried not to be shocked by the woman who'd raised Alec, though "raised" was a subjective term. Not his biological mother—his biological mother had abandoned him when he was just a baby—but the woman his father had lived with from the time Alec was very young until she'd disappeared when he was arrested at thirteen.

Raegan swallowed hard, trying not to pass judgment, knowing instinctively this was no kind of mother for any child. "I'm—"

"Just a friend," Alec cut in, never looking away from Charlene . . . or Charlie.

Charlie reached for the blue beer can on the plastic table to her left, her fingers as wrinkled and bony as her face, making her look eighty rather than the fifty she probably was. "Just a friend," she muttered. "You bring your *friend* all the way out here to meet your mama?"

"You're not my mother."

She stabbed her cigarette into an already full ashtray. "I was more a mother to you than that woman you call Mommy now, but you don't give a shit. Just let me rot out here like the ungrateful child you always was. I got health issues, ya know." She coughed for effect. "Children 'r' supposed to take care of their parents. But no, just 'cause I don't got a whole bunch a letters behind my name, you just forget all about me."

It both angered and frustrated Raegan that this woman—that these people from Alec's past—kept tabs on him, always waiting for the moment to sink their claws in and drag him back when he was nearly free.

Alec stepped toward Charlie. "I'm not here to talk about me. I want to know about Gilbert."

"John?" Her thin lips turned down, and she shook her head as she tapped another cigarette out of the pack. "I don't know nothin' 'bout John."

"Yeah, I heard you were asked about him, and that you said you haven't seen him."

"And I haven't," she answered, puffing out a line of smoke. "I wouldn't lie to the cops, or . . . who was that guy who called to talk to me?"

"A friend," Alec answered.

"Yeah, another friend." She leaned back in her chair and eyed Raegan as if she wanted to claw Raegan's eyes out. "You got all kinds a friends now, don'tcha, son?"

"Look." The bite to Alec's voice told Raegan he was heading quickly past his patience limit. "We both know you and my father have a sick sort of relationship. You're the first person he turns to when he's in trouble."

"What kinda trouble he in this time?" she asked, drawing the cigarette between her lips as if she were completely clueless, which they all knew she wasn't.

Alec stepped toward her. "Don't play games with me, Charlene. I know he came to see you after he got out the other day. I want to know what he wanted."

She stared up at him like a cat stares at a goldfish, waiting for the moment it accidentally jumps out of the bowl and into the cat's mouth. Long, tense moments passed that made the hair on Raegan's nape stand straight. Finally, Charlie tapped her cigarette on the edge of the ashtray and said, "Let's just say, for argument sake, that I heard . . . somethin'. What's in it for me?"

Alec's jaw clenched down hard. Reaching back for his wallet, he pulled a ten free and laid it in front of her. Her grayish-blue eyes went wide, and she licked her lips, but her gaze flicked back up to the wallet in his hand.

This was clearly a familiar game. Raegan watched with wide eyes as Alec laid another ten on the table.

Charlie scooped up both bills and stuffed them into her shirt. "He just wanted a place to stay for a few days. He left yesterday. I ain't seen him since."

"So you lied to the police."

She shrugged. "I omitted. Ain't the same thing. 'Sides, what 'r' you gonna do? Tell 'em? I know you won't 'cause you want my help."

"Where was he going?"

She shrugged and puffed on her cigarette.

Alec stared at her, then laid another ten on the table.

Charlie swiped it away to join the first two and grinned. "Don't know. He didn't say."

A muscle in Alec's jaw ticked as he laid another ten on the table. "He say anything about me?"

She giggled and grasped the money. "He said you was messin' things up for his job. You and some girl." She nodded Raegan's way. "Must a meant that one there. She's pretty enough." She leaned around Alec. "He give you that shiner, honey? I know good ol' John Gilbert's work when I see it. He got ya good, didn't he?"

Raegan's spine tingled, and she glanced at Alec, willing him not to break.

Alec stared at Charlie for several seconds, then pulled a twenty out of his wallet and held it up. "Who's he working for, Charlene?"

"Hell if I know."

He extracted another twenty and fingered the money in front of her. She reached for it, but before her grubby fingers could clasp it, he tugged the bills back.

Frustration lines creased Charlie's forehead and around her eyes as she glared up at him. "Some rich bitch in the city, okay?"

"What does he do for her?"

She sighed, her eyes never once leaving the cash in his hand. "I don't know."

When he didn't hand over the money, she glared up at him. "I'm tellin' ya the truth. I know what he used to do for her, 'fore he got sent up. By you. But that's it."

"And what was that?" Alec asked, waving the money in front of her.

Her gaze followed the cash. "Truckin' stuff. He moved stuff from place to place."

"What kind of stuff?"

The lines on her face deepened. Raegan could see she was struggling between her need for cash and her desire to stay quiet.

Alec must have seen it too, because he pulled out a hundred-dollar bill to join the twenties. "What kind of stuff was he moving, Charlene?"

She pursed her lips. Stared at the money. Her face turned as red as a tomato just before she jumped out of her chair. "Nothin'. He wasn't movin' nothing. I'm done with this." She twisted for the trailer's door. "You can show yerselves out."

Alec caught her by the bony arm before she could close her fingers around the door handle. She grunted as he jerked her back around and closed his other hand around her throat.

"Alec," Raegan jumped forward when she realized what he was doing and grabbed for his arm. "Oh my God, let go of her."

Alec didn't move. Didn't release the woman. "Tell me what he was moving, Charlene."

Charlie's eyes turned to hard black coals. "You're just like yer daddy."

"Yeah, I'm *exactly* like him. I learned everything from the master." He slammed her up against the side of the trailer, his voice turning to ice. "Tell me."

"I don't—" Her words died with a gasp. Wide-eyed, she struggled against his hold, but all it did was make her face turn redder and her eyes bulge even more.

"Alec." Frantic, Raegan pulled on Alec's elbow, desperate to get him to let go, but he was so strong she barely nudged his arm. "Alec McClane. This isn't the way. Let her go."

"No," he snapped, "it's the only way she understands." He focused in on Charlie with menacing eyes, his voice turning to a low growl. "I'm sick to death of you and my father fucking with my life. Tell me what he was moving."

"Brats," she gasped. "Like you."

CHAPTER SIXTEEN

Alec stilled. For a heartbeat, he didn't move. Wasn't sure he'd even heard the right words. *"Like you"*? She couldn't have meant that the way it sounded.

When Charlene gasped, he loosened his hold, his heart suddenly beating faster, sweat slicking his skin in the cool air. Against his arm, Raegan tugged at his elbow again, trying to get him to let go, but he ignored her.

He couldn't focus on anything but the sorry excuse of a human in front of him. "What did you say?" he whispered.

Charlene glared up at him even as she struggled. He wasn't hurting her—not yet anyway. She was the biggest faker on the planet. He'd learned that long ago. But he was ready to start hurting her if she didn't tell him what he wanted to hear. "You heard me."

The hold on all that rage he'd locked deep inside over the years bubbled up and over. Jaw tight, he tightened his fingers around her throat and squeezed.

Charlene's eyes flew wide when she realized he meant business.

"Alec!" Raegan yelled, pulling harder on his arm.

"Okay!" Fear lifted Charlene's raspy voice an octave. Alec loosened his grip, just enough so she could talk. "I said he was movin' brats like you for that rich bitch."

Raegan's hand dropped from Alec's arm. He knew her mouth was hanging open. Knew she was staring at the woman pinned by his grip, in utter shock, but he couldn't react. Didn't know what to trust or believe. Wasn't sure he'd heard that right. Slowly, mostly because he didn't trust himself, he released Charlene, but he didn't step back.

Charlene, ever defiant, rubbed at her wrist and glared up at him again. "Oh, don't you go gettin' all high and mighty. I might not like that bitch very much 'cause she looked down her nose at me, but yer father knew she was doin' the world a whole lotta good. Those kids came from crappy homes. She saved 'em, found 'em good families. And John was makin' nice money doin' it 'til you got arrested and sent to juvie. Then you ratted him out, and it all turned to shit."

Moving children . . . Finding them homes . . .

"You got nothin' to complain about, neither," Charlene snapped, taking one step to her left, closer to the trailer's door. "He saved you from one a those shitty homes. Brought you to me 'cause I couldn't have no kid a' my own. But you was always an ingrate. Even as a toddler. Always had this hoity-toity attitude, just like that bitch. Didn't surprise me none when you turned on your daddy. I told him you was gonna do it one day. He done gave you a better life than you deserved, and you shit all over him."

Alec's pulse turned to a whir in his ears, and his skin grew hot and tight as the impact of her words sank in.

Moving children . . . Finding them homes . . . "Makin' nice money doin' it . . ."

His vision turned red, and a rage like he'd never known whipped through his veins. He slammed his hands into the side of the trailer, inches from Charlene's head. "Did he take my daughter?"

Charlene jerked back, her eyes filled with true fear as she scrambled back, trying to slink away. "I—I don't know."

"Tell me!"

"I don't know!" Her voice trembled as she pressed her hands back against the siding. "I swear it. I only seen him a handful a times since he got out a prison. I didn't even know you lost your kid 'til last year. 'Fore I could ask him about it, he was arrested again on that probation violation. He was just trying to find work. He wasn't doin' nuthin' wrong. I tried to ask him 'bout it the other day when he was here too, but he wouldn't talk."

"Where did he go?"

"I—I don't know."

Alec lurched forward and grasped her by the throat again. Charlene gasped. This time, Raegan didn't even move at his back. "If I find out you're lying to me—"

"I ain't. I swear. He was actin' all nervous when he was here. Rantin' about that rich bitch makin' him do stuff he shouldn't be doin'."

"Moving more children?" Alec asked.

She shook her head. "I don't think it was that. He was only good at that before 'cause he had that big truck, ya know? It was easy to pick up kids on his delivery route, throw 'em in the back, and take 'em to the drop spot without anyone knowing. He ain't got that truck now, not since he got outta the clink. He said he was doin' somethin' else. Somethin' he didn't like. Somethin' he said was gonna get him in trouble with the cops if they ever found out."

For the first time since they'd arrived, Alec looked back at Raegan. And in her eyes he saw disbelief, shock, and horror.

Alec focused on Charlene once more. "When you see him again, you're going to call me. Do you understand?"

Charlene nodded quickly. "'Kay, I will. But he ain't comin' back here."

"How do you know?"

225

She pursed her lips as if she'd just realized she'd said too much.

Tightening his fingers once more on her throat, Alec said, "Talk."

"H-he said he was leavin' town. Said th-things are too hot for him now."

"Where? Where is he going?"

"I don't know."

"Charle—"

"North, okay? He said he was goin' north. He stole Bobby's truck across the street and split. That's all I know. I swear it. I swear that's all I know."

Alec knew she was no longer lying. He'd lived with her long enough to know when she was working him, and the last few minutes there'd been no manipulation in her words, only fear.

He released her. She stumbled forward but quickly righted herself and lurched for the trailer. The door slammed in her wake, and a click sounded on her flimsy lock.

Anger vibrated in Alec's veins as he stood in the silence, staring at the peeling metal siding, his mind tripping back over Charlene's words.

Moving children . . . Finding them homes . . . "Brats like you . . ."

Something soft touched his arm, jolting him out of the fast-forward replay. Raegan whispered, "Alec."

"Brats like you . . ."

His pulse raced faster until it was a roar in his ears. Turning away from the trailer, he moved toward the mud path on the side of the trailer, those three words spinning like a tornado in his mind. He needed air. Needed to think. Needed—

"Alec, wait."

Holy fucking shit. *"Brats like you . . ."*

Brats like *him*.

Shock gave way to disbelief, and finally, hysteria. Whipping out his cell phone, he checked the signal only to find nothing. "Dammit. No fucking signal."

He needed to call the cops. Needed to call the FBI. Needed to get someone out here before Charlene realized what she'd just done and tried to run. Needed—

"Alec." Raegan rushed in front of him, forcing him to slow his steps. Worry and fear swirled in her eyes. "Talk to me."

There were no words. Closing his arms around her, he pulled her against him and buried his face in her hair as the hysteria inside him turned to a laugh he couldn't contain.

"Alec." Her hands stilled against his chest. "Are you okay?"

"Am I okay? I'm better than okay. I'm fan-fucking-tastic."

"I don't underst—"

He knew she didn't. He was acting like a lunatic, but he couldn't help himself. The relief—the knowledge, the truth—was so sweet . . . "He's not my father," he said into her hair, holding her tighter. "You have no idea how that makes me feel. He's not my real father. He's nothing. He's . . ." He closed his eyes and breathed what felt like his first liberated breath of air. "I'm free. I'm so fucking free."

"Free?" Pushing back, she looked up at his face with confusion and disbelief. "You're relieved? I thought you'd be upset. Your whole life has been—"

"My whole life has been a lie, and I'm so okay with that." He framed her face with his hands. "All this time I thought . . ." Emotions tightened his throat, and he shook his head, fighting back the hitch in his voice. "But he's not my father. I'm not related to him. Everything I've fucked up, I've fucked up all on my own. It's not genetic. I'm not him. I'm never going to become him."

"I never thought you were like him."

God, he loved her. Loved her so damn much. Even when she'd just seen him at his worst, she was on his side. "Five minutes ago I proved the opposite."

"Why? Because you grabbed Charlie? She's lucky I didn't get a hold of her. I was ready to rip her limbs off if she decided to clam up."

Laughter rose in his chest again, and he closed his arms around her, holding her close once more, her heart racing just as fast as his. "I should have let you have a go at her from the beginning. Would have saved me some cash."

"She's a terrible human being," Raegan said against him, the humor gone from her voice, "and you are nothing like her or John Gilbert. Nothing."

Alec closed his eyes and just held her, knowing that wasn't true. His quick temper, the drinking, and the internal struggle he still waged on a daily basis that he wasn't good enough or smart enough or worthy enough were all things he'd gotten from Gilbert. They were things he was going to continue to fight. But at least now he knew it wasn't a losing battle. He wasn't going to become the man he hated more than any other.

A new emotion surged inside him. One he hadn't felt before. One that gave him strength.

Hope.

"You know what else this means? Don't you?" he asked, still holding Raegan against him. "It means she's out there. It means Emma's out there somewhere, and she's alive. If he took me, if he took those other kids, it means she's with another family right this minute."

Raegan drew back and looked up with shimmery eyes. "Oh, Alec."

"We're going to find her." He framed her face again, lowered his head, and pressed his warm lips against her cool ones. "We're going to find her and bring her home."

She wrapped her arms around him and kissed him back.

All he wanted to do was get lost in her, but they didn't have time. Releasing her, he closed his hand over hers and tugged her down the road toward his truck. "We need to get out to the highway where we can get a signal and call Bickam. I want Charlene picked up before she decides to run or ODs. She'll be itching to spend that money I gave her."

Raegan's feet shuffled to keep up with his longer steps. "What if she takes off after we leave?"

"We'll wait at the bottom of the road until the Feds show up. There's no other way out of here except the hills. And if she decides to go that way, she won't make it far."

He turned and smiled at her, and when she smiled back—a warm, happy, hopeful smile—his heart turned over and he knew that finally, *finally*, everything was about to be right.

He was getting his family back. And nothing and no one was going to stop him.

———

"Shit." John Gilbert stared down at the burner cell phone buzzing beside him on the ripped plastic bench seat as he drove. Only one person had the number to his new phone.

He ignored the call. He had enough cash left from his first payment to get him all the way to Seattle. There he could find a forger to create documents that would take him across the border. As for money to get to the border, well, he was a man who could always find a way. Charlie, the bitch, had been a total bust in the money department, but at least she'd helped him steal this beater F150.

Shifting against the seat, he reached for the knob on the radio. The phone buzzed beside him again.

Son of a bitch. He slowed the truck and pulled to the gravel shoulder. Staring at the phone, his heart beating hard, he debated his options, then decided the less they knew the better. If he didn't answer, they'd know he'd run. If he answered, they'd think he was still around doing their shit work.

He lifted the phone to his ear. "Yeah. I'm here."

"Mr. Gilbert," a terse voice said on the other end of the line. "You haven't been answering your phone."

He refrained from saying sorry because he wasn't. "I didn't hear it."

Silence, then, "A man named Alec McClane checked in to the emergency room the other night with a gunshot wound. You wouldn't know anything about that, would you?"

Gilbert's heart raced like a filly in heat streaking away from a stallion. "No. I don't know nothin' about that."

"Mm hm. Your job was to keep one nosy female reporter off a story that could be detrimental to our interests."

"By any means necessary," he huffed. "That's what I was told. I done exactly what I was told to do."

"Firing a weapon in broad daylight on a busy downtown street is not what we told you to do. And at your son, no less."

Anger burned a path straight up Gilbert's cheeks. "He ain't my son. He never was."

"Our employer wants to meet with you to discuss your progress. Ten o'clock tonight. There's a dock at the end of North Sever Road. Don't be late. And don't think about running, Mr. Gilbert. We know where to find you." The line clicked dead in his ear.

Blood pulsed in Gilbert's veins, making his hand shake against the phone. He was dead meat if he went to that meeting. A dock off a deserted road, late at night? No fucking way.

Lifting his gaze, he looked out the cracked windshield and tightened his hand into a fist around the phone, a new wave of rage roaring through him.

This was Alec's fucking fault. He should have killed the bastard with that bullet instead of injuring him. He'd wanted Alec to suffer and now that was coming back to bite him in the ass, just like the no-good kid he never should have taken in had come back to bite him more times than he could count.

The phone's casing cracked beneath his fingers. Realizing his knuckles were white, he let the phone drop to the seat beside him.

Fuck his employer. Fuck what the bitch wanted. He was done. He shoved the truck into gear and pulled out onto the highway. He was leaving this fucking town for good.

As soon as he did one last thing.

He whipped a U-turn and headed back to Portland.

———

Alec kicked the apartment door closed and pulled Raegan into his arms. She moved into him without hesitation and lifted her mouth to his, opening to his kiss with the same heat and need and hope thrumming all through his veins.

They'd waited thirty minutes for Bickam to show up at the trailer park. Alec had never been as happy as the moment he'd seen the Feds hauling Charlene out of the trees in handcuffs. She'd tried to run—as he'd expected—but she hadn't gotten far. And she was spitting daggers at him when she saw him standing there watching. Alec had wanted to sit in on her questioning, wanted to know exactly what she'd omitted when she'd spilled her story to him, but Bickam had quickly shut that down and sent him and Raegan home with the promise he'd call as soon as he had any information.

Any information . . . That could come tonight, or tomorrow. But for the first time in years he had hope that it would come. Until it did, all he wanted to do was savor every moment of this life he should have been living these last three years. This amazing, wonderful, perfect life he was never walking away from again.

Tipping Raegan's face up with his hands, he kissed her deeper and pressed her back against the wall in the entry. "Mm, Raegs . . ." He slid his hands down her arms, across her ribs, and around to her lower back. "I need you. Right now."

"Yes." She lifted to her toes and kissed him harder. "Yes," she mouthed against him, trailing her hands over his shoulders, careful to avoid his injured arm. Her fingers dropped to his waistband and the button on his jeans as if she couldn't wait.

His whole body trembled.

"I love you," she mouthed against him, flicking the button free and sliding her tantalizing fingers inside to graze his hip bones. "Have I told you that lately?"

He groaned at her wicked touch. "And I love hearing you say it." Shifting his hands lower, he lifted one of her luscious legs to hook around his hip and rocked against her. "Say it again."

She laughed and whispered, "I love you."

He smiled. Kissed the corner of her mouth. Nipped his way across her jaw until he found her throat. "Again."

"I love you." Her head fell back against the wall, and she flexed her hips, rubbing against his straining erection. "Oh, Alec. That feels so good. Don't you dare stop."

He had no intention of stopping. He kissed his way down the soft column of her throat, slid his hands under the hem of her shirt, and trailed his fingers up her rib cage until they brushed the satin of her bra.

She arched, offering him her breast, offering everything. "Alec . . ."

A humming sound hit his ears. Lifting away from her mouth, he stilled and listened, then realized that wasn't trembling he'd felt. It was his phone vibrating in his back pocket.

His adrenaline surged, and he reached back for it. "Hold on. My phone's going off."

"Already?" Lips swollen, face flushed, Raegan looked down at the phone in his hand. "Is it Bickam?"

"I can't—"

Alec froze when he saw the words "Unknown Caller" on the screen. A little voice screamed not to answer, but something else, some unspoken instinct deep inside, told him not to ignore this call.

He hit "Answer" and pressed the phone to his ear. "Who is this?"

"You know damn well who it is," Gilbert said.

Everything inside Alec went cold, and he straightened, letting Raegan's foot fall to the floor. "What do you want?"

"Alec?" Raegan's breathless voice whispered close, and he felt her fingers grazing his abdomen, but all he could focus on was the gravely voice on the other end of the line.

"Can't a father just call his son to see how he's doing?"

He was just about to toss the father comment in Gilbert's face when he realized Gilbert probably didn't know Charlene had been arrested or that she'd spilled everything.

"What do you want?" Alec said instead.

Raegan's fingers fell from his skin, and he looked her way. Her eyes grew wide and frightened. He squeezed her hand to reassure her everything was okay.

"Just calling to say good-bye. My ship's finally come in."

Yeah, his ship back to the big house. Again, Alec bit his tongue.

"Couldn't leave without a proper good-bye," Gilbert went on. "And a little somethin' for you to remember me by. Step outside onto your ex-wife's deck."

Alec's stomach tightened, and his gaze shot to the window.

"Yeah," Gilbert said in a smug tone. "I know you're there. I know everything, boy. I left a present outside for you."

Alec's adrenaline surged as he glanced toward the patio door in the living room and the city lights beyond. Was the fucker out there, watching? Was he somewhere close with another gun, waiting for the perfect moment to strike?

Pulling the phone away from his face, Alec covered the mouthpiece with his hand and whispered to Raegan, "Call nine-one-one."

"What's going on?" she whispered, panic quickening her voice.

"Gilbert's outside," he mouthed to her.

Her face went ashen. Pushing away from the wall, she took one step past him for the living room.

Alec caught her at the wrist and pulled her back. He shook his head. "Stay away from the windows," he whispered again, covering the mouthpiece once more. "Use the phone in the bedroom."

She nodded and rushed past him for her room.

When she was gone, Alec turned toward the patio doors. "Okay, you got my attention. What's out there?"

"Too afraid to look yourself?" Gilbert taunted in his ear. "You always was a wuss."

"I'm not afraid of you."

"No, you're afraid of the truth. Step outside, Alec."

Common sense screamed *don't do it*, but Alec moved into the living room and eyed the glass door anyway, careful to stay out of view of the windows. "Why is this so important to you all of a sudden?"

"Look and see. Unless you're too afraid."

Sweat beaded on Alec's forehead as he inched closer to the door, careful to remain in the shadows so Gilbert couldn't see him. When he was close enough, he peered through the glass. The small deck was empty but for two iron chairs and a small iron table.

Turn around. Don't fall for his games. Don't look.

His heart beat hard and fast as he crept closer. As he narrowed his gaze to see through the dark glass. As he spotted what looked like a plastic bag on the round table.

Raegan's hushed voice drifted from the other room, but Alec couldn't make out her words. Reaching the wall, he flipped the outside light on. A scrap of fabric in a sealed plastic bag sat in the middle of the small table.

The blood drained from Alec's face as he stared at a scrap of white fabric dotted with tiny pink hearts. Fabric stained red with dried blood. Fabric that matched the dress Emma had worn to the park the day she'd gone missing.

"I killed her," Gilbert said in his ear. "Your daughter is dead. You said you always wanted to know the truth. There's your fucking truth, *son*."

"No." Alec's throat closed as he struggled for an explanation like a drowning man fights for air. It was a trick. It wasn't real. It couldn't be real. Gilbert was fucking with him. Just like every other time he'd fucked with Alec. The phone shook in Alec's hand, and his legs grew weak. But the roar in his ears was all he heard. "No, I don't believe you."

"Oh, you will," Gilbert growled. "I told you I'd make you pay, son. You're about to. There's a logging road off Highway 26, just past Elsie up in the mountains. At the end you'll find a shallow grave and all the fucking answers you deserve."

———

"They're not going to find anything," Raegan said out loud, more for herself than for Alec. She shivered beneath the thick jacket and watched the team of FBI agents ahead, excavating through the snow at a spot near the end of the gravel road. "He was taunting you. The same as always. It's what he does. You said it's what he does."

Beside her, Alec didn't respond. Just stood stoic and silent as he watched the men digging beneath the spotlights.

Fear tightened Raegan's throat. He'd barely spoken since finding the bag of bloody fabric on her deck. Hadn't once turned to her the way he had after they'd left that trailer park. She tried not to read too much into that. She knew he was scared, just like her. But she couldn't stop the fear from turning to terror as it slid into her chest to wrap an icy hand around her heart.

It was happening. *Oh God . . .* She swayed on her feet, not to fight the cold but to keep her legs from buckling beneath her. Anger whooshed in, and she fought back the terror. She wasn't going to give up. She'd done that before. Walked away. Let Alec spiral. She wasn't going to do that again.

"Alec." She gripped his arm hard and turned him to face her. "Alec." She wanted—needed—the Alec back from a few hours ago. The one who'd been so full of hope he'd made her believe anything was possible. "Look at me, dammit."

His gaze slowly slid her way, but when his blue eyes met hers she didn't see fear or stress or even heartache as she expected. She saw nothing. Just a flat, blank stare she recognized from three years before.

"Don't do this," she whispered, gripping tighter to his coat. "Don't let him do this to you. Don't think the worst."

"McClane!"

Alec's gaze shot past her, and Raegan's heart pounded hard as she glanced over her shoulder toward Jack Bickam, striding toward them from the site.

Her stomach pitched. Bickam's face was drawn and tight as his boots crunched across the snow. Shrugging deeper into his tan coat, Bickam lifted the satellite phone in his hand. "Just got word. Washington State Police spotted Gilbert in that stolen F150 about thirty miles south of Olympia. He ran, of course. They pursued. He lost control of the vehicle. Flipped three times. He's being transported to Providence St. Peter Hospital as we speak."

"Is he alive?" Raegan's hope rushed back. If Gilbert was alive, he could tell them he'd been lying to Alec. This could be over. They could go home. Forget this had happ—

"For now," Bickam answered. "But he's not conscious. EMTs aren't sure he'll make it."

Raegan's stomach dropped again, and she looked back at Alec. Still no emotion passed over his face. Just that same blank stare she remembered all too well as he gazed past Bickam toward the lights.

Please, Alec . . . She squeezed his arm through the thick coat, hoping he could feel her. If he wouldn't look at her, she'd find another way to reach him.

"Look," Bickam said on a sigh. "This could take days. If there's anything out here, we'll find it, but I guarantee we're not going to find it tonight. Let me get someone to take you both home. I'll call you right away if anythi—"

"Here!" someone yelled beneath the lights. "I've got something here!"

Bickam turned and jogged away from them. Without a word, Alec pulled free of Raegan's grip and followed. Sweat broke out all along Raegan's spine, and her heart thundered in her chest as she rushed to catch up with him.

It's not her. It's not her. It can't be her, she repeated in her head as she drew close to the group of men staring down at a shallow hole in the frozen ground.

The voices turned to hushed whispers. The balding FBI agent who'd driven her and Alec up here turned and stared at her. The group slowly stepped back. Vaguely she heard, "Don't contaminate the scene," and, "We need to cordon off the area. No press gets in or out of here."

Alec stopped steps in front of her and stared down into the pit. Nothing about his body language gave anything away. His shoulders didn't tense or relax. He didn't even move.

Raegan's pulse thundered hard, pounding, pounding, pounding in her ears as she moved up at his side and looked over the edge.

Everything came to a screaming halt when she spotted the tiny skull and small bones of what she knew immediately had once been a child.

CHAPTER SEVENTEEN

"No," Raegan rasped beside Alec. "It's not her. I don't believe it." The forest moved in slow motion around Alec, turning hazy and ethereal. He watched as if in a fog as Raegan stepped back, shook her head, and said, "No. It's not her. She wouldn't have been up here. She's with another family. Charlie said they found kids new families."

Somewhere deep inside he knew she needed him. Knew he needed her too. But he couldn't reach that place. It was spinning away from him. Taking with it all the joy and happiness and hope he'd felt only hours before. Leaving behind nothing but . . . nothing.

His gaze drifted back down to the remains in the bottom of the pit, sticking out of the frozen mud. It was a child, he knew it was a child, but he needed to see everything. Needed to see what cloth was in the pit with those bones, needed to see the shoes. They'd still be there. Shoes wouldn't have decomposed yet. There had to be more. There had to be something—

"We can't tell gender from the bones of a child," Bickam said quietly at his back. "We'll need to run DNA tests against you and Raegan."

Somehow Alec found the strength to nod. Wasn't sure how he did. He felt as if he were moving through a thick soup, his limbs heavy, his eyes clouded, his heart—he didn't know what his heart was doing because he couldn't feel it. And he wouldn't let himself feel it until he knew for sure.

"It can't be her." Sobs caught in Raegan's voice as it grew higher. "It's not her. It's not her," she chanted, almost as if to reassure herself. "I know it's not her. Alec, tell them."

Snow crunched, followed by a hushed voice.

"No," Raegan said. "I don't need to calm down. I'm fine. No, I'm not leaving."

"Get her out of here," Bickam muttered.

"No!" More snow crunched, followed by the rasp of fabric. "Oh God, don't let it be her."

The heartache in her voice slowly brought Alec around, but he was still moving through that thick soup, unable to process things in real time. By the time he spotted her, an agent was already putting her in the back of a car and closing the door.

Go with her.

His heart raced. In the center of his chest. Right where he'd felt it come to life when Raegan had kissed him and loved him and come back to him. His breaths picked up speed as he watched the car's lights flip on.

Go with her.

With the heavy beats came a swift whoosh of blinding pain, right in the same spot, but somehow, somewhere inside, he knew he could live through it. As long as he was with Raegan.

He stepped toward the car, already backing up, and was just about to lift a hand to wave the driver down when an agent at his back, one standing over the shallow grave, said, "Does that look like a shoe to you?"

Alec's whole body froze.

"Yeah," another agent said in a grim voice. "A tiny shoe. Call Jack over here. We might be able to identify gender after all."

239

Raegan ran her fingers through hair still damp from her shower and stared at her reflection in the mirror. Dark circles marred the skin beneath her eyes from lack of sleep, but it was the overabundance of stress and worry that made her look as if she could break at any moment.

Be tough. You can get through this.

Her gaze drifted to her cell phone on the counter, and another wave of fear rolled through her blood. Fear she told herself not to succumb to. She sensed she was fighting a losing battle.

Alec hadn't come home last night. He hadn't even looked at her when those FBI agents had removed her from the scene. She'd waited up for him, expecting him to return to her at some point, but he hadn't. And now, at nine a.m. with no texts or calls in response to her efforts to reach him, she was afraid to think about where he was and what he was doing.

Panic pushed in, threatening to pull her under. She was walking a tightrope between freaking the hell out and trying to stay sane. Didn't he know that? Breathing deep, she told herself to stay calm, to think rationally, and to focus on the facts.

She'd spent a lot of time doing just that last night alone in her room, and the only truth she knew for certain was that nothing definitively pointed to that child in those woods being their daughter. If there were no other objects in that grave, identifying those bones would take weeks—maybe even months. And after researching online late into the night, she knew that no coroner could even tell them if the bones were male or female because bones alone couldn't tell gender unless a victim has passed the age of puberty. No, she wasn't going to believe the worst until she was staring at the proof in front of her. She just hoped Alec didn't believe it either and that he hadn't slipped out of her reach, lost in the same guilt and pain that had pulled him away from her so long ago.

Grabbing her cell phone from the counter, she dialed and headed for her living room.

"Hey," Hunt said, answering on the second ring. "I was just about to call you."

Her feet stopped near the couch, and the fear she'd been fighting all night welled inside her like a geyser. Was he with Alec? "You were?"

"I found some information about that dead social worker and a charity he was involved with. I tried to call Alec, but he's not answering."

Her eyes slid closed, and she breathed slowly, but it did nothing to alleviate the pressure in her chest. "He's not answering my calls either."

"Alec's not with you?"

"Not since last night." Raegan's hand grew damp against the receiver, and she didn't want to say the words but knew she had to. "The FBI found a child's body in a shallow grave in the mountains off Highway 26 last night."

"Oh shit."

It was shit. Everything about this was shit, and it was eerily similar to the shit of three years ago, but she wasn't going to focus on that. She was going to focus on the here and now and what she could do to prove that wasn't her daughter. "Tell me what you found on the charity."

"Raegan—"

"Tell me about the charity, Hunt." Her eyes burned, but she refused to cry. Turning into her kitchen, she stopped in the sunlight streaming through the kitchen window and blinked several times, letting the warmth give her strength.

Hunt sighed, and she heard the worry in the sound but refused to give in. "It wasn't easy to find, but I've got a name. The Children Are Our Future charity is managed by a corporation. BLK Conglomerates. It's an import/export business. They move products all over the world. They have offices in LA, New York, London, and Shanghai. The CEO is Arnold Kasdan."

The name was vaguely familiar. "Does he live in Portland?"

"No. Primary residence is in New York. But he's from Portland."

"He grew up here?"

"Yeah. Forty-two years old. Father's deceased—he's the one who started BLK Conglomerates fifty-some years ago. Only child, unmarried. His mother still lives in Portland."

"What's her name?"

"Miriam Kasdan."

The name rolled around in Raegan's head. She'd heard it before. Knew she'd heard it recently. A spark flared when she remembered where. "I saw her the other day at the news station. They were interviewing her for a segment about the arts. She's a huge supporter of fine arts in the community."

"Yeah. That's what I found too. She's on the board of directors for both the children's museum and the Portland Ballet Company."

"Is she involved with Children Are Our Future?"

"No. BLK Conglomerates manages their funds, but I haven't found anything linking her to CAOF. Except for a photograph of her son, Arnold Kasdan, standing with Conner Murray in front of the children's museum she supports with a bunch of kids from CAOF. It could be nothing, but it looks like Arnold Kasdan definitely knew Murray, even if only briefly to tour the museum."

It wasn't a direct link, but it was something worth looking into. "I'll call her later today and try to set up an interview. Maybe I can find out if her son is more directly involved with CAOF and how well he knew Murray."

"Okay. I had a thought this morning about Gilbert."

"What kind of thought?"

"Well, after Alec called yesterday afternoon and told me about your meeting with Charlene, I started thinking . . . If Gilbert was working for someone, there has to be a record of that, right? Bank accounts, deposits, that kind of thing."

"Yes, but he hasn't been out of jail that long. Do you think he'd take time to set up accounts? He's on the run. He'd want cash."

"True, but when Alec was a kid, he wasn't. If what Charlene said is true, Gilbert was working for these people back then. I think it's worth checking into."

"It is, I agree." And she couldn't believe she hadn't thought of that herself. *Of course, yesterday you were dealing with the fallout from that meeting with Charlie and learning Alec was an abducted kid himself, then Gilbert's phone call and the bag he left on your deck, and finally the remains found in those woods.* Was it any wonder she hadn't thought of it? There hadn't been much time to think about anything besides fear.

She stiffened her spine, determined not to give in to that fear.

"I'll keep looking into Gilbert's funds and let you know if I find anything," Hunt said, drawing her back to the conversation. "There wasn't a lot left of Murray's car after he went over that embankment. His death is being attributed to alcohol. My contact at PPD said they did find an odd blue paint on his bumper that didn't match his paint job, leading them to think maybe there was another car on the road behind him when he went over, but they haven't been able to find any witnesses."

"You mean they think he was rammed from behind?"

"That was their initial thought, but they couldn't find any other evidence supporting that theory. Several cars have gone off the road at that spot. It's possible his vehicle scraped a rock or something that was already streaked with paint from an earlier accident."

Possible but highly unlikely as far as Raegan was concerned.

"I'll try to call Alec," Hunt said softer, "and give him this info too."

"Okay." Raegan's heart ached all over again. She didn't want to drag Hunt into their relationship. She'd already leaned on him too much the other day in the hospital, but she knew if Alec reached out to anyone, it would probably be him. "If you hear from him, would you tell him to call me, please?"

"Of course I will. Maybe he's just trying to process it all."

"Maybe." She looked down at her feet and forced back the tears. "But I've texted and called him a dozen times since last night, and he's not responding. I'm afraid—" Her voice cracked, and she swallowed hard. "I just want to know that he's okay."

"I know you do. I'll try to see if I can figure out where he is."

"Thanks." She wasn't going to break. Not now. She had too much to do. Blinking into the sunlight again, she breathed deep. "Look, I gotta go. Call me when you know more about Gilbert's funds."

"Will do. Stay strong, Raegan."

She clicked "End" and stared down at the phone. Staying strong was exactly what she planned to do.

Right after she found Miriam Kasdan's number and set up a meeting.

———

Every inch of Alec's body hurt, from the top of his head to the tips of his toes. A blinding, burning ache that consumed every muscle.

He rubbed a hand over his mouth as he sat on the barstool in the dimly lit dive bar he'd wandered into an hour ago and stared at the shot of whiskey in his hand. He'd had every intention of going home with Raegan last night. Of doing what she did every damn day and being resilient, but as soon as he'd heard those agents talking about that shoe, he hadn't been able to move.

It had been black from the earth when they'd pulled it out of the ground. A tiny toddler Converse tennis shoe. None of the agents could tell what size it was, and they couldn't even agree on what color the shoe had originally been, but all Alec had been able to think about was the fact that Emma had been wearing a pair of white Converse shoes the day he'd taken her to that park. From that moment on he hadn't been able to do anything but stand and watch, waiting to see if they pulled anything else that belonged to his daughter out of that pit.

He swirled the amber liquid in the shot glass and watched it stick to the sides and gradually peel away. An image filled his head of skin peeling away from bone as it decomposes.

Sickness rolled through his stomach, threatening to come up. Fighting it and the image back, he breathed through his nose until the nausea eased. But the pain was still there, pummeling his chest like a prizefighter attacking a speed bag. The sight of that grave, the bones, the snow, that shoe . . . all of it flashed behind his eyelids again and again until he wanted to scream.

That was how he'd ended up in this bar instead of going to Raegan's apartment. As he'd driven back into the city this morning, the pain had been so unbearable he'd had to pull over. And before he'd realized what he was doing, he was sitting on this barstool, staring at this drink.

His cell on the bar next to him buzzed, and he glanced down to see Hunt's name on the screen.

Shit, Hunt had probably heard the news from Raegan by now. Alec knew she had to be wondering where the hell he was and why he hadn't come home yet, but he couldn't face her until he pulled himself together. What was he going to tell her? He didn't have any answers for her yet, and every time he remembered the panicked sob in her voice when those agents had taken her away from the scene last night, that pain in the middle of his chest intensified until it hurt to even breathe.

He looked back at his whiskey. One drink. He could have one drink to take the edge off, kill a little of this pain and numb him out. Then he'd have the strength to face Raegan and Hunt and his siblings and parents—all the people he knew would inevitably be phoning next.

He lifted the shot from the bar and had a memory flash of Raegan standing in the middle of that muddy road after they'd gone to see Charlene, looking up at him with soft, loving green eyes as she said, "I never thought you were like him."

Just as quickly, that memory was followed by another. Of Gilbert hollering when Alec had been about ten to get him his "drink." Of Alec going into the filthy kitchen in that trailer they'd lived in with Charlene. Of pushing aside dirty dishes and climbing onto the counter to find the bottle of Jack Daniel's. Of staring at it and wondering what about the amber liquid was so appealing. Of pulling off the cap and taking a long swallow that burned a path of fire to his gut and made him cough. Of Gilbert laughing maniacally from the doorway and sneering, "That's right, boy. You're no better'n me, you little shit."

He stared at the whiskey in his glass, remembering how the Jack Daniel's had settled like a lump of coal in his belly that day. How he'd wanted to puke it all back up. How he'd swallowed another mouthful just to spite the man. And how he'd felt ten minutes later. Like he no longer gave a shit about anything Gilbert said or did.

That had been the start of a lifelong addiction he was still battling. Yes, the alcohol numbed the pain, but it never got rid of it completely. When the buzz wore off, when his eyes cleared, it was all still there. Alcohol hadn't fixed things for Gilbert, had it? It hadn't done anything but turn the man into a mean son of a bitch, one Alec never wanted to be like.

He set the shot glass on the bar. His white-knuckled fingers released their death grip on the glass, and he drew his hand back to watch the color slowly seep back into his skin. Much as the life had slowly seeped into his soul starting with the day he'd met Raegan.

His pulse picked up speed as he thought about the last few days with her, how she made him feel alive, how he didn't want to be numb when they were together. He wanted to feel everything with her—the pleasure, even the pain, because with her the pain was never quite so bad as it was when he was alone. And staring at this glass now, he knew why. Because she believed in him. Because she supported him. Because she loved him in a way no one ever had before.

His heart felt as if it came to life in his chest, picking up speed until the rapid thump against his ribs was all he could feel. He could sit here and be like Gilbert, blame others for his agony, wallow in the guilt, lose Raegan for good, or he could make a choice. To hurt and grieve and live. Live through the highs and lows and joys and heartache of this crazy thing called life. And he could do it all with Raegan. If she hadn't given up on him yet.

His hands shook as he climbed off the stool and pulled a twenty from his wallet.

The bartender looked up from the dishes he was scrubbing at the end of the bar. "You leaving? You didn't even touch your drink."

"No, I didn't." And he never would again. "Thanks."

He pushed the heavy steel door open and blinked against the blinding glare of the morning sun. He hadn't showered since yesterday. Needed to go to his house and get a clean change of clothes. But he needed Raegan more. He ached to tell her that he loved her and couldn't live without her. Pulling his cell phone from his pocket, he dialed her number and pressed the phone against his ear with trembling fingers.

The line rang five times before flipping to voice mail. "This is Raegan Devereaux. Sorry I missed you. Leave me a message, and I'll get back to you as soon as I can."

She didn't want to talk to him. He couldn't blame her. He hadn't been there for her last night. But he was determined to make it up to her now.

He headed for his truck and waited until the line beeped. "Raegs, it's me. I'm sorry I didn't call you back earlier. I've been . . . processing." Tears burned the backs of his eyes as he climbed into the cab and stared out the windshield at the dumpy tavern. Owning every ounce of the pain, he scrubbed a shaky hand through his hair. "I don't know anything. I don't know if that was our baby or not." His voice grew thick, but he forced himself to go on. "I just know that I love you and need you. I'll be there in ten minutes."

He hit "End" and shoved the truck into drive. And knew that no matter what happened now, he was never going back to the bottle again. He just prayed he hadn't pushed Raegan so far this time that she'd closed the door on them forever.

CHAPTER EIGHTEEN

Raegan's heart raced as she sat in the front seat of her car with the door open and watched Alec's name disappear from her screen.

She'd wanted to answer, was desperate to talk to him, but had been too scared to hit that button. Guilt pressed like a heavy weight on her shoulders. If she heard even the slightest slur to his voice, she knew it would wreck her, and she couldn't be wrecked right now. Not when she was about to meet with Miriam Kasdan.

Telling herself she was doing the right thing, that she would call Alec back when she was done here, she slid the phone into the change compartment on her console so she wouldn't be distracted by it during her meeting, climbed out of her car where she'd parked in the brick circular drive, and slipped the strap of her purse over her shoulder. After dropping her keys in her pocket, she tied her trench coat around her waist, hit the lock on her fob, and headed up the wide concrete steps of the stately Tudor mansion in the southwest hills.

When she'd called earlier and spoken with Miriam Kasdan's secretary, the woman had said Mrs. Kasdan would be happy to provide a few follow-up answers to her interview at the station. Raegan just hoped the elderly Mrs. Kasdan hadn't seen her photo the day the woman had done her on-screen interview.

She rang the doorbell, eyeing the mansion with a mixture of awe and disgust. The three-acre property was meticulously cared for, something straight out of the British countryside with low hedges and envy-inducing English gardens that, even in the middle of winter, looked pristine. Raegan doubted the people who lived inside were as picture perfect as the property, though. Her parents owned properties like this, and their lives were nothing but giant, chaotic, soul-crushing messes. There was more to life than image. More than accumulating objects and showing off. She'd never felt as alive as she had the day she'd moved out on her own and finally walked away from this kind of wealth.

No, that wasn't true. She'd felt more alive. When she'd been with Alec. Even when life had been cruel and heartbreaking, she'd always felt alive with him. Through the good and the bad, through the ups and downs, through every moment of every day. And she didn't want to lose that. She wanted it back. Wanted it all. Wanted him with all his flaws and struggles because they were as much her flaws and struggles as they were his.

Her chest tightened, and she turned for her car, desperate to call him back now instead of later. The front door of the stately mansion pulled open before she reached the first step, though. Whipping around, she stared at a young woman in a long black skirt and white blouse with blonde hair pulled back into a bun.

"Ms. Chapman?" the woman asked.

Raegan forced a smile. "Yes. Anna Chapman," she lied. "Ms. Hennessy?" When the blonde nodded, Raegan smiled. "We spoke earlier."

"Of course." Miriam Kasdan's secretary moved back so Raegan could enter. "Come in, please."

Raegan stepped into the marble entry and glanced up at the soaring ceiling above with its intricate sky painting, then over the expensive artwork on the walls, not a speck of dust anywhere to be seen.

"Mrs. Kasdan is awaiting your arrival in the library." The secretary led Raegan through an expensively decorated sitting room and down a wide hallway before stopping in front of a set of double doors. Opening both doors, she stepped back and said, "I'll be in the kitchen if either of you need me."

Raegan nodded and moved into the library. Hundreds of leather tomes filled the cherry bookshelves that circled the room. A wall of windows looked out across the stone patio and vast green lawns. Across the way, a fire crackled in a giant fireplace, and seated on the couch facing the fire, a salt-and-pepper-haired woman dressed in a crisp navy suit turned toward Raegan.

Miriam Kasdan's hair was cut in a perfect bob to her chin, and the skin near her eyes crinkled underneath her flawless makeup as she smiled, laid her book on the couch next to her, and rose. "Ms. Chapman?" she asked.

"Yes." Raegan rounded the couch and offered her hand. "Call me Anna."

"It's very nice to meet you." The woman's slate-gray eyes narrowed. "I don't believe we crossed paths at the station the other day."

"No, we didn't." Relief rushed through Raegan that she hadn't been recognized. "Thank you for meeting with me."

With a curt nod, Miriam Kasdan gestured for Raegan to sit. "You actually caught me at the perfect time. I don't have to be at the children's museum until two o'clock."

"Wonderful." Raegan set her purse on the floor near her feet and her notebook on her lap. "This won't take long." She flipped to a blank page and pulled a pen from her bag. "I know your on-tape interview focused on all the wonderful things you're doing for the arts community in Portland."

"It did. We spoke at length about the Portland Ballet Company and where the company is heading."

"You've also done a lot to make the children's museum more accessible to the less fortunate in our city."

"I have." Mrs. Kasdan folded her hands on her lap, sitting up straight and proper. "I always wanted the children's museum to be a place for all of our city's youth, the privileged as well as the underprivileged."

"Can you speak a little about the things you're doing to open the museum up to at-risk children?"

"Of course. The board and I have been working with various charities to bus inner-city children to the museum. As you know, the museum sits up on the hill outside downtown. Not exactly easy to get to if a child lives on the east side. This summer we're also planning two one-week summer day camps, which will provide transportation for children to and from camp from the outlying areas."

She wasn't specifically mentioning the Children Are Our Future charity. Raegan bit her lip, choosing another approach. "Is this drive you have to help the less fortunate something that's specific to you, or do others in your family share the same passion?"

Mrs. Kasdan tipped her head. "I'm not sure what you mean."

Raegan shifted against the expensive fabric. "I mean, was community service work, specifically regarding the plight of children, something your husband cared deeply about before he passed?"

"Walter?" She considered a moment. "Walter cared about a great many things."

"And what about your son?"

Mrs. Kasdan's slate-gray eyes narrowed. "I thought this was a follow-up interview regarding my work with the arts."

"Oh, it is," Raegan covered quickly. "My director was just so impressed with your charity work that he asked me to get a more rounded picture about other things you're doing in the community. You and your family, that is."

"Hm." Mrs. Kasdan eyed her skeptically. "My son, Arnold, is a very busy man, but he believes in the power of giving back to the community. He always has."

Not what Raegan was hoping for. She scribbled the son's name for effect. "Are there any charities here in Portland that he's involved with?"

"I'm not su—"

The double doors pushed open, and Ms. Hennessy stuck her head in the room. "I'm sorry to interrupt, Mrs. Kasdan, but you have an important phone call."

"Who is it, Claire?"

"Tony. He says it's urgent."

Miriam Kasdan's jaw tightened. It was a very subtle move, but Raegan caught it.

Flashing Raegan a tight smile, Mrs. Kasdan rose. "I'm sorry. This will only take a moment."

The older woman moved toward the doors with hurried movements, her expensive heels tapping across the inlaid wood floor like nails being hammered into a coffin. Terse, hushed voices echoed from the hallway, followed by Mrs. Kasdan's heels clicking into silence.

Raegan's stomach rolled as she set her notebook on the table in front of her and stood. The interview was not going well. Mrs. Kasdan wasn't giving up anything, and worse, she was starting to grow suspicious.

Raegan scanned shelves for anything personal she could talk about to form a connection with the older woman and cut the tension. Maybe if she could get Mrs. Kasdan reminiscing or talking about family she would open up a little more.

Raegan moved through the room, professionally decorated with spendy furnishings and trinkets that looked as if they'd come straight from the pages of Pottery Barn. There were no personal photos on the shelves or the walls. None of the Kasdan family or Mrs. Kasdan's son. None even of Mrs. Kasdan's professed loves—the ballet company or the children's museum.

Raegan found that odd. If this were her home, she'd have pictures of Emma and Alec all over those shelves. Her heart rolled when she thought of Alec again, but she drew a breath and kept scanning. At the end of the library, she spotted a heavy wood door that made her stop.

Common sense told her Mrs. Kasdan would be back at any moment and that Raegan shouldn't snoop, but she was curious. Glancing over her shoulder toward the hallway, she waited and listened. No voices or footsteps echoed her way. Closing her hand around the knob, she twisted. To her surprise, the knob turned all the way, and the door pushed open.

A personal office sat before Raegan with a long cherry desk occupying the center of the room, the surface spotless but for a Tiffany lamp and gold pen. A plush chair was pushed up against the desk. Another wall of windows behind the desk looked out across yet another immaculate lawn, and on the far side of the room, a trio of chairs was grouped to form a sitting area. But what captured Raegan's attention hung on the walls. Over the fireplace and along both sides. Rows and rows of small black frames, each holding a heart-shaped scrap of fabric in a rainbow of different colors.

There were dozens of hearts. At least forty that she counted. Turning, she spotted more framed hearts on the walls near the windows, so many they made her blink as if she were seeing stars.

"I see you found my collection."

Raegan startled and glanced toward the door where Miriam Kasdan stood with a blank expression on her perfectly made-up face. "I-I'm sorry. I didn't mean to snoop. I just . . . I was looking for a restroom."

She winced because the excuse sounded lame to her own ears.

Mrs. Kasdan stepped into the office and glanced over the walls. "I suppose to an outsider it may seem silly. To me, though . . ." A look of profound pride spread across her features. "Some old women knit, others quilt. I find relaxation in framing objects I find beautiful."

Raegan wasn't sure about the beautiful comment, but as she looked to her right where a heart-shaped piece of faded, pinstriped denim sat on a small table, surrounded by several lengths of picture frame molding waiting to be snapped together, her stomach pitched because she realized these were more than just beautiful objects.

"It's . . . really amazing," Raegan said, fighting back the heat prickling her spine. All these hearts . . . All those missing kids . . . The image of that scrap of fabric Gilbert had left in the plastic bag on her porch flashed in front of her eyes. "H-how many hearts have you framed?"

"Fifty-eight, Ms. Devereaux."

Raegan froze.

Miriam Kasdan tipped her head. "That was the head of my security team on the phone, wondering why Raegan Devereaux, the mother in a high-profile missing-child's case, was caught on surveillance video entering my property."

Raegan slowly turned to face the woman. She was at least thirty years younger than Miriam Kasdan, but the woman outweighed her by a good twenty pounds, and blocking Raegan's only door of escape, the woman looked like someone who'd not slowed down at all in her later years.

Think, quickly. She had to get out of here before Miriam Kasdan knew what she suspected. "I . . . I lied about my name. I'm sorry for that. I didn't think you'd see me if you knew my real name, given that I no longer work for KTVP."

"I'm well aware you no longer work there." All pretense of friendliness fled Miriam Kasdan's voice. "What are you doing here, Ms. Devereaux?"

Sweat slicked Raegan's spine. If this woman knew she no longer worked at the station, and she knew about Emma's disappearance, lying wasn't going to work. The only play she had was to pull the mother card and hope Miriam Kasdan could empathize, considering she was a mother herself. "My daughter went missing three years ago. We looked everywhere for her but never found her."

"I remember hearing about your daughter's abduction on the news. I'm sorry for your loss. It has nothing to do with me, however."

The words were crisp and terse, and they made Raegan's stomach roll because she didn't believe them. "I know. And thank you. I apologize for bothering you like this, but I saw you at the station the other day, and after I got home, when I realized who you were, I thought"—*come on, lie to her*—"well, I thought someone like you, with such a high-profile status in the community and with all your charity work, might be able to help me out."

"Help you out," the woman said speculatively.

"Yes." Heat spread up Raegan's neck as she grabbed hold of the lie and ran with it. "Starting a charity. I want to start a charity to help families of missing children. Searching for a child is time-consuming and expensive. Not to mention emotionally taxing. Families in those situations need counseling, they need time off from their jobs, they need money to continue their search. Before I left KTVP I was looking into a case where a two-year-old disappeared from his yard, and I couldn't stop thinking about what the family was going through and how—"

"Why?"

The elaborate lie Raegan had concocted faltered on her tongue. "Excuse me?"

"Why are you continuing to look into cases that do not concern you? Especially when your job no longer requires you to do so?"

The question threw her. "B-because I know what those families are going through. They just want answers about their children."

"And you believe you're the person to provide those answers?"

"I don't know. Maybe. Someone needs to help them."

Mrs. Kasdan stared at Raegan for several moments, then again said, "Why?"

"I'm not sure I follow you."

"Why do those parents deserve answers? Oh, I follow the news too, Ms. Devereaux. I'm well aware that most of the children who disappear are either neglected or fall victim to their parents' selfish lifestyles. Drug addicts, immigrants, prostitutes . . . those kind of people don't deserve to have children if they can't take care of them, wouldn't you agree?"

That tremble of unease in Raegan's belly turned to a hard rolling wave as she watched Miriam Kasdan step toward the small table and run her pink manicured nails over the heart-shaped piece of denim. In that moment she knew for certain that it wasn't a beautiful object at all. It was a trophy, one that sent bile shooting up Raegan's esophagus.

"I—I don't understand what you mean," Raegan lied, knowing exactly what the woman meant. Her gaze flicked to the door behind Miriam Kasdan as she contemplated her exit route and how fast she could contact the police.

"And what about the children?" the woman went on as if Raegan hadn't even spoken. "What do they deserve? A life in squalor like their older siblings, nothing more to look forward to than the next gang fight down the road or learning to turn their own tricks? That's no life for a child." She lifted the pinstriped denim heart in her hand and caressed it as a mother caresses a child's hair. "If those children were given a second chance, if they were with families now who not only cared for them but who gave them the best of everything—the finest educations, summer trips abroad, a future of wealth and privilege—would you still want to help their selfish biological parents find them? Would you take away every opportunity they've been given to rise up from the ashes of poverty and sentence them back to a life of despair and hopelessness?" She pinned Raegan with a hard look. "I don't think you would."

"Yes, I would," Raegan said, fighting hard to stay in control and not give herself away. "Because those children still have parents and siblings and people who lo—"

"People who neglected them," Miriam Kasdan snapped, slapping the heart-shaped piece of fabric on the table. "I see their older siblings. I see those children come into my son's charity offices looking for a handout. His staff tries to partner them with mentors in the community, but by the time a child is nine or ten, it's too late. Their environment has shaped them as much as their DNA."

Anger exploded inside Raegan. She couldn't hold it back any longer. "So you, what? You steal their younger siblings? Child trafficking is a felony."

"I don't see it that way," Miriam Kasdan said calmly. "I see it as an act of heroism. I save children from horrible lives and even worse futures. Every single child I've helped is in a better place now because of me." She smirked and lifted her hand to point toward a frame on the wall. "Even that one."

Raegan turned to see what the woman was pointing at and focused on a white scrap with tiny pink hearts that she hadn't noticed before in the sea of framed hearts—the same fabric in the dress Emma had been wearing the day she'd disappeared.

The blood drained from Raegan's face, and her own heart felt as if it came to a stuttering stop in the middle of her chest. "No."

"Yes," Miriam Kasdan said with a smug grin. "Instead of judging me, you should thank me. I saved your daughter from that degenerate Gilbert, and I'd do it again if I had the chance."

———

Raegan wasn't in the apartment.

Alec walked out of her bedroom and into the living room, glancing around to see if she'd left her keys or cell phone in the hope she'd only run out for a minute and would soon be back. Both were missing, along with her purse.

He tugged his phone out of his pocket and checked to see if she'd texted or responded to his voice message. She hadn't.

"Damn."

He was just about to call her when the phone in his hand buzzed. Instead of Raegan's name, though, Bickam's flashed on the screen.

His heart rate sped up. A mixture of fear and dread spiraled through his stomach, and he thought of that whiskey again, but he knew he wouldn't reach for it no matter what he heard. With shaking fingers, he hit "Answer" and lifted the phone to his ear. "Yeah."

"McClane? It's Bickam. I was about to call Raegan but thought I'd let you know first. I'm looking at the lab report on that scrap of fabric you found on Raegan's patio."

"And?" He closed his eyes and focused on his breath. In, out. One lungful at a time.

"The blood isn't human."

Alec's eyes popped open. "What?"

"It's cow blood."

"What does that mean?"

"It means it's not your daughter's blood."

Hope wiggled between Alec's ribs like arcing bolts of lightning electrifying his heart. "The bones in the mountains. Have you—"

"We don't have any answers for you there. We still can't say if they're male or female. Boys and girls that young are structurally the same."

Alec knew that. Bickam had told him the same last night. But then Alec had been so sure those remains belonged to Emma, he'd barely listened. Now . . .

Now knowing that the blood hadn't been hers, he realized it was highly likely Gilbert had been fucking with him the same way Gilbert had always fucked with him. The bastard had wanted a reaction to the bloody fabric, and when he hadn't gotten it from Alec, it was only then that he'd given up the location of those remains.

Alec's heart beat even harder when he thought about how many kids wore Converse shoes. They were wildly popular, and they were unisex. He also realized if Gilbert was involved in some kind of child-abduction ring as Charlene had claimed, those remains could belong to any child.

He didn't want to think of another child suffering, but he couldn't stop that hope inside from twining around his heart to give him strength. "When will you know . . . if it's Emma?"

"A week. Maybe two. I've put a rush on the DNA tests, but it will depend on how backed up the lab is. Is Raegan with you or should I call her to give her this info—"

Alec didn't hear the rest of what Bickam had to say. He hit "End" and dialed Raegan's number. He needed to talk to her. Needed to tell her the news himself. Needed to tell her he was a fool and beg her not to give up on him.

Her phone rang over and over, then finally clicked over to voice mail. "Son of a bitch." Why wasn't she answering?

"Raegan, it's Alec again. It's important. I need you to call me right away." Frustrated, he hit "End." Looked around the apartment. Tried to figure out where she could have gone. She'd quit her job at the station. She clearly wasn't with Bickam. She didn't have any family in the area. Since he hadn't spent more than a week with her recently, he didn't even know who her friends were now.

His gut told him someone at KTVP might know who she socialized with. She'd mentioned a girl bringing her home the other night after she'd been attacked in that alley. Ashley, Amy . . . no, Anna.

He moved for the front door. The phone in the kitchen rang, stopping his feet. Hope burst inside Alec as he shoved his cell into his pocket and jogged across the room.

"Raegan?"

"No, it's Hunt. That you, Alec?"

Shit. "Yeah." Alec glanced toward the front door, fighting the urge to hang up on his friend so he could search for Raegan. "It's me."

"Okay, then." Surprise rippled through Hunt's voice. "Can I talk to Raegan?"

Confusion pulled Alec's brows together because there was no reason for Hunt to call Raegan. The two had never been what anyone would consider friends, mostly because Hunt thought Raegan was the reason his addiction had gotten the best of him. "What's going on? Why are you calling her?"

"Because I'm not a dick like you."

Alec winced. He deserved that. Raegan had definitely talked to Hunt this morning. "Point taken. Thanks for checking on her."

"I tried to call you several times earlier, dumbass, but you didn't answer. Are you drunk?"

"No." Alec raked a hand through his hair, irritated they were having this conversation when all he wanted to do was find Raegan. "I haven't been drinking."

"Are you lying to me? I'll find out if you are. You're a shitty liar, you know."

"I'm not lying." Alec braced his hand on the granite counter. "Look, I went to a bar. I ordered a drink. I didn't drink it."

"Not at all?"

"Not even a drop. I'm not going back there. What did Raegan say to you this morning?"

"She said you were a dick. A little tiny one, just like the one in your pants."

Alec frowned. "I get it. Move on already."

"Gladly. Since you finally pulled your head out of your ass, I'll tell you what I called to tell her. I have some financial info on Gilbert. She and I discussed checking into it this morning and seeing if we could trace who Gilbert was working for before you got sent to juvie."

Alec's pulse sped up. While he'd been wallowing in his pain, Raegan had been strategizing and fighting and never once giving up on their daughter, just like always. Awe rippled through him. Awe and love. "What did you find?"

"Some interesting shit. Before Gilbert was sent to prison eighteen years ago, he was receiving payments from Rightways Trucking."

"I'm not following you. He drove a truck. We know that."

"Yeah, but Rightways Trucking is a subsidiary of BLK Conglomerates, the same company that manages the Children Are Our Future charity. The same charity Conner Murray was connected to."

"How?"

"Not totally sure yet. Arnold Kasdan is the CEO of BLK. I told Raegan about a picture I found of Kasdan with Murray in front of the children's museum here in Portland. I can't find any payments to Murray via BLK, but the secretary I talked to at the CAOF charity office remembers seeing Murray in their building at least once a month. She said she thought he was a volunteer, but there are too many coincidences here for that. I'd bet you money Kasdan was the mastermind behind the whole thing. Murray was probably his contact with the families. A social worker like Murray would know where those kids would be at what times. Gilbert, I'm guessing, was the one who handled the pickups and drop-offs."

Alec's stomach twisted as he pushed away from the counter. Hunt was talking about abductions. Gilbert was the one who'd kidnapped those unsuspecting kids and hauled them away. "I need you to get this information to Jack Bickam at the FBI."

"I will. I wanted to tell Raegan not to go meet with Miriam Kasdan first, though."

"What?"

"Tell her not to go. The FBI will have enough information here to question Arnold Kasdan about Gilbert and this whole thing. We don't want to tip him off or give him a reason to run. I can't seem to locate the guy, so I don't know if he's here in Portland or halfway around the globe."

"Slow down. You're confusing me. Who is Miriam Kasdan?"

Hunt sighed. "Arnold Kasdan's mother. She lives here in Portland. Raegan was going to meet with her this morning to feel her out."

The blood drained from Alec's face as a new fear rushed through him. "Oh shit."

"What?"

Alec glanced around the empty apartment. "Raegan's not here."

"She already left?"

He pulled his cell from his pocket and stared at the blank screen. "And she's not answering either of our calls."

CHAPTER NINETEEN

Raegan rounded on Miriam Kasdan and only barely held back from strangling the woman. "Tell me what happened."

The older woman folded her hands in front of her and moved back to stand in the doorway, blocking Raegan's exit from the office. "Your daughter was not the type of child we normally rescue—no older siblings, educated and successful parents—but one of our couriers picked her up by mistake."

"A courier," Raegan repeated as she stared at the older woman, disbelief swirling like a tornado in her gut. "You mean John Gilbert. We both know he didn't take her by mistake."

"Yes. Gilbert." Kasdan's lips turned down in disgust. "He was adept at moving inventory, but he was a liability when it came to his personal life."

The woman was speaking about these children as if they were objects rather than living, breathing people. Sickness swirled along with the disgust inside Raegan.

"Unfortunately for you," Kasdan went on, "Mr. Gilbert's personal affairs were intertwined with your husband's. By the time I learned what Gilbert had done, it was too late to correct the error. The repercussions would have been innumerable. Then I looked into your husband's background, and, well, I knew the child was better off being relocated."

"What do you mean better off?" Raegan snapped. "She's not better off anywhere but with me."

"Oh, but she is. You see, with her new family, there is never any threat of John Gilbert touching her ever again. You know how dangerous that man can be. Look at the bruises on your face, Ms. Devereaux. Is he the sort of man you'd allow near a young, vulnerable child? Imagine what he would have done to that poor girl had I not stepped in to save her."

A new wave of understanding hit Raegan as she lifted her hand to the yellowing spots near her temple. "Did you hire him to make me back off these cases?"

Mrs. Kasdan pursed her lips. "A very unpredictable man indeed. I hear he was involved in a car accident last night." She glanced down at her manicure. "Knowing him, he'll likely survive. Pity, isn't it? Your daughter is still not safe."

The last of Raegan's patience erupted in a fury that colored everything red. Her hand closed into a fist at her side as she stepped toward Miriam Kasdan. "Where is my daughter?"

"Careful, Ms. Devereaux. If you harm me in any way, you'll never find your daughter. If, on the other hand, you agree to cooperate, I can take you to her."

Raegan's heart stuttered, drawing her up short. "What does 'cooperate' mean?"

"It means exactly what you think it means. You agree never to speak of what you know to anyone. In exchange for your silence, I'll give you your daughter. All you have to do then is leave the country. I have powerful friends, Ms. Devereaux. We can give you new names, new identities. Say the word, and you can both have the same new start I've given dozens of children."

"Disappear." Raegan's gaze skipped over the framed hearts on the walls. The woman wanted her to disappear just as those children had disappeared.

"Disappear with means. There's a big difference. Come, now. If you love your daughter the way you say you do, you'd want her safe from the likes of John Gilbert, and we both know so long as Gilbert is alive, she will never truly be safe. His need for revenge is never-ending. He will use your daughter however he can to get that revenge."

Raegan's mind swam. Could this be real? Could this woman really take her to Emma? She looked back at Miriam Kasdan. "W-what about her father?"

"Mr. McClane? Isn't he an alcoholic?"

"He's been sober almost three years."

"That's not what my sources tell me."

Raegan's eyes narrowed. "What do you mean?"

"My sources informed me that he was seen just this morning entering a tavern on the west side. He stayed there for over an hour. What does one do in a tavern in the morning besides drink, Ms. Devereaux?"

Raegan's heart cinched down hard. No, she wouldn't believe that. She knew Alec had been upset last night when the FBI had dug up those remains, but he'd told her he didn't want to drink. He'd told her he'd never spiral back to that dark place he'd been in before.

Except . . . he'd also told her that every day was a struggle and that he would always be an addict. And he hadn't come home last night. Swallowing hard, she realized that he could have very well gone to that bar. He could have been drinking. He could be drunk right now.

Her pulse beat hard, picking up speed until it was a roar in her ears, but not because she was afraid of where he was or what he could be doing right this minute. It raced because she loved him, for better or worse. That's what she'd said. That's what she'd meant. She wasn't going to walk away from him now or ever. And she wouldn't let him push her away again either.

She met Miriam Kasdan's emotionless stare with very focused eyes. "I don't care."

"Well, I do." The older woman's jaw tightened, and for the first time since she'd admitted to her horrendous crimes, Raegan saw a glimmer of anger. "I've thoroughly vetted each family. No parents addicted to any kind of vices will ever be approved for relocation. You might turn a blind eye to the reality that your *ex*-husband is a stinking drunk, but I won't. If you want this new start with your daughter, Ms. Devereaux, you'll have to take it without him. Choose now."

Raegan's mind skipped with what-ifs. But before the first even registered, she found her answer in the other woman's steely gaze.

There was no choice. Miriam Kasdan was never going to take Raegan to Emma. She was going to con Raegan into leaving this mansion with her, and then she was going to get rid of Raegan, probably the same way she'd gotten rid of Conner Murray.

Instinct curled in her belly. An instinct that made her abandon any plan of running and told her she was dead if she tried to leave this room. An instinct that also told her the answer to her daughter's whereabouts could be found here. In Miriam Kasdan's personal office where the woman flaunted her trophies of children stolen and sold.

"Okay."

The older woman lifted her perfectly threaded brows.

Raegan nodded. "I'll go with you. I need my Emma. That's all that matters."

"More than your husband?"

"Yes. More than . . . Alec," she lied. "If he was in a bar today, I've already lost him. I can't lose Emma again."

Miriam Kasdan studied Raegan speculatively, then slowly nodded. "Wise choice. Follow me. My associate is waiting to take you to your daughter."

Raegan waited until the woman's back was turned, then she reached for the lamp from the edge of the desk and jerked the cord from the wall.

"What on ear—"

Miriam Kasdan only made it halfway back around before Raegan slammed the base of the lamp into the side of her head. The older woman's body sailed sideways, hit the doorjamb, and slumped to the ground.

Raegan's head came up, and she stilled, listening for the secretary or anyone who'd heard what she'd just done. When only silence met her ears, she set the broken lamp down, stepped over Kasdan's limp legs, and grasped the woman by the arms to pull her all the way into the room.

Her hands shook as she dropped the motionless woman on the floor behind the desk, stepped over her once more to pull the office door closed, and locked it. No guilt consumed her as she checked Kasdan's pulse. Death was too simple for this woman. Raegan wanted her to suffer. In prison for the rest of her life, surrounded by all the same unsavory people she believed didn't deserve a child. Finding the woman's pulse slow but steady, she rose and scanned the office for a phone but couldn't see one.

Damn. Hers was in her car. She didn't have time to look for a phone. She only had minutes before someone came looking for the bitch.

She yanked drawers in the desk open one by one, knowing there had to be files somewhere. All she found was computer cords, pens, cardstock, and a small key.

Shoving the last drawer closed, she looked around again. Fear grabbed hold of her throat and squeezed. There were no file cabinets in the room. There was no computer. Only the desk, sitting area, the fireplace, and a row of shelves. No place even to store files.

Her stomach twisted as she zeroed in on the shelves. Moving quickly across the room, she scanned titles. Most of the books were paperbacks. Romance novels. Mysteries. Not classic leather tomes like the ones she'd seen in the library. These, obviously, were Miriam Kasdan's personal books. Lifting her hand, Raegan pulled a stack from the shelf and flipped through each one.

Just normal, publisher-produced paperbacks. No notes crammed inside, no photos, nothing.

Dropping them on the floor, she reached for another stack. And another. In a matter of minutes she had the entire shelving unit stripped of books. Stepping back, her hands shaking from defeat, she stared at the empty bookcase. And realized . . .

The section of shelving three rows up on the right looked different from the others.

She jerked forward and narrowed her gaze on the wood one shade darker than the rest of the unit. Lifting her hand, she ran her fingers over the back until they passed over a keyhole. One you'd never find unless you knew it was there because it was camouflaged to look like the rest of the wood.

Keys . . .

She whipped back to the desk, jerked the top drawer open, and grasped the key she'd found earlier. Pulse thundering, she rushed back to the shelf, slipped the key into the hole, and turned.

A click sounded in the silent room, but Raegan's pulse pounding as loud as a marching band was all she could hear. The false backing popped open. She shoved it aside and stared at a stack of files in the hidden safe.

Her fingers shook as she yanked them out and scanned the file tabs. No names, just numbers. She flipped open the top file. "William" was printed at the top of the first page.

She set the folder on a shelf, reached for another. Multiple first names. No last names. "Jacob." "Linda." "Sally." She stopped when she came across the name "David." She shuffled through folders until she found the name "Mary."

Billy Willig, David Ramirez, and Mary Coleman. The three missing children whose parents she and Alec had interviewed this past week.

Breathing faster, she flipped through files frantically until she located the one she'd been hoping for.

"Emma."

Her lungs constricted. She tore open the folder and stared down at the background information typed neatly on the white sheet.

Her name. Alec's. Their addresses. Names of each of their parents and siblings. Under Raegan's father's name, the words "Wealthy but not a threat. Estranged from daughter" were typed neatly as if it were part of her description.

Raegan's heart thundered as she flipped page after page outlining Gilbert's connection to Alec and Alec's stint in rehab, what the McClanes each did for a living, and how their association with Alec might cause trouble. The last page was headed by the word "Relocation."

She jerked the page out, dropped the file on top of the others, and frantically scanned the words. Emma's name wasn't listed anywhere on the page, but another name was.

"Emily Waldorf."

There was also an address. An Oregon address in a wealthy area outside the city of Sherwood.

Sherwood . . . Conner Murray had been killed when his car had gone over an embankment on a windy road near Sherwood.

Voices echoed beyond the doors in the library, jolting Raegan's attention from the page. The door on the far side of the room rattled.

"Mrs. Kasdan?"

Fear spread like ice through Raegan's veins. Shoving the paper into her coat pocket, she looked around for an escape. There was no door. Only windows. All probably connected to a central alarm.

The doors shook harder, and the voices outside doubled and grew louder.

Raegan's gaze shot back to the windows. She had only one way out, and she was taking it.

———

Alec pounded his fist on the door of Miriam Kasdan's mansion for the third time, frustration curling like fire in his gut because they were being ignored.

"Raegan's car's not here, man," Hunt said beside him, glancing over the immaculate lawn. "Maybe she stopped somewhere before her appointment. Or maybe she's already been here and left."

The already-been-here-and-left part was what worried Alec. "She'd answer her phone if that were the case." Turning, he skipped over the steps and headed down the drive.

"Where are you going?"

"Around back. To see if someone left a door open."

"That's breaking and entering."

"Only if someone catches me."

Hunt muttered curses as he hustled to catch up. They followed a paved road around the side of the house. A long carpet of green lawn spread out from the house down the hillside. To the right, a raised verandah was framed by a concrete balustrade, and to the left, three cars were parked behind a large detached six-vehicle garage—a shiny silver Rolls-Royce convertible, a sleek black Jaguar, and a twenty-year-old blue van with a dented front end.

"Shit," Alec muttered quietly, eyeing the van. "Didn't you say cops found blue paint on Murray's vehicle at the accident scene?"

"Yeah, I did." The side door on the garage opened, and Hunt pressed a hand against Alec's arm, shoving him back into the rhododendron bushes. "Someone's coming."

Two burly-looking men exited the garage. One held a cell phone to his ear. It was hard to hear over the distance, but Alec was sure the guy said, "Yeah. We're on it. I'll call when it's done."

They watched as the two men climbed into the van. The engine revved. Seconds later they swept past Alec and Hunt in the bushes and turned down the long, curved lane toward the road.

Alec glanced toward his friend. "When it's done?"

Unease drifted over Hunt's usually congenial features. He pulled the .45 he carried at the small of his back from its holster. "I don't like the sound of that."

Alec didn't like it either. Worry curled through his chest as they moved around the back of the house and up onto the raised patio. Broken glass lay shattered across the decorative concrete.

Alec's heart jumped into his throat, and he rushed to the broken window and peered inside what looked to be an office. The gap in the window was large enough for a person to climb through. Tucking his hand into the sleeve of his coat, he broke a large piece of glass aside to make the gap bigger, then climbed through the opening and stared at the dozens of file folders and paperbacks scattered across the floor.

Hunt was breathless when he reached Alec. "Okay, now we're really breaking and entering."

Alec knelt for the closest folder and opened it. Names and addresses, birthdates, and work histories. He flipped pages, unsure what he was seeing. He came across what looked like a contract, and behind it, a receipt of sale.

"What is that?" Hunt asked.

"I don't know." Alec kept flipping pages. The second-to-last page looked like a return receipt, but he couldn't tell for what. His fingers stilled on the last page. No name was listed, just a date. And below that a stamp that read "Deceased."

"Holy shit," Hunt muttered. "Is that what I think it is?"

"I—I don't know." Sickness churned in Alec's stomach as he knelt and lifted another folder. Flipping to the back he found another date, followed by a name and address.

"It's in here," a woman's voice echoed from beyond a door slightly ajar across the room. Alec and Hunt both looked up. The door pushed open just as Hunt raised his gun. "We have to get this cleaned up before someo—"

The elderly woman with salt-and-pepper hair wild around her bruised face and a wrinkled suit jolted when she spotted them. "Oh my goodness." She pressed a hand to her heart. "Who are you? How did you get in here? Ms. Hennessy, call the police. We've been burgled."

The blonde just behind the older woman stepped back with wide eyes. Hunt shifted the gun her way and muttered, "Uh-uh. Stay right here."

The blonde froze.

Fear filled the older woman's slate-gray eyes, but the emotion was quickly masked by a wave of rage that made her whole face red. Almost as red as the blood trickling down her temple. "You can't just waltz into my home. Do you have any idea who I am? The police are already on their way."

Alec's blood pumped hot as he stepped over the paperbacks and lifted the folder in his hand. "Good. I'm sure they'll be more than interested in this, Mrs. Kasdan. Where is my daughter?"

Every inch of color drained from Miriam Kasdan's face as she glanced from the file in his hand up to his eyes. "Y-your daughter?"

"And my wife. I know she was here this morning."

Kasdan glanced toward the gun Hunt held, pointed right at her. "I—I don't know what you're—"

The phone in Alec's pocket buzzed. He whipped it out, a burst of relief rushing through him when he saw Raegan's name on the screen. "Raegs, where are you?"

"Alec, listen to me." Her voice was distant, as if she were talking into a speaker. "It's Miriam Kasdan. The charity socialite. She's the one behind the whole thing. She took those kids and—"

"I know. I'm standing in her office right now. Raegan, where are you?"

"I'm going to get Emma before they move her. She's in Sherwood, Alec. 49273 Ridgeview Lan—" Her voice cut off with a muffled scream.

"Raegan?" Fear clamped hard around Alec's throat. "Raegan?" he asked again when she didn't answer. "Raegan!"

The line went dead.

"What happened?" Hunt asked, gun still trained on the two women.

Wide-eyed, Alec looked up at his friend, remembering the two thugs they'd spotted jumping into that blue van and tearing off down the drive.

"I have to go." Urgency spurred him back toward the broken window. "I have to get to Raegan before it's too late."

"Go." Hunt pulled a cell from his pocket and dialed with one hand. "I've got this." He lifted the phone to his ear. "Yeah, I need to speak with Special Agent Jack Bickam immediately."

CHAPTER TWENTY

Raegan swerved on the two-lane road that wound up through the hills above Sherwood. The blue van had come out of nowhere and slammed into her from behind, the force of the hit shooting her forward and sending the cell phone in her hand flying across the car.

She gasped, gripped the wheel tighter, and pressed on the gas to take the next turn as her adrenaline surged. The neighborhoods on her left disappeared. Now all she could see were thick trees on both sides of the road. One glance in the rearview told her the older van couldn't keep up with her Audi. It had dropped back, but she knew she hadn't lost whoever was in it. If she didn't get to Emma first, they would. And if that happened, she knew she'd never find her daughter.

Flooring it, she swerved around corners, holding on tightly so she didn't lose control. Her heart pounded hard. Her palms grew damp against the steering wheel. The car banked to the left. Ahead she spotted a paved drive, blocked by a wrought-iron gate. The stone address marker read "49273."

She slammed on the brakes, swerving off the road onto the gravel shoulder. Shoving the car into park, she threw the door open and jumped out. Her muscles contracted as she raced toward the arced metal gate, flanked on both sides by two towering stone columns topped with decorative lights.

There was no time to buzz the intercom. Heart in her throat, she grasped the top of the gate at its lowest point, stepped up on the bottom rung, and pulled herself up. Metal cut into her hands. Her knee cracked against the top of the gate as she threw herself over. Her body sailed through the air as she dropped down the other side and landed hard against the concrete.

The sound of an engine revving echoed on the road. She stepped back. Then turned and ran.

The drive dropped down to the left and curved to the right. Her feet pounded hard against the concrete as she ran downhill, trying not to stumble and fall. At the bottom of the drive, she spotted a giant, contemporary mansion set on a cliff overlooking a sea of trees. Pushing her muscles harder, she raced toward the portico and rushed up the three elongated steps to the twelve-foot, ornate, double wood front doors.

She pounded her fist against the doors and yelled, "Hello?" Not waiting for an answer, she grabbed the iron handle and pressed down on the latch, but the door was locked. Slamming her hand against the door again, she hollered, "Hello? Is anyone in there?"

A rush of heavy footsteps sounded on the driveway. Whipping around, Raegan spotted two burly men in black racing toward her. Her eyes flew wide. She let go of the door and ran back down the steps, sprinting around the side of the three-car garage.

A flat concrete pad spread out behind the garage. Three steps led up to a back door. She jiggled the doorknob, only to find it locked. Jumping off the landing, she followed more elongated steps down the side of the house. Her pulse roared as she hustled to the bottom level. A staircase swept up to a deck that ran all along the back of the main level of the house. She paused to catch her breath and scanned the deck. There would be nowhere to hide up there. Heart thundering, she rushed underneath to the patio below.

The patio at the lowest level gave way to another deck that arced out over the cliff. No lights shone down here, and even in the middle of the day, with the trees all around blocking the daylight, it was hard to see. Her feet skidded to a stop just before she went sailing through a giant octagonal-shaped hole in the decking.

She jerked back several steps and gasped. The wood around the hole was fresh, unstained, as if it had been recently laid in preparation for a hot tub. Raegan scanned the railing on the far side, realizing there was nowhere here to hide either. She turned to go back the way she'd come when a voice shouted from the deck above.

Her heart shot into her throat as she froze and looked up. She strained to listen, but all she could hear was her pounding heartbeat. And then . . .

At her back, footsteps shuffled just before another voice chuckled close.

"There you are," a man said behind her. "Feisty, aren't you?"

Raegan swallowed a scream and whipped around. She couldn't see more than a silhouette, but she knew the man was big, at least six three and over two hundred pounds. Panic built in her chest, making her skin prickle and her breaths shallow. She glanced to the right and left, only to find she was trapped.

The man moved toward her. "Come on, now. You've had your fun. It's time to go."

Defiance rose up inside Raegan. She wasn't leaving. Not without her daughter. Swiveling away, she ran. The man behind her swore and sprinted after her. His hand darted out, grazing her elbow. Pushing her muscles as hard as she could, she jumped and prayed he didn't jump with her. A grunt sounded at her back as she flew through the air, followed by a strangled scream and, finally, a thud.

Raegan's body slammed into the wrought-iron railing. The air whooshed out of her lungs as she gripped the banister tightly, holding on as she looked over the cliff. The man sailed through the hole in the decking and hit the rocks far below.

Gasping, Raegan stumbled back from the railing and turned before she fell through the hole too. But she didn't have more than a moment to catch her breath. A shout echoed on the verandah above, followed by the rush of footsteps. Her adrenaline spiked all over again, and she knew she had only a split second before the other thug found her. Looking across the deck, she spotted French doors on the house. She quickly rounded the hole, raced forward, and grasped the door handle, praying it had been left unlocked. The knob turned in her palm.

Relief sparked in her veins like a live wire. She stumbled inside the house, whipped around, and locked the door. Stepping back, she looked up and around. The game room was decked out with a giant TV along one wall and a bar along another. An archway past the bar opened to another room. To her left she spotted stairs that ran up to the main level.

She bolted toward the stairs, grasped the railing, and used it to help pull herself up. The stairs curved up to the right. Skipping steps, she rushed up to the main level and screamed, "Emma!"

No answer met her ears. No voices. She sprinted through rooms on the main level, searching. "Emma!" The elaborate kitchen opened to an enormous great room. Still no voices, no sounds met her ears, nothing to indicate anyone was home. "Emma!"

Fear tightened her throat as she checked one room after another—formal dining room, office, library, guest room—finding each empty and silent. In the marble entry, she scrambled up the ostentatious curved staircase and hurried across the bridge flanked by railings that looked over the entry on one side and the great room on the other. A whir sounded near her ear, followed by a thwack in the Sheetrock to her right.

Raegan's eyes grew wide as she jerked forward, twisting around to see a hole where a bullet had torn through the wall. Her adrenaline surged. One glance over the side confirmed the man she'd heard outside had found a way in. In the center of the great room below, he lifted the gun again and pointed it right at her.

Another whir sounded. She yelped and threw herself around a corner.

"Little bitch," the man yelled. His footsteps pounded against the marble in the entryway. "Come back here."

Fear closed like a noose around Raegan's throat. She lurched forward and raced down the hall, searching for a place to hide. A set of double doors at the end of the hall sat open. She rushed inside, turned, and slammed the doors closed behind her. Pulse thundering, she flipped the lock with shaking hands and stumbled back.

"Where did you go?" the man hollered. "You can't hide from me! I'm not going back empty-handed."

Sweat beaded on Raegan's brow as she backed farther into the room. The lock wouldn't hold him for long. She was trapped unless she found another way out. Turning, she quickly scanned the master bedroom. A wall of curved windows looked out over the trees. A massive bed sat against the far wall. She spotted doors to her left, and turned that way only to discover a closet. Panic built in her chest, making her body shake. He'd look there first. Whipping around, she lurched for the massive bathroom. A huge glass-enclosed shower took up one whole corner. A raised whirlpool tub sat in front of an arched window. Frantic for something—anything—to camouflage her, she dashed across the marble tiles, ready to climb inside a cabinet if she had to, when she spotted an open door off the bathroom that led to another room.

Exercise equipment surrounded her. There was nowhere to hide in here. But on the far side of that . . .

. . . a back staircase that led down. Relief pushed her a step forward.

Wood splintered and cracked in the bedroom, pulling a yelp from Raegan's throat.

"I know you're in here, bitch."

Fear stabbed through Raegan with the force of a thousand daggers, and she jolted forward, racing around a stationary bicycle and treadmill toward the staircase on the far side.

A whir sounded just as she reached the top step. The decorative molding just to the left of her head exploded in a burst of fragmented wood.

Raegan screamed and lost her footing. Her body cracked against the wall and dropped to the stairs. Pain shot into her shoulder and across her back as she tumbled end over end. Her face smacked into the steps, the staircase spun around her. She grappled for the railing to stop herself, but her fingers only grazed the spindles as the force of her body pulled her down two flights of curved steps to the bottom level of the house.

The back of her head cracked against a marble floor. Something warm and wet trickled down her temple. Groaning at the pain stabbing into every inch of her body, she shifted her hands beneath her and tried to push herself up, but her arms ached and didn't seem to be working. The sharp scent of pool chemicals filled her nostrils. Struggling to see where she was, she lifted her head and looked around, but the room was spinning, and the black dots in her vision made it hard to focus.

Footsteps pounded somewhere above, bringing her focus around. Fear surged inside her again, but her energy lagged, and she struggled to stand. Grunting, she finally managed to reach her feet, but her head felt light, and she swayed. She grappled for the wall and stumbled back. A voice echoed in the stairwell. Followed by a curse and a shout.

No, she realized, squinting up the stairs, shaking her head to get rid of the spots. Not one voice but two.

Another crack sounded, but this one was different. It wasn't the sharp thwack of a bullet digging into wood. It was more dull, like a fist hitting flesh and bone. Like—

A series of thuds echoed down the stairwell, and Raegan had a split second to jerk backward before two tangled bodies hit the marble floor and rolled, fists flying.

Shaking, Raegan scrambled back from the stairs, out of the way. The man who'd shot at her landed on his back with a grunt and threw a right hook up. Raegan yelped as his big fist slammed into another man's face above, and she flattened herself against the wall, praying they hadn't spotted her. Blond hair whipped through the air as the second man's head snapped to the side, but just before Raegan turned to run, her eyes caught the shape of the man's jaw and nose and the curve of his neck. And in a heartbeat of horror she realized that the second man wasn't another thug chasing after her. It was Alec.

"Alec!" she screamed, her eyes growing wide.

Alec grunted, bared his teeth, and shoved his forearm hard against the man's throat. The man gasped and struggled against the hold, face red, muscles straining. Alec only glared down at him with wild eyes. "Son of a bitch. You're fucking done."

The man grunted and threw his weight to the side, dislodging Alec's arm and shoving him over to his back.

Raegan screamed, paralyzed against the wall with fear as she watched them roll across the floor again. Out of the corner of her eye, she spotted the thug's gun on the ground at the base of the stairs, a silencer screwed on to the end.

A rush of adrenaline pushed her forward, and she scrambled for the gun. Her hand closed around the hilt just as a splash sounded. Looking up, she fumbled with the gun and caught sight of Alec wrestling with the other man in the rectangular lap pool. The man got the upper hand and threw his weight onto Alec, forcing him under the water. Alec sputtered and splashed. Fear sucked all the air out of Raegan's lungs as she watched the hulking man holding Alec under.

He was going to kill Alec if she didn't do something fast. Hands shaking, she lifted the gun and pointed, praying she was aiming in the right direction, that Alec wouldn't pop up out of the water too soon, that there were still bullets in the chamber to fire.

Sucking in one last breath, she pulled the trigger.

The gun recoiled in her hands, thrusting her back. She gripped the gun tightly so she wouldn't drop it. A whir sounded, followed by a thwack. Her spine hit the wall, and she scrambled to keep from falling over. The man jerked back in the water and went under. A split second later, Alec broke the surface and stumbled to the wall of the pool, gasping for air. Waves sloshed onto the travertine tile and ricocheted back.

The gun in Raegan's hands shook as her arms dropped to her sides, but her adrenaline was still pumping, and the fear was still real, tightening around her throat, keeping her from being able to think or speak or move. Her legs wobbled.

Alec's head turned her way, and his gaze found hers. "Raegs." Brushing the water out of his face, he slogged through the pool and up the steps.

His arms closed around her before she hit the ground. In a daze, she was aware of his wet body pressing against her, of his hands carefully taking the gun from her trembling fingers, of his strength pulling her in and holding her up. But she still couldn't speak. Couldn't do anything but hold on.

"I've got you," he whispered. "You're okay. I've got you."

A tremble rushed through her, and she knew it was the adrenaline crashing, but she couldn't stop it from happening. "I . . ."

"You're okay." He held on even tighter, one arm locked around her waist, the other at her shoulder blades, his warm, wide hand threading into her hair to cradle the back of her head. "I've got you," he said again, almost as if he needed to reassure himself of that fact, not her.

Her cheek pressed against his damp shoulder. She closed her eyes and breathed through her nose, trying to ease the shakes. The instant her eyes were shut, though, a hundred different emotions pummeled her chest, the strongest of which was terror.

"I thought . . ." She curled her fingers into the back of his wet shirt and clung to him. "I thought he was going to kill you."

"He didn't." He rocked her gently, his heartbeat just as fast and erratic as hers. "I'm okay. You're okay. Scared the shit out of me, though, when I came inside, saw those bullet holes and heard you scream. I thought . . ." His voice trailed off, and a shudder rushed through him, but he only held her tighter.

Her fingers tightened in his dripping shirt. "I should have waited for you, but . . ." Feeling a little steadier, she drew back and looked up at him. Water ran from his hair down the side of his handsome face, making her heart pinch because . . . he'd come after her. He'd saved her life. And she'd failed.

Her stomach dropped, and tears welled in her eyes. "I was afraid if they got here first they'd take her. She's not here, though. No one's home, and I don't know where she is."

"It's okay." He brushed the hair away from her temple and tipped her face up so her eyes met his. "We'll find her, Raegan. The FBI is on their way, and Hunt's not letting Kasdan out of his sight until the cops get to her place. I saw the files. They can't hide Emma from us anymore. It's over. We'll find her. I promise we'll find her."

She swallowed the dread threatening to consume her and sank against him, hoping and praying he was right. But the fear didn't seem to want to let go, and she felt as if the fight was being sucked right out of her, draining her of energy, of strength, even of hope.

Alec's arms closed around her once more, pulling her in. She sank against him and turned to press her cheek to his wet chest as she just tried to breathe, as she told herself this wasn't the end. Emma was out there somewhere. They had proof now that she was alive. They were going to find her. Her gaze drifted across the pool area and landed on the man who'd attacked her. His big body floated facedown in a sea of red water.

"Oh my God." Sickness welled in her stomach at the sight, and she closed her eyes quickly, turning her face against Alec's shirt.

He stilled, muttered, "Shit," and shifted so he was between her and the pool. "Don't look."

Voices echoed somewhere in the house. Raegan heard them but couldn't turn to look. She was too fixed on not losing the contents of her stomach.

"Down here!" Alec hollered, massaging his fingers against the back of her head while she just tried to breathe.

Footsteps echoed in a nearby room—many—followed by shuffling and the sounds of cloth rustling.

"Damn." Bickam. That was Jack Bickam's voice somewhere close. "You two okay?"

"Yeah," Alec said, still rubbing the back of Raegan's head. "We're okay. Just a little banged up."

"Raegan," Bickam said gently. "Can you talk?"

Swallowing hard, Raegan lifted her head and looked to her left where Jack Bickam stood nearby, his face filled with concern. Behind him, several people moved into the room, talking quietly as they stepped toward the pool. "I-I'm okay. H-he chased me through the house. I tried to run, but he had Alec in the pool, was holding him under the water. I grabbed his gun from the ground. I just wanted him to let Alec go. I—"

"Sh," Bickam said in a soothing voice. "It's okay. We'll work it all out." He looked to Alec. "You see anybody else?"

"No."

"There was another one." Raegan swallowed hard, fighting back the image of that body hitting the rocks. "H-he chased after me outside. He went over the cliff."

Bickam smirked. "You took down two attackers? I may need to recruit you for the FBI."

Alec chuckled against her, but Raegan didn't find any of it funny. She was too busy trying to get the images of those men out of her head.

Voices picked up in the room. Alec and Bickam spoke quietly about what had just happened, but all Raegan could think about was her daughter. "Jack," she said, interrupting them. "Emma's not here. She's not here and—"

"Don't worry," he answered, pulling a notebook from his pocket. "We'll find her. The owners of this house are Rob and Jennifer Waldorf. He's in finance, and she's an interior decorator. We ran a check on them after O'Donnell called from Kasdan's place. They reported a private adoption about three and a half years ago. A little girl." He shoved the notebook back in his pocket. "I've already got officers on the way to both their places of work. It's the middle of the day. Assuming Kasdan didn't tip them off after you left her, Raegan, that little girl is probably in a day care or preschool right this minute."

Alec looked down at her and said, "See?"

Hope burned a path of fire through Raegan's belly, giving her strength. She was almost too afraid to grasp it. "And what if Kasdan tipped them off?"

"They won't get far. I've issued arrest warrants for both of them. The team I sent over to pick up Kasdan told me the files you found prove the Waldorfs knowingly purchased a child. That's a felony in this county. We'll find them, Raegan. It's just a matter of time."

Alec had said the same, and Raegan wanted to believe it, but she was afraid. Yes, they'd uncovered an abduction ring, and the people involved would all soon be prosecuted, but she still didn't have her daughter.

Her energy waned again, and she sagged against Alec. His arm was right there to hold her up.

"Why don't you two head upstairs?" Bickam said. "McClane, have one of the guys up there get her a bandage for that cut on her forehead."

"Will do." Alec's arm tightened around Raegan's shoulder as he steered her toward the doorway. "Come on, baby."

Raegan wasn't sure how they made it back up to the main level, but she did notice the number of people they had to step around as they walked. Moments ago, the house had been empty and she'd thought she was going to die. Now it was swarming with police and FBI, and all she could think was that the one person who was supposed to be here wasn't.

The back stairs opened off the kitchen. Alec guided her around the granite island and through the great room toward the entryway. Daylight burned her eyes as they moved down the wide steps and into the circular drive. Someone rushed over, took her by the arm, and drew her away from Alec's warmth to sit on the backseat of an open police cruiser.

She blinked several times, trying to shake herself out of this fog. When a burn cut across her forehead, she hissed in a breath.

"Sorry," the young twentysomething officer said. "Just cleaning the wound." He dropped a bloody piece of gauze in a bag at his knees that made her stomach pitch. "This might need stitches. Paramedics are on their way. I want you to let them take a look at it."

Raegan nodded as the officer placed a bandage over the cut, searching for Alec in the sea of faces. The officer checked her other cuts and bruises. Several minutes later, he finally stood and stepped back. Just as quickly Alec's broad shoulders and chiseled features came into sight, and just knowing he was close calmed Raegan and brought everything into focus.

She held out a hand to him. His long fingers curled around hers, and then he was there, on his knees in front of her, gazing up at her with so much love and warmth in his light-blue eyes, her heart contracted hard.

"You okay?" he asked, squeezing both of her hands in his.

She nodded, but tears pricked her eyes.

"Oh, baby. Come here." He wrapped his arms around her.

Her hands slid over his shoulder. Closing her eyes, she focused on him, on them, on the fact they were okay and closer than ever to finding Emma, and just held on.

"You heard Bickam," he whispered. "We're gonna get her back. You were right all along. You said she was still alive, and I didn't believe you. I was such a fool. Can you ever forgive me for that?"

"There's nothing to forgive."

"Yeah, there is." He eased back and looked up at her. "I should have trusted in you—in us. I never should have given up on her. And I shouldn't have left you alone last night." He reached for her hands, gripping them against her lap as his gaze searched her face. "I should have gone home with you."

Home. Their home.

Warmth filled her chest, pushing aside the fear, giving her strength. Lifting her hand from his, she skimmed her fingertips over his jaw. "I know you were upset and that you needed some time. I don't care where you went or what you d—"

"I didn't drink." His clear blue eyes held hers. "I wanted to. But I want you more. I'll always want you more."

Those tears came rushing back, filling her eyes and blurring her vision before she could stop them. "I want you too. All of you. For better or worse."

He pushed up on his knees and kissed her, his hand sliding into her hair, his strong body warm and solid against hers. "For better or worse," he whispered, holding her tight. "I won't leave you again. I will never, ever leave you again, Raegan. You're my everything."

She closed her eyes. Breathed in the scent of him. And felt an inner peace solidify inside her, because two things were certain now: Whatever happened, however long it took, they wouldn't give up on their daughter. And they'd never, ever give up on each other again.

An engine sounded in the distance, then grew silent. A car door slammed. Voices echoed around them, but Raegan didn't turn to look because she had what she needed right here.

Alec lifted his head, and his body stilled against hers. Near her ear, he whispered, "Oh my God."

"What?" Raegan drew back and searched his face. His eyes widened as he gazed through the back windshield of the car at something behind her. Twisting in her seat to see what he was looking at, she said, "What are y—"

The words caught in her throat when she spotted the slim, blonde twentysomething woman standing beside a Toyota Camry Raegan didn't remember being in the drive when she and Alec had walked out of that house, speaking with two FBI agents. And perched on the young woman's hip, looking around with wide eyes, was an auburn-haired four-year-old girl.

"Alec," Raegan gasped, reaching for his shoulder.

Alec stood quickly and pulled Raegan to her feet, his eyes never once leaving the little girl. "I don't believe it."

Raegan rushed around the back of the squad car with him. Others had noticed the woman and child too, and several officers moved toward the woman, blocking Raegan's view. Her pulse shot up. Against her hand, Alec's palm grew damp. An FBI agent on the outside of the group spotted them drawing close and stepped back. He tapped another agent on the shoulder to make room. As the sea of bodies parted, Raegan heard the young woman's voice saying, "No, I'm not Jennifer Waldorf. I'm the Waldorfs' nanny. My name is Lisa. Lisa Schneider. No, I don't know where they are. Mr. Waldorf is away on business right now. I don't know where Mrs. Waldorf is, probably at the spa. What's going on here? Would someone please tell me why there are so many cops here? What's happened?"

The last agents moved out of the way, and Raegan's chest drew tight as a drum as she stared at the little girl in the young woman's arms. The little girl with Raegan's auburn hair and Alec's mesmerizing blue eyes.

"E-Emma?" Raegan asked in a voice just above a whisper.

The woman's forehead wrinkled, and a worried look passed over her features as she glanced from Raegan to the girl in her arms and back again. "No. Her name is Emily. Who are you and what do you think you're doing here?"

The little girl blinked several times as if she had no clue what was happening. Her small hand fisted in the puffy fabric of the woman's coat sleeve. But slowly, as her gaze darted between Alec and Raegan, a hint of a smile pulled at her lips. And when she tipped her head to the side in that shy, sweet way Emma always had, Raegan spotted the small, strawberry birthmark near the corner of her eye.

In a rush, all the fear and agony and longing inside finally slipped away. Raegan squeezed Alec's hand, and tears blurred her vision all over again as she looked up at his shocked and joy-filled eyes, then gazed back at their daughter.

"We're her parents," Raegan managed, finding her voice. "And we're finally here to take her home."

EPILOGUE

Six months later . . .

"Stupid bastard doesn't know when to quit," Alec said into the phone pressed to his ear when he heard the news that John Gilbert had finally awoken from his coma nearly six months after he'd run from the cops and rolled his stolen pickup off I-5.

"No," Jack Bickam said on the other end of the line. "He sure doesn't. Miriam Kasdan is still blaming him for everything, saying he was the mastermind behind the whole abduction ring, not her."

Alec huffed as he crossed one arm over his chest and tucked his hand against his side. "Gilbert isn't smart enough for all that."

"Don't worry, her story isn't flying. But it's gotten Gilbert singing like a canary. He's talking. A lot. According to him, Arnold Kasdan, the son, was the first abduction. I guess the Kasdans couldn't have kids of their own, and Walter Kasdan, Miriam's husband, was too busy building his empire to care much about his wife's desire to be a parent. So she started volunteering with inner-city youth, trying to fill the void. They lived in Spokane back then. Arnold was one of the kids she came across during her volunteer work. The way Gilbert told it, Arnold's biological mother was a meth addict, and his father wasn't really in the picture. Good ol' Miriam bonded with the kid and was so appalled by his living situation she decided to take him with her when she and her husband moved to Portland. She saw it as an extension of her 'good work.' I guess she told her husband Arnold's mother had died of a drug overdose and that he had no other family. The husband agreed to let her keep the kid, and they passed him off as their son. We're checking into the story. Gilbert also told us that when she got to Portland she continued her charity work and came across more kids like Arnold. She couldn't adopt them all—nor did she want to—so she made it her life's work to find them 'better homes.' Arnold has been involved in the operation for a long time. He, apparently, sees Miriam as his savior and totally bought into the whole 'saving kids from a terrible life' crap. He's the one who got Gilbert released early, by the way. He's also the one who arranged for Conner Murray to disappear when Murray got nervous after you and Raegan talked to him. It was a real family business all around."

A family of psychos. "What about the kid you found in the mountains?"

"Just got a positive ID yesterday. It was a two-year-old boy named Kyle Jackson. He went missing in Seattle. Mother was a prostitute; father unknown. His disappearance didn't garner a lot of press coverage. He was diabetic, though. According to Gilbert, he went into some kind of seizure, and his handlers—he claims he wasn't one of them, by the way—didn't know what to do. When the boy died, they disposed of the body in the Coast Range."

Alec's stomach churned. "And yet Gilbert knew exactly where to find the body. I don't buy his I-wasn't-involved story for a second."

"Neither do we. We also found out why Emma was in Sherwood. None of the other kids were relocated that close to the city where they were taken. Kasdan didn't arrange Emma's relocation. Gilbert did. Taking her was revenge against you, as you know. As soon as he had her, though, he knew he had to get rid of her fast. He picked the Waldorfs from Kasdan's files and dropped her off unbeknownst to Kasdan. Guess she was pretty ticked when she found out, but the Waldorfs were willing to pay three times what she charged other families, so she let the transaction stand."

Bile churned in Alec's stomach over the way Miriam Kasdan had sold children as if they were objects.

"Anyway," Bickam said, "Gilbert will never see light outside a prison wall, and the Waldorfs will be spending a long time behind bars as well. You and Raegan don't have to worry about any kind of retaliation from either of them. Mr. Waldorf still claims he knew nothing about the illegal adoption, but the wife already broke down and spilled everything. Guess guilt finally got to her. That or fear."

Alec guessed fear. The Waldorfs had to know Emma had come from somewhere. Whether they'd turned a blind eye mattered little to him. They'd still broken the law, and they'd put another family through hell.

"You and Raegan did a good job bringing this all together," Bickam went on. "It'll take us some time to locate all the biological parents of the fifty-plus files we found in Kasdan's office, but you've brought a lot of closure to a lot of people."

Alec's heart pinched as he moved to the window and gazed out at Raegan, who was smiling in the afternoon sunlight in an off-white sundress, her curly auburn hair hanging down her back while she pushed Emma, with matching hair and a miniature version of Raegan's dress, on the swing Alec had built in their backyard. His sister, Kelsey, decked out in an off-the-shoulder jumpsuit, stood nearby with a glass of wine in her hand, along with his mother and Ethan's fiancée, Sam, who were chatting away and waving at a giggling Emma on the swing. His gaze skipped over to Ethan and Rusty tossing a football nearby with the newest McClane, Thomas, then to his father, who was already starting up the grill on the patio while Hunt held a beer, feigning interest in Michael McClane's inane chatter about the perfect way to sear a steak.

Yes, everything he and Raegan had uncovered would bring closure to a great many families, but not all of them would find the happily ever after he and Raegan had. Kyle Jackson's mother wouldn't. His gaze slid back to Raegan, and his heart filled with more love than he'd ever thought possible. It didn't matter where a mother lived or what job she performed. She would always be a mother, and that bond between a mother and child could never be broken.

"Speaking of Raegan," Bickam said in his ear. "I haven't seen her on the news. Is she planning to go back to work anytime soon?"

"She is working." Alec smiled because Raegan was smiling and because her infectious energy lit him up all over. "Just not at any news station. She's staying home with Emma and writing."

"A book?"

"Yeah."

"Bet I can guess what it's about."

Alec's heart turned over again when he thought of Raegan's strength. She'd never let her doubts show. He knew now that she'd had them—way more than he'd thought she'd had—but she'd never let those doubts destroy her hope. "It's therapeutic for her to get it all out. I've read some of it. It's powerful."

"I have no doubt it'll be a bestseller. How's Emma?"

His gaze drifted to his daughter in the swing, pumping her little legs, the buckles on her white sandals glinting in the sunshine. His heart filled even more. "She's good. Really good. The child psychologist she's been seeing has helped a lot. The first few months were rocky, but it's better every day."

"She see the nanny anymore?"

The Waldorfs' nanny, Lisa Schneider, had agreed to stay on with Alec and Raegan after Emma had come back to live with them. Since she'd been more a caregiver to Emma than either of the Waldorfs, she was the one Emma had been the most attached to. The nanny had moved in with them, but because Raegan's apartment was only a two bedroom and not big enough for all of them, he and Raegan had decided to relocate to his farmhouse outside the city. Alec's father and brothers had chipped in and helped finish the renovations in record time, and after three months, when Emma had grown used to her surroundings, the nanny had slowly transitioned out of Emma's life.

"Not since Memorial Day. She starts college in the fall and got a job with a new family for the summer in Portland. She's good about checking in with Emma, but she doesn't really need to anymore." His smile widened as he watched his daughter lean her whole body back on the swing and laugh upside down at her mother. "I don't think Emma can understand any of what happened at this point, but she will someday."

"Yeah, she will," Bickam said. "And she'll know how many people love her. You're a lucky man, McClane. Don't forget that."

"Trust me, I won't."

They said their good-byes, and Alec hung up, thankful for the update from the FBI, even more thankful that everything was finally behind them. The Feds could sort out all the details. He'd leave them to it. The only thing he wanted to focus on now was his family.

He pulled the back door open, crossed the porch, and jogged down the steps to the patio. His father glanced up from the grill. "Everything okay?"

Alec slapped a hand on his dad's shoulder, reached around, and grabbed a blueberry from the fruit tray his mother had set out on the counter earlier. "Everything's great." He grinned and stepped away. "Everything's better than great."

Michael McClane chuckled in his "I didn't wash my hands" apron, the one he always wore when he played grill master because he thought the silly joke was funny. "That's good to hear, son. Hunter, why don't you go see if those women need more wine."

"Sure thing, Mr. McClane." Hunt set his beer on the counter and reached for the bottle of white Alec's parents had brought. Under his breath to Alec, he muttered, "You didn't mention I was playing glorified waiter all afternoon."

Alec grinned and walked across the patio with his friend. "Minister, waiter . . . what's the difference?"

Hunt huffed. "Careful. I get to stand up in front of all these people and talk about you." His eyes narrowed in a sinister way. "Maybe I'll tell Raegan about the time you got arrested in college for sneaking into that sorority's sleeping porch."

"Go for it," Alec said. "She's already heard that story."

Hunt shook his head as he stepped out onto the grass and headed toward the women. Thankfully, Kelsey's dick of a husband had decided not to show today. None of them liked the guy, but Hunt especially had no use for the man. Today of all days, Alec was grateful he wouldn't have to break up any tense moments.

Ethan heaved the football toward Rusty. Just before it landed in Rusty's hands, Alec jumped sideways in front of him and caught it. At his back, Rusty muttered, "Show-off."

Alec turned and pitched the ball toward Thomas. "It's all talent."

Thomas laughed.

"Old talent," Rusty called. "You don't have the moves you did back in high school, loser."

No, he had new moves. Alec's smile widened when he remembered showing Raegan those moves last night in their bed.

"Daddy!" The sweetest voice he'd ever heard echoed around him, followed by chubby little arms encircling his legs and holding tight.

Alec swept Emma up into his arms. The doll his mother had given her this morning dangled from her hand. "Hey, princess."

"Did you see me on the swing? I'm awbsum."

He chuckled. "Yes, you are. You're very awbsum." His gaze drifted past her to Raegan, who was striding toward him across the lawn. "And your mom's pretty awbsum too."

Smiling, Raegan wrapped her arms around both of them and looked up. Love shimmered in her gorgeous green eyes. Love and a trust he was never going to betray again. "That's because she's got two awbsum people for parents," Raegan said.

Alec leaned down and kissed her. In his arms, Emma made a *bth-bthtbthbt* sound and giggled.

Raegan eased back. Around them, the family that had saved Alec from a life of misery laughed and chatted, but all he could see was the woman who'd rescued him from the darkness inside himself. She brushed a hand over his shoulder and down the sleeve of his pale-blue dress shirt. "Are you nervous?"

"No."

"That's good, because they're going to love you."

Alec really didn't care if they loved him or not. "Even if they don't, I've got everything I always needed right here. I've got you—"

"And me," Emma piped in.

Alec smiled and kissed his daughter's cheek. "Yes, and you, princess." He looked back down at the woman who'd agreed to marry him again today in a simple backyard ceremony, and a wave of love swept through him. "I wouldn't be here if it weren't for you, you know. You never gave up on me."

Raegan's eyes went all soft and dreamy. "I never gave up on us. And I never will."

He leaned down to kiss her once more.

"Alec?" His mother's excited voice drifted to his ears. "They just drove up."

Raegan drew back and grinned.

"They're here?" Emma asked in a high-pitched little voice.

"Yes, they're here," Raegan answered with the same anticipation.

"More grandmas and grandpas?" Emma's blue eyes widened. "Do you think they brought me presents too?" She wiggled against Alec's hold, and he set her down. As soon as her sandals hit the grass, she tore off across the backyard toward the gate where Hannah McClane waited with a smile.

Alec watched the only woman he'd ever considered his mother swoop Emma up into her arms and thought about the people climbing out of their car on the other side of that gate. It had taken several months, but Hunt had helped him track down his biological parents. His mother had been a fledgling college kid in Idaho when he'd been born, working two jobs and going to school, his parents unmarried, neither with means. She'd taken him to a park with her books one afternoon to study and had fallen asleep in the shade while he played. When she'd awoken, he'd been gone. Alec had no memory of that day. No memory of her. But in the months since he'd found her, he'd gotten to know her through e-mails and texts; and his father too, who'd stuck around even after Alec had been taken.

They'd stayed together through trauma and heartbreak. They'd proved that love never died. It grew and changed and survived. Just as Hannah and Michael's love had grown and changed and survived when they'd adopted four—correction, five—screwed-up kids from horrible backgrounds, never knowing how it would all work out.

The same way Alec's love for Raegan had grown and changed and survived, even when he'd done everything wrong along the way.

His stomach twisted. "Okay, I lied. I'm nervous."

Grasping his shoulders, Raegan turned him toward her as she smiled, lifted to her toes, and kissed his cheek. "About meeting your biological parents, I hope. Not about marrying me again."

He looked down at her and smirked. "Never about marrying you."

"Good." She lowered to her heels, grasped his hand in both of hers, and pulled him with her as she stepped back. "Because I am never letting you go again, Mr. McClane. You're stuck with this life now, husband."

He smiled as they moved toward the gate. Partly because she'd called him "husband" again. But mostly because this life, with her and their daughter and his crazy, messy, incredible family was all he'd ever truly wanted.

And he was never letting it go.

ABOUT THE AUTHOR

Before topping multiple bestseller lists—including those of the *New York Times*, *USA Today*, and the *Wall Street Journal*—Elisabeth Naughton taught middle school science. A voracious reader, she soon discovered she had a knack for creating stories with a chemistry of their own. The spark turned into a flame, and Naughton now writes full-time. Her books have been nominated for some of the industry's most prestigious awards, such as the RITA and Golden Heart Awards from Romance Writers of America, the Australian Romance Readers Awards, and the Golden Leaf Award. When not dreaming up new stories, Naughton can be found spending time with her husband and three children in their western Oregon home. *Gone* is the second book in her Deadly Secrets series, following *Repressed*.